About Alison Stuart

Alison Stuart began her writing journey halfway up a tree in the school playground with a notebook and a dream. Her father's passion for history and her husband's love of adventure and the Australian bush led to a desire to tell stories of Australia's past.

She has travelled extensively and lived in Africa and Singapore. Before turning to writing full time, she enjoyed a long and varied career as a lawyer, both in private practice and in a range of different organisations, including the military and emergency services.

Alison lives in a historic town in Victoria.

Also by Alison Stuart

The Postmistress

Lord Somerton's Heir

Guardians of the Crown series

By the Sword
The King's Man
Exile's Return

The
GOLDMINER'S SISTER

ALISON STUART

mira

First Published 2020
Second Australian Paperback Edition 2021
ISBN 9781867237754

The Goldminer's Sister
© 2020 by Alison Stuart
Australian Copyright 2020
New Zealand Copyright 2020

Published by
Mira
An imprint of Harlequin Enterprises (Australia) Pty Limited (ABN 47 001 180 918), a subsidiary of HarperCollins Publishers Australia Pty Limited (ABN 36 009 913 517)
Level 13, 201 Elizabeth St
SYDNEY NSW 2000
AUSTRALIA

® and TM (apart from those relating to FSC®) are trademarks of Harlequin Enterprises (Australia) Pty Limited or its corporate affiliates. Trademarks indicated with ® are registered in Australia, New Zealand and in other countries.

A catalogue record for this book is available from the National Library of Australia
www.librariesaustralia.nla.gov.au

Printed and bound in Australia by McPherson's Printing Group

MIX
Paper from
responsible sources
FSC® C001695

This book is dedicated to the love of my life, David, without whom this story would never have come into being.

One

'Out of the way, woman!'

Eliza Penrose jumped back, tripping on the wooden boardwalk as a chestnut horse careered down the road, avoiding bullock carts and pack horses and sending pedestrians jumping for safety. She fell backwards into an undignified heap, gasping for breath as a small crowd began to gather around her. A child laughed.

'Are you 'urt?' Amos Burrell, the coachman who had brought her to Maiden's Creek, crouched next to her, concern written on his broad, friendly face, a beefy hand outstretched to help.

Only her dignity.

'Don't you have eyes in your head?' The rider's angry voice was tinged with the soft consonants of a Scottish burr.

Her face burning, Eliza allowed Burrell to help her to her feet and managed a shaky thanks to the coachman before turning to the inconsiderate rider, who had brought his horse to a halt and now glared down at her.

1

'Look what you've done!' She held out the mud-streaked skirts of her green travelling coat, her anger masking a sudden, irrational urge to burst into tears. She had not come all the way from England to greet her brother in this dishevelled state.

The Scotsman looked her up and down. Even in the saddle he sat straight and tall, his broad shoulders straining beneath a heavy woollen jacket. Brown hair curled beneath his wide-brimmed felt hat. He leaned on the pommel of his saddle and said, 'And you, madam, shouldn't have been standing in the middle of the road.'

'Now then, Mr McLeod,' the coachman said, 'be fair—you were riding like the devil.'

'And with good cause.' McLeod swept his hand toward a dray making its ponderous way down the treacherous road that wound into Maiden's Creek. A massive iron boiler, no doubt bound for one of the mines, had been strapped to it but now appeared to have slipped, threatening to take the entire dray over the side of the descent.

At the end of the long, tiring coach journey that had begun in Melbourne two days ago, the Shady Creek to Maiden's Creek coach had passed the dray on the narrow track some miles back. Eliza had leaned out of the window, fascinated by the sight of the ten huge bullocks straining at their collars as the bullocky's whip circled their heads. It had taken all the coachman's skill to steer a safe course between the dray and a plunge down the steep slope.

'I am looking for someone. Besides, where am I supposed to stand?' Eliza demanded, indicating the narrow boardwalk outside the Empress Hotel, which was stacked with luggage.

'Melbourne?' McLeod's lips curled in a wry smile. 'Now if you'll excuse me, I must see to my boiler.' He touched his fingers to his hat and put his heels to the horse, leaving Eliza standing on the boardwalk in her ruined travelling clothes, seething with impotent fury.

'Who was that oaf?' she asked Burrell.

He smiled. 'McLeod. 'e's the mine superintendent up at the Maiden's Creek Mine.'

Eliza's heart lurched and she turned to watch the rider. He had reached the stricken dray and dismounted, lending his shoulder to right the heavy boiler. Mine superintendent at Maiden's Creek had been the position her brother William had held until the opportunity to invest and manage a new mine, the Shenandoah, had come his way more than twelve months earlier.

She huffed out a breath. Regardless of the situation, there had been no call for the man to be so rude. She looked forward to sharing her thoughts on the manners of the citizenry of Maiden's Creek when her brother turned up.

From the safety of the boardwalk, she adjusted her fashionable green hat with its now bedraggled red feather and glanced up and down the bustling main street, looking for her brother's familiar face among the strangers. Plenty gave her a curious glance but she could not find the person she sought. Punctuality had never been Will's greatest virtue and from what she understood of the local geography, Pretty Sally, where he now lived, was some miles out of Maiden's Creek. Perhaps he had simply misjudged the distance he needed to travel. Or had a problem at the Shenandoah Mine required his urgent attention?

Maybe he hadn't received the letter she had sent from Melbourne? A missive addressed merely to Mr W J Penrose C/- Pretty Sally General Store did seem somewhat vague.

Eliza's chest tightened with disappointment that Will wasn't here to meet her. She had spent the uncomfortable coach trip imagining their reunion after all these years. So much to say … and, of course, sad news to impart. Will had always been close to their mother and her death would be a grief to him.

'Are you expecting someone to meet you?' Burrell asked.

'I thought my brother …' She cleared her throat and raised her voice to be heard over the cursing and shouting of the bullockies and the incessant thump from several batteries of gold stampers. It had been years since the cadence of the mines had marked the passing of her days, the rhythm of the stampers as familiar as her own heartbeat.

She squared her shoulders beneath her fashionable, but now ruined, coat and addressed the coachman. 'Would you be so good as to direct me to the house of Charles Cowper?'

Burrell raised an eyebrow. 'Charles Cowper? What would be your business with 'im?'

'He's my uncle.'

'Your uncle?' Burrell scratched his nose and frowned. His eyes widened as he made the connection. 'Then you'll be Will Penrose's sister? Should've seen it when I took you on board at Shady Creek.'

A wave of relief washed over her. 'Yes, I am. I thought he would be here to greet me. I sent him a message, but as he appears to be detained, I'll go to my uncle's house and wait for him there.'

Burrell's gaze slid to the coach and he cleared his throat. 'I'd best be seeing to me 'orses. Cowper's 'ouse is up there.' He indicated a neat white weatherboard house on the hill above the town. 'You'll be after some 'elp with your luggage?'

He signalled a couple of men who were leaning against the wall of the Empress Hotel and indicated Eliza's heavy iron-bound trunk and leather portmanteau. 'You two. Be so good as to carry this lady's luggage up to Mr Cowper's 'ouse.'

The men regarded the trunk and cast a quizzical look at its owner. 'Travelling light are we, lady?'

'There'll be a shilling in it for you,' Eliza said.

The older of the two rasped his beard and glanced up the hill at her uncle's house.

'Hope you've got a stout pair of boots in there,' he said. 'You're going to need 'em.'

Eliza glanced down at her mud-caked leather town boots and sighed. Perhaps it was just as well Will had not been there to meet her.

She thanked Burrell for his assistance and lifted her bedraggled hem. Dodging puddles, pack horses and wagons, she made her way up the main road to the zig-zagging track that led to her uncle's house, followed by the two men carrying her luggage. She arrived breathless from the exertion of the steep climb to the front door. As she waited for her knock to be answered, Eliza glanced back at the way she had come. The town lay below her, snaking its way haphazardly along the line of what had once been a stream but now looked—and smelled—like an open sewer. A large tailings heap at the north end of the town marked the existence of a sizeable mine, the newly crushed rock bright against the older slopes that rose behind the buildings and machinery. That had to be her uncle's mine, the Maiden's Creek Mine that Will had described in his infrequent letters. The slopes that rose above the town had been largely denuded of vegetation, apart from occasional clumps of raggedy eucalypts and sad tree ferns, and she had a clear view of the troublesome bullock dray, its load now righted, picking its way down the road into the town, guided by the disrespectful Scot on his chestnut horse.

Melbourne indeed! She had no intention of going back to Melbourne or England or anywhere else. After the years cast adrift from her family, her place was here beside her brother, building a new life together.

'Yes? Can I help you?'

Eliza started and turned back to the house. A small, neat woman in a brown gingham dress under a spotless white apron held the door open, her brow creased in suspicion.

Eliza summoned a smile. 'Good afternoon. My name is Eliza Penrose and I'm here to see my uncle.'

The colour drained from the woman's face and she took a step back. 'Miss Penrose? Mr Cowper said nothing about expecting you.'

'I presumed my brother, William, would have told him that I had left England and would be joining him here at Maiden's Creek,' Eliza said, too exhausted to be polite.

The woman took a breath and shook her head. 'No. Mr Penrose said nothing to us.' She ran her hands down her apron and, as if remembering herself, said with stiff formality, 'I'm Mr Cowper's housekeeper, Mrs Harris. Mr Cowper's at the mine but it's the work of a moment to fetch him. Come in, Miss Penrose, you look all done in—and what happened to your pretty coat?'

'Some ill-mannered oaf on a horse knocked me into the mud.'

Mrs Harris clucked her tongue in sympathy. 'Weather's been foul this last week. Folk are saying it's going to be a bad winter. Now give me that coat and hat.'

Eliza gratefully divested herself of her sodden coat, hat and gloves into the hands of the housekeeper, who showed her into a small but well-furnished parlour with a pretty bay window. She settled Eliza into a comfortable chair beside a cheerful fire and left her with a promise of tea.

Eliza sank into the chair, conscious of her aching muscles and lack of decent sleep for nearly two days. She closed her eyes, grateful for the warmth and glad that the long journey that had commenced when she sailed from Liverpool in early March had at last come to an end. She dozed, waking to the rattle of tea cups.

'I should've let you sleep.' Mrs Harris set the tray down. 'It's a trek to get here, isn't it?'

Eliza managed a smile. 'It is, but nothing a good cup of tea won't cure. Tell me, is Pretty Sally far from here? Is there some sort of transport I can hire to take me up there?'

Mrs Harris stood quite still, her smile frozen on her face. 'Don't you worry about that for now,' she said. 'I've sent the boy for your uncle; he'll be here presently. You just sit quiet and enjoy your tea. There's some Dundee cake for you too. I'll be in the kitchen if you need me.'

Alone again and revived by the tea and cake, Eliza rose to her feet and examined her appearance in the mirror by the door. She pulled out her handkerchief and rubbed at a mud smear on her cheek. She took the pins from her hair and tried to restore it to an orderly knot. She had barely finished the rough toilette when the front door crashed open.

'Where is she?'

Her heart jumped at her uncle's familiar voice. She didn't hear Mrs Harris's response as the parlour door opened and Cowper stood in the doorway, flushed and panting as if he had run from the mine. She barely recognised him. Before Charles Cowper left England he had worked with her father and been very much a part of her life, but it had been years since she'd last seen him. The years had added inches to his waist and seen the loss of most of his hair. Only a luxuriant moustache compensated for the lack of locks on his head.

'Eliza, my dear ...' he began but had to pause to catch his breath. 'What in the good Lord's name are you doing here?'

Eliza frowned. 'Didn't Will tell you I was on my way?'

Cowper coughed. 'Will was want to keep his own counsel.'

Eliza caught the past tense and her nerves tingled. Something was wrong. 'Where is he?' She glanced at the door, half expecting her brother to walk through it.

Charles Cowper placed a hand under her elbow and guided her back to the chair by the fire. He drew another chair up and, holding her hands in his, sucked in his moustache. 'My dear, you cannot have got my telegram or letter …'

She shook her head. 'I've been on a ship for over three months. We only docked a few days ago in Melbourne. Has something happened—'

She saw the answer in Cowper's face even as he said, 'Will is dead.'

Will? Dead?

'But he wrote to me …' she began uselessly, as if saying it made the fact of his death no longer true. She pulled her hands free from her uncle's grasp and he sat back in his chair. 'When? How?'

'Barely six weeks ago,' Cowper said. 'An accident at the mine.' He glanced out of the window. 'The Maiden's Creek, not the Shenandoah.'

Eliza shook her head. 'I don't understand. What was he doing at Maiden's Creek? Didn't he cease working there a year ago?'

'He did, and it is as much a mystery to me as to everybody else. The fact remains he was found dead at the foot of the tailings. The doctor was of the opinion that he had been dead at least six hours before he was discovered by the early shift.'

Eliza tore at the strings of her purse, pulling out Will's last letter to her, dated May the previous year and crumpled and stained from much re-reading. She handed it to Cowper but she knew every word by heart.

Dearest Liza,

Fortune has smiled on us. I have settled our father's debts with my uncle and left his employ to strike out on my own as manager and shareholder of a mine outside Maiden's Creek. The Shenandoah is already showing great prospects and I am confident in suggesting that you join me in this brave new country. We can make a good life for ourselves here. When you have made your plans, you can write to me care of the General Store at Pretty Sally. Come as soon as you are able.

   Yr. Loving bro
   W J Penrose (Will)

Her uncle read the letter and shook his head. 'He was a fine young man and a brilliant engineer. He had such a promising future.' He sighed as he returned the letter to her. 'Sadly, we were not on the best of terms in recent months. We argued about him throwing away his prospects at Maiden's Creek for such a risky venture as the Shenandoah Mine and once he had removed himself to Pretty Sally, we met only on very few occasions. At no time did he mention the prospect of you joining him.' He ran a hand over his eyes. 'I regret my angry words, but it is too late now to tell him how proud I was of him and of the remarkable work he had done with the Maiden's Creek Mine and the Shenandoah.'

Eliza hardly heard him. She focussed on her hands, twisting them in her lap, fighting the resolve not to howl her grief to the wind. In the last few months, she had lost her mother and now her brother. With the exception of this man and her aunt in Bath, she was entirely alone in the world. Disbelief, anger and despair caught in a knot in her throat.

Cowper coughed. 'The fact we did not know of your coming does not make you any less welcome, Eliza. I have a spare room and I'm sure Mrs Harris is already heating water for a bath.' He reached over and patted her hand. 'You must be exhausted, my dear. Even in good weather the journey over the mountains is difficult.'

She nodded and stared into the fire for a long time before finding the courage to impart the sad news she in her turn brought with her.

'I would have come sooner but Mama's health was failing. At my aunt's request, I gave up my position at the school to go to Bath to be with her.' She raised her brimming eyes. 'She died in late January. I would have written but we agreed it would be better to bring the news to you and Will in person.'

Charles Cowper nodded, his mouth a hard, thin line. 'So, it seems we are both bearers of bad news. Did my sister suffer?'

'It was not an easy death. The doctors said it was a cancerous growth. They could do nothing to save her and all Aunt Margaret and I could do was watch as it consumed her. I have a letter from my aunt for you in my luggage.' Eliza looked away, pressing her hand to her mouth to stop the tears. 'She is all alone too. I hated leaving her ...'

Cowper stood and laid a hand on her shoulder. 'You've had a terrible shock. There will be time enough for talk later when you have had a chance to compose yourself. Unfortunately, I have a business to run so, if you will excuse me, dear girl, I must return to my duties.'

After he had left her, she sat staring into the flames, too tired and numb to truly comprehend that, without Will, she was alone in this strange and unfamiliar country. All the plans, hopes and dreams that had sustained her on the long voyage were gone. Her future loomed before her like the flames in the hearth, wavering and dancing, falling into embers.

Two

The winter evening had already begun to close in as Alec McLeod joined the mine foreman, Enoch Trevalyn, to watch the team manhandle the new boiler into place on its carefully prepared brick bed in the massive cavern that served as the mine's plant room.

Trevalyn nodded his approval. 'That's going to change things.'

'It means we can drive the steam-driven drills,' Alec said without much enthusiasm. The revolutionary pieces of equipment had been ordered by Charles Cowper and were already on the way. Alec had seen the drills in operation on the Ballarat goldfields and disliked and distrusted the noisy pieces of equipment, particularly the amount of dust they produced. However, they would improve the speed of tunnelling and reduce the accidents caused by the mallet and drill bit.

Trevalyn pushed his greasy felt hat to the back of his head and scratched his bald spot. 'Did you hear Will Penrose's sister's come looking for him?'

Alec's stomach lurched. He had come to know and like his predecessor at the Maiden's Creek Mine in the months before Will's death. They had spent many a long evening discussing the intricacies of the mining industry. Will had mentioned he had a sister, but the girl was thousands of miles away back in England. She couldn't be here in Maiden's Creek.

'The Harris boy came looking for Cowper this afternoon. I heard him telling the boss that Miss Penrose had been knocked over in the street and was in a fearful state.'

Alec almost swore out loud. He had sent the niece of his employer flying into the mud? Half the town must have witnessed his appalling behaviour and if it got back to Cowper … Then again, the only thing that really seemed to matter to Cowper was the price of his shares.

'She can't know about her brother,' Trevalyn continued. 'What a welcome.'

The two men stood in a silence punctuated by much cursing from the men installing the boiler.

'You know Penrose's father was one of the biggest mine owners in Cornwall?' Trevalyn said.

'No.'

'Fell on hard times. No one wanted tin any more.' Trevalyn shrugged. 'Many a Cornishman found his way to these shores, me included. Penrose was a good boss.' He glanced at Alec. 'Not saying you ain't a good boss.'

'Thank you,' Alec said in a voice dripping irony.

Suddenly the boiler tipped to the side, causing one of the men to jump out of the way to avoid his foot being crushed. Alec lunged forward to help steady the machine. It wavered but fell no further and the men finally manoeuvred it back in place.

'Take a break,' Alec said, and the workers stepped back from the heavy piece of machinery, mopping their brows.

A crib room had been cut into the side of the plant room, furnished with a rough table and bench. The men laughed and chatted among themselves as they opened lunch pails. Many of the miners were Welsh or Cornish like Trevalyn and those with wives gladly shared griddle cakes and pasties with their less fortunate single mates.

'Come and join us,' David Morgan called to Alec, in the singsong accent of the Welsh. 'You've not lived till you've tasted me wife's baking.'

Alec drew up a stool at the end of the table and accepted the offer of a pasty and mug of tea.

'You married, sir?' Morgan asked.

'No.' Alec paused. 'Not any more. Wife died four years ago.' They said grief dulled with time but every day he still felt the pain of the loss of his wife—his Catriona—and their child like a knife in his chest.

The atmosphere around him shifted like sand, but Alec merely tapped the pasty he had been given and continued, 'Bridget O'Grady keeps house for my brother and me. A good woman in so many ways, but she can burn porridge just by looking at it.'

That provoked laughter and broke the tension. Alec brushed the crumbs from his shirt and rose to his feet, cracking his head on the low ceiling. He rubbed the injury and silently cursed his mother's tall genes.

'I can tell you weren't born a miner,' Trevalyn said. 'You'd have lasted five minutes at Geevor.'

Alec let the comment pass. His family had been coal miners in Lanarkshire for more generations than he could count. He'd been born the son of a miner. *And I'd have followed him down the mines, but for a sharp-eyed clergyman who had encouraged me to apply for a scholarship.*

As each man finished his pasty they broke off the end and tossed it into a dark corner.

'You'll be attracting rats doing that,' Alec said.

The youngest of the trio, Tregloan, grinned. 'It's for the Knockers,' he said, then, seeing the puzzled frown on Alec's face, added, 'Do you not have the Knockers in the mines in Scotland?'

Alec shook his head.

'They're little dwarfish creatures that inhabit the mine and watch out for us poor miners. If you hear them a-knock-knock-knocking, that's their way of warning you that there's trouble,' Trevalyn said.

Alec laughed. 'You mean that the knocking that foretells a collapse is those little fellows?'

Every man around the table nodded.

'In Wales, we call them the Bwca,' Morgan said. 'And there's some that say the knocking is them hammering away and causing the fall.' He shrugged. 'Me, I prefer to think they're on our side, so they get our pasty to keep 'em happy.'

Alec shook his head. Miners were a superstitious lot and no less so where he had come from, although the Knockers were new to him. The men returned to work and as the day ticked into evening, Alec glanced at his watch. 'It's late. Call it a day, boys.'

As he followed the crew out of the mine, he paused to glance down the dark shaft that had been sunk in the floor of the cavern. Only the faintest light showed where a team of men were working on a new lead, sweating in the cramped, dust-filled tunnel. The echo of the mallet striking the drill bit drifted up the shaft in a steady cadence. One man would hold the drill bit, the other strike it. Strike ... turn ... strike ... turn. The new pneumatic drills would change mining forever.

Outside, Alec shrugged on his coat, shoving his hands into its pockets as he walked down the hill toward the light of his small cottage where his brother would be waiting for him. He thought about his childhood in Wishaw and the life of the coal miners—and the deaths. Had he moved so far from that life? He had substituted coal dust for gold dust and a pick for a pen, but his days were still spent in the dark and damp. He wanted to move into the light and the fresh air, turn his hand to the land, but that was a dream beyond the salary he earned.

As he turned onto the path leading to his front door, he took a breath and looked up at the pinpricks of the stars in the velvet sky. He stretched his stiff shoulders, grateful for the welcoming light that burned in the window and the curl of smoke from the chimney.

'You're late, Alec.'

Ian McLeod sat at the table, the old family bible open in front of him, making notes on a sheet of paper.

Ignoring his younger brother's disapproving gaze, Alec sank into a chair beside the fire and let out a heavy sigh. Windlass, the large ginger cat who had adopted the brothers on their arrival, immediately jumped onto his lap, circled several times and settled with his big head on his paws. Alec let his fingers stray over the cat's soft fur, finding its warmth and gentle purring soothing after his long, difficult day.

Rising from the table, Ian came to stand on the hearth, his back to the fire and his dark eyes scanning Alec's face. 'That bad?'

Ian had lost his hearing following a childhood illness but, as long as he could see the person he was talking to, he could read their lips. Those meeting him for the first time might only notice a slightly ponderous tone in his voice to indicate anything was amiss.

'We nearly lost the boiler on Little John's. One of the ropes snapped. If the others hadn't held ...' Alec shuddered.

'That's why you're the engineer and I'm not.' Ian gestured at the stove where a pot sat exuding the smell of burned food. 'Bridget left a stew if you're hungry.' A smile caught the corners of his mouth as he resumed his seat at the table. 'Up to her usual standard.'

Alec pushed an indignant Windlass off his lap and stood. He lifted the lid on the pot and sighed. Even if he had come in earlier his dinner would not be anything else but burned. He thought of the delicious pasty he had shared in the crib room and his stomach growled. Despite his misgivings, he spooned some of the blackened mess onto a plate, broke off a hunk of bread and joined Ian at the table. He poked tentatively at something that may have been a carrot and wondered what beast the grey, leathery pieces of meat had come from. At best wallaby, at worst possum, but if a man was hungry enough he would eat anything, even Bridget O'Grady's cooking.

'What are you doing?' he asked his brother.

Ian tapped the bible. It had been their mother's and was almost falling apart with use across the generations. 'Reverend Donald has asked me to give the homily on Sunday.' His mouth twisted in a self-deprecating smile. 'At least I'll not be able to hear the congregation snoring when I send them to sleep.'

It surprised Alec that despite everything he and Ian had been through, Ian retained an unshakeable loyalty to the Presbyterian faith and was now an elder of the St Andrews congregation. Alec only attended church for weddings and funerals. His belief in God had largely died with Catriona and the baby.

He changed the subject. 'How was your day?'

Ian shrugged. 'Same as any other. Books to keep, letters to write.' Ian had a good head for figures and when Alec had taken the position at Maiden's Creek Mine, he had secured the job of company clerk for Ian, a temporary position that seemed to have become permanent as his brother had proved his worth.

'One interesting thing happened. Cowper's niece arrived in town. The boy came with a message and Cowper shot off. Came back an hour later with a face like thunder,' Ian said.

Alec paused, fork halfway to his mouth. 'I know. I sent her flying into the mud this afternoon and I was probably less than polite.' The memory of the encounter with the small, angry woman in the green coat came back with startling clarity.

Ian laughed.

'It's not funny,' Alec said.

'Yes, it is.'

'Cowper's niece of all people,' Alec muttered and sank his head into his hands.

Ian studied his brother. 'If she's Will Penrose's sister, she can't know that Will is dead.'

'I think you can assume Cowper told her.'

'Cowper certainly wasn't happy. He actually swore.'

Ian worked in the main office, which was separated from Cowper's by a half-glass partition wall. While the partition itself was hardly soundproof, Ian kept his ability to lipread from his employer, who had got into the habit of handing his clerk written instructions. Ian could make out most conversations conducted in the privacy of the mine manager's office as long as the participants' faces were visible. Thinking he could not be overheard by his deaf clerk, Cowper tended to be less discreet than he would otherwise be. Fortunately for his employer, Ian had a strong sense of integrity and unless he felt it was something Alec should know, he kept his own counsel.

The thought of the awful news that Cowper would have imparted only intensified Alec's guilt at his ungentlemanly behaviour toward the bereaved Miss Penrose and when he had eaten, he searched out the bottle of Scotch whisky he kept for these occasions. Ignoring Ian's sharp glance, Alec took the glass he'd poured to his seat by the fire. Undeterred by his previous eviction, Windlass jumped on to his lap and settled again.

Ian closed the book he had been working on and joined Alec. 'You drink too much.' As a good Presbyterian, Ian disapproved of drinking for whatever reason.

'Aye,' Alec agreed. 'I do.'

'Drinking will not—' Ian began but closed his mouth as Alec glared at him.

It was a conversation the brothers had many times and it was true, drinking wouldn't bring Catriona back, but it eased the pain and helped him forget, if only for a little while. Alec lifted the glass, watching the reflected flames from the fire leap and dance in the soft amber liquid.

He turned his thoughts back to Cowper's niece, Will Penrose's sister. Her neat little figure in her green coat and some sort of ridiculous hat with a red feather, standing in the road looking for a brother who would not be there to meet her.

'What's the girl's name?' he asked.

'What girl—Oh, Cowper's niece? Eliza.'

Eliza Penrose. Alec turned her name over in his mind. She would surely be the young engineer's legal heir. The guilt that coursed through him cut deeper. Will had trusted him with a secret—a secret that lay concealed beneath a floorboard in Alec's bedroom—but now Will's closest relative had arrived, Alec was left with a dilemma, a crisis of conscience.

On the morning Will Penrose had been found dead, Alec had discovered an envelope pushed under his door labelled, 'Keep this safe for me'. Alec had thought it puzzling but simply set the envelope to one side, intending to ask Will what he meant when they next met.

Will's trust in him had only become significant when he arrived at work to the news that Will lay dead at the foot of the tailings. When Alec opened the envelope later that evening and sorted through the papers, he recognised what his friend had left for him: meticulous diagrams and mathematical calculations that comprised a new design for an industrial boiler that would revolutionise the mining industry—if not all industries.

He waited until Ian went to bed and he heard the gentle snores that indicated his brother was sound asleep. Alec retrieved the oilskin-wrapped package that he had hidden on the day of Will's death.

In the living room, he set the package on the table and unwrapped it, to reveal a large, stout, buff-coloured envelope from which he pulled the much folded and slightly grimy papers that had been Will's passion. A new and more efficient heat exchanger that would double the power output of the industrial boilers.

When Will died there had been no one to claim the plans and Alec had lain awake many a night, wrestling with his conscience. The devil on his shoulder had whispered in his ear and told him that, if he still believed in God, this would be the answer to his prayers—he had left Lanarkshire and come to Australia for the promise of a better life and the proceeds from the patent on such a machine would mean he and Ian could live like kings. All he had to do was lodge the patent in his name.

There were just two small problems. Although he had discussed some aspects of the concept, the design rightfully belonged to one William Josiah Penrose, not Alec James McLeod. And the second problem? The design had a fundamental flaw that Will had been agonising over. In their discussions, Will had mentioned a problem but had not confided the details of the flaw. As Alec studied the papers again, trying to make sense of Will's scribblings and deletions, he had the sense that they had indeed missed something important. Until the issue had been identified and resolved these designs were worthless.

He folded the papers, replaced them in the envelope and poured himself another whisky.

Keep this safe for me.

The devil on his shoulder had been wrong, and Alec had always known it. With Will's death, the design rightly passed to his next of kin: his sister, Eliza Penrose. It had been easy enough to dismiss

Eliza when she was safely back in England but now she had come to Maiden's Creek. The voice of Alec's conscience had Catriona's soft, Highland lilt: *You know 'tis the wrong thing to do, Alec McLeod. Now the lass is here, for the love of your friend, you have to make this right for her. What she does with it is her business, not yours.*

All very well, he told his conscience, but why had Will Penrose chosen that night to leave the plans with him for safekeeping? Had Will had a premonition of his own death or were there more sinister forces at work that had prompted him to entrust Alec with the precious plans?

The thought had nagged at Alec in the weeks since Will's death but as time passed, he had pushed it aside. The coroner had found that Will's death had been an accident and Alec had nothing to prove anything different.

Despite the warmth of the room, he shivered.

Three

21 June 1873

Eliza sat on the edge of the single bed and looked around the sparsely furnished bedroom into which Mrs Harris had shown her the previous evening. Exhausted, Eliza had been able to do little more than wash before falling into the comfortable bed and into a deep, dreamless sleep.

She had woken at first light, momentarily confused as she looked at the pressed metal ceiling above her. She'd sat up, hugging her knees to her chest as she looked around the room that had been Will's while he'd worked for his uncle. Surely he must have left some essence of himself, of his laugh and his bright eyes? Was it possible for someone with so much life and love in their soul to just cease, as if they had never existed?

But within these four walls, decorated only with a faded and yellowed needlework sampler proclaiming the biblical text *My help cometh from the Lord, which hath made heaven and earth*, it was as if Will had never been.

She dashed her tears away and set her bare feet on the rag rug beside the bed. Her breath frosted in the cold air and she shivered.

Her travelling clothes, which she had draped over the chair, had been spirited away, no doubt by Mrs Harris. Eliza rummaged in her leather portmanteau for clean linen and the mourning gown she had purchased after her mother's death and which by rights she should still be wearing. She had deliberately chosen not to arrive in Maiden's Creek in deepest mourning. To do so would announce without words the sad news of their mother's passing. Little had she thought that now she would be wearing mourning for both Will and Mama. Another sob gathered in the back of Eliza's throat and she sank onto the bed, clutching the crumpled gown to her chest.

There was a tentative knock on the door before it opened and Mrs Harris entered the room. She set a cup of tea on the small table by the bed, then sat beside Eliza and handed her a clean, neatly folded handkerchief.

'You poor lass,' she said. 'It was a shock for us all.'

Eliza blew her nose and wiped her eyes properly. 'I don't understand how it could have happened. Will was brought up around mines. He would never—' She hiccupped into the sodden handkerchief.

'It was a terrible thing to happen. Such a shock for the whole town.'

'What am I going to do?'

Mrs Harris patted her shoulder. 'Today's a new day and the world will look brighter after a wash. You can join Mr Cowper for breakfast.' The housekeeper rose to her feet, all brisk efficiency. 'Now let's get you organised. Oh dear, look at the state of that dress. Well, it will have to do for now. I'll press it up nice and neat for church tomorrow.'

Eliza took a deep breath and tried to find a dry corner of the handkerchief but after Mrs Harris left the room, the tears returned. The act of dressing strengthened her a little, but her reflection in the washstand mirror revealed a washed-out ghost of herself, her eyes lost in dark smudges of grief and exhaustion. She took a steadying breath and smoothed down her crumpled skirt before joining her uncle in the small dining room.

'You look a little pale, my dear,' Cowper remarked as Eliza took the seat across from him. 'Did you not sleep well?'

'I slept very well, thank you, Uncle.'

He rubbed his hands together as the door opened. 'Ah, Mrs Harris, breakfast. I hope you have a good appetite because Mrs Harris is one of the best cooks in the town,' Cowper said to Eliza.

Eliza thanked Mrs Harris as she set down a substantial breakfast of bacon and eggs. 'And thank you for your assistance this morning.'

The woman nodded. 'If you have anything else to wash, I will attend to that this morning. In this weather it takes a little while for things to dry properly, so the earlier I get started the better.'

'She has been very kind to me,' Eliza said as the housekeeper shut the door behind her.

'She has a good heart.' Cowper picked up his knife and fork and attacked his breakfast with the enthusiasm of a man who had not eaten for days.

Eliza cut a piece of bacon. It was excellent but in her present mood it tasted like boot leather. She set her fork down and looked at her uncle. 'Tell me a little more about Will,' she said. 'And the accident.'

Cowper shook his head. 'Oh, my dear, what is the point of talking about it? To be honest, I have nothing to add to what I told you yesterday. Will left my employ a year ago and he's been living up at Pretty Sally, working on the Shenandoah Mine.

I know he came into town every now and then, but I rarely saw him.'

'Then who did he meet? Who were his friends?'

Her uncle forked more egg and bacon into his mouth, a dribble of yolk adhering to his overlong moustache.

'Friends? This is not the sort of place where friendships as a woman would think of them are formed.'

'What of the night he died?' Eliza persisted.

'They said he'd been seen drinking at—at one of the many establishments in this town, but he had left by midnight and what he did after that, no one can say. The coroner concluded he slipped on the tailings and fell to his death.'

'But why did he go up to the mine so late at night?'

'No one knows. Now, do eat up. Mrs Harris will be mortally offended if you don't send back a clean plate.'

Eliza forced herself to finish the plate of congealing egg, conscious she had eaten hardly anything over the last couple of days, but the food sat heavily in her stomach. She laid the knife and fork neatly on the plate and pushed it to one side. 'Where is he?'

'What do you mean?'

'Will. Where is he buried?'

'In the town cemetery. I was on the point of arranging a memorial stone but maybe that is something you wish to do?' He paused. 'I will pay, of course.'

Eliza nodded. 'Thank you, that would be a kindness.' Her uncle did not need to know that her finances were in a parlous state. What she had managed to save and what she had been left by her mother had nearly all gone. The only thing of any value she possessed was the gold locket around her neck, given to her by her father on her eighteenth birthday. She would have to seek some sort of employment as a matter of urgency, unless—

Everyone she had met in Melbourne and on the coach had told her how well the Maiden's Creek goldfields were doing, and Will had owned shares in the Shenandoah Mine. Perhaps there might be a small legacy, enough to sustain her for a little longer?

'Did my brother have a will?'

Charles Cowper ran a hand over his balding head. 'He did. My solicitor in Melbourne is dealing with its execution.'

Hope flickered in her heart but faded with his next words.

'The fact is, it is not worth the paper upon which it is written.'

'What do you mean? There is the Shenandoah Mine. His shares—'

'Indeed, but sadly Shenandoah is failing to live up to its early promise. Any money Will saved he ploughed into the mine and at the time of his death the shares were worth a fraction of their value. In fact, Will was so disappointed with the prospects for the mine that, under the terms of his will, he left the shares in the Shenandoah to me, rather than burden you with a worthless investment. Everything else was left to you, of course, but I am afraid that amounts to nothing more than his personal possessions.'

'Why would he leave the mine to you?' she asked through stiff lips. 'You said yourself that you were not on the best of terms.'

Cowper spread his hands. 'Professional differences, nothing more. But he was always a sensible young man and he recognised that management of a mine is not a job for a woman, particularly as it looks like the Shenandoah will need to be wound up. That is more than a gently born girl like yourself should have to deal with.'

'Please don't patronise me, Uncle. I am not a girl. I am twenty-five years old and I have been making my own way in the world for the last five years.'

Cowper regarded her for a long moment. 'I did not intend to patronise you, but all the indications are that the Shenandoah is indeed worthless. It started off well, with a good find of surface gold but the reef has petered out. Out of respect for your brother and the other shareholders—who are presently overseas—I've kept a crew up there, and while there is always the hope of finding another seam, we doubt there is anything more. Will probably hoped to spare you the disappointment and the responsibility.' He reached over and patted her hand, a gesture which made Eliza's teeth clench with irritation. 'I'm sorry, my dear, but that is the gamble of trusting in gold. It is high-risk mostly for little reward. A decision will be made about its future when the major shareholders return from their travels. But for them it is no great loss. For your brother, alas, it was everything.'

Eliza withdrew her hand. In one of his letters, Will had described the mine as an investment in their future—both their futures—the restoration of the Penrose family fortunes. It must have been a bitter disappointment for him to have made the decision to leave his share to his uncle and not her. 'And his possessions?' she asked in a small, tight voice.

'I had them packed up. The box is in the shed, I'll have the boy bring it in for you. Hopefully it contains things that will bring you some comfort.'

'Thank you.' She looked up. 'Uncle, if you could spare some time this morning, can you show me where he is buried? I would like to pay my respects.'

Cowper wiped his moustache and pushed back his chair. 'I have business at the mine this morning, but I will be pleased to take you after lunch.'

Eliza summoned a smile and thanked him.

Eliza knelt on the ground beside her brother's grave, the sharp stones digging through her layers of petticoats and stockings. She scarcely felt the pain of them, or the icy wind blowing down the valley, as she laid a gloved hand on the raw earth that marked Will's final resting place. She covered her eyes with her other hand as tears welled again.

Five years ago, she and her brother had stood on the dock at Liverpool, a very different winter wind blowing up the Mersey, at the crossroads of their lives: Will headed for a new life in Australia and Eliza for the post of governess at a great house in Yorkshire. Their days would be a far cry from their comfortable home in Cornwall.

He had taken her hand, squeezing her icy fingers. 'Give me some time, Eliza,' he'd said. 'You have my word—as soon as I am settled, I'll send for you. There is a future for both of us in Australia, I know it in my heart. England holds nothing for us any more.'

His letters had always repeated his intention they be reunited. She had never dreamed it would be like this.

'What do I do now?' she whispered to the cold dirt of Will's grave.

The white cross bore the neat black painted inscription: W J PENROSE, Died 27 April 1873. Despite its bleak appearance, the grave seemed well looked after. Not a weed sprouted from the fresh earth, still piled high on the grave, and a wilted posy of flowers had been placed in a chipped blue-glass ink bottle at the foot of the cross. Eliza had not thought her uncle senti-mental; the posy seemed the gesture of a woman. Maybe Mrs Harris?

Gathering up some of the earth in her gloved hand, she let the dirt and stones fall back on the grave and stood up, brushing the mud off her skirt.

The wind picked up, tugging at her shawl. She drew it tighter around her as she looked around the quiet cemetery. With so little flat ground in the valley, the innovative citizens of Maiden's Creek had cut the graves in terraces just wide enough to accommodate them. The place seemed far removed from the hustle and bustle below; the ceaseless thump of the stamper batteries muted in the peaceful atmosphere.

Her uncle had retired a little way up the hill to talk with the gravedigger, who leaned on his shovel, resting from the labour of digging a new grave in the hard earth. The murmur of their voices drifted down toward her.

Seeing she had risen from her knees, Cowper slithered down the slope to join her. Removing his hat, he stood beside her for a long moment in respectful silence. Above them, the grave digger returned to his labour, the sharp clang of his shovel striking a discordant note.

'Who is he digging the grave for?' Eliza enquired.

'A woman died in childbirth yesterday.' Cowper looked around the already well populated cemetery and shook his head. 'The weak and the vulnerable don't survive long up here.'

She cast her uncle a curious glance. It seemed an odd remark from a man not given to shows of emotion.

He pulled a gold pocket watch from his waistcoat and snapped it open. 'Let me escort you home, my dear, and then I really must return to the mine.'

Eliza shivered as the chill wind seemed to cut through her. The Cornish would call it a lazy wind—too lazy to go around. She had not expected Australia to be so cold or so damp. Bruise-coloured clouds roiled above the ridgelines of the steep valley. It had rained on and off during the day but the clouds seemed higher now, the threat of rain a little more distant. The limbs of the young deciduous trees in gardens across the valley—planted, no doubt, by homesick residents—were bare. So strange to think of June as being winter and not the start of summer. In England the land would be green and lush and it seemed to her that she had lived this year in perpetual winter.

She tugged at her gloves, settled the veil back over her face and took a deep breath. 'If you don't mind, Uncle, I will stay here a while longer.'

'Do you wish company?'

'No. You have duties at the mine, and I would like to be alone.'

He nodded and looked around. 'If you're inclined to exercise, do watch your step. These hills are a honeycomb of mines.' He pointed to a stand of trees above the cemetery. 'There is a good view of the town from up there. It is a rough-and-ready place not without beauty and charm, but don't linger too long, it is sure to rain again within the hour.'

Eliza watched her uncle stride away. On their way to the cemetery she had noted how people greeted him by name and he raised his hat in acknowledgement without breaking stride. It seemed strange to see him as a person of some importance in this place so far from her mother's drawing room in Cornwall.

Charles Cowper had been a frequent visitor to the Penrose home, following the marriage of Eliza's parents, until he had moved to Australia to make his fortune on the newly discovered goldfields. After Eliza's father's disgrace and death, it had been Charles Cowper who had come to the rescue, settling the family's debts and offering Will the opportunity to escape England. Will had gone but had discovered that the price of joining his uncle was the repayment of the debt the Penroses owed him. Although the debt had been discharged, it had taught Eliza that whatever the future held, she knew better than to allow herself to become beholden to Charles Cowper.

The rasp of the gravedigger's shovel kept time with the distant stampers. *Thud, thud, thud*, a sound that echoed her own heartbeat. She looked down toward the town. The main street seemed alive with a stream of men and beasts. Despite the noise, the bleak, denuded hills and the stench from the creek, there was, as Cowper had said, a charm to the valley.

Her wandering thoughts were diverted by a woman coming up the path to the cemetery. She wore a dark bonnet and a shawl over a plain blue gown and in her hand she carried a nosegay of greenery. The woman paused at the start of the row of graves that led to where Eliza stood and glanced back down the hill as if undecided about proceeding. Their eyes met, the woman's chin lifted and, with a purposeful stride, she came toward Eliza, stopping on the far side of Will's grave.

'It's you, isn't it?' Eliza said. 'You have been placing the flowers on his grave?' Up close she could see the woman was young and pretty with full, red lips and high cheekbones, but her eyes had a glittering hardness to them. Eyes that had seen too much.

The young woman knelt and tipped the dead flowers from the improvised vase, replacing them with the fresh posy of native foliage. Satisfied that the vase stood straight and the greenery was neatly arranged, she rose to her feet.

'Can't find flowers this time of year,' she said. She studied Eliza for a long moment. 'You're his sister, aren't you?'

'Yes. How do you know?'

A half-smile lifted the woman's features but there was no humour in her eyes. 'Whole town knows,' she said. 'There are no secrets in Maiden's Creek.'

'You have the advantage of me. Who are you?'

'Me?' The woman brushed the top of the cross with her hand. 'I'm no one.'

'Were you a friend of Will's?'

The woman coughed then took a breath and brought her gaze up to Eliza's. 'A friend? Aye, I would hope that would be how he'd think of me.'

'If you were a friend of my brother's, I would like to think of you as a friend of mine. Please, allow me to know your name?'

'Sissy.'

'Sissy …?'

'Just Sissy.' She turned and hurried away.

Eliza started after her, but the woman moved fast and the ground beneath Eliza's feet was too uncertain. Frustrated and annoyed, she abandoned the undignified pursuit and climbed the hill to speak with the gravedigger.

He paused as she approached, leaning on the long handle of his shovel. 'Miss Penrose,' he said. 'I was sorry for your brother. He were a fine man.'

She thanked him and pointed down the hill. 'Did you see that woman who was just here?'

A guarded expression crept onto the man's gaunt face.

'You couldn't miss her.'

The gravedigger scratched his unshaven chin. 'Aye. That'd be Sissy. She comes every day. But you don't want to be dealin' with the likes of her, Miss Penrose.'

'Does she have a last name?'

'Not that I know of.'

'Where would I find her?'

The man picked up his shovel and drove it into the earth, turning his back on her. 'Nowhere you belong. Now, I best be gettin' back to me work. Funeral's in the mornin'. Good day to you, Miss Penrose.'

Eliza stood watching him for a little longer, fascinated by the practised rhythm of the gravedigger as he dug into the unforgiving earth, sparks rising when the metal hit the rocks. She thought of Will, her brilliant, laughing brother, entombed forever in the cold ground, and turned away.

Four

'The fundamental theorem of calculus states that the integral of a function f over the interval a, b can be calculated by finding an antiderivative F of f.' Alec turned to the blackboard and scribed the formula in his swift, impatient hand.

'That is something of a generalisation, Mr McLeod. The Kelvin–Stokes theorem carries the proposition much further.'

Alec nearly dropped the chalk as he turned to face the diminutive woman standing in the doorway, a book clutched in her hand. His students swivelled in their seats and gaped at the unexpected visitor.

He took a breath and set the chalk down on the table in front of him. 'Yes it is, and we will be covering the Kelvin–Stokes theorem in the next lecture,' he said, rather too quickly. 'Thank you, gentlemen, that will do for today.'

The six young men rose and shuffled past the woman in the doorway with polite greetings. The front door to the Mechanics' Institute shut with a thump, leaving Alec alone with Miss Eliza Penrose.

'I'm sorry, I didn't mean to interfere,' she said. 'I am passionate about calculus in all its purest forms.'

Alec stared at her. He had no idea how one addressed a woman who had just declared her passion for calculus. He cleared his throat. 'That is admirable.'

She entered the room and held out her hand. 'We didn't meet under very favourable circumstances yesterday, Mr McLeod. I am Eliza Penrose. You may have known my brother?'

Alec dusted his palms on his trousers and took her small hand in its black glove. 'I owe you an apology for my boorish behaviour.'

'You had an emergency and I was in the way,' she said. 'It is I who owes you an apology. I trust you managed to right the boiler?'

He nodded. 'Aye, we got it up to the mine in one piece.' He turned back to the blackboard and began rubbing away the lecture.

'What are you teaching?'

'I give the occasional Saturday afternoon lecture on physics and calculus and sometimes geology to those who are interested. Ours is an industry that often relies on such fine detail, but I suspect you know that, Miss Penrose.' He set down the rag and considered his next words. 'I didn't answer your question. I did know your brother and considered him a friend. Please accept my condolences on his loss. It must have come as a shock.'

She sniffed and looked at the floor as she gave a brisk shake of her head. 'It did. There was no way I could have known ...' She looked up at him, her mouth twisted in anguish and her grey eyes smudged by grief. 'That was why I was standing where I was in the road. I had expected him to meet the coach and when he didn't come ...' She cleared her throat and looked away.

'He was admired by all who knew him,' Alec said, adding, 'and he is missed.' The words seemed trite and inadequate. He had no idea what he could say that would ease this woman's pain. The only words that came to mind sounded like what they were: empty platitudes. 'I'm sorry.'

'I've just been to pay my respects at the cemetery. I saw there was a lending library here and thought it would be good to borrow a book.' She looked at the well-worn volume in her hand, George Eliot's *The Mill on the Floss*, Alec noted. 'I heard your lecture and curiosity got the better of me. I'm sorry about my interruption. My father always said curiosity would be my downfall.' She managed a thin smile.

'Curiosity is an admirable concept,' Alec said, 'but it's not often I come across a woman familiar with the theorems of calculus.'

The smile broadened. 'I told you, I love mathematics,' she said. 'I teach it, but not very successfully. I am yet to find a child who finds the same pleasure in it that I do.'

'Your own education must have been quite unusual.'

'My father had liberal views on the education of women and allowed me to attend Will's lessons with his tutor, until he went away to school. Then I just read as much as I could.'

'The Mechanics' Institute committee would be interested in anything you are able to teach, Miss Penrose. There is, alas, no remuneration attached to the work, but there's great satisfaction.'

Eliza Penrose's smile slipped. 'Unfortunately, I cannot afford to work for nothing,' she said. 'Neither Will nor my mother left me enough to live on.'

Alec frowned. 'But the Shenandoah Mine should provide you with some income?'

'My uncle Cowper tells me it's failing. And, it seems, Will left his interest in it to my uncle.' She squared her shoulders. 'You can't miss what you don't have. I am sure there are teaching positions in Melbourne I can take up.'

'Something will come your way, Miss Penrose,' Alec said, conscious of the package concealed beneath the floorboards in his cottage. He pulled his watch from his pocket and glanced at it. 'Please excuse me. I had best return to the mine and check on the installation of that boiler.'

As if remembering why she had stepped through the door of the Mechanics' Institute, Eliza held up *The Mill on the Floss*. 'And I had better see to the borrowing of this book. Good afternoon, Mr McLeod.'

Alec pulled on his hat and coat and stepped out into the cool air, pulling up his collar and thrusting his hands into his pockets as a cold gust of wind swept down the valley.

The elderly gentleman who looked after the library at the Mechanics' Institute had an idiosyncratic method of filing the books that seemed to have more to do with the colour of the binding than any other logic. Under the eagle eye of the library's custodian, Eliza had managed to locate the novels, gratified to find a good selection of reading. She had not seen a book in her uncle's house, not even a bible.

Clutching *The Mill on the Floss*, she wandered back up the main street, stopping to look in the window of the large double-fronted store proclaiming MACKIE'S GENERAL STORE, EVERY PROVISION FOR HOUSE AND MINE. From the display in the windows, it did indeed appear to sell everything from gold pans to handkerchiefs. Passing the post office, she recalled that she needed to write to her aunt in Bath and tell her of Will's death. Another grief for the poor woman to bear.

Eliza entered her uncle's quiet house by the back door, coming into a comfortable, well-scrubbed kitchen. Through a half-open door, she glimpsed a small bedroom off the kitchen with a neatly made single bedstead covered in a patchwork quilt.

Mrs Harris sat at the table shelling peas and a boy sat by the fire polishing a man's boots, a large wooden box open beside him. He looked up and smiled. He had the round, flat face of a child suffering from what she had heard described as 'Mongolian idiocy'.

Seeing the gentle honesty of his smile, her heart lifted, and she smiled in return.

'Good afternoon,' she said. 'What's your name?'

'Tom.' He held up the boot he had been polishing. 'I keep Mr Cowper's boots so shiny he says he can shave in them. Do you have any boots that need polishing?'

Eliza looked down at her footwear, still muddied from the previous day. 'I do,' she said, 'but I'm afraid they're very dirty.'

'Then best take them off at the door,' Mrs Harris said. 'Tom'll see to them. You're traipsing mud all over my clean floor.'

Eliza turned to the woman and apologised. Balancing against the door jamb, she removed her boots and handed them to Tom.

He turned them over in his big hand. 'So small,' he said. 'I won't be able to get my hand inside them.'

Eliza smiled. 'I know. I keep hoping I will wake up one day and be six inches taller but I'm always the same. Now, Mrs Harris, if you have a cloth, I will see to the mess I have made.'

The woman coloured. 'Oh, you don't need—'

'Yes, I do, and I will make us both a cup of tea. Would you like tea, Tom?'

The boy glanced at the housekeeper.

'What do you say, Tom?'

'Yes, please, and can I have some cake too?'

Mrs Harris's smile betrayed the relationship. Mother and son without a doubt.

'How old are you?' Eliza asked as Mrs Harris handed around cups and plates laden with sizeable hunks of cake.

'I'm fifteen years old.'

'And do you go to school?'

Tom shook his head and his mouth turned down. 'No. Mr Emerton says there is no place at his school for idiots like me.'

Eliza bristled. 'Who is Mr Emerton?'

'Schoolmaster. Right old so-and-so he is,' Mrs Harris said with such vehemence, Eliza couldn't help but stare at her.

'Is Tom your son?'

Mrs Harris raised her eyes to meet Eliza's and lifted her chin with a practised defiance. 'He is, what of it?'

'Perhaps I can help him with a little schooling.'

'Why'd you want to do that?'

'I'm a schoolteacher, Mrs Harris, and I have no time for intolerance such as this Mr Emerton has shown.'

Mrs Harris glanced at her son. 'We'll see,' she said. 'No good making promises you won't be in a position to honour.'

'What do you mean?'

'You've no reason to stay in Maiden's Creek,' she said. 'You'll be off to Melbourne soon enough.'

'I've not made any decisions.'

The housekeeper gathered up the dirty cups and plates and set them on the sink. She turned back to Eliza. 'I do my best by the boy,' she said quietly, 'and Mr Cowper is good to let him stay on and do the odd jobs around the house.'

'Does he pay him?' Eliza asked.

Mrs Harris turned back to the dirty dishes in the sink, her silence answering for her. Tom was tolerated on a grace and favour basis.

'Tom's brought your brother's box in from the shed,' she said. 'Key's in the lock. I'm afraid we took the liberty of donating his clothes to the Ladies' Committee for charity and his books to the Mechanics' Institute Library. We weren't—'

'You weren't expecting me to turn up in person and claim them?'

The woman flushed.

'You did exactly what I would have done.' Eliza glanced out the window. The day seemed to be closing in already. 'Please excuse me, I have letters to write.'

'There's a fire in the parlour. It will be warmer than your bedroom.'

Eliza thanked her and walked down the corridor that ran from the front door to the kitchen. The sizeable parlour and dining room were to the left, Eliza's bedroom was at the front of the house along with a second, closed door adjoining her room—that must be her uncle's bedroom. As she passed, she tried the handle of the second bedroom and found it locked.

In her own room a battered travelling box had been placed beside hers. The initials WJP had been stencilled on the lid and she traced them with her forefinger before turning the brass key in the lock and lifting the lid. Eliza sat back on her heels and considered Will's meagre possessions. There seemed little to show for his life. The contents barely took up the base of the trunk and, despite what she had said to the housekeeper, Eliza wished that his clothes had not been so quickly given away. She longed for something tangible, something that still carried the essence of him.

The first object she took from the trunk, neatly wrapped in a silk handkerchief, proved to be Will's gold pocket watch. Their father, Josiah, had given Will the timepiece when he had turned twenty-one and Will had always worn it tucked into his waistcoat pocket. She opened the dented and scratched cover and traced the engraved inscription with her finger.

WJP from JEP
7th August 1854
Punctuality is the politeness of kings

The glass had cracked and the hands stopped at just past twelve-thirty. It took her a long moment to realise that the damage may well have occurred during Will's fall and the frozen hands marked the hour of his death. The thought turned her blood to ice. Her fingers closed over the cold, hard object, willing it to tell her the story of what happened that night.

Chiding herself for being a sentimental fool, she rewrapped the watch and put it away in the pretty little inlaid jewellery box that had been her mother's. So little to show for our lives, Eliza thought. A few pieces of paste jewellery, her locket, her mother's wedding ring and a broken watch.

The brown leather writing box that she had given Will when he left for Australia contained the letters she had written to him over the years, bundled up and tied with a piece of frayed string. They were crumpled and smeared with mud and she could imagine him taking them out and rereading them in quiet moments in the mine or sitting before the fire of an evening. With her back propped against the iron bedstead she started to read them, reliving the loneliness and despair of a young woman cut off from her family that had poured from her pen. Will had never been much of a correspondent himself but she had cherished his letters and, like Will, carried them with her.

She stood and brought out the leather folio where she kept his letters and arranged the two collections on the bed covers in date order. Seeing his familiar scrawl brought on tears, an unstoppable flood that poured from her, and she fell across the bed, crumpling the papers in her hand.

It had gone dark when she rose, cold and stiff. She washed her face and gathered up the scattered letters, tying them together with the string. She placed them in the leather folio and replaced it in the bottom of her travelling trunk. As she did so, she resolved not to bring them out again—they belonged to the past and spoke of a future that had been nothing more than a dream. She couldn't dwell on the might-have-been, she needed to make plans for a future that no longer included her brother.

She closed the lid on Will's chest and turned the key in the lock. It occurred to her that she had found no reference to his work over the past years. Will had adopted his father's work practices and kept detailed notebooks, including a daily journal, with conversations, calculations, predictions and outcomes noted with his engineer's eye for detail. She would have to ask her uncle what had become of them.

But when she raised the subject with Cowper over dinner, he just shrugged. 'If they're not there, then your brother didn't have them,' he said. 'Tehan assures me that everything belonging to Will was packed in that trunk.'

'Who's Tehan?'

Cowper looked up from his dissection of the rather tough mutton. 'Tehan is the chap who is managing the Shenandoah for me. The men call him Black Jack. He'd been working as foreman for your brother so he knows the mine and seemed a sensible choice as mine superintendent. Obviously he's not got your brother's education but he has a good instinct and he's steering the mine on a steady course.'

'But you said it has no future.'

'And neither does it. But until the majority shareholders return, I am obligated to keep it operational.'

'And this Tehan saw to Will's belongings?'

'After your brother's accident, I suggested he could have the use of your brother's cottage at the mine and left it to him to pack up Will's possessions. Next time I see him, I'll ask about the notebooks.'

Eliza turned back to her meal. While Mrs Harris may have been considered a good cook, the sheep from which the mutton had been taken must have been extremely elderly. When she looked up she found her uncle watching her, a frown creasing his forehead.

'Is something troubling you, Uncle?'

'You know, Eliza, as your only surviving male relative, you are now my responsibility—'

'Not at all. I do not consider myself anyone's responsibility. Least of all yours.'

'Nevertheless, there is nothing for you here. I will be happy to pay your passage back to England and provide a small income sufficient for you to keep a small cottage, perhaps.'

Eliza stared at him. She had just travelled thirteen thousand miles to come to this country—nothing could possibly induce her to go back and live out her days in lonely spinsterhood in a cottage in some tiny village, teaching Dame School if she was lucky.

'That is exceedingly kind of you, Uncle, but I have no wish to return to England. I am sure there is some useful employment I can find here in the colony.'

Cowper speared pieces of carrot and potato with his fork and chewed them slowly, his eyes fixed on her face. 'Very well. If you don't wish to go back to England, at least let me assist you in setting up in Melbourne—or Sydney, if you prefer. Maybe a little business, or if you are set on teaching, I could assist in finding a position at a respectable ladies' college, somewhat like the one you left?'

Eliza thought of the forbidding stone walls of Miss Drury's Academy for Young Ladies on the edge of Dartmoor. It had been a lonely life, but she had enjoyed teaching and that alone had provided some consolation. But now she needed time—time to mourn Will and to recover from the rigours of the long journey.

'That is very kind of you but if I am not an inconvenience, may I stay here for a little while? Will loved this place and I owe it to his memory not to desert him the moment I arrive.'

Cowper set his plate to one side and nodded. 'Of course. You are not an inconvenience and I welcome the company. Stay as long as you wish. And if there is anything I can help you with, please do not hesitate to ask me.'

Eliza set down her knife and fork. 'I would like to see the Shenandoah Mine.'

Her uncle blinked. 'I beg your pardon?'

'Will's mine, the Shenandoah.'

'Why? It's just a mine. No place for a lady.'

'Because … because it was important to Will.'

A muscle twitched in her uncle's cheek and he glanced at the window, where icy rain lashed the glass. 'Bear in mind it is winter and, in this weather, the road up to Pretty Sally is well-nigh impassable, but next time Tehan is in town, I will mention your wish and we will see what can be done.'

'We've spoken of the Shenandoah, but what of your mine, Uncle? The Maiden's Creek. Is it doing well for you?'

Cowper sat back, lacing his fingers over his waistcoat. 'We have hit the main reef in the deep lead and our yield is improving already. I have assured the other shareholders we can expect a good return this year. You have to understand, it can be years before a mine can pay a good dividend. The investors have to have a lot of faith in it.'

'My father always said that it's a form of gambling.'

'Indeed, and look what became your father. But I can assure you there is nothing to concern yourself about. It's a man's business.'

Eliza bit her tongue. She had been brought up in a house where the main topic of conversation around the dining table had always been mines and mining. Tin or gold, the story was the same, and she probably understood more than many men about the risk/reward proposition. That had been her father's undoing.

'Take my advice, gold mining is no business for a woman, Eliza,' Cowper continued, 'and this is a hard place to live. My offer stands. While you are welcome to stay as long as you wish, I will provide every assistance for you to leave Maiden's Creek and find something more congenial.'

Eliza forced a smile. 'Are you trying to get rid of me, Uncle?'

He held up a hand. 'Not at all, not at all. It is merely your own health and sensibilities I am concerned about. Once winter really sets in, it will be hard to leave and the weather can be harsh.'

'I will just have to purchase some flannel underwear,' Eliza said, and was rewarded with a look of horror on her uncle's face.

$\mathcal{F}ive$

22 June 1873

Alec rolled over in bed and lay for a long time listening to the sound of ... nothing. On Sundays the stampers fell silent and the inhabitants of Maiden's Creek complained of the unnatural peace and quiet. In the deafening silence, Alec thought through the tasks for the following day until a loud rapping on his bedroom door reminded him he had promised Ian he would accompany him to church.

The smile on Ian's face when Alec had told him he would attend the service caused a stab of guilt. He had to remind himself that in Ian's world, the approval of his older brother equalled that of a father; and Alec was inordinately proud of Ian, who always found joy in everything and whose faith in a God who had failed Alec in so many ways remained unshakeable.

They stepped out into a cold, damp morning. Mist wreathed up from the gullies to shroud the tops of the hills that surrounded the valley. The tolling of bells called the faithful of Maiden's Creek to worship: St Thomas on the Hill summoned adherents to the Church of England; St Mary's, the Roman Catholics; and

St Andrew's, the Presbyterians. The Methodists and others of the non-conformist faiths met in the Mechanics' Institute. For them, the use of such fancies as bells was frowned on.

As they entered St Andrew's, they encountered the eldest of Angus Mackie's many daughters, Susan, who worked in her father's general store and played the harmonium at the church service on Sunday,

'Good morning, Mr McLeod.' She lowered her eyes, before modestly looking up at Ian from under lashes.

To Alec's surprise, Ian's cheeks reddened. 'G-good morning, Miss Mackie.'

She greeted Alec but not with quite the warmth she had shown his brother. 'I'm so glad you will both be joining us for luncheon,' she said.

Alec quirked an eyebrow at his brother.

Ian had the grace to avoid his brother's unspoken question and turned back to Susan Mackie. 'We are looking forward to it.' He glanced at Alec with entreaty in his eyes.

'Aye, that we are,' Alec said. Even though this had been the first mention of luncheon at the Mackies, if nothing else, a decent meal would be more than welcome.

Ian and Susan still stared at each other with what Alec's mother would have called cow eyes.

'I like your hat,' Ian stuttered.

Susan Mackie blushed and hid a giggle behind her hymnal. Alec bit back a sigh. She really was a remarkably silly young woman and, not that he was an expert on hats, he thought the particular shade of burgundy clashed with her red hair.

A tall, thin woman with her dark hair coiled on top of her head in a tight, unflattering bun approached the group. Flora Donald, the assistant teacher at the school and sister of the minister, James Donald, held out a hymnal to Alec.

'Good morning, Mr McLeod. We don't often see you here at St Andrew's. Have you come to hear your brother preach?'

Alec took the hymnal. 'I have. How are you, Miss Donald?'

Two spots of colour bloomed in her pale cheeks. 'Passing well, thank you, Mr McLeod. And you?'

The inane conversation on weather and the state of the roads stumbled on for a few more awkward minutes before Alec managed to escape and find a place at the back of the church. He endured the interminable droning of the Reverend Donald before Ian rose to preach. Much as he loved his brother, Alec failed to share his enthusiasm for the parable of the prodigal son. He crossed his arms and tried to pay attention but his sympathy had always been for the older brother, left behind to keep the farm going while his younger sibling went off carousing. He found himself nodding off, jerking awake when someone dropped a book. He hoped Ian hadn't noticed.

After the service he stayed to help Ian pack away the hymnals and together they walked down to the Mackies' residence behind their substantial store.

'What did you think?' Ian asked.

'Inspiring.'

His brother whacked him playfully on the arm. 'You fell asleep.'

'Did not.'

'I saw you.'

'I was resting my eyes. It helps me concentrate.'

Angus Mackie had six daughters, all red-headed and freckle-faced. The eldest had married and left Maiden's Creek, Susan worked in the store and the other four were still at school.

Alec's disquiet about the lunch deepened when Flora and James Donald joined the party and he found himself seated next to Flora. Ian was next to Susan, who seemed overcome and barely addressed a word to him throughout the meal. The two youngest girls giggled and whispered to each other, casting Susan quick glances.

Having exhausted another conversation about the weather, Alec asked Flora about her work at the school.

Her already thin lips tightened. 'The school is closed. Mr Emerton was taken ill last week and there's no saying when he'll return.'

Angus Mackie, who, among his other civic duties, also sat on the school's Board of Advice, waved a fork in the air as he spoke with his mouth full. 'Aye, we've a serious problem there, Miss Donald. Dr Sims says it's the man's heart and Emerton will not be fit for duty for months, if at all. The school will have to remain closed for the time being, until a replacement teacher can be found.'

Flora straightened. 'But that could take months.'

Mackie shrugged. 'The Board of Advice will discuss what is to be done. Don't fret, Miss Donald.'

'I'm not fretting, but I am concerned that the children's education will suffer.'

Flora Donald fidgeted, her long, thin fingers tightening on her cutlery but before she could respond, Mrs Mackie changed the topic of conversation. 'I hear Will Penrose's sister has arrived in town, the poor lassie knowing naught about her brother's accident.'

Flora sniffed. 'Waltzing into town not even wearing proper mourning for her poor dead mother, Mary Harris told me.'

Her brother glared at her. 'Flora. You've no right to be listening to such tattletales, let alone repeating what they say.'

But Flora Donald would not be deterred. 'And that's not all Mary Harris told me. She comes from bad blood. Her father was a wastrel and we all know her brother to be a drunkard who consorted with whores.'

Alec stiffened. 'William Penrose was my friend, Miss Donald.'

'That's as may be, but the fact remains, their father committed the sin of taking his own life and there's nothing to say Will Penrose didn't follow where his father led.'

'Are you suggesting Penrose committed suicide?'

As Alec uttered the word, the whole table froze.

'Mr McLeod,' Angus Mackie chided. 'This is not the place to discuss such matters.'

Alec bridled. It had not been him who raised the issue, but Flora Donald seemed to be finding her meal of the utmost interest and would not meet his eyes.

Ian had missed the exchange and cast his brother a questioning glance. Alec glared but his brother's attention had already been diverted by Susan Mackie's fingers lightly brushing his sleeve as she reached for the basket of bread.

There was no reprieve at the end of the meal. The McLeods were invited to linger and hear Susan playing the piano. Ian was deputed to turn the music and Alec persuaded to sing 'Will Ye Nae Come Back Again'. He generally enjoyed the music of home but today he just wanted to escape. And every time he tried to catch Ian's eye and make their apologies, his brother ignored him.

Finally released, they tramped back to their own cottage, Alec sunk in a deep gloom.

When they shut the door on the world, Alec searched out his whisky bottle. The lack of anything stronger than cordial at lunch had been almost more than he could bear.

'Don't ever do that to me again,' he grumbled.

Ian's eyes widened in innocence. 'Do what?'

'Inflict the Mackies on me. It's plain they are after matching you with Susan.'

Ian stared at him, his mouth cast down. 'Don't you like Susan?'

Ian's doleful reaction confirmed Alec's suspicion that the attraction was mutual. He coughed. 'Do you like her?'

Ian shrugged and looked away.

'You do.' Alec grasped his brother's shoulders and turned him so Ian could read his lips. 'I am an ill-tempered old curmudgeon, just ignore me. If you like Susan Mackie, then I wish you well.'

'I want what you and Catriona had,' Ian said.

Alec smiled. 'Aye, and that's what I wish for you. It's plain the girl likes you and if you feel the same way, then good luck to the both of you.'

Ian beamed. 'Thank you. Your blessing means a lot.' He poked Alec in the chest. 'And you. You've mourned Catriona long enough. It's time for you to find a lass.'

Alec laughed. 'Hah! If you think I'm going to be matched with Flora Donald then you—and she—can think again.'

'You don't like Flora?'

'Can *you* imagine being married to her?' Alec said. 'With her sharp tongue?'

'Maybe that's because she's unhappy? She's strong and healthy and properly raised. That's all you need in a wife.'

'No, it's not. I need a companion who shares my interests.'

Ian laughed. 'Machinery and mines? Really, Alec?'

'My point exactly, Ian.'

On the other side of the valley, Eliza had accompanied her uncle, Mrs Harris and Tom to the service of Matins at St Thomas on the Hill. Cowper marched her to the front pew of the church and the heat rose in Eliza's face as the eyes of the congregation of Maiden's Creek Church of England bored into her back.

The single brazier and the hot bricks under each pew did little to dispel the chill of the building and when the service concluded, Eliza found herself unable to feel her toes. At the door, Cowper introduced her to the Reverend Johnson, a tall man with thinning hair and a prominent Adam's apple who greeted her heartily, taking her hand in both of his. Like his church, they were icy.

'Delighted to welcome you to our little flock, Miss Penrose, and my deepest condolences on the passing of your brother. My word, his funeral was one of the biggest we've ever seen in this town. We could not fit everyone in the church.'

Eliza swallowed the lump of grief that rose in her throat and thanked the man. Cowper drew the vicar away, leaving Eliza standing by herself. A large woman trailed by a smaller, mousy woman sailed up to her.

'How remiss of your uncle not to introduce us properly,' the large woman said. 'Mrs Russell—Mrs Osborne Russell. My husband is the manager of the Bank of Australasia, and this is Mrs Jervis.' She indicated the mousy woman, who bobbed her head. 'Mr Jervis manages the Bank of Victoria. On behalf of the Ladies' Committee, please accept our condolences on your brother's passing.'

Eliza thanked them and Mrs Russell continued, 'We heard what happened on your arrival. Such a greeting to our little town.' She tutted. 'McLeod is such an oaf, not at all like your poor dear brother, but then your brother was raised as a gentleman, which is not the case with McLeod.' She leaned in to Eliza. 'Dragged himself up out of the coal mines by the straps of his boots. Once a miner, always a miner, I say.'

'Oh, I—' Eliza began.

'I do hope you will join the Ladies' Committee, Miss Penrose. We are committed—'

'Committed!' put in Mrs Jervis; it was the first time Eliza had heard her speak.

'—Committed to doing good works among the less fortunate among us.'

'Very commendable—'

'But of course, we wage a continual battle, in the good Lord's name, against the evils of drink and the scourge of loose women.'

'I …' Eliza cast around for a suitable answer to that assumption. 'I understand the good work you ladies do, but you will have to accept my apologies. I fear I must seek some sort of employment. I cannot be beholden to my uncle indefinitely.'

'Employment? A lady such as yourself?' Mrs Jervis could not have looked more shocked if Eliza had taken off all her clothes and ridden down the main street of Maiden's Creek.

'Unfortunately, I am a lady fallen on hard times, Mrs Jervis,' Eliza said with barely concealed irritation. 'I must take paying work where it offers.' And because the pious sanctity of the two ladies had annoyed her, she added, 'As must the women who you dismiss as "loose". They are only trying to make their way in a world that is not kind to women who lack the protection of a man.'

'I never did!' Mrs Jervis put a hand to the snowy white lace cravat around her neck.

Mrs Russell's chins shook. 'Miss Penrose, *really*. I can only assume such plain-speaking comes because you are tired and strained from the long journey and the shock of the news that awaited you. Come, Mildred, we must discuss the reverend's sermon with him.'

Eliza let out a breath as the two formidable matrons pushed through the crowd in the direction of the unfortunate vicar.

'Bless you. That's the best laugh I've had in weeks.'

Eliza turned to face her eavesdropper, a small woman, not much taller than her.

The woman smiled. 'Nothing gives me greater pleasure than seeing those two biddies brought down a peg or two.' She held out her hand. 'Berenice Burrell, but I'm Netty to my friends. My husband, Amos, told me you'd arrived.'

'The coach driver?'

'The same. Will told us all about you. He was so excited at the thought you were coming to join him here. He couldn't wait to show you the country.'

'Did you know him well?'

Netty Burrell nodded but her pleasant, cheerful countenance crumpled. She produced a handkerchief from her sleeve and dabbed at her eyes. 'I'm so sorry about your brother. I suppose you had no way of knowing that … that …'

Eliza shook her head, sparing the woman further distress. 'No. My uncle had to break the news.'

'It shook the whole town.' Netty looked around at the little gatherings of worshippers lingering by the church. 'Will Penrose was greatly liked. You should have seen his funeral. Hundreds turned out to pay their respects.'

'So the vicar told me. That is some comfort.'

Netty took Eliza's hands in both of hers. 'Come and take tea with me this afternoon?'

Eliza clutched at the first real thread of friendship that had been offered to her since her arrival. 'I would love to,' she said. 'Where do I find you?'

'I have the dressmaker's shop. The residence is behind it. Come at three?'

'Thank you,' Eliza said. 'I will look forward to it.'

She turned to find her uncle coming toward her, Mrs Harris behind him.

'I am so sorry,' Cowper said. 'I didn't mean to abandon you with no proper introductions, but unfortunately the duties of warden …' He spread his hands apologetically. 'Never fear, I have arranged for the more important people in town to dine with us tomorrow evening. You will meet everyone you need to know then.'

As they descended the steep path away from St Thomas's, Mrs Harris said to Eliza in a low voice, 'That Mrs Burrell.'

'What of her?'

'Too common for the likes of you.'

'Thank you for the advice,' Eliza said, 'but I think I will be the judge of who I consort with, Mrs Harris.'

The woman sniffed and hurried on several paces, leaving Eliza and Tom to bring up the rear. The boy chatted about Sunday School and showed Eliza the special bookmark he had been given. As he talked, Eliza realised that the currents of social tension that flowed beneath the fabric of Maiden's Creek were no different from those in any small community and she had better watch her sharp tongue, or she risked alienating every woman in town by the following Sunday.

Six

Eliza ignored the housekeeper's advice and, braving the rain that had set in for the afternoon, kept her social engagement with Netty Burrell. On her explorations of the town, she had passed the neat shopfront with a half-curtained window in which a mannequin dressed in a fashionable plaid dress with matching bonnet and pelisse had been placed. A sign propped against the glass read: MRS B BURRELL, SEAMSTRESS AND DRESSMAKER. Eliza found a narrow path that ran down the side of the building leading to a red door with a gleaming brass knocker.

Netty greeted her at the door with a smile that warmed Eliza's heart. 'Come in, come in. Thank you for coming out in this vile weather.'

Netty took her umbrella and wet coat and Eliza stepped into a homely parlour. Two chairs and a little table had been placed in front of a fire burning in the shining grate. 'I've just put the kettle on. Take a seat by the fire and warm yourself.'

'You're very kind, Mrs Burrell,' Eliza said, gratefully drawing herself up to the fire.

'Netty. Everyone calls me Netty. May I call you Eliza? I feel like I know you so well.' Netty busied herself with the tea, pouring two cups and handing one to Eliza.

'I am sure Will had other topics of conversation.'

'He did, of course he did.'

A tear dripped into Eliza's tea cup as she lowered her head. Netty produced a neat square of lace-edged cambric from her sleeve.

'I hadn't seen him for five years,' Eliza said with a shuddering breath as she set the cup down and wiped her eyes with Netty's handkerchief. 'I do apologise. I seem to have been awash since I arrived.'

'Nothing to apologise for. It must have been a terrible shock to you.' Netty patted her hand. 'And then for that Alec McLeod to be so rude to you. But he's not a bad lad, that one, just hard to get to know. Keeps himself to himself.' Netty took a sip of her tea. 'What's your uncle told you about Will's death?'

'He was found at the foot of the tailings and the coroner concluded it was an accident,' Eliza said. 'But I don't understand why he was up at the Maiden's Creek Mine in the middle of the night.'

'That no one knows. There was some suggestion that maybe he had drunk a little more than usual that night.' She sighed. 'All I know is that Amos and I lost a good friend and the community lost one of its best men. He had an instinct for mining that few have.' She paused. 'If you don't mind me asking, what's become of the Shenandoah? We haven't heard anything down here.'

'My uncle tells me he has put in a crew to work it but he says it is worthless, and I suppose he should know. It's his responsibility now.'

Netty set her cup down with such force it rattled in its saucer. 'His responsibility? I don't understand. It was common knowledge that Penrose held shares in the mine. They'd be yours now?'

'No. He left them to my uncle. If it is worth nothing but trouble, then maybe I am well rid of it.' But the thought of losing the

Shenandoah left a hollow ache in Eliza's heart. It had meant so much to Will.

Netty stood and paced the floor. 'But that's not right,' she said, her hands on her hips. 'What about the Shenandoah's other shareholders? Do Caleb and Adelaide know about this?'

'Will told me all about them, and Mrs Hunt did write to me when they were in England, but we could not arrange a meeting. Are you well acquainted with them?'

Netty laughed as she resumed her seat. 'Aye, you could say that. I was nursery maid to Adelaide from when she was a wee bairn and Caleb ... well, Caleb is Caleb and it is a true blessing that they found each other. It was Caleb's mine, you know. He won it in a game of chance. Will convinced him that it had good promise and when they discovered the gold, they went into the business together. That's how it all began.'

'Will believed in it enough to put everything he owned into it,' Eliza said.

Netty studied her for a long moment and her mouth turned down. 'Amos and I have a few shares in the Shenandoah, a wedding present from Caleb.'

'I'm sorry.'

'Nought to do with you, lass,' Netty said. 'You don't miss what you don't have, but it'll be disappointing for Caleb and Adelaide. They believed in it as much as Will did.'

'Do you know where they are now? I should have liked to meet them, but I had obligations at the school and couldn't get up to London,' Eliza said, remembering the frustration at not being able to escape even for a few days.

'They've been travelling but are on their way home. When Adelaide last wrote, they were in America. I suppose Caleb wanted to show her his birthplace.'

'I didn't know he was American.'

'Oh, yes. A proud Virginian, he'd tell you. He is a fine doctor and the town misses him, not that he'll come back to that. Dr Sims is competent enough, but we all miss Caleb.' She looked around her comfortable parlour. 'They were generous to me. I've always been good with a needle, so Adelaide set me up with the business before she left Maiden's Creek. She says every woman should be able to make their own way in the world.'

'That's true,' Eliza said. 'I have found my vocation in teaching.'

'Do you truly enjoy it, though?' Netty cast her a doubtful look.

Eliza considered her answer. 'I do. There is enormous satisfaction in seeing a child understand something about the world that was previously hidden from them. Although I would never go back to being a governess. I hated that.'

'It depends on the family,' Netty said. 'Miss Adelaide had some wonderful governesses. One of the better things Sir Daniel did for his daughter.'

'I started as a governess,' Eliza said, 'but the son of the house viewed any woman, particularly if they were young and pretty, as his personal property—' She broke off. She'd said too much.

From the flash of anger in Netty Burrell's blue eyes, she knew the woman understood.

Netty lifted the lid of the teapot and peered inside. 'More tea?'

'What do you know about a girl called Sissy?' Eliza asked as Netty handed her the fresh cup.

Netty paused, her hand outstretched. 'Sissy? Did Will mention her in his letters?'

'Not once. I met her at the cemetery yesterday. She's been leaving flowers on his grave.'

Netty took a sip from her cup and set it back on the table. 'I'm sorry to say this, Miss Penrose, but your brother treated her most heartlessly.' The words came out in a rush.

'Will? How?'

Netty opened the sewing box beside her chair and picked up a fine muslin chemise. 'Will you excuse me? I have to get this done by tomorrow morning.' She began sewing with small, neat stitches. 'There's an establishment in town run by Lil White. You'll hear it referred to as Lil's Place.'

'What sort?' One look at Netty's face gave her the answer. 'Oh, a house of ill repute?'

Netty cleared her throat. 'Lil brooks no nonsense from anyone and the girls are well looked after.'

'And Sissy is one of the girls?'

'She is.'

Heat rose in Eliza's cheeks. 'And Will patronised this place?'

Netty shrugged. 'He was a young man and Sissy's a pretty girl. He made the mistake of falling in love with her and he promised her marriage and respectability.'

Conscious her mouth had fallen open, Eliza snapped it shut. How would she have reacted if Will had told her he planned to marry a—a whore? A nagging voice of conscience reminded her that she had defended such women only that morning.

'My parents would turn in their graves,' she said.

Netty nodded. 'That's as may be, but Sissy, poor fool, was head over heels in love with him. He kept her stringing along for months, over a year, but once he had the Shenandoah and was free of your uncle, he cast her off.'

Eliza frowned. 'While I find it inconceivable that he would have proposed marriage to such a woman, Will was never wantonly cruel.'

'I can't say for certain what passed between them, but she's not been the same sweet creature this last year. And you may call her "such a woman", Miss Penrose, but I count her, as I do every other girl at Lil's, as a friend. So does Miss Adelaide.'

Chided, Eliza looked down at the cup in her hands. Whatever her occupation, Sissy was still a human being with feelings and hopes and dreams, and it sounded like Will had dashed them. And now Will had left them both.

'I didn't mean to sound so judgemental,' she said. 'She must have loved him because she tends his grave and lays flowers on it.'

'For all of his disregard of her, she took his death hard,' Netty said.

Eliza sat back in the comfortable chair, soothed by the crackling fire as Netty continued her stitching in silence.

Then, without looking up, Netty said, 'So, your uncle has the mine and your brother left you nothing of value. What will you do now?'

Eliza sighed. 'It seems I have no choice but to go to Melbourne or Sydney and try and find a position as a schoolteacher. There's nothing to hold me in Maiden's Creek but a grave.'

Netty nodded. 'That's a pity, but that's our lot in life isn't it?' She smiled. 'Still, you're a pretty girl, you should find yourself a husband.'

Eliza gave a humourless laugh. 'I am twenty-five and I fear my best years are well behind me now. I'm good for nothing except teaching or being a companion to some elderly, and hopefully wealthy, lady.'

'Don't say things like that,' Netty said with surprising ferocity. 'Miss Adelaide never gave in. She trained as a telegraphist and ran the post office in this town for five years. She kept her son Danny and I fed and shod by her own hard work.' A fierce pride in her friend's achievements shone from Netty's eyes.

'I hope to meet her one day,' Eliza said.

'Oh, you will. She'll be back by year's end.' Netty stood up. 'Now, if you've nowhere else to be, bide a while. I can see you are a lady of fashion and there are precious few of those in this town. I would love to have a good look at how that skirt is gathered.'

Eliza looked at the black wool of her skirt. 'This? It is very plain. I had it made in Bath, but the dressmaker assured me it was the latest silhouette.'

She lingered until the afternoon began to draw in, happy to pore over the plates in Netty's out-of-date ladies' magazines, discussing how the modes could be adapted to suit the current fashion.

Seven

23 June 1873

Unrelenting rain kept Eliza indoors all day. She occupied her time by writing letters, reading, and helping Mrs Harris in the kitchen, whether the woman appreciated her assistance or not. Any attempts Eliza made to draw her into conversation were met with monosyllabic answers. Mrs Harris was proving a hard person to get to know.

With guests expected for dinner, Eliza dressed carefully, choosing an elegant black evening gown that had belonged to her mother. She had spent the voyage altering it to a more fashionable style and fit but when she entered the parlour, one look at the assembled guests made it clear she had overdressed. The other women were attired in what she would describe as 'Sunday best' and none of the gentlemen wore evening dress.

Her uncle stepped forward. 'Eliza, my dear, so pleased you could join us. Allow me to introduce you ...'

She turned to each guest as Cowper made the introductions. A short stout man was introduced as Angus Mackie, who kept the general store, and his red-headed wife, Leonora, was equally as short and stout. She recognised Mrs Russell and Mrs Jervis from church. Osborne Russell looked exactly as a bank manager should, tall and silver-haired with a magnificent moustache and neat beard, and Mr Jervis was a shorter rounder version of Russell. The other guests were introduced as the Reverend Donald, minister of the Presbyterian church, St Stephen's—a thin man in a clerical collar who wore round, wire-rimmed glasses—and his sister, Flora Donald. Miss Donald inclined her head, her hard eyes appraising Eliza's evening gown. From the tightly drawn lines around her long nose, the woman clearly disapproved of what she saw.

Cowper indicated that Eliza should take the place of lady of the house at the opposite end of the table, with an empty place on her left, set for a tardy guest. Cowper glanced at his watch and then the door, where Mrs Harris hovered. 'I invited McLeod, but he must be held up at the mine. We won't wait on him,' he said. 'You can serve, Mrs Harris.'

Flora Donald turned to Eliza. 'Please accept my condolences on the death of your brother, Miss Penrose, but take comfort in the fact he is with our Lord now.'

Eliza thanked Flora with an appropriately doleful inclination of her head. She had met this type before. The woman probably slept with a copy of the bible under her pillow.

'Of course, Miss Penrose, we were all deeply saddened by your brother's death,' Osborne Russell said. 'May I enquire as to what you were doing before your move to the Antipodes?'

'I am a teacher,' Eliza said.

'As is my dear sister, Flora,' Reverend Donald said with a fond smile in the direction of his sister.

Flora returned the smile and a pang of regret cut to Eliza's heart. She would never be called 'dear sister' again.

'And were you teaching in England?' Mrs Mackie asked.

'Yes, I was the senior teacher at Miss Drury's Academy for Young Ladies in Devon,' Eliza said.

Jervis leaned forward. 'What did you teach?'

'Whatever was required of me: English, history, geography, Latin, mathematics and needlework. I had the benefit of an excellent education, which I have been able to pass on to my pupils.'

'Very commendable,' Russell said. 'You should have no difficulty securing a good position in Sydney or Melbourne with those qualifications.'

Eliza turned to Flora. 'Where do you teach, Miss Donald?'

'I am the assistant teacher at the Maiden's Creek Public School,' Flora replied. 'Although it is presently closed and the children are running wild, as they are wont to do. Their fathers work in the mines and drink in the pubs and their mothers are too busy to instil proper discipline.'

'They're not all bad children,' Mrs Mackie said.

Flora turned her attention to the woman. 'They lack the fear of God,' she said, 'but under the new Act, we cannot impart the word of the Lord in our teaching.'

'Why is the school closed?' Eliza asked.

The Reverend Donald answered for his sister. 'Unfortunately, the head teacher is unwell and we were forced to close the school last week while we considered the situation.' He gestured around the table. 'Under the new Education Act we have a Board of Advice. Mr Mackie and Mr Russell and I comprise the Board and it is our duty to see to the appointment of a replacement.'

Eliza frowned. In her walks around the town she could not recall seeing a school building. 'Where is the school?'

'Just beyond the mine entrance to the north of the town. It was only built five years ago and is already inadequate for the number of children,' Russell said.

'How many students do you have?'

Flora answered, 'We've just over seventy children, aged six to fifteen. I have the infant classes and Mr Emerton had some fifty children in the older classes.' Her lips tightened. 'There's a wildness about this town, Miss Penrose, as you'll learn. More public houses than churches, and as for that deplorable establishment Lil's Place ...' She spat out the words as if they tasted foul.

'I was telling Miss Penrose about that unfortunate place yesterday morning,' Mrs Russell said.

Flora Donald turned back to Eliza. This time there was no sympathy in the harsh lines of her face. 'Sadly, your brother was something of a patron of Lil's Place, Miss Penrose. You should know he had taken up with one of those ... those women.'

'Miss Donald!' Mrs Mackie scolded. 'Do not speak ill of the dead.'

'Aye, well, it's best she knows what sort of man her brother was—or had become.'

The animosity in the woman's voice surprised Eliza. 'Will was never a saint, Miss Donald,' she said. 'He left a trail of broken hearts behind him in England.'

Mrs Russell looked at Cowper. 'All I can say is that it is a mercy you put an end to that nonsense, Charles. As I was telling you yesterday, Miss Penrose, the Ladies' Committee provides the social and moral fibre for our little community.'

'Indeed,' Mrs Jervis agreed. 'We have been battling to control the drunkenness and immoral behaviour in this town. We have the full support of the churches, do we not, Reverend?'

'We do,' Reverend Donald said. 'We are as one on the subject.'

'Indeed. Those women are a scourge on this town,' Mrs Russell said. 'They should all be packed up and sent back to Melbourne.'

Charles Cowper cleared his throat. 'In an ideal world you are correct, Miss Donald, but we do not live in such a place. Lil keeps a good, orderly house. Would you rather the men rampaged through the streets looking for anything in a skirt?'

'I would rather the men were in church where they belong,' Flora retorted. 'My brother has an excellent sermon on the temptations of the flesh.' She glanced at the minister, who seemed very intent on his soup.

'Where is this establishment?' Eliza asked.

'Out past the mine and the school house,' Mrs Russell said. 'On the outskirts of town, where it should be.'

Flora Donald clucked her tongue. 'I visited once to impart the word of the Lord to the godless souls. I gave Mrs White a copy of the New Testament and she threw it back at me.'

Fortunately, a sharp rap on the front door interrupted any further discussion on the evils of Lil's Place.

'Ah, that must be McLeod,' Cowper said with what Eliza suspected was relief.

A flushed and slightly dishevelled Alec McLeod entered the dining room, running a hand over his damp hair as if trying to restore it to some sort of order. 'Sorry I'm late,' he said. 'We're having a problem with the new boiler.'

Cowper frowned. 'Nothing serious?'

'No. Trevalyn's got it under control.'

Cowper gestured at the empty chair next to Eliza. 'I don't believe you've met my niece, Miss Penrose. Eliza, my mine superintendent, Alec McLeod.'

'Miss Penrose and I have met, sir.' Alec took the hand she held out to him, crushing her fingers in his large, square grip.

He took the seat beside her and gave her a rueful smile. 'Although I am embarrassed to say, not in the best of circumstances. I am responsible for ruining her coat.'

'From the account I heard, I believe that you were extremely rude,' Mrs Russell said.

Eliza came to the man's defence. 'It was an accident. I was in the wrong place and Mr McLeod was attending to an urgent problem. Mrs Harris has done a fine job of getting the mud out.' No need to mention their subsequent encounter at the Mechanics' Institute.

'You are very gracious, Miss Penrose,' Alec said as Mrs Harris set a bowl of soup down in front of him.

'It's cold,' she said.

Alec mumbled an apology to the housekeeper.

Flora Donald, seated on the other side of him, said, 'Your brother gave a fine homily on Sunday, despite his affliction.'

'He did indeed,' the Reverend Donald said. 'You must be very proud of him.'

Alec paused, soup spoon halfway to his mouth. 'Aye, that I am.'

But Mrs Mackie had already turned her attention to Eliza. 'Mr McLeod's brother, Ian, is one of the less fortunate among us.'

Alec's soup spoon clattered in the bowl. 'My brother is deaf, Miss Penrose.' He cast Mrs Mackie a dark look. 'But in no way would I describe him as less fortunate than the rest of us.'

'Indeed not. He does an excellent job as my clerk,' Cowper said.

'I'll tell him you said that,' Alec said.

'Yes, well. Probably something I have needed to say for a while.' Cowper coughed.

'Oh, I meant only—' Mrs Mackie's flustered apology was interrupted by the arrival of the main course.

As Cowper carved the chicken, Flora Donald addressed Osborne Russell, asking when the school would reopen.

'Dr Sims is arranging for Emerton to be sent down to the hospital at Sale, away from the noxious fumes and noise. As if there is anything we can do about those. But Miss Donald is right, we can't leave the school closed indefinitely.' Russell tugged at his beard. 'I'm at a loss as to what to suggest. We have a new Act but no real guidance about how it is to be implemented. The children have missed more than enough schooling over Mr Emerton's heart problems. I have written to the Department of Education in Melbourne but we will need to advertise for a permanent replacement teacher as a matter of urgency.'

His wife puffed out her not inconsiderable chest. 'You men.' She gestured at Flora Donald. 'The answer is sitting here at the table. Appoint Miss Donald the acting head teacher, then at least the school can reopen.'

'No, that will never do,' Mackie said. 'With all due respect to Miss Donald, a man's hand is needed at the school, and until we can find a suitable male teacher, it will need to stay closed.'

Eliza looked at the pompous, self-satisfied faces of the men at the table and fought back a mounting anger. 'My apologies, gentlemen, but I fail to see why the appointment of a man to this position is so important? If Miss Donald is qualified and capable then why should she not be allowed to fill the position?'

Flora Donald cast her a sour look. 'I don't need you to speak for me, Miss Penrose.'

'Flora is a certified teacher under the old Act, why can't she be appointed as temporary head teacher and a new assistant found?' Reverend Donald said.

Russell stroked his beard and sat back in his chair, the fingers of his other hand beating a silent tattoo on the table. 'On reflection, if it means the school can reopen, I agree it seems sensible to put Miss Donald in charge for the time being with a suitable assistant. Do you think you can manage such a responsibility, Miss Donald?'

'Of course I can.'

'However, the question remains of an assistant. It is too much to expect you to manage with just a pupil assistant,' Russell continued.

'But how do we find someone qualified?' Mackie asked.

Russell rolled his eyes. 'We are a small town a hundred or so miles from Melbourne, we will make do.'

Mrs Jervis raised a hand. 'What about Miss Penrose?"

Everyone turned to look at Eliza and her heart began to race. If she could secure a position at the local school, it would give her the time she needed to consider her future. She cleared her throat. 'I would like to be considered for such an appointment,' she said.

'Eliza, my dear, there is a big difference between having the care of a few well-bred young ladies and a school of over seventy boisterous boys and girls,' Cowper said. He shook his head. 'No, I cannot possibly countenance such an appointment.'

His disapproval took her by surprise. 'With the greatest respect, Uncle, it is hardly your decision.'

'This is not a discussion to have in front of our guests, Eliza.' His eyebrows rose in warning but Eliza ignored him.

'It is not a discussion to be had at all. I'm qualified and experienced and if it is intended to be a temporary position, then I fail to see why I should not be considered. I'm very good with children and I'm not afraid of hard work. I have references from my previous positions.'

'Being good with children is one thing,' Mrs Mackie said, 'but I am afraid many of the children—our own dear girls excepted of course—are not what you are used to back in England.'

'I hear your concerns gentlemen—and ladies,' Russell said. 'But in the absence of any other alternative, I agree that Miss Penrose is a godsend. While we advertise for a new head teacher, isn't it better that the children are in school, rather than running amok in the town?'

'You cannot, of course, expect to be paid,' Angus Mackie said.

Alec McLeod, who had seemed more intent on the food than the conversation, looked up. 'Of course she can be paid,' he said. 'Good God, man. Do you expect her to work for nothing?'

Eliza shot him a grateful glance.

The store owner's mouth open and closed several times. Clearly he *had* expected her to be an unremunerated volunteer. He looked at his fellow board members but got no support.

'It will be cheaper if we were to use the pupil teacher. My own Agnes is more than capable,' he said at last.

Russell gave the storekeeper a long, thoughtful look before clearing his throat and addressing Eliza. 'In the circumstances, as the situation is only temporary, how would it be if we were to offer you three days at the school, Miss Penrose? We can, as Mr Mackie points out, manage with the pupil teachers on the other days, but if Miss Donald requires more assistance, we can negotiate something further.'

Eliza would have preferred at least five days' paid work but it was better than nothing. As long as she could stay with her uncle without paying board, she could set aside a little money to pay her way back to Melbourne.

She summoned a smile. 'Of course that would suit me, if it suits Miss Donald.'

'Miss Donald?' Russell turned to the newly appointed acting head teacher.

Flora Donald's lips tightened so hard that her mouth became a disapproving slash. She took a breath and gave Eliza a smile not echoed by her eyes. 'It seems an acceptable arrangement,' she said.

Russell smiled at her. 'As the Board of Advice are all present— gentlemen, are we in agreement?'

A murmur of assent went around the table.

Eliza glanced at Flora Donald, expecting a nod of acknowledgement at the very least, only to be met by a glacial stare. Clearly Flora Donald had taken against her. Eliza summoned a smile. 'I look forward to working with you, Miss Donald. When do we reopen the school?'

'Today is Monday. Word will need to go out to those families in remote communities, so … shall we say Wednesday?' Russell said.

'Wednesday will be fine,' Flora Donald said. 'If that suits you, Miss Penrose?'

'Of course. Shall we meet tomorrow and discuss how best to proceed?'

Flora Donald sniffed. 'Very well, come to the school house at eleven.'

Russell clapped his hands. 'Excellent. Thank you both, ladies. You have retrieved a difficult situation. Now, are there any more of those excellent potatoes?'

As the chatter around the table turned to more mundane matters, Eliza watched Alec McLeod covertly heaping another serve of vegetables and potatoes onto his plate. She leaned toward him.

'Mr McLeod,' she said in a low voice, 'you eat like a man who hasn't seen food in weeks.'

The man had the grace to pause, spots of colour appearing on his high cheekbones as he looked at his plate. 'Not food like this. I have a housekeeper who cooks for Ian and me, but …'

'Her repertoire is limited?'

'Aye, that is one way of putting it.'

Flora Donald turned to him. 'I cannot help but overhear, Mr McLeod. I would be more than happy to help with some proper meals for you and your dear brother. Scotch broth, colcannon, neeps and tatties …'

Eliza saw it all written in the woman's desperate eyes. No wonder Flora Donald had taken against her, she saw her as a potential rival for Alec McLeod's affections. The thought almost made Eliza laugh aloud. She had met the man precisely three times and their first acquaintance had hardly been auspicious. She had no idea if

Flora Donald and Alec McLeod had any sort of understanding, but Flora had no reason to fear her.

Alec looked from one woman to the other. 'Thank you,' he said. 'Bridget O'Grady does fine by us but I'm sure we'd not say no to a bowl of good broth every now and then.'

Flora beamed but before she could respond, Angus Mackie claimed her attention, leaving Eliza and Alec staring at each other.

'Have I got something on my nose?' she asked.

Alec turned back to his nearly empty plate. 'I was just thinking you don't resemble your brother.'

She shook her head. 'No, William was a typical Cornishman: dark haired and fine-boned. Before my uncle lost his hair, he had the same chestnut colouring that I have. All my mother's family had it.' She glanced at the other dinner guests and lowered her voice, 'You missed the discussion on my brother's failings and his association with an inappropriate woman.'

'Oh, you mean Sissy?'

'Is it true? Did he offer her marriage?'

Alec's gaze flicked to her uncle. 'A conversation for another time, Miss Penrose.'

'Eliza,' she replied. 'May I call you Alec?'

He smiled, the lines at the corners of his eyes crinkling.

'What are you talking about?' Flora Donald's strident tones cut across them.

'The weather,' Alec said. 'I was just telling Miss Penrose that it can snow here in July.'

Flora's narrowed eyes flashed from one to the other.

'Perhaps you could advise me, Mrs Mackie,' Eliza said. 'I need to find a bootmaker. My footwear is not up to the rugged paths or hard weather.'

Mr Mackie beamed. 'Of course, Miss Penrose. We keep a stock of hardy boots and you'll be needing an oilskin too. It is an inelegant form of clothing but effective against the cold and wet.'

'You are encouraging,' Eliza Penrose said as the others nodded agreement.

Alec smiled. 'And in summer you will roast. This is a country of extremes.'

Mrs Russell straightened in her chair. 'I hope we will see you at the dance on Saturday night, Miss Penrose?'

Eliza glanced at her uncle. 'Dance?'

'A celebration of the anniversary of our dear Queen's coronation. The Ladies' Committee believes regular social engagement makes for a happy community,' Mrs Jervis said.

'Miss Penrose is in mourning,' Flora Donald said.

Eliza had momentarily forgotten that her official status as the bereaved daughter and sister precluded social invitations. 'I think my life is my concern,' she said stiffly.

Flora Donald drew a sharp breath but nothing more was said.

As she closed the door on the last guest, Eliza turned to find her uncle standing behind her in the dimly lit hallway.

'Eliza, I really must object to this mad idea of taking on the school.'

'I don't understand why. I thought you would be pleased to have me independent.'

'I would be happier to see you comfortably set up in Melbourne. Maiden's Creek is no place for you.'

'So you keep saying, but I have seen no evidence that it is unsuitable. The people who dined here tonight were perfectly respectable, and as for taking a position at the school, if you wish me to pay board, of course I shall, within the limits of my earnings.'

He took a step back. 'No. That's not what I meant.'

'Then what did you mean?'

'I had to watch Will become corrupted by this town,' he said. 'I won't stand by and watch the same thing happen to you.'

'I am hardly likely to take up with a prostitute, Uncle. Or spend my nights in drunken maundering in one of the public houses.'

'Of course not,' he said.

She touched his arm. 'Just give me some time. You heard the board members tonight, they have no intention of allowing a woman to remain as head teacher. As soon as a new man is appointed, Miss Donald will go back to being assistant teacher and I will no longer have employment here.'

He patted her hand. 'I worry about you, Eliza.'

He hadn't concerned himself about her for the last five years, but she smiled. 'Please don't trouble yourself,' she said.

'If you are set on it, I'll bid you good night, my dear, and thank you. It was a pleasure to have a lady gracing my table tonight.'

Eliza shut her bedroom door and lay down fully clothed, letting her thoughts drift over the events of the evening and, in particular, the terrible accusations against Will. What could she do to salvage her brother's reputation?

'I need to understand,' she whispered aloud. 'I need to understand why you died, Will, and I'm not leaving until you are at peace.'

Eight

Alec returned home to find Ian slumped in Alec's chair, staring at the fire. He looked up as Alec closed the door behind him, shutting out the winter evening.

'Problem?' Alec employed the simple sign that the two used, a question mark drawn on the palm of the hand.

Ian nodded. He hauled himself out of the chair and fetched his satchel from his bedroom. He set the bag on the table with a thump.

'What have you got in there, rocks?'

'I need your advice.' Ian unbuckled the satchel and removed two heavy ledgers. Alec recognised the Maiden's Creek Mine gold register. He picked up the second ledger—that belonging to the Shenandoah Mine.

'What are you doing with these? Cowper will dismiss you on the spot if he knows you have them.'

'Tell me what you think,' Ian said and opened the Maiden's Creek ledger.

Alec ran a finger along the rows of numbers and frowned.

Ian studied his face intently as he said, 'It shows production of gold is up for the last couple of months—by a lot.' He shook his head. 'That can't be right. We've made no major finds. Production should be similar to what it was in March. This is showing a yield of three ounces to the ton.'

Ian nodded. 'That's what I thought,' he said. 'Now look at this.'

Ian opened the Shenandoah ledger. With a pang, Alec recognised Will Penrose's neat copperplate, which ended abruptly with his death. The writing changed to an unknown hand, a rougher, heavier hand. That of Jack Tehan, Alec surmised.

'Where did you get this?'

Ian looked away. 'I took it from the safe in Cowper's office. Tehan brought it in this morning. I have to do the reports for the Mine Inspector and it struck me as strange that one mine was showing a leap in profits while the other seemed to be declining.'

Alec studied the figures and looked up at his brother. 'I agree, this shows a decline in production at the Shenandoah for a couple of months before Penrose's death and since then—' he let out a low whistle, '—it's almost tailed off to nothing.'

'Does that seem strange to you?'

Alec nodded. Surely the mine inspector would notice such a discrepancy, or could the differences be accounted for if the figures were viewed in isolation? He ran a hand through his hair. 'Are you suggesting that gold from Shenandoah is being used to bolster the returns of Maiden's Creek?'

'That's exactly what I think. Why would Cowper do that?' Ian reached for the paper and pencil he kept handy on the mantelpiece and handed it to Alec. There were times when their conversation became too complex or Ian was simply too tired to lipread. Now was one of those times.

Alec saw all too clearly how Cowper benefitted and he wrote, 'Two reasons. The increase in gold production from Maiden's

Creek bolsters the shareholdings of that mine while lessening the value of the shareholdings for the Shenandoah. He's already got Penrose's shares and when the other shareholders return from their travels, they will find their investment worth nothing and he can buy them out for a pittance.'

Ian stared at him. 'That's ... ruthless.'

'Cowper IS ruthless,' Alec wrote. 'Remember how he moved on the Blue Sailor after the fires last year?'

Ian nodded, his brow creased. 'What do I do? What else is Cowper lying about?'

Alec looked into his brother's troubled face and his conscience lashed him. He thought about Will Penrose's design for the boiler. If Cowper was a thief, stealing gold from the Shenandoah, was he any better?

He put his head in hands and groaned aloud.

'Alec?'

Alec drew his hands down his face and looked into his brother's clear eyes. He chewed the end of the pencil and wrote, 'I have a question for you. What would you do if you knew something you intended to do would make your fame and fortune and would mean you would never have to live in poverty again?'

He passed the note to Ian, who read it and looked up. 'But?'

Alec wrote, 'By doing so you were depriving an innocent party of what was rightfully theirs?'

Ian shook his head. 'That would be wrong. It breaks at least two commandments.' He paused and realisation dawned in his eyes, 'You're not talking about Cowper, are you? Alec, what have you done?'

'I haven't done anything yet,' Alec wrote.

Ian cast him a questioning look.

'I want to tell you, but I can't. I don't know how to make it right,' Alec wrote.

Windlass jumped onto Alec's lap and he absentmindedly stroked the tom's broad head.

'Start by telling me the truth,' Ian said. 'Perhaps I can help.'

Alec dislodged Windlass as he stood up. He fetched Will Penrose's folder from its hiding place and unfolded the plan on the table for Ian to study. Ian knew enough about engineering to recognise what he was looking at. His long fingers ran over the detailed drawings.

'Who did this?'

'Will Penrose. I helped with some of the calculations but it is all Penrose's work.'

'What does it do?'

'It's a design for a boiler. I won't bore you with the details, but it will revolutionise the amount of power a boiler can put out. Though there's a fundamental flaw in one of the calculations that I haven't resolved yet.'

'So it's worthless?'

'Worse than that. It's dangerous.'

Ian looked at his brother and frowned. 'Why do you have it?'

'The morning Penrose was found dead, I found this pushed under our door.'

'I don't understand. Why would he give it to you?'

Alec shook his head and said aloud. 'I don't know.' He paused and wrote, 'Yes, I do … Safekeeping. Penrose must have suspected someone knew about it and wanted it.'

Ian studied him for a long moment, his clear, wise eyes searing Alec's soul. 'You were going to register the patent?'

Alec did not reply.

'But it's not yours.'

'I know.' Alec wanted to say that it seemed so straightforward when the reality of the legal heir, or in this case, heiress, to the plans was not a tangible presence in Maiden's Creek.

Ian shook his head and said, 'You have to do the right thing, Alec. This design belongs to Miss Penrose and you know it.'

'Yes,' Alec agreed. 'But what if this was the reason Penrose died?'

Ian stared at him and his lips moved silently. He swallowed. 'Murder?'

The word fell into the silence between them. The word that had been nagging at Alec since Will's death.

'It's worth a fortune—more than a fortune. Enough to kill for. Enough for me to consider ...'

'Stealing it?'

Alec nodded.

Ian paced the room. He stopped at the table and laid a hand on the plans. 'On the day he died, Penrose came to his uncle's office. They argued. They had their backs to me so I couldn't see what was said but is it possible that if the discrepancies were starting to show before he died, Penrose suspected something?' He tapped the plans. 'And now this. It seems to me there are at least two good reasons why someone would want Will Penrose dead.'

The brothers stared at each other. 'Why didn't you say something at the inquest?' Alec asked.

Ian shrugged. 'What could I say? I didn't hear what was said. Besides, what court takes the testimony of a deaf man seriously?'

'Ian—' Alec began but his brother dismissed him with the wave of the hand. It was old well-trodden ground.

'Does anyone know you've got the plans?' Ian said.

'I don't believe so.'

'Alec, you have to tell Miss Penrose. Not just about the design but also the missing gold from the Shenandoah.'

Alec grimaced as he imagined that conversation. He picked up the pencil and wrote, 'Of course you're right, but what can she do about it? She has no interest in the Shenandoah, Penrose left it to

Cowper.' He looked up from the notepad. He'd seen Cowper in action, seen the cold-blooded way he had swooped on the shareholdings in the Blue Sailor after the disastrous fires of the previous year. He would stop at nothing to get hold of something he coveted and it stood to reason he coveted the successful Shenandoah and, if he knew about it, Will's plan for the boiler.

His blood ran cold. The man could be ruthless, but would he resort to theft and murder?

He shut both ledgers with a decisive thump. 'This is all speculation,' he wrote. 'You're talking about our livelihoods, mine and yours. We can't be a party to any further conversations like this. We both have jobs to do and we have to get on and do them without asking questions.'

'Penrose was your friend—' Ian began.

'This is none of our business, Ian. You shouldn't have involved yourself. Pack those ledgers away. You have to get them back to the office before Cowper notices them missing.'

'What is the matter with you?' Ian said. 'He is stealing gold from the Shenandoah.'

Alec turned on his brother, seizing him by the forearms and looking straight into his eyes. 'Ian, if Cowper even suspects we know what he is doing, we'll be out of here with no jobs, no references. I have to think about what's best for you and me.'

Ian shook off his brother's hands. 'And what about you? These plans belong to Eliza Penrose. The eighth commandment—'

'Don't quote God and commandments at me,' Alec wrote, the lead in the pencil snapping in his anger.

'Will Penrose is dead. You owe it to him to do right by his sister,' Ian said and Alec recognised the stubborn cast to his brother's mouth. Ian's sense of right and wrong had got him into trouble before now.

'How do I make you understand? If Will died for the boiler plans or, if he suspected Cowper of stealing his gold, we may end up in the cemetery as surely as Penrose did.'

Ian's eyes widened as realisation dawned. 'Cowper? Surely you don't think …' Ian paused. 'Are you saying you think Cowper killed—'

'I'm not saying anything, but where money is at the heart of a crime, lives don't matter.'

'But Cowper—'

Alec shook his head. 'I don't know, Ian. I don't think Cowper himself is a killer, but there are men on these goldfields who are and, for the right price, would think nothing of pushing a man down a tailings heap.'

The colour drained from Ian's face. Ian, who only saw goodness in his fellow human beings.

Alec laid his hand on his brother's shoulder, but Ian shook it off and went into his bedroom without another word, shutting the door behind him.

Alec stared at the closed door for a long moment, cursing his blunt talk. With a heavy sigh he turned away and fetched the whisky bottle. He set it on the table along with a glass and stared at it. Ian was right, he couldn't keep reaching for the bottle every time a problem became too hard.

A door creaked and he looked around. Ian stood in the doorway to his bedroom.

'Pour me a glass.'

The brothers sat across from each other with the whisky bottle and Ian's notebook and a newly sharpened pencil between them. From the tight lines around Ian's mouth, Alec knew his brother was exhausted.

'I'm sorry,' Alec wrote. 'I spoke bluntly.'

'Do you really think Penrose's death may not have been accidental?'

Alec shrugged. 'I am beginning to have my suspicions.'

'Is Miss Penrose in danger?'

Alec blew out a breath. 'No.'

'You—we—have to help her.' To emphasise his point, Ian tugged at Alec's cuff.

'You.' Alec poked his brother in the chest. 'Do nothing. Keep your head down, do your job, ask no questions. Understood?'

Ian sat back. 'So you *are* going to help her?'

Alec mirrored his brother's posture. 'Do I have a choice?'

Ian shook his head. He took a sip of the whisky, pulled a face and pushed the glass toward Alec. 'I will make copies of the ledger entries,' he said. 'Keep them with the plans.' He reached for the ledgers. 'And you have to tell her about the plans or you are no better than Cowper.'

Alec tipped the remnants of Ian's whisky into his glass and stared morosely into the whisky's beguiling amber depths. 'When the time is right.'

He looked up at his brother. If looks could kill, Ian had just consigned him to the depths of hell.

Nine

24 June 1873

The door of the school house creaked as Eliza pushed it open to reveal a large vestibule with rows of hooks running along the wall. She took a breath as she stepped inside, inhaling the musty scent of chalk dust and unwashed bodies. The main room had been equipped with rows of desks with attached benches, each seating four children. By her reckoning, the schoolroom could accommodate fifty children at desks with a further row of benches at the front for another twenty.

A large blackboard dominated the end of the room where the head teacher's desk stood on a raised platform. A map of the world had been pinned to the wall between the high windows and two fireplaces stood on opposite sides of the room about halfway along. A second teacher's desk had been placed at the rear of the room.

Flora Donald stood at the head teacher's desk, studying a ledger and tapping a long, flexible cane in her hand.

'Good morning,' Eliza said.

The woman started and closed the book with a thump. 'Good morning, Miss Penrose.' Flora Donald set the cane down on the desk. 'I've considered the curriculum and consulted the board. We are agreed, you will only be required three days a week to teach the senior classes arithmetic and natural science. That will be Tuesday all day and Wednesday and Thursday mornings.'

'I see. Are you sure you do not wish me to do more?' Eliza's hopes for earning sufficient money to stand on her own feet and not be reliant on her uncle's charity were fading.

'On the other days, I will have the assistance of the pupil teacher, Agnes Mackie. She is hoping to gain her certification in teaching next year. As it stands for a school this size, the rules allow one assistant and one pupil teacher and the pupil teacher is cheaper, but there may be days you will be needed, if you can make yourself available.'

'I have no other commitments.' Eliza hoped she didn't sound too eager.

Flora Donald pointed to the second tall desk at the rear of the classroom. 'Your desk will be that one.' She turned and indicated a door behind her, 'The head teacher's office is through there. That's where Mr Emerton kept the supplies, such as they are. If you require anything you are to ask me for it and I shall see whether we have it.'

Eliza's footsteps echoed as she walked the length of the room. She stopped before the head teacher's desk and looked up at Flora. There were times she felt her lack of inches and this was one of them, as Flora Donald towered over her from her position on the platform. Eliza squared her shoulders, swallowed her pride and forced a smile.

'Miss Donald, I fear that you may have formed an unfavourable opinion of me and I would very much like us to set whatever differences there are between us to one side.'

'You're mistaken, Miss Penrose. I have not known you long enough to have formed any opinion of you whatsoever.'

'If we cannot be friends, then I would like us to be able to work together for the sake of bringing learning to the children of this town.'

Flora's mouth twitched. 'That is an admirable sentiment.'

Eliza wondered what it would take to break down the woman's antipathy. 'Please be assured, Miss Donald, I have no interest in assuming the role of head teacher. You are in a much better position than I to fulfil that responsibility, but the truth is, I have no one to support me and as my brother has left me nothing, I must find my own employment. I am quite content to help you for as long as I am needed.'

'Aye, well, your brother's death was a tragedy and it must have been a terrible shock to you.' Did Eliza detect a small degree of unbending in Flora's expression? 'In the circumstances you are holding yourself together bravely, Miss Penrose. We shall see how you manage for a couple of weeks and perhaps the matter can be revisited with the Board of Advice.'

'Thank you. I would be grateful.' Eliza smiled. 'Now that our relative positions are understood, can you explain the curriculum to me?'

'Under the new Education Act, our curriculum is clearly set out and quite simple. Reading, spelling and explanation, writing and dictation, arithmetic, grammar, geography, needlework for the girls and when we have time and the weather is fine, we undertake military drills and gymnastics in the yard.'

Eliza nodded. 'I enjoy teaching arithmetic but if that is your preference—'

'No,' Flora said with an alacrity that indicated that mathematics was not her preference. 'I would be delighted for you to assume that responsibility, particularly with the older children. I enjoy teaching writing and dictation.'

And the military drills, no doubt, Eliza thought ungraciously.

Flora spent some time going through the roll book with Eliza, a very instructive exercise as each child's graded mark was recorded in meticulous detail. The names meant little to Eliza, apart from one Agnes Mackie, age fifteen, who seemed to excel at everything and was the logical choice for a pupil teacher.

Dark clouds were rolling in as Eliza left the school. The cold wind blew dry leaves around her ankles as she stood looking up at the forbidding mass of the Maiden's Creek Mine tailings, which cascaded down from the workings on the far side of the creek. Will had died on that mountain of loose rocks. As she stared at it, one question repeated in her mind: Why?

She pulled her shawl tighter around her neck and shoulders and turned back to the town and the warmth of her uncle's parlour. Mrs Harris would be serving tea and cake and Eliza could read one of the books she had borrowed from the library and forget her woes for a little while.

25 June 1873

Eliza rose before dawn and forced herself to eat something for breakfast, even though the bread and cheese turned to dust in her mouth and the tea tasted like dishwater.

Just a hint of warmth in the sun crept over the hills, dispersing the mist from the gullies, but Eliza barely noticed. A rabble of butterflies chased each other in her stomach as she approached the school. Several small, rotund ponies had been turned loose into the small paddock beside the playground and knots of children were already playing together in the school yard. They stopped to look at their new schoolmistress, casting her curious glances as she opened the gate. Eliza bade them good morning and was rewarded with uncertain smiles and nods before they turned back to their amusements.

Flora Donald, dressed in a sober brown woollen gown and a spotless white apron, waited at the door. Eliza greeted the acting head teacher with a smile that was not returned. Flora's unblinking gaze raked Eliza from head to toe—she knew it had been a mistake to choose her favourite dark blue gown and not the black gown, but she only had the one suitable mourning dress and she was damned if she was going to be disapproved of by this woman.

'Good morning, Miss Penrose. You are responsible for ringing the bell at eight sharp. Any child arriving late is marked as such. You are to wear this.'

Flora handed her an apron similar to her own.

'I'll just put my coat away,' Eliza said and stepped into the schoolroom. Mean fires in the fireplaces did little to alleviate the chill of the large room. Eliza shivered and went to add some more wood.

'What are you doing? We cannot afford the wood for the fires and we'll need it for when the weather gets really cold,' Flora chided.

Eliza tied on the apron and pulled her shawl tighter around her shoulders. She rubbed her hands together and stamped her feet, her breath clouding in the cold air. Maybe once the room was filled with warm bodies it would heat up.

The clock above one of the fireplaces struck eight.

'Please ring the bell, Miss Penrose,' Flora said.

Picking up the school bell, Eliza threw open the front door. Hefting the bell in her right hand, she stood on the front step and gave a half-a-dozen short, sharp rings. The clanging resounded off the steep valley walls, echoing into its darkest corners and momentarily drowning out the beat of the stampers.

Girls and boys of all ages in clean but much mended clothes clattered past her, jostling and pushing each other as they hung coats and satchels on the hooks in the vestibule.

'Close the door, Miss Penrose.'

Eliza looked up and down the street and, satisfied that no more children were coming, shut the door. She took a breath, straightened her shoulders and strode down the aisle between the desks where the children had found their seats. Seventy pairs of eyes bored into her back.

Show no fear, Will would say and at the thought of him, she smiled, feeling his sardonic presence with her.

Mounting the platform, she stood beside Flora Donald, folded her hands in front of the starched apron and surveyed the schoolroom.

Flora said, 'Good morning, children,' and seventy voices droned, 'Good morning, Miss Donald.'

'Children, I would like you to meet Miss Penrose, who will be our assistant teacher while Mr Emerton is indisposed. Now, say good morning to her.'

'Good morning, Miss Penrose.'

'We'll begin by singing the national anthem.'

Eliza had never heard 'God Save the Queen' sung so discordantly, but the schoolroom lacked a musical instrument for accompaniment.

At the conclusion of the anthem, the children resumed their seats. As the room settled, one of the older boys at the back of the room rose to his feet, struggling to get his long limbs out from beneath a desk that was too small for him.

'When's Mr Emerton coming back?' he asked.

'Mr Emerton remains quite unwell and will not be returning. A new head teacher will be appointed in the fullness of time,' Flora replied.

'Miss Penrose? My pa says you've never taught a school like this before,' a red-headed girl in the same row as the boy said without standing.

The butterflies in Eliza's stomach redoubled their effort. She asked the girl's name.

'Martha Mackie,' the girl replied, her chin rising.

'Firstly, Martha, you will stand, or raise your hand, if you wish to talk, and secondly, I will not have you questioning my qualifications to teach you. Did your parents teach you no manners?'

The girl coloured and looked down at the desk. 'Sorry, miss,' she mumbled.

Eliza's gaze swept the room, defying the other children to question her right to be there. 'You may only be five feet tall,' her father had told her, 'but you must show the world you are two yards high and will not take nonsense from anyone.'

'Please take the roll, Miss Penrose,' Flora said.

Eliza lifted the lid of the head teacher's desk and jumped back, stifling a yelp as a spider as large as her hand stared back at her from the top of the roll book with dark, fathomless eyes.

Don't show weakness, don't scream, don't give them the satisfaction.

She caught her breath and closed the desk lid with deliberate care. 'It seems one of our students has misplaced his or her pet, Miss Donald,' she said.

Before Flora could glance at the arachnid, Eliza addressed the children. 'Miss Donald and I will leave the room for five minutes and when we return, we shall expect the animal to have been removed and there will be no repercussions. If it is still there on our return, you all stay in over lunchtime.'

With as much dignity as she could muster, she retreated to the office, Flora in her wake.

Flora shut the office door and turned to Eliza, her eyes blazing. 'May I remind you, Miss Penrose, that *I* am in charge and it is up to me to say who will or will not suffer repercussions for their impertinence.'

Eliza returned Flora's furious glare. 'And are you partial to spiders, Miss Donald?'

'I am not, but I will not have my authority undermined.'

Through the half-open door, uproar arose—the children laughing and shouting. Eliza closed her eyes and forced herself to breathe. Was the laughter at her expense or that of the perpetrator of the failed practical joke? She thought of the spider with its eight huge, hairy legs. She had never in her whole life seen such a large beast. What else did this strange country have in store for her?

She checked her watch and, on the dot of five minutes, she threw the door open and the two women returned to the classroom, ignoring the last-minute scrambling as children returned to their desks. The head teacher's desk lid stood open and Eliza lifted out the roll book, now free of the spider, and began calling out the names.

The large boy was Bert Marsh. Eliza would have laid odds that Bert had been behind the spider. As well as the prissy Martha there were another three Mackie girls. The eldest, Agnes, had been appointed the pupil teacher and, to judge from her sullen glare, resented having *her* position of authority usurped by Eliza.

As she closed the book, the schoolroom door burst open to admit a latecomer. Eliza took the child for a boy until Flora Donald said, 'Charlotte O'Reilly, you are late. You will stay in over the dinner hour and write out fifty times "I shall not be late for school".'

The child looked down at her feet, clad in boots that had begun to come apart, revealing her toes. With her short brown hair and patched boy's clothes, it was little wonder Eliza had mistaken her for a boy.

'Yes'm, sorry'm,' Charlotte mumbled.

Eliza glanced down at the roll book, looking for the child's name. Charlotte O'Reilly, aged ten. The ten was followed by a question mark. A number of gaps against the child's name indicated she had missed a great deal of schooling.

'Take a seat, Charlotte,' Flora said. 'Make room for her.'

No one moved.

Martha Mackie stood up. 'No one wants to sit next to her, miss. She smells.'

The O'Reilly child stared fixedly at the floor and shuffled her feet.

'She can sit next to me,' a large boy of about twelve, who had answered to the name of Joe Trevalyn, stood up and moved along his bench. He gave the ragamuffin a smile and Charlotte O'Reilly shuffled onto the bench, perching precariously on the very edge.

'Thank you, Joe,' Eliza said.

'Now, Charlotte, why are you late?' Flora demanded.

The child raised her chin. 'Me name's Charlie,' she said.

'In this room, you will be called by your given name: Charlotte. What is the reason for your tardiness?

'I had to help Ma with a brew.'

Eliza heard one of the girls say, 'Mad Annie's mad daughter,' and the room erupted in laughter. Colour burned in Charlie O'Reilly's cheeks and she stared at the desk.

Flora clapped her hands, bringing the room back to silence. 'We've had enough interruptions. Miss Penrose, please take your position with the older children for their mathematics class.'

Eliza walked the length of the room to the tall desk with a blackboard on an easel beside it. Pausing only to check there were no stray arachnids in her own desk, she turned to face the children.

'Thank you to whoever introduced me to that particular species of spider. Could someone please tell me what genus it is?'

Silence. Then one of the boys spoke up. 'Please, miss, it was a huntsman. They don't bite.'

'Yeah, not like a redback,' Bert Marsh said. 'Bite from one of those can kill you.'

Eliza looked at Flora, busy writing on the blackboard, and said, 'You probably all know that I am new to Australia, so let's start the day with a nature lesson. I want you to teach me about the animals.'

'But we should be doing mathematics. We are learning percentages.' Martha Mackie half-rose from her seat in indignation.

'Mathematics can wait. Who wants to start? What is the largest animal you have seen?'

As the children contributed the names of the local fauna, Eliza wrote them on the blackboard: wallabies (good eating); wombats and possums (not so tasty); bats; the strange platypus that lived in the quiet creeks; parakeets; bellbirds; and snakes. She asked the children to draw their favourite animal on their slates and tell her where they had seen them. A couple of the boys drew snakes and by the end of the morning she learned that the tiger, brown and black snakes, along with redback spiders, were to be avoided at all costs. It had been a most instructive lesson.

'Remember when the tiger snake bit Danny Greaves?' one of the children said.

'He nearly died!'

'He's got a beauty of a scar,' Bert Marsh said with what sounded like grudging admiration.

The name Danny Greaves did not appear in the roll book so Eliza assumed that he had left the town at some point.

Over lunch she watched from the school steps as the children played in the yard. Inside the schoolroom, the strange ragamuffin, Charlie, stood at one of the blackboards, scrawling her lines. While the others ate lunches packed into pails or tied up in cloth by their mothers, Charlie did not appear to have anything. Eliza cut off some bread and cheese from her own lunch and took them over to the child with an apple.

'There you go.'

Charlie looked up, a pair of startling green eyes shining brightly from her dirty face. 'For me?'

'Yes. You won't learn if you're hungry. Please stay after school, I would like to talk to you.'

But as soon as the clock struck four and Eliza rang the bell, Charlie bolted and was the first one out the door. Eliza watched her scampering away, her brown legs flying in her haste to be away from the school. With a thoughtful sigh she turned inside to prepare the room for the following day.

'Don't waste your time on Charlotte O'Reilly, Miss Penrose. That child has no place among decent folk,' Flora said as she inscribed 'Cleanliness is next to Godliness' at the top of the board: the worthy thought for the next day.

'Why do you say that?'

'If it were up to me, that child would be banned from the school, but the Board of Advice tells me that every child has to receive an education.' She gesticulated with the chalk. 'She is always late, always dressed in boy's clothes and is generally unwashed. The chance of some nasty infection spreading to the other children is not to be borne.'

'So your objection to Charlotte is simply that she is inadequately dressed and bathed?'

'Don't be ridiculous, her mother is—' Flora Donald broke off. The chalk she held in her hand snapped with a crack.

'Her mother is what?'

Flora's lips curled in distaste and she returned to her blackboard, furiously rubbing at the day's work. 'Her mother, if you can call her that, has a grog shop up on the Aberfeldy Road. Little more than a bark hut. Brews her own disgusting beer and, from what I hear, grog is not the only thing she sells, if the price is right.'

'How far out of town?'

'A couple of miles at least. It's on the turn-off to Pretty Sally.'

'So to get to school, Charlie walks into town?'

'I suppose she does.'

'And is no one doing anything to help them?'

'The Ladies' Committee have tried to take food and clothes but the last time, Mrs O'Reilly saw them off with a rifle. There is no helping them.'

'And yet the child keeps coming to school?'

Flora shrugged. 'It won't last. You'll see.'

'Is there no father?'

'No. The mother probably couldn't even give you a name if you asked her.'

A number of questions swirled in Eliza's head but she had tried Flora's Christian righteousness far enough. She didn't need to antagonise the woman any more than she already had done, so she changed the subject and they discussed the day, an exercise which included a resounding telling off from Flora for Eliza's impromptu nature lesson.

Eventually Eliza took her leave.

A man on a horse had turned into the track that ran past the school, leading up to the mine, and as Eliza shut the gate, he slowed, pushing his hat to the back of his head.

'You must be Miss Penrose,' he said.

She looked up at him. He had light brown hair, a trimmed beard and a pair of grey-green eyes that crinkled at the corners as he smiled.

'You have the advantage of me, sir.'

'My apologies.' He swept the hat from his head. 'Jack Tehan. I had the honour of working with your brother.'

'*Black* Jack Tehan?'

He laughed. 'Ah, you've heard me called Black Jack? The nickname is, I'm afraid, ironic. I am black in neither looks nor temperament.'

'And how did you know who I was, Mr Tehan?'

'Oh, 'tis a small community and word travels fast.' He glanced back to the main road. 'Also I met young Charlie on the way down here and she told me there was a Miss Penrose teaching at the school so I made the connection.'

Eliza remembered where she had heard the name. 'And you are the man currently managing my brother's mine, the Shenandoah?'

A muscle twitched in Tehan's cheek. 'Yes, your brother employed me as foreman and after … Now I work for your uncle.' He cocked his head to one side and considered her for a long moment. 'Forgive my impertinence, Miss Penrose, but you're not much like your brother.'

'No. He got the dark Cornish looks, I got the English,' she said and frowned. 'And am I wrong in thinking you're Irish?'

Tehan shook his head. 'Born and bred in this country,' he said. 'Or Tasmania at least. Not sure whether we Tasmanians consider ourselves Australian or not. We're something of a law unto ourselves, but my dad was Irish and the brogue may have rubbed off.' He looked up at the darkening sky. 'Now, if you'll be excusing me, your uncle is expecting me.' He paused and gave her an appraising look. 'Will I be seeing you at the dance on Saturday night?'

'I've not made up my mind. I'm officially in mourning, Mr Tehan.'

'Aye, you are too, but there's precious little fun to be had out here so we take it where we find it.' He tipped his fingers to his hat. 'Good day to you, Miss Penrose.'

'Goodnight, Mr Tehan.'

He replaced his hat and gave a curt nod. 'Pleasure to make your acquaintance.'

Eliza followed his progress up the hill toward the mine.

'Don't you be having anything to do with that man.' Flora Donald's acerbic command cut across her reverie. 'He has the charm of the Irish about him but there are several girls in these parts who are nursing hearts broken by Mr Tehan.'

Eliza turned to face her. 'I am quite capable of forming my own judgements, thank you, Miss Donald.'

'Well, don't say I didn't warn you. I will see you tomorrow morning, Miss Penrose.'

And with that, Flora left, her shawl wound tightly around her.

Eliza remained by the gate, waiting until both Flora and the enigmatic 'Black' Jack Tehan were out of sight before turning for her uncle's house.

As she made her way up the hill, her thoughts were filled with Charlie O'Reilly. Why did Charlie keep coming back to school when everything from her home life to the antipathy of her fellow students and teachers seemed set against her? Surely there could only be one reason: she wanted to learn. The child thirsted for knowledge.

'To hell with Flora Donald,' Eliza muttered as she closed her bedroom door behind her and flung her hat onto the bed. Every child deserved an education and she would do whatever it took to ensure Charlie O'Reilly had every opportunity, if for no other reason than to ensure she escaped her mother's fate.

Ten

Alec thrust his hands into his coat pockets and hurried across the yard to the adit, the entrance to the mine, which led into a long passageway. He found Trevalyn in the plant room. The foreman stood beside the new boiler in conversation with the mine's black-smith. He turned to Alec with a furrowed brow.

'We've a problem with the welding.'

The men discussed the issues and once the men were back at work, Alec and Trevalyn adjourned to the crib room.

Alec asked the foreman what he had heard about the Shenandoah Mine.

'You'd know more than me,' Trevalyn said.

'Just interested in hearing what's being said about it since Penrose's death.'

Trevalyn bit into a cold pie, no doubt lovingly packed by Mrs Trevalyn. Alec's nose twitched. The best he could put together was stale bread and cheese.

'From what I hear it was showing good promise,' Trevalyn said. 'After Penrose's accident, Cowper promoted Jack Tehan to manage it and if anyone has a nose for gold, it's Black Jack. Made his fortune in Bendigo and lost it just as fast. I've heard he'll bet on raindrops running down a window pane. Do you know him?'

'Met him a couple of times. Penrose thought he did a good job.' But he had sensed a reluctance in his friend when he spoke of Tehan. 'Got in a foreman straight off the Bendigo field,' Penrose had said a few months before he died. 'He came recommended by Cowper. Seems to know his stuff—' The *but* had remained unspoken.

Alec looked at the boiler without really seeing it while he brooded on the question of how Black Jack had come to be at the Shenandoah. If he had been recommended by Cowper it made some sense. Charles Cowper had started out on the Bendigo gold-fields and must have come across Tehan during his time there, but it raised the question of why Cowper would be recommending a mine foreman to Penrose when the two were barely speaking.

Alec left Trevalyn to finish his pie and descended one of the ladders that lined the shaft to the deep lead. At present the winch was only used for bringing up the extracted rock but with the new boiler they could look at putting in a proper cage to trans-port the miners to the new level; they had dropped the shaft fifty feet, which made it quite a climb on ladders alone. The reef had widened at this point and now they were striking out westward, following the quartz seam. The early crushings were promising and for the first time in several years of hard rock mining, the Maiden's Creek Mine was finally producing a marketable quan-tity of gold, but it was not enough. Not yet.

Alec ducked his head under a beam that had once been a mag-nificent Huon pine, bought in at some expense from Tasmania. Light but strong and rot resistant, Huon made the best mine supports.

Noticing him, the team at the end of the tunnel stopped work and straightened as best they could, wiping their sweating, grimy faces and pulling their hats from their heads.

'Afternoon, Mr McLeod,' David Morgan said.

'How's it going?'

Morgan pushed his cap to the back of his head and scratched his chin. 'Slow work today, boss. We've hit hard rock.'

'Don't let me stop you.'

Morgan nodded and picked up the yard-long drill bit. George Tregloan swung the mallet and struck the end of the bit. Morgan turned the bit, Tregloan hit it. After a while they would swap places and the third member of the team, John Marsh, would take the bit and Morgan the mallet. It was hard, slow work but at the end of the week they would have drilled the holes into which explosives would be placed. On Saturday the explosives would be blown, the dust allowed to settle and the debris carted out to be crushed by the five-headed stamper below the mine on Monday.

Alec watched the three men. They had been working together so long, they almost moved as one, each alert to the others' movements. Away from the mine they could be found in the Britannia, slaking the mine dust with a beer. He picked up a piece of quartz, turning it over in his hand. Every time he did this, his heart thrilled to the possibility that this innocuous rock may hold the elusive and seductive glint of gold. He pulled his geologist's hammer from his belt and struck it, the quartz fracturing into three pieces. He held each piece up and studied it in the light of the lantern that had been hammered into the wall of the tunnel.

'Anything?' Marsh said.

Alec shook his head. 'Where do you think this reef is heading?'

The men downed their tools to discuss the possible line of the seam they had been following. Despite its current westerly direction it could easily change direction and run the risk of running into an adjoining lease. Cowper had been gradually buying out the smaller leases, which made Maiden's Creek the biggest mine in the district.

Alec listened to the men's opinions; they had an instinct for mining and he trusted their judgement. They agreed that the reef was heading down, away from the creek and town. Another lead to be sunk, Alec realised with a thrill of anticipation as he left the men and returned down the tunnel, his heavy boots slopping in the mud and puddles between the rail lines that carried the little carriages filled with broken rock.

At the shaft level he stopped to inspect the pre-cut lengths of wood propped against the wall, ready for installation when the next blast extended the tunnel. He unslung one of the lanterns and held it up. Bits of bark still adhered to the lengths and the hairs on the back of his neck prickled. He knew wood and something was missing: the warm honey smell of Huon pine. He held the lantern up close to the supports. These were not Huon, but sugar gum, a notoriously brittle wood, unsuitable for heavy work in such damp conditions. This had not been what he specified.

He rehung the lantern and took the ladders several rungs at a time, intent on speaking to Trevalyn. Failing to find him, Alec stormed out of the mine, the mounting anger roiling in his heart. In the yard he found the woodcutters, the Benetti brothers, unloading their cart. They greeted him with broad smiles.

'Signore McLeod, how are you today?'

Alec took a breath, bringing his temper under control. 'Do you know anything about the sugar gum supports?'

Giuseppe glanced at Salvatore and shrugged. 'We were told to provide sugar gum for the support posts.'

Alec thanked the Benetti brothers and left them to their work. Only one person would have overridden his specifications. He threw open the door to the administration building and stormed past Ian in the outer office, entering Charles Cowper's wood-panelled sanctum without knocking.

Cowper rose from behind his desk, his mouth open to protest Alec's invasion of his office.

'Where are the Huon supports that I ordered last month?' Alec said.

'What do you mean?'

'You know damn well what I mean. All I can see are useless sugar gum logs.'

Cowper's chin came up. 'I decided that the Huon was too expensive,' he said. 'I sold it to another mine.'

Alec stared at the man. 'You *sold* it?'

'At a tidy profit.'

Alec balled his fists. 'This is not about profit. This is about the safety of the mine. We've had this argument before. Sugar gum is too brittle.'

'I needed the money to pay for the boiler,' Cowper said. 'You can't have everything you want in this business, McLeod. Compromises need to be made.'

'Not at the risk to the men's safety.'

'Nonsense. The wood is perfectly sound. It'll do for the time being. Once we start turning a decent profit we can replace it with Huon.'

When Alec opened his mouth to protest again, Cowper banged his fist on the desk. 'My decision, my responsibility. Your job is getting the gold out, McLeod. Leave me and get on with it.'

Still seething, Alec stormed out of the office.

Ian looked up as his brother passed, a questioning quirk to his eyebrow.

Alec shook his head. 'I'll tell you later,' he said. 'Got to get back to the mine.'

As he put his hand to the door, it opened. Alec took a step back and Jack Tehan sauntered in, his hands in his pockets. The recently promoted mine superintendent of the Shenandoah Mine hung his coat and hat on the hook and turned to Alec and Ian with a smile.

'Good afternoon, gentlemen. How are the McLeod brothers today?'

'Tehan. What brings you into town?' Alec said.

Tehan jerked his head at the manager's office. 'As your brother will tell you, Cowper likes me to report in on a weekly basis, McLeod.' He scratched his beard. 'Between us, it's a hell of a hike down the hill every time I want a decision made, but that's how Cowper wants it.'

'Report on what? I've heard the Shenandoah is going nowhere.'

Tehan shrugged. 'The valley runs on rumours, you know that. But I'm pleased to run into you, McLeod, I've a technical problem and I wouldn't mind your advice. I know you and Penrose used to exchange thoughts.'

That had been different—Penrose had been a friend. Still, it would be churlish not to offer advice when it was requested, so Alec nodded.

'That's grand. I'll be staying at the Britannia tonight,' Tehan said.

'I'll join you for a drink,' Alec said. He sensed, rather than saw, the other man's hesitation.

'A drink? I didn't think you Prezzies were up for drinking?'

'You think just because I'm a Scot, I've taken the pledge?' Alec forced a laugh and glanced at his brother. Ian, sensing he was being addressed, looked up. 'I leave that to my brother. A good Scottish whisky is my idea of heaven.'

'As an Irishman, I would have to disagree,' Tehan said with a laugh. 'Very well, McLeod, I'll meet you at the Britannia at eight.'

Alec forced himself to eat the shepherd's pie left by Bridget O'Grady. The meat was swimming in fat and the potato burned black. Even Ian—who would eat anything without complaining— ate slowly, his face screwed up in a grimace.

'We have to find a better cook,' Alec said. 'Bridget'll kill us at this rate.'

Ian nodded and pushed his plate to one side. 'Why are you meeting Tehan?'

'He says he wants my advice on something. Besides, it wouldn't hurt to get to know him better. Maybe I can get to the bottom of the ledger discrepancies. Did you hear anything of his conversation with Cowper this evening?'

Ian shook his head. 'They had their backs to me. Although as he was leaving, Tehan did say something about Eliza Penrose.'

'What?'

'I don't know, it's hard to read his lips through his beard.'

Alec found Jack Tehan ensconced at a small table in the corner of the bar of the Britannia Hotel, a whiskey already in his hand. To judge by the man's high colour and relaxed demeanour, he was several drinks ahead of Alec. Alec ordered a beer from Yorkie Oldroyd and joined Tehan.

'I thought you said you were a whiskey man,' Tehan said.

Alec looked down at the beer. 'Start slow and work up to it,' he said. In truth, he wanted to keep a clear head in this conversation. 'So, who looks after the Shenandoah when you're away?'

'I've a decent foreman. Most of the men came with me from Bendigo. They're experienced and they know how I like things done.'

Alec nodded. 'What's the problem you want my advice on?'

Tehan pulled a notebook from his pocket and Alec recognised the handwriting immediately.

'That's Penrose's notebook,' he said. 'How did you come by it?'

'Cowper had them. Figured I'd need them and a godsend they are too, but I don't have the learning you and Penrose had and I was hoping you could explain this calculation to me?'

He indicated the complex mathematical calculation with a finger, its nail encrusted with dirt. Alec considered the page. When he had worked it out, he turned to a blank page in the notebook and set out the calculation in diagrammatic form. Tehan nodded and asked the right questions. Whatever Tehan's past may be, he had a sharp mind and he quickly grasped what Penrose had intended. Tehan took the notebook back from Alec and stowed it in his pocket with a gruff thanks, and before Alec could protest, he ordered two whiskies—one Scotch and one Irish. Yorkie Oldroyd set them down with a thump that sloshed liquid onto the table.

Tehan raised his glass. 'Here's to gold mining,' he said. 'May it bring us the fortune we so richly deserve.'

Alec drained the glass and set it down. As he began to rise from his seat, Tehan waved him back into the chair.

'Stay a while, McLeod. I prefer doing me drinking in company.'

The whiskey had worked its magic and Alec found no pressing need to return home. 'What took you to the Bendigo fields?' he asked.

'What is anyone doing on the goldfields, McLeod? I came over from Tasmania about eight years ago, looking for me fortune. Nothing to hold me there.'

'Did you come from mining stock?'

Tehan laughed. 'Me father was a convict. Served his time, but he was good for nothing. It was me mother who ran the farm and kept us fed. I went to Bendigo knowing nothing about mining, but you learn quickly enough.'

'Is that where you met Cowper?'

Tehan's eyes narrowed. 'Aye. Met him when I first arrived. He was managing the Central Deborah. Saw a young lad with potential and encouraged me to up me knowledge with courses at the Mechanics' Institute. What about you, McLeod?'

'Family were coal miners in Lanarkshire. My brother and I emigrated five years ago. I had a couple of years in Ballarat.'

'Then what on earth induced you to leave a place like that for this carbuncle on the arse of the world?'

Alec smiled and raised his glass to his lips. 'The money,' he said. 'Cowper was prepared to pay me well to move to this carbuncle. Why did you leave Bendigo?'

A smile flickered at the corner of Tehan's mouth. 'A lady,' he said. 'Judged it prudent to beat a retreat before her husband chased me out with a shotgun.' He raised his glass. 'God bless the fairer sex, but they lie at the bottom of all our troubles.'

'And there I would have to disagree with you,' Alec said. 'My wife was my partner in everything.'

Tehan swilled the liquid in his glass. 'Didn't know you were married, McLeod.'

'I was. My wife's dead.'

Tehan mumbled an apology as Yorkie slapped another round in front of them. The men drank in silence.

'If you've any sense,' Tehan said after a long moment, 'You'd be courting Cowper's niece. She's his only relative, isn't she? He'll worth a pound or two when he passes over to the other side. You could have a fancy house in Melbourne and everything you want at the click of your fingers.'

'Got to find a bit more gold first,' Alec said.

'Maiden's Creek is doing all right,' Tehan said.

'Better than Shenandoah, I hear.'

Tehan's lips tightened and he shook his head. 'Can't talk about Shenandoah.' He considered the dregs at the bottom of the glass. 'Yorkie, another ... please.'

Yorkie cocked an eyebrow at Alec, who shook his head. There was no distance between enough and one too many and that could lead to regrets.

'Why not?' Alec asked. 'I hear it's failing.'

Tehan shrugged and sat back as Yorkie set the fresh glass down in front of him and held out his hand for payment.

'Come on, Yorkie mate,' Tehan said. 'I'm good for a bit of credit.'

'Pay up,' the barkeeper said.

Tehan fumbled in his pocket and counted out some coins.

'Not enough.'

'Here.' Alec made good the shortfall.

Tehan clapped him on the shoulder. 'You're a good man, McLeod. Now, what were we talking about?'

'The Shenandoah.'

'That'll be what it'll be.' He leaned forward. 'What I'd like to know is what your mate Penrose did with his plans for the new boiler.'

Alec kept his face neutral while every nerve in his body tightened. 'What plans?'

Tehan leaned forward, his eyes sharp. 'You're no fool, McLeod. You and I both know that Penrose had been working on the design for some new fandangled boiler.' He tapped the table. 'That's where the money is. Not in these bloody hard hills.'

Alec pulled his wits together, wondering exactly how much Tehan knew about the plans. 'He mentioned something of the sort but I can only assume that, if they were in Penrose's possession, then Cowper has them.'

'Cowper and I went through Penrose's possessions the day he died. If he had those bloody plans we would have found them.'

Alec shrugged. 'Can't help you. Besides if they exist, aren't they the property of Miss Penrose? They should be of no interest to you or Cowper.'

Silence fell again as Alec fought off the tug of his own conscience.

'On the subject of Miss Penrose,' Tehan said. 'I heard you tried to run her down. That's never a good way to make a girl's acquaintance.' A sly smile curled his mouth. 'Mind you, I think she likes me.'

'Oh? And when did you meet her?'

'I made a point of making her acquaintance this afternoon. Pretty little thing. Are you a betting man, McLeod?'

'No.'

'Pity, because I would bet you a month's wages that I will bed her within …' He paused, gazing up at the ceiling as if doing a calculation in his head.

Alec stood. 'That's enough, Tehan. Miss Penrose is a respectable woman and I'll not have her spoken of in those terms.'

'Hah,' said Tehan. 'I was right, you do like her.' He pushed back from the table and stood, his hands resting flat on the table as he leaned over Alec. 'There is a challenge in bedding a virgin and a virgin with her uncle's prospects is a challenge worth accepting.' He tapped his nose. 'Watch me, McLeod.'

Alec's hand balled into a fist and it took all his willpower not to break that very nose. He did not need to make an enemy of Black Jack. If anything, he needed Tehan to think of him as a friend and ally—if only for the sake of Eliza Penrose's reputation.

Chuckling to himself, Tehan weaved out of the bar, leaving Alec alone with his dark thoughts.

Eleven

28 June 1873

Alec had no intention of going to the dance at the Mechanics'
Institute but Ian's obvious eagerness to attend swayed him. If Ian
had not planned a tryst, he at least expected to meet up with Susan
Mackie, and while his brother did not need a chaperone, Alec knew
Ian was not comfortable among large, overwhelming gatherings.

A sizeable crowd had already filled the hall at the Mechanics'
Institute by the time the brothers arrived. Ian's step faltered and
the rise and fall of his chest told Alec what it cost his brother to
attend. He caught Ian's arm and turned him in the direction of the
trestle tables where the ladies were setting out a substantial supper. Susan, wearing a green sprigged dress with a lace collar, was
arranging plates. As if aware she was being observed, she looked
up and her smile left Alec in no doubt as to the depth of her feelings. Ian glanced at his brother and Alec nodded.

'Go on. I don't need your company.'

He watched his brother wend his way through the crowd and
smiled. With eyes only for each other, Ian and Susan could have
been alone in the room.

'Good evening, Mr McLeod.'

Alec looked down at the slight figure who stood beside him and caught his breath. For all her diminutive height, Eliza Penrose outshone every woman in the room in a midnight blue satin dress that would have graced the ballroom at Government House.

'E-evening, Miss Penrose.'

'I think I overdressed,' Eliza said, glancing around the crowded room. The other women were gathered in little knots, casting glances in her direction.

'You look bonny,' Alec managed and was saved by the band striking up a lively polka. He gathered his courage in both hands. 'Will you dance with me?'

She smiled. 'Thank you.'

He led Eliza into the space that had been reserved for dancing. Trevalyn and his wife passed them. The mine foreman had a grin on his face and his eyes shone as he danced his flushed and smiling wife around the floor with gusto.

'I would never have guessed Trevalyn liked a dance,' Alec said.

'Is he Joe Trevalyn's father?'

Alec nodded. 'Joe? Is he the one with the club foot? He's the youngest. A good lad.'

'He has a good heart,' Eliza agreed, 'and I think he's Charlie O'Reilly's only friend. So shall we dance, Mr McLeod?'

'I warn you, I've two left feet.'

'I'll help,' she said as he set his large hand on her slender waist. Her fine fingers twined with his and he caught his breath. He could barely remember the last time he had touched a woman.

Eliza gazed up at him, her eyes sparkling and her lips parted, as she tapped out the beat on his arm with the fingers of her right hand. 'Now,' she said and led him off.

Alec had never felt more awkward or clumsy in the company of the diminutive Miss Penrose. He fixed his gaze on a corner of the room to avoid looking straight down her décolletage, which showed an indecent amount of shoulder and creamy flesh. No wonder the matrons of Maiden's Creek looked scandalised.

'Who's Charlie O'Reilly?' Alec asked once he felt confident enough to venture a little conversation.

'Strange little thing. Dresses in boys' clothes and lives alone with her mother way out of town.'

'Oh, you mean Mad Annie's child?'

A slight flush rose to Eliza's cheeks. 'Why do they call her Mad Annie?'

Alec shrugged. 'Maybe because she chooses to live by herself out there—' He turned to see who had bumped into him and his brother gave him a sheepish grin of apology before whisking Susan away. Ian may not have been able to hear music but he had once told Alec that he sensed it through the vibrations in the floor and, with an able partner like Susan, no one who didn't know him would suspect his deafness.

'Who is that?' Eliza asked.

'My brother Ian. I'll introduce you later.'

'I'd like that. And you lied—you dance well.'

The polka ended and the band moved into a more sedate waltz. Eliza smiled up at him.

'Shall we continue?' she suggested.

Alec awkwardly shifted his position, drawing Eliza closer. As they stepped off, a hand on his shoulder made him pause and he looked around. Jack Tehan grinned at him.

'You can't monopolise the only attractive woman in the room, McLeod.' Tehan bowed in an almost courtly manner. 'If I may, Miss Penrose.'

As manners dictated, Alec ceded his place and retired to the table of punchbowls. Nothing alcoholic, of course, but he still poured himself a cup and stood watching Eliza Penrose circle the floor in the arms of the Tasmanian. They made a handsome couple and Jack Tehan had a grace and talent for dancing that Alec knew he lacked.

'Good evening, Mr McLeod.'

At the sound of Flora Donald's voice, Alec took a deep breath and forced a smile. 'Good evening.' They stood for a moment in awkward silence, before Alec gathered his courage. 'Do you dance, Miss Donald?'

'Aye, of course I do. Are you asking me, Mr McLeod?'

Alec steeled himself and waltzed Flora onto the floor. He had no sense of a woman beneath his hand, just the whalebone of her corseting, and unlike Eliza Penrose, Flora's careful steps, while competent, lacked fluidity and grace. He may as well have been dancing with a broom.

He greeted young Tregloan and his pretty wife, who were acquitting themselves with grace, then excused himself at the end of the dance, heading out into the clear night for some fresh air.

'I told you. That Miss Penrose is a sweet handful.' Jack Tehan came to stand beside him, lighting a cheroot.

'Don't be crude, Tehan.'

'I mean it. She doesn't belong in Maiden's Creek.'

'What are you doing here?'

'The lads are entitled to a bit of a fun, McLeod.'

'The lads? You've brought your crew into town?'

'Some of them. A couple of them decided to stop at Lil's on the way in.'

The music drifting from the hall abruptly stopped, only to be replaced by raised voices.

Alec and Tehan exchanged glances and went back into the building. The crowd seemed to have flattened themselves against the wall as two burly men faced off in the centre of the dance floor. Alec recognised one of his men—George Tregloan—but the other man, squat and dark-haired with a heavy black beard, was a stranger.

Tregloan's eyes blazed. 'The lady said she didn't want to dance with you.'

The lady in question stood on the side of the dance floor, ashen faced, rubbing her left wrist—Eliza Penrose. If she had hoped to stay out of the notice of the matrons of Maiden's Creek, whatever had occurred had definitely pushed her to centre stage.

'What happened here?' Alec demanded of Tregloan.

'He grabbed her wrist and tried to pull her onto the dance floor,' Tregloan said. 'Wouldn't take no for an answer.'

'I just asked the lady for a dance,' the black bearded man responded.

'Outside, Jennings,' Tehan said in a voice that brooked no argument.

'One of yours?' Alec enquired.

Tehan grunted and Jennings balled his fists at his side, hot angry eyes going from his boss to Eliza before he stomped outside with Tehan following. Alec watched them go with a feeling of disquiet. He knew Jennings' type. They were trouble.

The master of ceremonies for the evening hurried to the bandstand and cleared his throat. 'Ladies and gentlemen, time for a reel.' His voice sounded unnaturally high and it took a moment or two for the band to resume playing.

Slowly the crowd relaxed and the dance floor filled again while those not dancing gathered in knots to discuss the altercation that had just occurred, casting furtive glances at Eliza Penrose, who stood in the company of Netty Burrell, and the Tregloans.

Alec joined them. 'Are you hurt, Miss Penrose?' he asked.

'See for yourself,' Netty said, holding up Eliza's right wrist, where the deep red marks were already beginning to purple into bruising.

'The man was drunk,' Eliza said. 'He tried to drag me on to the dance floor.'

'He pulled her right over and when Tregloan here went to help her, he threatened to hit him. That's when you came in,' Netty said.

Eliza looked up at Tregloan and smiled. 'Thank you for intervening.'

Tregloan shuffled his feet. 'Don't like to see a lady imposed on like that. I knew your father, Miss Penrose. My cousin worked at Tregear. He was a good man.'

Eliza gave him a tremulous smile and she laid a hand on his arm. 'Thank you, Mr Tregloan.'

The young man smiled. 'This here's my wife, Jenny.'

Jenny Tregloan held out her hand. 'Pleased to make your acquaintance, Miss Penrose.'

'Go back to the dancing,' Eliza said. 'I'm all right.'

The Tregloans moved away, taking up a place in a set of the Lancers, and Eliza turned to Alec. The gas lights caught the unshed tears that glistened in her lashes.

'I think I would like to go home,' she said.

Alec looked for Ian. He was participating in the set to the best of his ability and his eyes were only for Susan Mackie. He didn't need Alec to be his nursery maid. With Jennings somewhere in the dark, Eliza Penrose needed him more.

'I'll escort you home,' he said. 'Netty, if you have a chance, could you tell Ian to make his own way home?'

Netty smiled, her gaze also on Ian and Susan. 'I think the lad is more than capable of finding his own way home, Mr McLeod.'

'Did you come alone?' Alec asked Eliza as they threaded their way to the door.

Spots of colour appeared on her cheeks. 'As you probably know very well, Uncle Charles is in Melbourne and Mrs Harris had no wish to attend, but I came with Netty Burrell.'

Relieved that the young woman's reputation was not irretrievably damaged, Alec offered her his arm and they stepped into the night.

The shock of the cold after the warm press of the hall caused Eliza to catch her breath. The whole evening had been a disaster, from her choice of gown to the incident with that man, Jennings. A respectable grieving woman wouldn't even have considered going to a dance, let alone actually taking to the floor.

After her lack of proper mourning and her eagerness to take the position at the school, the matrons of Maiden's Creek would surely label her a troublemaker.

'Take my arm, Miss Penrose, the road's a bit uncertain in parts and I'd hate for you to twist an ankle in a pothole.'

She hesitated before slipping her hand into the crooked arm he offered her. His warmth and solidity provided a reassuring presence and walking next to him, she had a sense of safety and security she had not felt since her father's death.

'I'm sorry to have spoiled your evening,' she said.

'You haven't,' he said. 'I only went for Ian's sake. I'm not one for dances.'

'I can't get used to the fact that it is the end of June and midwinter,' Eliza said. 'Such a back-to-front country.' She could see only the profile of his strong face in the dark. 'How long have you been in Australia?'

'Five years. After the hills and mists of Scotland, I wondered what I'd come to. It was midsummer and the country around Ballarat was baked hard, the bush tinder dry. Then we nearly froze in winter. But I've learned to love the Australian bush and the strange seasons.'

'Do you miss the Highlands?'

Alec laughed. 'I'm not from the Highlands,' he said. 'Never been further north than Fort William. No, I was born and bred in Lanarkshire in the heart of the coal mines.'

'And I come from the tin mines of Cornwall.'

'Aye, but the difference is you were the lady in the grand house on the hill, while I and my family lived in a two-up, two-down row house in Wishaw.'

'What does that matter? I don't have the grand house any more. I have nothing. My father and his hubris saw to that. You are an educated, intelligent man. The mine superintendent, no less. How did you escape?'

'Escape,' he said. 'I hadn't thought of it like that. I would call it luck.'

'Why?'

'My father was a great believer in education. He fought for Ian and me to attend school, even though my contemporaries were already going down the mine at the age of twelve. But that would have been my fate if it hadn't been for my schoolmaster. He spoke to my father and persuaded him I should apply for a scholarship. My father worked extra shifts to ensure I attended the Scottish Episcopal College of the Holy and Undivided Trinity of Glenalmond.'

She smiled. 'It sounds more like a bible college.'

'It was intended to train young men for the ministry of the Scottish Episcopal Church, but beggars cannot be choosers. From there I won another scholarship to university in Edinburgh. I studied geology and spent some time in Germany learning engineering. I had no intention of going back to mining.'

'But you did?'

'I had no choice. My mother died and my father was in poor health so I had to return to Wishaw for Ian's sake. I count myself lucky.'

'Some people,' Eliza said, 'can be lucky and for others such luck as they may have had trickles out of their fingers. That wasn't luck, Alec McLeod, that was your own hard work.'

'And you, Miss Penrose?'

'Eliza,' she said.

'Eliza.'

'I am not one of the lucky ones,' she said. 'If anything, the opposite. Did Will tell you the sad story of the Tregear mine?'

'He mentioned that your father made some poor investments.'

'Tregear itself was just about worked out so he cast around for other opportunities. When they failed, we lost everything. *Everything*. Will came out here to work for our uncle and my mother moved in with her sister in Bath. As for me ...' She shrugged. 'When you are trained for nothing, you have to make do with what you have. In my case I had two choices: either a lady's companion or a governess. I chose the latter. I found that while I loved teaching, being a governess was not to my liking, so I have been teaching at a ladies' academy for the last three years. Then came Will's letter about the Shenandoah ... The rest you probably know.'

Alec said nothing, but the muscle in his arm tensed beneath her fingers and he seemed to draw her closer. They had reached the path leading up to Cowper's house and she slipped her hand from his elbow.

'I can make my way from here,' she said.

He didn't move. 'I wouldn't be a gentleman if I didn't see you safely to your door, Miss Penrose.'

Eliza recognised a stubborn man when she met one so she chose not to argue but set off up the path with Alec following.

Halfway, she caught the toe of her shoe on a rock and nearly fell, but Alec caught her arm, righting her.

'Such silly shoes,' she said apologetically. 'I knew I should have worn something more sensible. They're ruined now.' It seemed everything about this harsh landscape conspired against the pretty and frivolous.

The front door was locked and Eliza gave a tentative knock.

It was answered by Mrs Harris, dressed in her nightgown and a man's dressing gown, her hair in a long plait over her shoulder. She held up a lamp. 'I didn't expect you home so soon,' she said and her gaze drifted past them to the Mechanics' Institute below where the music drifted up on the still night air.

'I—I … felt a little unwell and Mr McLeod was good enough to walk me home,' Eliza said in the full knowledge that Mrs Harris would hear the whole ghastly story in due course. One thing Eliza had learned very quickly in her short time in Maiden's Creek: gossip ran around the town like mercury through the crushing tables.

Mustering her last shred of dignity, Eliza turned and thanked Alec for escorting her home. He turned away, taking the steep path with the ease and agility of a man used to the hills. She lingered at the door until the night swallowed him up before turning inside to the warmth of her own bed.

Rather than return to the dance, Alec went home. Even as he approached the cottage, his instinct prickled. The door to the cottage stood ajar. He paused and called out Ian's name, a habit, even though he knew Ian wouldn't hear him, but the cottage was in darkness and he had no reason to assume his brother had returned early.

He pushed the door fully open and took a step back, allowing his eyes to adjust to the darkness inside. A plaintive meow announced the presence of Windlass and he could make out the shape of the cat crouched under a bush. He clucked encouragingly but Windlass did not move, voicing his displeasure to Alec.

Alec swallowed and stepped into the cottage, fumbling for the candle and safety matches they kept just inside the door. His shaking fingers closed on both and he lit the candle with diffi-culty before holding it up. The small flame illuminated a scene of devastation.

While the town had been at the dance, someone had broken into the cottage and every room had been ransacked. The drawers in the dresser had been pulled out and upended, and the cupboard doors stood open, crockery, pots and pans strewn across the floor. The bits and pieces on the mantelpiece, including the McLeod family clock that they had brought from Scotland, had been swept onto the floor. The glass and the casing of the old clock were smashed beyond repair.

A gasp behind him made him start and he nearly dropped the candle as Ian stepped across the threshold. He stood for a long moment beside Alec, his gaze darting from one corner of their humble home to another.

Ian moved first. He stooped and picked up the studio portrait taken of their parents on their wedding day. The frame was in splinters and the glass shattered. He looked at Alec with tears in his eyes. 'Who would do this?'

Alec shook his head and checked the two bedrooms. Like the living room, both had been thoroughly turned over: the mattresses pulled from the bed and slit open, shedding stuffing across the room like snow, the chest of drawers upended, and on the floor was every item of clothing. Alec's travelling box had been pulled from under the bed, the lock forced open and his personal papers torn and scattered. The image of Catriona and himself on their wedding day, which he kept by his bed, lay face down on the floor.

He turned it over, his chest constricting at the sight of the cracked glass that now obscured Catriona's beloved face.

He sank to his haunches in the middle of the detritus of his life and ran a hand through his hair. His bed had been shifted in the search and, fortuitously, the clod who had moved it had dragged one of the legs onto the loose board that concealed the plans. He shifted the bed and lifted the floorboard, relieved to see the oil-skin package still secure in its hiding place.

Ian's footfall creaked on the floorboard behind him. 'Who would do this?' he asked again.

Alec lifted the package out and twisted to look up at his brother. 'I think I know.'

'Who?'

'Black Jack Tehan and his men.'

Ian looked down at the package in Alec's hand. 'Were they after the plans?'

'I suspect they were.'

'I told you they would bring trouble.' Ian's normally calm eyes flared with anger. 'Have you told her about them yet?'

Alec shook his head. 'I need to find an appropriate time.'

Ian snorted and turned back to the living room where he began to restore order with much banging of pots and scraping of furniture. He had every right to be angry.

Alec stood and set the package down on the ruin of his bed. He joined his brother, stooping to pick up the broken clock. Every Sunday night his father's ritual had been the winding of this clock to ensure the gentle tock would carry them through another week.

'Where's Windlass?' Ian asked, turning in a circle.

'Outside and very cross,' Alec said.

'I suppose we should be grateful that the thugs didn't take out their frustration on him.'

A lump rose in Alec's throat. Whoever had been sent to look for the plans did not need to inflict so much damage and killing a defenceless animal could well have been part of the sport. 'He's smart,' he said. 'He knew to stay out of sight. He'll be keeping low and will be back when he's hungry.' Or at least he hoped so.

It didn't take the brothers long to restore order to their simple home. Ian, who was handy with a needle, even managed to mend the mattresses sufficiently to allow them somewhere to sleep.

Just as they were about to go to bed, Windlass appeared at the back door, demanding an apology for the inconvenience.

Alec lay awake on the now lumpy mattress, his arms behind his head and the purring cat on his chest, staring up at the ceiling while his mind roiled. If anyone was responsible for the sacking of the McLeod house it had to be Tehan.

Tehan was the only other person who knew of, or suspected, the existence of Penrose's plans and it could be no coincidence that he and his crew had come into town that night. The question that went unanswered was whether Tehan was acting for himself or for Cowper.

Alec needed to talk to Eliza but he just didn't know when or how.

'Face it, you're a coward, McLeod,' he told the cat and suspected Windlass probably agreed.

Twelve

8 July 1873

During the week following the dance, Eliza settled into a routine at the school, where Flora Donald had—with a great show of reluctance—increased her two half-days to full days. Between navigating the treacherous waters of Flora Donald's ongoing antagonism and a number of students who simply did not want to be tied to a school desk, Eliza found she returned to Cowper's house exhausted at the end of a school day.

Charlie O'Reilly managed three or four days a week at most and as she was always the last to arrive and the first to leave, Eliza could never keep the child long enough to learn more about her. The child seemed to have no friends. During breaks she perched on a log on the far side of the yard, never invited to join in the skipping games or hopscotch by the other girls. The only one who showed her the slightest kindness was Joe Trevalyn. Joe was hampered from joining in the boy's rough-housing games by his club foot but, the other children seemed to accept and like the boy and he was no outcast, unlike Charlie.

One damp Tuesday morning, Charlie arrived very late. She skulked into the room and before she could slide onto the bench next to Joe, Flora called Charlie up to the front of the room. Charlie went slowly, her gaze on the floorboards, dragging her feet.

'You're late again, Charlotte. And where were you yesterday?'

'Sorry, miss,' Charlie said.

Eliza took a breath—up close she could see the child had a blackened eye. It was probably a few days old, already yellowing.

'As writing lines seems to do nothing for your punctuality, hold out your hand.'

Charlie's mouth tightened and she held up a shaking hand. The children behind her seemed to hold their breath as Flora brought the cane down with well-practised strokes on the child's palm, twice, sharply. Charlie hissed with the pain but otherwise made no sound.

'Let that be a lesson to you,' Flora said. 'Go back to your seat.'

Charlie returned to her place beside Joe. The boy leaned over and whispered something to her. Eliza hoped they were kind words.

At the end of the day, Eliza positioned herself at the door and managed to catch Charlie by the frayed and filthy collar. She pointed at the child's desk in the schoolroom. 'Wait there for me,' she ordered.

When she had seen the last student safely off the premises, she returned to Charlie, who sat biting a filthy fingernail. She reminded Eliza of a half-tamed animal, seeking human contact but ready to flee at the first threat.

'I gotta go,' Charlie said. 'Ma'll kill me.'

'Who gave you the black eye? Did your mother hit you?'

'Nah, that was one of her customers. I was too slow. Ma doesn't hit me unless I've done something real bad. Please can I go, Miss?'

'I won't keep you long,' Eliza said. 'I would just like to know more about you. Let's start with your age.'

Charlie shrugged.

'You must know how old you are?'

'I think I'm ten,' Charlie said grudgingly. She was so small she could have been mistaken for a six-year-old.

'What am I to do with you?' Eliza wondered, flicking through the results of several short tests she had given the child. 'Your arithmetic is well in advance of your age but your reading is that of two levels below and your letter hand is appalling.'

'I suppose you're going to try and stop me coming like that bastard, Emerton,' Charlie said, turning a face full of defiance to Eliza.

'You do not, under any circumstances, swear in front of me or any of the other children, Charlotte.'

'Charlie.'

'Very well, Charlie. And you're wrong, I would very much like you to keep coming to school,' Eliza said and the naked hunger in the child's face almost made her want to weep. 'But you can't keep missing days. Do I need to talk to your mother?'

'No. No, Miss, please don't talk to me ma. She don't want me coming to school. She says it gives me ideas above me station.'

As Charlie's station in life could hardly be any lower, a surge of anger rushed through Eliza. Charlie's eyes slid away to the door and Eliza recognised she had pushed the child as far as she could, so she let Charlie leave, the child scampering out of her reach like a frightened rabbit.

'She's a lost cause, that one.'

Eliza turned to face Flora Donald, who stood in the doorway to the teacher's office with her arms crossed. 'I don't agree,' she said. 'Look at these tests. She is capable of mathematics years ahead of that for a ten-year-old.'

Flora studied the test results and her eyes widened. In that fleeting moment Eliza glimpsed the teacher beneath the prickly exterior, before Flora turned to the examples of Charlie's other work Eliza had set out and her mouth tightened.

'But look at this, Miss Penrose. My first-year students have better handwriting.'

'I suspect that is because she's missed so much school over the years. With regular attendance, and maybe a little extra help, she could catch up.'

'The child needs to be taken in hand,' Flora said and her fingers twitched as if she still held her birch cane.

'Corporal punishment is not the answer. Did you see her black eye? She has enough of that at home. Perhaps we could go and talk to her mother?'

'You've not met her mother. I wouldn't go near her without a police escort.'

Eliza stared at her colleague. 'But surely she has to understand how important her daughter's education is?'

Flora snorted and turned away, picking up the abandoned slates from the desks and stacking them neatly on the table at the front of the room. She waved in the direction of the front door. 'Can you lock up?'

Eliza shot home the bolts and returned to the schoolroom. Flora waited by the side door, tapping her foot with impatience.

'Go and visit Mad Annie, if you think you can help,' she said, 'but in my opinion you will just make the child's position worse. You're a fool if you think you can change that girl's life.'

'At least I can say I tried.'

As they left the building, Eliza said, 'I wish you would call me Eliza when we are alone.'

'Why would I do that?' Flora said. 'Given names are the privilege of friends. Good evening to you, Miss Penrose.' She strode down the path, leaving Eliza with nothing to do but watch her go.

At the mine manager's house, Eliza found her uncle in front of the fire in the parlour reading a news sheet, his foot propped up on a stool. As he generally kept long hours at the mine, clearly something was not right.

'Are you quite well, Uncle?' she asked.

He looked at his foot. 'Gout. This cold weather brings it on. Dr Sims suggested I should rest it.' He glanced out of the window and his lips tightened. 'As Mrs Harris's boy is out on errands for our good housekeeper, I wonder if I could prevail on you to run a message up to McLeod?'

'Is he back?' she asked, her heart skipping a beat. After the disquieting break-in at the McLeod brother's cottage, Cowper had despatched Alec to Port Albert to see to the arrival of some mine equipment.

'Yes, got in last evening with the new drive shaft. Pass me paper and pen.'

She obliged and left him scrawling his note while she wrapped herself back in her outdoor clothes.

Cowper handed her the folded paper and said, 'I am expecting Jack Tehan this afternoon so if you see him at the mine, send him over here, or leave a message with the clerk.'

'Mr McLeod?'

A woman's voice interrupted Alec's consideration of the heavy burlap-wrapped object he'd a spent a week nursing up from Port Albert. Women were a rarity at the mine and he turned to see Eliza Penrose. She stood watching him from a distance, a neat figure in her dark dress and a fringed tartan shawl.

'How was your journey?'

Alec huffed out a breath. 'Hellish. This is not the best weather for bringing in heavy equipment over the mountains, but we got it here. What brings you to the mine, Miss Penrose?'

She held out a note. 'My uncle is indisposed and sent me to give this to you.'

He took the paper, unfolded it and read the contents. Nothing important, just some fresh instructions regarding a shipment of fuel for the boilers. Nothing that couldn't have waited until the following day but Cowper liked to keep control even in his absence. He stuffed the note in his pocket, conscious that she waited.

'Did he want a reply?'

She shook her head. 'He didn't say so.'

'Is there something else I can help you with?'

She glanced at the mine's adit and turned back to face him, her eyes bright. 'I would like to see where William worked—the things that were important to him.'

It took a moment for him to comprehend what she was asking. 'You want to see the mine? Why?'

Her chin lifted. 'I was brought up in a household where mines and mining were the main topics of conversation,' she said. 'Mining runs in my blood.'

'I apologise, Miss Penrose, I didn't mean—'

She waved a hand. 'What happened to, Eliza? I didn't mean to snap at you. I miss my brother, more than I thought possible. This is where he lived, worked and died. It will help to understand something of his life during the years we were apart.' She coughed and reached into her sleeve for a handkerchief. 'Dust,' she said, wiping her eyes.

Considering the damp day and the sodden state of the yard, Alec let the remark pass. This woman had travelled around the world only to have her hopes dashed by the news her beloved brother was dead.

'I understand.' He glanced at his watch. 'If you don't mind the mud and inconvenience, I would be happy to show you the mine.'

She shook her head and lifted her skirt slightly to reveal a pair of stout leather boots and a tantalising glimpse of a slender ankle. 'I've been shopping,' she said. 'I am quite well equipped for mud and inconvenience.'

He smiled and gestured at the adit. 'Then come this way, Miss Penrose.'

At the entrance, he lit a candle and set it in a lantern he took from the shelf.

'You don't use Davy lamps?' Eliza asked and his opinion of her rose a notch.

'No. Unlike the coal mines, we don't have explosive gases.'

The hard-packed dirt beneath their feet was slimy from the damp conditions. Puddles had formed between the rails used by the carts and the scent of damp earth drifted in a miasma from the dark hole before them.

Eliza held back, staring into the darkness.

'Have you changed your mind?' Alec asked, but she shook her head.

'I was thinking about my father's mine, Tregear. It was one of the most profitable tin mines in Cornwall in its day. He first took me into it when I was five years old. There is something about the smell of a mine that reminds me of him. He carried the scent with him when he came in from a day's work.'

Alec thought of the mine at Wishaw where his father had worked. His father had returned home at the end of the day, black from head to toe and carrying more than just the scent of earth.

Eliza straightened her shoulders and gathered up her skirts. Then, smiling at him, she said, 'Lead on, Mr McLeod.'

He lifted the lantern and she followed him into the main tunnel, which ran two hundred yards into the heart of the mountain.

There were only a couple of places where he had to duck to avoid cracking his forehead on the ceiling or a beam. Eliza passed beneath them without hindrance.

'William wrote that when he first came to the Maiden's Creek Mine the main tunnel resembled the hind leg of a dog,' she said.

Alec laughed. 'Aye, I've read his notes and yes, you can see where it veered off.' He pointed at a dark tunnel leading from the one they were in. 'They followed a lead that petered out. He did a fine job straightening the tunnel.'

Faint light and the sound of hammers on metal echoed down the mine. 'This was his idea too,' Alec said as they came out into the enormous cavern that served as the plant room. 'We've sunk a shaft to follow the lead but we need to power the winding gear. Most conventional mines would have a poppet head above ground but we have a couple of hundred feet above us before we even hit this level, so Penrose decided we would simply move the equipment needed underground.'

He gestured at the two iron boilers. The older, smaller boiler was in operation, its firehole casting a red, angry glow around the cavern. The new boiler had still not been commissioned as they'd been waiting on the drive shaft that he had brought up from Port Albert. Every time Alec looked at the huge piece of metal, he thought of Penrose's design, which would deliver a boiler half the size with twice the power output.

He brought his attention back to his guest. Eliza turned on the spot, taking in the scale of the man-made cave.

'Will did this?'

Not by himself, Alec was tempted to answer. In fact, he doubted Will had even picked up a shovel, but the cave had been constructed according to his plans.

'He had a good instinct but we need fresh air as we go down so we are starting to cut ventilation shafts from the top.' Alec patted the new boiler. 'We'll have this one running soon and then we can improve the access to the lower levels and use the smaller boiler for the pumps.'

Eliza laughed, a gentle, sweet sound at odds with the industrial surroundings.

'What's so funny?'

'You have the same light in your eyes Will used to have. He was always scribbling in his notebooks. Ideas for machines and bits and pieces to make the mines safer and easier to work.'

Alec gave the boiler one last, loving caress. 'I love machines. I'm fascinated by their workings.'

Eliza smiled. 'Just like Will.'

As she appeared to be genuinely interested, he took some time explaining the plans for the mine and how Bride's Reef sloped diagonally from where it had come through at the mine entrance, all the time watching her face for signs of boredom. But her eyes were bright and she nodded and asked questions that revealed her knowledge of mining did indeed run deep.

'Your brother picked the direction of the reef and had started the deep lead before he left his position here. Again, his instinct was correct. We've hit a good seam and we're following it out.'

Eliza's eyes narrowed and she drew a deep breath. 'If his instinct was so good, then why was he so wrong about the Shenandoah Mine?'

Alec frowned. 'Who said he was wrong?'

'My uncle. He said the extruding dyke that Will found petered out.'

Alec had never heard a woman use the correct geological term for a quartz reef before. Eliza Penrose went up even further in his estimation.

He shook his head. 'That wasn't what he told me.'

'Have you been up to Shenandoah?'

'Only the once. Will had a problem with accessing the seam the deeper it went and we discussed the options. I would have said it was a good seam.'

'Is Jack Tehan any good at what he does?'

Whatever his personal feelings for Black Jack, Alec had to admit, 'Aye. He's not got the education your brother had, but they tell me his instincts are good.'

'But if there's no gold, then keeping Shenandoah going seems a waste of time and effort.'

Alec wondered how best to answer this observation. He knew Cowper was keeping it going because there was still gold and that gold was being used to bolster the Maiden's Creek figures. He debated whether Eliza needed to know that but here, where there were plenty of eyes and ears, was not the place to have that talk.

'It's taken three years to get any appreciable gold out of this mine and that's only because we've gone down, so until such time as the other shareholders are in a position to make a decision, he may as well keep going.'

Eliza seemed to accept that explanation. She walked over to the shaft and peered into the inky blackness. 'How far down?'

'Near fifty yards so far. Puts us about in line with the creek. We're running the tunnel away from it and there's some good colour down there but we will need to go down further. To do that we need good pumps to keep the water out, so I need to get this boiler working … Sorry, I'm boring you.'

She shook her head. 'No, you're not. Where did you say you were you before Maiden's Creek, Alec?'

'Ballarat. Very different terrain to this field,' he said and added, 'If you've seen enough, Eliza, I best get back to work.'

She nodded. 'Thank you. It's meant a great deal to me.'

Back in the outside world it had begun to rain again, water puddling in the rough cobblestones of the courtyard. A horse stood tethered outside the office, its colour obscured by the mud which had covered its legs and spattered up its flanks. The dispirited animal shook its head, sending sprays of water into the air.

'That's Tehan's beast,' Alec said. He had questions for Jack Tehan concerning the break-in at the cottage. He also had business with Eliza Penrose. First things first.

He glanced at her and cleared his throat.

'Miss Penrose—Eliza, if the weather is fine on Saturday afternoon, would you care to come for a ride with me? I'm sure you've not seen any of the better sights of the valley and there's a waterfall up one of the gullies that should be flowing well after all this rain.'

Her lips parted in a smile. 'I would like that. Thank you, Mr McLeod.'

'Aye, well, I'll call for you on Saturday.' He paused. 'You do ride?'

She nodded and began to speak but they were interrupted by Trevalyn striding across the courtyard, his brow furrowed.

'You didn't take her into the mine, did you?' he demanded of Alec.

Alec had never seen his unflappable foreman quite so angry. 'Aye, what of it?'

'Beggin' your pardon, miss,' Trevalyn said, pulling his hat from his head, 'but it's terrible bad luck to bring a woman into a mine, particularly a redhead.'

'Superstitious nonsense,' Alec snapped. He paused. 'I don't like the tone of your voice, Trevalyn.'

Trevalyn turned to Eliza, his anger abating. 'I meant no offence, Miss Penrose, but there's plenty of men working here who believe that superstitious nonsense.'

The colour had drained from Eliza's face and she looked up at Alec. 'I'm sorry, Alec, I didn't think ... I'd forgotten about the superstitions. Father took me down the Tregear Mine once. The men were furious, and he never took me again. Then there were stories about the Knockers.'

'It's all nonsense.' Alec glared at Trevalyn. 'I would like to think we left such folklore behind in the old country, Trevalyn.'

The foreman's lips twitched. 'Aye, well, as Miss Penrose knows, those Knockers are cunning little folk. They could've stowed away with any of us. As for the other, my apologies, miss, I spoke out of turn. Good day to you.'

Trevalyn sprinted back across the yard to the workshops.

'I'm sorry, Eliza. That's not like Trevalyn,' Alec said.

'But he's right. I should have been more respectful,' Eliza said. 'I was brought up around such stories.' She paused and gave a humourless smile. 'I don't suppose it was a tommyknocker that pushed Will to his death?'

Alec hesitated, unsure of how to answer.

'What was Will doing up here the night he died?' she asked.

'No one knows.'

'Where did he—' She swallowed. 'Can you show me?'

The rain had reduced to a few sprinkles so he nodded. 'If you wish.' He led her down the lane that ran between the administration office and one of the workshops to the head of the tailings heap that spilled down the hillside to the creek. A drop of fifty yards or so, almost vertical.

'He wouldn't have stood a chance,' she murmured.

'The men found some dislodged rocks over here.' Alec pointed. 'It seemed to indicate that he lost his footing on them and—'

'Plunged to his death?' She took a deep breath. 'Is it possible that he may have been depressed about the failure of the Shenandoah, and ...'

Alec stared at her. 'Are you asking if it is possible he took his own life? There are easier ways for a man to kill himself than throwing himself off a tailings heap.'

Her eyes widened and Alec cursed himself. 'Pardon my blunt speech.'

'No apology needed. You're right, but did you know my father shot himself? It is at the back of my mind that maybe Will ...' She shook her head. 'I suppose I'll never know what happened that night.'

As they turned back to the yard, the rain intensified and they took shelter under the eaves of one of the workshops.

'Perhaps you need to speak with our police sergeant, Maidment,' Alec said. 'He'll have the coroner's records and maybe he can put your mind at rest.'

Eliza thanked him for the suggestion and indicated the horse. 'Are you sure that's Tehan's horse? I have a message for him.'

'He'll be in the office. We'll have to make a run for it.'

Eliza and Alec burst through the door to the main office, shaking rain from their hair and clothes. Ian McLeod rose from this desk and held out his hand, 'Pleased to make your acquaintance, Miss Penrose.'

Eliza smiled and shook his hand. 'Very pleased to meet you, Mr McLeod,' she said, unconsciously adopting a deliberately slow and precise speech to accommodate Ian McLeod's deafness.

'It's all right, Miss Penrose,' Ian replied. 'I can understand what you say as long as you look at me and speak clearly.'

Embarrassed, she smiled at him. 'I'm sorry, I didn't mean to patronise you.'

Ian shrugged and Alec said, 'Ian surprises people.'

'Another two drowned rats.'

They turned to the manager's office, where Jack Tehan lounged against the door jamb. Water gathered in a puddle at his feet and his damp hair had begun to dry, curling at the ends into unkempt light brown waves.

'Is that your horse out there?' Eliza asked. 'You'll kill it if you don't get it into the dry.'

Tehan shot her a sharp glance. 'My horse is my business, Miss Penrose.'

'My uncle is at home, laid up with the gout. He told me if I were to see you that I should tell you to come over to the house.'

Tehan straightened. 'As he commands,' he said. 'If you are returning home, Miss Penrose, allow me to accompany you?'

'It's still raining,' Alec said. 'You'd be best to bide here until the rain lessens, Miss Penrose. You go on ahead, Tehan, I'll see her home safely.'

'It's getting late,' Eliza said. 'I would rather go home.'

'Take my oilskin,' Ian said, lifting the heavy slicker from the hook by the door.

Tehan opened the door, admitting a shower of rain. He shut it again.

'Before you go, I've got business with you, Tehan.' Alec said.

'Have you? It will have to wait. If you're ready, Miss Penrose? Good day to you, McLeod.'

Swamped by Ian McLeod's oilskin, Eliza walked beside Jack Tehan, who led his horse. As they passed through the mine's gate, she glanced back. Alec McLeod stood on the steps to the office, his hands thrust into his pockets.

'So you've been on a tour of the mine. Impressive, isn't it?' Tehan said. 'Your brother knew what he was doing.'

'I'm curious to see the Shenandoah Mine.'

'Are you now? I'm afraid, Miss Penrose, as you can see from the state of meself and me horse, the track up to Pretty Sally is hardly fit for travel at the moment and it will get worse before the winter's done. I suggest you wait until the warmer weather before venturing up to the mine. And at the end of the day, it's just a mine. Nothing to see.'

They passed the school house and crossed the bridge spanning the swollen creek. 'How long did you work for my brother?'

'That would be going on six months or more. He was a good boss. The men liked him. More importantly, they trusted him. This is a dangerous business, Miss Penrose. Trust is very important.'

She met his eyes. 'Indeed, Mr Tehan, trust is important.'

'You can start by calling me Jack,' he said. 'No one calls me Mr Tehan. It's plain Jack or Black Jack.'

At the house, Tehan took the horse around the back to the stable, allowing Eliza time to restore herself to order and ensure that Mrs Harris had tea organised.

When Tehan entered the parlour, Eliza was sitting with her uncle beside the fire.

'Sorry to hear about the gout,' Tehan said as he joined them. He looked down at his stockinged feet and grimaced at the sight of one toe protruding through the wool. 'I apologise, but Mrs Harris wouldn't let me in until I had removed me boots.'

Cowper harrumphed and told Tehan to sit down as Mrs Harris set down a tray, poured tea and handed around plates bearing still warm cake, which Tehan devoured in two mouthfuls.

Eliza cleared her throat. 'I understand that you kindly packed my brother's belongings after—' she paused, '—after the accident.'

Tehan took a noisy gulp of tea and set down the cup. 'That was me sad duty. I hope you found everything in order? He didn't have much to call his own.'

'I am missing his notebooks,' Eliza said.

Tehan glanced at Cowper, who gave a barely perceptible shrug.

'His notebooks?' Tehan said. 'There's no mystery. I have them, Miss Penrose.' He tugged his beard, which had dried to the colour of new mown hay. 'I am relying on them at the moment, but if you would like them ...'

Eliza shook her head. 'Not if they are of use to you, but I would like to see them.' Maybe Will had written personal notes? But she doubted it. He was, after all, an engineer.

She gathered her courage to ask the question that had been nagging at her since she had seen the place where Will had died. 'Mr Tehan, as the person who probably saw him the most, did it seem to you that Will may have been depressed or worried about something?'

Cowper frowned. 'What are you implying, Eliza?'

'Are you asking if took his own life?' Tehan said.

She started, surprised both by Tehan's perception and his honesty. 'Please understand, it's difficult for me … You see my father—'

'Eliza, really,' Cowper began.

Tehan shook his head. 'I don't know what you want me to say, Miss Penrose. We were not friends. He was me employer. If I'm honest with you, he seemed more distracted than usual but otherwise, I couldn't say I saw anything unusual in his behaviour.'

'What nonsense, girl,' Cowper said. 'The coroner concluded it was an accident and that is all it was. The stupid fool went too close to the tailings and they gave way under his feet. Damned dangerous. I have a running battle with some of the children who like to scavenge the tailings for flecks we missed. Now if you'll excuse us, Eliza, Tehan and I have business to discuss.'

Eliza stood, prompting Tehan to rise. She held out her hand to him. He had elegant hands with long fingers but the dirt of his profession was ingrained in his nails and the pores of his skin. He held her hand for a little longer than propriety demanded, only releasing it when she pulled away.

At the door she turned back. 'There is one more thing. As I have no interest in the Shenandoah, it is none of my business, but with the major shareholders still abroad, I am curious as to how you are financing the running of the mine if it is in such a parlous state?'

Her uncle stiffened, half rising from his chair but subsiding with a grimace. 'That is, as you say, none of your business, Eliza,' he said, 'Please close the door behind you.'

Eliza retreated to the warmth of the kitchen. The smell of cooking banished the miserable evening that had settled over the valley. Tom sat by the fire, polishing Tehan's boots. He looked up and smiled at her. Over the last few weeks she had spent some of her spare time with the boy, helping him with his reading and writing.

Mrs Harris, her sleeves rolled up and her face pink and shining from exertion, stood at the kitchen table, kneading bread for the morning. She straightened and wiped her forearm across her forehead, leaving a smear of flour.

'Anything I can do?' Eliza asked.

'You can peel the potatoes.' Mrs Harris pointed at a bowl on the other side of the table.

Eliza found the paring knife and set to work.

'Don't you be taken in by that Jack Tehan, Miss Penrose,' Mrs Harris said. 'Handsome is as handsome does.'

Eliza paused in her task. 'I've no intention of being taken in by him. I can see for myself that the man is a rogue.'

Mrs Harris nodded and returned to pounding the dough. 'He's got the Irish charm and from all accounts, he comes from bad stock. I've heard tell his father was a convict sent to Tasmania for murder.'

'Really?'

'Forgery,' Tom said. Both women looked at him. 'His dad was a forger.'

'And just how do you know that, Tom Harris?' his mother demanded.

Tom stuck his chin out. 'I hear things,' he said. 'No one pays me much mind so I hear what they say and I heard Mr Tehan telling the master his da were a forger.'

Mrs Harris wagged a floury finger at the boy. 'Eavesdroppers hear no good of themselves.'

Tom shrugged and returned to polishing Jack's boots.

'There's many a girl who's set her cap for Jack Tehan and regretted it.'

'But he's only been here six months. It seems a short time to have acquired such a reputation.'

'I knew him in Bendigo,' Mrs Harris said. 'Had to leave town hurriedly on account of a husband not taking kindly to finding Tehan in bed with his wife.'

'Ah,' Eliza said. 'I don't think you need to fear for my virtue, Mrs Harris. I'm hardly a catch for any man and I think the likes of Tehan would be after a girl with a bit of money and prospects. I have neither.'

'Aye, but you've a pretty face, and who's to say you don't have prospects? Your uncle is a wealthy man and he has no other relatives that I'm aware of.'

Eliza wondered if she caught a faint tone of bitterness in the woman's voice. 'Barring the gout, he's hale and hearty and I can't live my life on the presumption of his generosity in the event of his death.' She plopped the last potato into the pot. 'I'm on my own, Mrs Harris, and that is how it will stay.'

Jack Tehan left before supper and after Eliza and her uncle had eaten, they sat in the parlour, enjoying the warmth while the rain slammed against the tin roof and the windows. She had stockings to darn, a job she hated.

'How's the foot?' she asked, fitting the darning mushroom to the heel of her stocking.

He grimaced. 'Plagues me like the devil and I've too much work to do to sit here like an old man, but doctor's orders are doctor's orders.'

'Will's business partner, Caleb Hunt, was doctor here for a while, wasn't he?'

'A damn fine doctor too. We had our differences but I can't deny he had a skill that Sims lacks.'

'What's that?'

'It's the instinct that you're born with that distinguishes a genius from the rabble.'

'Some people tell me that Will had something similar.'

Cowper nodded. 'He did.'

'You must have been angry when he left Maiden's Creek for Shenandoah.'

'It's never easy to lose a good employee but I recognised Will had to make his own way in the world, and I found an excellent replacement in McLeod.'

Eliza let a few beats of the stamper pass before she looked up. 'What did you and Will fight about?'

Cowper stiffened. 'Who told you that?'

'This is a small town, Uncle.'

'Then the rumour-mongers must know that we fell out over that woman he was keeping company with.'

'Sissy?'

Cowper rolled his eyes. 'Good God, he had promised her marriage! A Penrose married to a fallen woman? You say this is a small town, well, it is a small *colony*, Eliza. It would have meant social ostracism for your brother, his wife and the rest of the family, you included. I tried to make Will see sense, and I think I succeeded to a degree. I believe that he broke contact with the girl, but he never forgave me.'

Eliza smiled. That would be Will. He could hold a grudge.

Cowper sighed. 'I am sorry he passed away before we had a chance to make amends.'

They sat in silence, only the crackling of the fire disturbing the peace of the room as it sent sparks up the chimney.

Thirteen

11 July 1873

Charlie did not attend school on Wednesday or Thursday and on Friday, Eliza resolved to visit Annie O'Reilly and see what could be done about the child.

She found Mrs Harris in the kitchen, churning butter. 'Can you tell me where Annie O'Reilly lives?' Eliza asked.

The woman stopped her work and wiped her forearm across her forehead. 'Why would you want to know that?'

'I have to talk to her about her daughter.'

'She don't like the townswomen. Calls 'em busybodies.' She paused. 'Actually, she calls 'em something else but I'm too much of a lady to say.'

Eliza straightened. 'Nevertheless, I must try to talk to her. The situation with Charlie can't continue.'

Mrs Harris frowned. 'What situation?"

'The child is clearly intelligent. She has an aptitude for maths far greater than children in the most senior classes, but while she misses school, she will never learn.'

'And you think that a quiet chat with Mad Annie will change things?'

'She needs to be made aware of Charlie's position.'

'Oh, I think you'll find Annie is fully aware of her daughter's position,' Mrs Harris said. 'But if you're set on talking to her, then you're a braver woman than I am. You'll find her hut on the Aberfeldy Road, just about on the turn-off to Pretty Sally. It's a couple of miles to walk out past the Chinese gardens. You can't miss it. Do you want to take Tom for company?'

Eliza hesitated. If Annie's reception was to be as hostile as everyone seemed to think it would be, then maybe a second person could be useful. But she was doubtful what help Tom would be in a difficult situation and she intended to visit Sergeant Maidment on the way, so she declined the offer.

North of the town on the Aberfeldy Road. It shouldn't be too hard to find, Eliza thought. After all, there was only one road heading north out of the town. 'If you want to hire a horse, Sones Livery stable has good, solid beasts,' Mrs. Harris said.

'That's a luxury I can't afford and besides, it's a lovely day for a walk.'

At the Maiden's Creek Police Station, a sturdily constructed building in the centre of town, she disturbed a large constable engrossed in a newspaper.

'Can I help you, madam?' he asked.

'Yes. I'd like to speak with Sergeant Maidment.'

The constable glanced at a closed door behind him. 'May I enquire as to the nature of your business?'

'My name is Eliza Penrose. I wish to speak with him about my brother's death.'

'Penrose, did you say? You wait here, miss, and I'll see if he is available.'

Before the constable could knock on the door, it opened and a tall, cadaverously thin man with sergeant's stripes on the arms of his serge police uniform appeared in the doorway.

'It's all right, Prewitt, I heard. Come through, Miss Penrose.'

Eliza took the seat Maidment offered. After extending his condolences for her bereavement, he sat down at his desk and studied her with bright, intelligent eyes.

'What is it I can do for you?'

'I believe there was an inquest into my brother's death. Do you have a copy of the coroner's report?'

Maidment nodded. 'I do, but may I ask why you want to see it?'

'I am curious to find out all I can about my brother's death.'

Maidment studied her. 'The coroner concluded it was an accident.'

'Nevertheless I would like to see it.'

Maidment opened a drawer in a cabinet in the corner of his office and pulled out a slender file. From it he extracted a couple of sheets of paper and handed them to Eliza. The report was scribed in an elegant copperplate and was surprisingly brief.

Coroner's Report into the Death of William Joseph Penrose

Mr Penrose, the mine manager and shareholder of the Shenandoah Creek Mining Enterprise, was discovered by two miners at approximately 6.30 on the morning of 26 March 1873.

The body was found at the foot of the tailings of the Maiden's Creek Mine, an establishment at which Mr Penrose had been previously employed, within a couple of feet of the creek. A quantity of dislodged rock found in the vicinity of the body caused the sergeant of police of the Maiden's Creek settlement to conclude that Mr Penrose had dislodged the loose stones when he fell from the mine site some fifty feet above the creek.

Dr Sims examined the body and concluded that the cause of death was a blow to the back of his head. On questioning, the doctor stated that such an injury, along with other non-fatal breaks and bruising, could easily have been sustained in the fall.

Witnesses report that Mr Penrose had been seen earlier in the evening drinking at the hostelry known as Lil's Place. Mrs White, proprietor of that establishment, confirmed that Mr Penrose had been present but seemed unable to recall any further details. She did, however, offer the observation that he left at approximately 11 pm but did not indicate where he intended to go.

No witnesses could be produced to explain why he was present at the Maiden's Creek Mine so late at night. He had been employed as mine superintendent at that establishment until a year previously but there had been no recent contact with the mine.

Mr Charles Cowper, manager of the Maiden's Creek Mine and Mr Penrose's uncle, advised that he and Mr Penrose had little contact since Mr Penrose had left for the Shenandoah Mine. Up until that time, Mr Penrose had been living in Mr Cowper's house. Mr Cowper confirmed that they remained on good terms.

No one present at the mine on the night in question recalled seeing Mr Penrose, although one miner, George Shaw, reported seeing a light in the mine manager's office around midnight. He described it as moving as if the person holding it were walking around the office. The night watchman was in his hut, having returned from a tour of the site. Owing to the noise from the stamper and his own deafness, he did not recall hearing anything untoward.

It is my conclusion that Mr Penrose's death is an unfortunate and tragic accident and no further action in respect of this case need be taken.

'Thank you.' Eliza handed the papers back to Maidment, conscious that he was watching her, no doubt waiting for hysterics. But she had no more tears for her brother—at least, not for the moment. 'Do you agree with the conclusion?' she asked.

Maidment frowned. 'I have no reason to think it was anything other than an accident.'

'What about the blow to his head?'

The police sergeant sat back in his chair and looked up at the ceiling. 'Miss Penrose, I presume you've seen where he fell? There are large rocks and an unstable surface. He could easily have hit his head on his way down, just as the doctor states.'

Eliza glanced out of the window. From where she sat she could see the spill of rocks cascading down to the creek, a harsh scar against the hillside. The conclusion of the report seemed quite reasonable in the circumstances. Will had been alone and he had been drinking, or at least that was the assumption drawn from Lil White's evidence. A misjudgement in his step and he could easily have tumbled to his death. Except it still did not explain what he had been doing up at the mine site or why a mysterious light had been seen in Cowper's office.

She stood and thanked Maidment. He saw her to the door and she strode out of the police station onto the northbound road. To call the uneven track a road seemed a little like calling a flower seller a duchess. As Eliza dodged the puddles and ruts, she thought of Charlie O'Reilly, who made this trek daily for the sake of a little learning. Little wonder the child's attendance was erratic.

Passing through a forest of blackened trees sprouting new life, Eliza crested a ridge and paused to catch her breath. Her new boots had started to rub blisters on her heels but she'd come too far to turn around so she limped on.

Ahead of her the road dipped into a heavily wooded valley and as she rounded a bend in the road, a rough bark hut came into view. Twenty or so yards before the hut, another track led off to the right, a handpainted sign indicating the road to Pretty Sally, and beyond the hut, the road forded a wide fast flowing creek.

The hut had a low verandah on the front with rough benches propped either side of the only door. Behind it she could see a precarious outbuilding, probably used as a stable and a small yard enclosed by rough-hewn railings. A thin thread of smoke escaped the crooked stone chimney. A sign had been hammered to a verandah post proclaiming BEER AND FOOD. The scent of hops, wood smoke, and boiled cabbage hung heavily in the air.

In contrast to the rough setting, a sweet, clear singing drifted from the glassless windows of the shabby hut. As Eliza approached, a scruffy dog tied to the verandah by a long rope rose to its feet, barking a warning. She gave the animal a wide berth and stepped onto the verandah and knocked on the crooked door.

'Is anyone at home?' she called.

The singing stopped.

'Who's there?'

'Mrs O'Reilly, my name is Miss Penrose. I'm the school-mistress in Maiden's Creek.'

'Who's with you?'

'No one. I came by myself.'

A bolt scraped back and the door opened a few inches. 'You must be the school ma'am that Charlie's been blatherin' on about. What 'appened to old rod-up-his-arse?'

Eliza blanched at the description of her predecessor. 'He is unwell. Miss Donald and I are standing in for him.'

'That dried-up old 'ag? She's worse than Emerton. So, 'ave you come to tell me that my Charlie can't attend again?'

'No, but I do want to talk to you about Charlie.'

'What's she been up to now?'

'Nothing.'

'So you've walked all this way for nothin'?'

'Please, may I come in? My feet hurt—'

'Poor you,' the woman said, her tone dripping sarcasm.

The door opened and Annie O'Reilly stepped out into the daylight. She wore a brown woollen gown, open at the neck, and a dirty apron tied high over the unmistakeable bulge of advanced pregnancy. Lifeless black hair, barely constrained in a rough knot, hung in lank strands around her face.

'Ain't you never seen a pregnant woman before, Miss 'igh and Mighty?' Annie said, green eyes narrowed, her chin lifted defiantly.

Embarrassed at being caught staring, Eliza looked at the woman's face and realised with a shock that Annie was probably only her age.

'I'm sorry, I didn't mean to—that was unforgivably rude,' Eliza said.

'Yeah, well ... sit down and take the weight off your feet.'

Eliza sank down on one of the benches and Annie sat beside her, awkwardly positioning her heavy body on the lumpy bench. She ran a hand over the bulge beneath the apron.

'Reckon it won't be long now.'

'No,' agreed Eliza, who had little experience with pregnant women. She wondered who the father was, or if this woman even knew who among her gentlemen callers was responsible.

'So, what can I do for you, Miss Penrose with the sore feet?'

'Charlotte—'

Annie stiffened. 'What about 'er?'

'She's very bright.'

The antagonism faded from Annie's face and she blinked. 'Bright? What do you mean by that?'

'I mean, she could do brilliantly at school, if she was given half a chance.'

'Could?'

'Yes, her education seems to have been interrupted and while she is very quick to grasp mathematics, her reading and spelling is very far behind others of her age.'

'Is that so? Well, it ain't my fault she's behind. The schoolmaster said she wasn't fit to be at school. Told 'er to stay away.'

'That has all changed. Attendance at school is now compulsory.'

'So they tell me. Well, I don't give a tinker's curse.' She caressed the bulge of her stomach again. 'When this one comes, Charlie'll have to stay 'ome and 'elp. I can't do it all by myself.'

'No, she can't miss any more school,' Eliza said.

Annie O'Reilly rose to her feet, not without difficulty, steadying herself on one of the verandah posts. 'No? That's too bad, Miss 'igh and Mighty, because that's 'ow it is for the likes of Charlie and me.'

Eliza stood up. Annie was taller by a few inches and as they faced each other, Annie's eyes hardened and her mouth set in a thin line.

'Please, Mrs O'Reilly,' Eliza said. 'I am sure we both want what's best for Charlie. Until the baby is born, can you make sure she doesn't miss any more school?'

Annie tossed her head. 'What good's it goin' to do 'er? You're just goin' to put notions into 'er 'ead.'

'With a bit of decent education, Charlie—' She was going to say *has a chance of escaping this* but she caught the words. 'Charlie could go into service or work in a shop.'

The defiance faded from Annie O'Reilly's eyes. 'You think so? You really think she could do that?'

'I wouldn't have walked all this way unless I truly believed it.'

'You've said your piece, now you can turn and walk back the way you came.'

'Mrs O'Reilly—'

'I've a brew on the boil and I can't be talkin' to you.' Annie turned and waddled back into the hut, slamming the door behind her.

Eliza stared at the crudely made door with mounting frustration. What chance did Charlie have in these circumstances? Then again, what chance did Annie O'Reilly have with another mouth to feed? The desperation of the woman's situation clawed at Eliza's heart and conscience as she turned back to town.

She distracted herself from the pain of her blistered feet by reviewing Charlie's situation. Had her mother, 'Mad Annie', made her choices or had they been thrust on her by circumstance? What would it take to give Charlie the chance to escape the drudgery her mother envisioned?

She started at the sound of whistling and a horse's hoofs behind her, moving to the far side of the track to let the rider pass.

'Deep in thought, Miss Penrose?' Jack Tehan looked down at her from the back of his tall bay gelding.

'I was.'

'May I ask what you're doing out here?'

'I've just been to visit Mrs O'Reilly.'

Tehan swivelled in his saddle to glance back up the track in the direction of the O'Reilly's grog shop. 'You keep strange company,' he said.

'I wanted to speak to her about Charlie.'

The humour drained from his face. 'What about Charlie?'

'Do you know her?'

'Of course I do. I pass the O'Reilly place every time I go up and down to Pretty Sally. She's a good-hearted child.'

'And a very bright one.'

'Is that so?'

'I've said too much.' Eliza straightened. 'It's none of your concern.'

'No, it's not.' The flickering of genuine interest in his eyes belied his words but in a heartbeat the cynical, world-weary look had returned. 'Can I offer you a ride back into town?'

She thought of the blisters and considered his sturdy horse. 'Will your horse take two?'

Tehan laughed. 'He'll hardly notice the weight of you. It won't be comfortable but you've a way to go yet and you seem to be limping.'

He kicked his foot out of the stirrup. Eliza placed her left foot in the iron and Tehan grasped her arm, hauling her up behind him. She swung her right leg over the horse and found herself pressed up hard against the man's back, her skirts hitched around her knees in a most unbecoming fashion. She breathed in a familiar and not unpleasant scent of horse and leather and man.

'Hold onto me belt,' Jack said, and she obediently twisted her hands into the worn brown leather.

With a laugh, he kicked the horse into a canter. Despite herself, Eliza let out a sharp cry and clung tighter, pressing her body against the wool of his jacket, feeling the smooth flow of muscle beneath the rough cloth.

'What are you doing?' she protested breathlessly.

His shoulders lifted in laughter and he turned slightly to look at her. 'I think you need a little fun and laughter in your life, Miss Penrose.'

And despite herself, Eliza laughed.

He slowed the horse to a more dignified walk and darkness began to close in as they climbed the last hill before town.

Eliza tapped her Galahad on the arm. 'Let me down here. I'll walk the rest of the way.'

Tehan glanced over his shoulder. 'Fearful for your reputation, Miss Penrose?'

'Yes ... no ... It is probably best I am not seen riding like a hoyden behind a man who has something of a reputation in this town for breaking hearts.'

'Is that what they say about me?'

'They do.'

'Very well. I'll save your good name.'

He halted and held her steady as she slid off the back of the horse.

'Thank you for the ride. You saved my feet.'

'The pleasure was all mine.'

They had stopped on the road beside a ruined house. Not much remained but the brick chimney, rising starkly against the lowering sky. It seemed a little distant from the line of the fire that had ravaged the bush to the north of the town.

Eliza shivered. 'What is this place?'

'Before me time but I hear tell that a smallpox victim died here and the house had to be burned to the ground to prevent infection.' Tehan pointed up the hill to the left of them. 'She's buried up there. Couldn't even be carried to the cemetery.' He leaned toward her and said quietly, 'They say her ghost still haunts her old home and she can be seen in the ruins, wringing her hands and wailing.'

Eliza took a step back. 'Really, Mr Tehan, you don't believe in such nonsense?'

He shrugged. 'I'm Irish, Miss Penrose. Far be it from me to question things we don't understand. Good evening to you.' He touched his fingers to his hat and kicked his horse into a trot.

Eliza lingered on the side of the road for a moment or two, her eyes drawn to the ruins of the house. In the gloaming, the place had an eerie feel. As she turned to walk the last few hundred yards into town, she thought she caught a flash of movement in the ruins. She whipped around but saw nothing except the blackened outline of a chimney. The chill wind caught at her skirt and she shivered again. The walls of the valley seemed to close in on her and her breathing sounded loud in her own ears. Eliza caught her skirts and ran, ignoring the blisters, not stopping until the warm, welcoming lights of Maiden's Creek came into view.

Fourteen

12 July 1873

Alec's intentions of confronting Tehan about the ransacking of his house were frustrated by his commitments at the mine. Installing the new drive shaft and commissioning the boiler meant he was working from before sunrise to almost midnight all week, but by Friday night, the bulk of the work had been accomplished and preliminary testing of the boiler looked promising. He felt quite able to take Saturday for himself and in truth, he couldn't face Ian's reproachful looks any longer. Eliza Penrose had to be told about her brother's invention.

By the time Alec had hired two horses from Sones Livery Stables and led them down the main street to Cowper's house, he felt physically ill. He just hoped he could frame the revelation in such a way so as to not incriminate his own suspect motives or frighten her with the knowledge that Black Jack Tehan also knew about the plans.

The thought of Jack Tehan, with his green eyes and his Irish charm, made Alec seethe.

What hope did a bluff Scottish engineer have? What hope did he want?

Eliza waited for him beside the road below her uncle's house. He stared at her. She was dressed in some sort of formal riding habit of rich dark green velvet with black frogging on the tightly fitting jacket. An outfit completed by a black velvet hat trimmed with a green feather and neat black gloves. She would have been quite at home on a grand estate back in England.

She had once come from a grand estate in England, Alec reminded himself.

Eliza frowned and looked down at her attire, holding out the long, impractical skirts. 'Is there a problem, Alec?'

Alec managed a smile. 'Forgive me saying this, but you look as if you are settling for a gentle canter in the park, not a ride in the Australian bush.'

'Oh dear.' Eliza frowned. 'I didn't have anything else. My father gave this to me and I have always loved it, but there has been precious little opportunity to wear it in more recent years.'

'You look lovely,' Alec said, and she did. The colour suited her and made her grey eyes sparkle. 'If I'd known you were going to be so grandly dressed, I would have asked Sones for a side saddle.' Alec gestured at the smaller of the two animals, a grey pony, with its standard English riding saddle. 'Although I doubt he has one. No one rides side saddle out here, it's too damn dangerous.'

Eliza's eyes widened and Alec felt the heat rising to his face. 'I apologise for swearing.'

'I thought as much. I will manage with my skirts astride.' She ran a gloved hand down the pony's nose. 'She's lovely. What's her name?'

'Nobby.'

Eliza shot him a sharp glance and he shrugged. 'Sones is not one to give his beasts fancy names.'

He bent and cupped his hands. Eliza placed a polished black riding boot in them and he hoisted her up with such force she almost flew off the other side. He apologised and caught at the trailing skirts to steady her as she settled into the saddle and arranged her skirts decorously around her. He wished himself anywhere else. She must think him a clod.

He swung into his saddle and twitched the horse forward. Alec had not been born to the saddle and he had an engineer's deep distrust of horses. Unlike machines, the beasts had minds of their own.

'My parents would have confined me to my room on bread and water for a week if they ever caught me riding astride,' Eliza said as they set off down the main street. 'Where are we going?'

Alec tipped his hat to the back of his head. 'I know a pretty spot on the Thompson and—' he patted his saddle bag, '—I have packed provisions.'

'Oh, a picnic. How wonderful. What about the waterfall?'

'I asked one of the lads and he told me the creek is flooded. It will have to wait till finer weather.'

The wooded hills closed in on them as they headed away from the township, the mountain ash tall and straight, while tree ferns bowed and dipped like graceful dancers.

'It smells wonderful,' Eliza said, taking a deep breath. 'I suppose in a few years all these lovely trees will be gone?'

Alec sighed. 'The mines are hungry beasts.'

'It will be such a shame. What will become of the animals and birds?'

Alec had no answer for that, so they rode on in silence until Eliza gave a soft cry and drew her horse up. Leaning toward Alec, she said, 'Is that a kangaroo? The sweet thing.'

The little animal had stopped on the track ahead of them, standing upright, ears forward, regarding the interlopers with curious eyes.

'A wallaby,' Alec corrected, refraining from adding that if he'd had a rifle with him, the 'sweet thing' would be dinner for him and Ian for a week.

The wallaby shook its head and went down on its forepaws, lolloping slowly into the underbrush.

'Have you not seen one before?'

Eliza looked at him, her eyes still bright with wonder. 'No. The children at the school told me about them and I've seen pictures in books, but to see one in real life … It was magical.'

Alec explained the difference between wallabies and kangaroos as the track descended toward the river. Eliza chatted about the children at the school. Drawn out by Alec's comfortable presence, she voiced her concerns for Charlie O'Reilly.

'Have you seen how they live?' she asked.

Alec nodded.

'Charlie has so much potential and it can't be safe for a woman and child out there in the middle of nowhere. I wonder if Annie could be persuaded to move into town?'

'Are you trying to change the world?'

'If I had the means, but I'm as poor as the proverbial church mouse.'

They reached a curve in the river where a grassy bank sloped down to a small cliff eaten away by the river. Alec slid off his horse, took the reins of Eliza's horse and helped her to dismount. She straightened, stretching her arms above her head.

'I haven't ridden in so long, I shall be quite sore tomorrow.'

Alec secured both horses and took out the blanket and food he had purchased from Draper's Bakery. He spread the blanket over a fallen log as Eliza stood watching the river. After the winter rains, the Thompson River was high, curling around the boulders and cutting corners in its haste to reach the sea.

'This is lovely,' she said.

He joined her and they stood side by side, revelling in the fresh, clean air and the silence, broken only by the distinctive call of a whip bird, answered by a chatter of parrots. They were north of the confluence so the filthy water flowing from the town and mine was swept away. Here the water was still pure, coming straight from the mountains. It was possible to forget the depredations man had inflicted on the landscape around Maiden's Creek.

'You were right about this impractical outfit,' Eliza said, hoisting her skirts over one arm to sit on the log. Alec set down the satchel, leaving Eliza to spread out the picnic: bread and cheese, bottles of ginger beer, a fruit cake and apples. Hands in pockets, he returned to the river, summoning the courage to tell her that he had her brother's plans.

'Aren't you hungry?' Eliza said and he turned to her.

Set against the muted colours of the bush rising behind her, Eliza could have been posing for a portrait, her chestnut hair curling around her face, and he realised with a jolt she stirred something in him he had thought he would never feel again. And now he was going to tell her that he had been contemplating stealing the only thing of value she had to her name.

He cleared his throat as she took a bite from an apple. 'Eliza—'

She looked up expectantly.

'I believe I have something that might belong to you.' The words came out in a rush.

Her brow creased. 'What do you mean?'

'Just before his death, your brother was working on a design for a new boiler.'

'He was always working on something, Alec. It wouldn't be Will if he wasn't scribbling in his notebooks.'

'This was more than just scribbling in a notebook. It was a meticulous plan which he intended to lodge with the Patents Office when he next went to Melbourne.'

'And how do you know this?'

'We talked about it and I helped him with some of the calculations. With his death, legally they belong to you.'

She frowned. 'Why haven't you mentioned this before?'

He had no answer for that question. 'The night he died he gave it to me for safekeeping. He slipped it under my door and I only found it the next day. By then it was too late to ask him why he had left it with me.'

'Is it any good?' she asked.

'It has the potential to revolutionise the industry.' Her eyes brightened and he ploughed on before she could speak. 'The thing is, Eliza, the plans are not complete. There are problems with some of the calculations that we hadn't been able to solve.'

Her shoulders slumped. 'A worthless plan and a worthless mine,' she said. 'I don't seem to have much to thank my brother for.'

Alec shook his head. 'I don't believe it's worthless, I just need some time to work through the calculations again. I'm not speaking lightly when I say it could be worth a fortune.' He swallowed. 'And as for the mine, I have good reason to believe that it is producing a good return, but the gold is being taken from the Shenandoah Mine and used to boost the finds from Maiden's Creek.'

'I don't understand.'

He took a deep breath before plunging on, 'I believe your uncle is diverting the gold finds from Shenandoah to increase the value of his stake in Maiden's Creek.'

'Why?'

'It has the effect of devaluing Shenandoah to the point where he can buy it for a fraction of its real worth from the Hunts when they return to Australia.'

Eliza stared at him. 'You mean he is stealing the gold? He wouldn't—'

Alec crouched in front of her and took her hand. It seemed so small and fragile, like a trapped bird. To his surprise, she made no move to withdraw or chastise him for his impropriety. 'I'm afraid he would. When it comes to business, he's ruthless, Eliza.'

'Do you have proof?'

'I have the figures for the two mines. As for the boiler design, I just need time to work through the calculations again. It could be worth a fortune, providing the capital can be found to make a prototype.'

She shook her head, pulled her hand free of his and rose to her feet. She walked down to the river and stood looking out over the dark, cold water with her arms wrapped around herself. 'And where would I get the capital I need to do that? I barely have enough to pay for a night's lodging.'

'Investors can be found.'

She turned to face him, eyes wide, her mouth a thin line. 'Alec, what you've just told me—the gold, the plans—would it be worth killing for?'

He hesitated. 'It could be,' he said slowly.

She continued to stare at him for a long moment. 'Does anyone else know about the design?'

Alec nodded. 'Jack Tehan. There was a break-in at my house the night of the dance—I'm sure it was his men.'

Eliza gasped. 'Looking for the plans?'

He nodded. 'They didn't find them ... or the evidence Ian found that the gold from Shenandoah is being counted in with that of Maiden's Creek.'

'How does he move the gold?'

'I think Tehan brings it in with him on his weekly visits to your uncle and the gold is salted into the battery.'

Eliza paced the clearing then stopped and returned to the log, head in her hands. 'I am struggling to believe my uncle guilty of such offences. He's shown me nothing but kindness.' She paused and looked up. 'But from the moment I arrived, he has seemed very anxious for me to leave.'

Alec sat beside her, the log creaking under his weight. 'How well do you know him?'

'I thought I knew him, but now it seems it was a different man.' Her mouth downcast and her eyes troubled, she asked, 'What am I going to do, Alec?'

· He hesitantly slid an arm around her shoulders, expecting her to rear back, but when she leaned her head against him, he held her close and breathed in the fresh, clean scent of rosemary and soap. He longed desperately to kiss her. The thought startled him.

As if reading his thoughts, Eliza straightened and he dropped his arm, pulling his thoughts back to the problem before them.

'Alec. Let me see the plans. Perhaps between us we can work through the problems and then I can go to Melbourne and lodge it.'

He nodded. 'It will take a few nights of hard work, but with your help we should be able to get it done.'

She touched his arm. 'Thank you.'

'You have no reason to trust me,' he said and meant it.

'I have to trust somebody, and Will trusted you.' Her eyes narrowed as realisation dawned. 'Tell me something, Alec, were you tempted to take the plans as your own?'

His hesitation must have given her the answer.

To his surprise, she smiled. 'So you're only human, after all. You weren't expecting me to appear so the temptation must have been there, but I think that the conscience of the young man schooled by the Scottish Episcopal Church would have troubled you for the rest of your days.'

Alec allowed himself to smile. 'Ian would agree with you.'

'Ian is wise beyond his years.'

Alec nodded. 'Aye, he is.' He sighed. 'When I lost my wife and bairn, I swore I would make a better life for Ian and myself. Will's plans seemed like a godsend.'

She stared at him. 'Your wife and child?'

He could do no more than nod and her fingers tightened on his arm. 'What was her name?'

'Cat—' He cleared his throat. 'Catriona. We'd been sweethearts since childhood. I lost her in childbirth, and the child with her.'

'Oh, Alec …' Eliza leaned her head against him.

'I couldn't find the midwife and the doctor refused to come. He was in the middle of his dinner and would not be disturbed … By the time he came, it was too late.' He hefted a sigh. 'It was a long time ago and another world.' He stood abruptly, forcing Eliza to straighten. 'It's getting cold. We should get back before dark or your uncle will have some choice words for me.'

Eliza rose from the log and stooped to pick up the rug. 'My uncle—' she gave the rug a vigorous shake, '—has no claim on me.' She paused. 'Is it possible that the will could have been forged?'

Alec hadn't even considered that possibility.

He lifted her onto her horse and she looked down at him. 'I am beginning to believe Will's death was no accident, Alec.'

Alec hesitated for a heartbeat. 'And I have to agree with you.'

Eliza bit her lip. 'I've read the coroner's report and it seems to me that the one person who may be able to tell me a little more about what happened that night was never called as a witness.'

'Who do you mean?"

'Will's girl, Sissy.'

Alec laid a hand on her arm. 'I'm worried for you, Eliza. If your uncle knows you suspect him ...'

'Oh, I'll give him no cause to be concerned,' she said, 'but it seems to me that I have more than one reason to go to Melbourne now, and the sooner the better.'

Fifteen

14 July 1873

Despite her best intentions, Eliza found her natural honesty made it difficult to conceal her knowledge in her dealings with her uncle. However, if he noticed she was unusually quiet, he made no comment. She attended church with him on Sunday and spent the rest of the day working on some embroidery she had promised to do for Netty.

On Monday, with Cowper at work, she told Mrs Harris that she would return the work to Netty. The day being unusually fine and almost mild, she walked down to the cemetery. There were no flowers to be found in Maiden's Creek in the midwinter so she visited her brother empty-handed. In the weeks since she had first come, the grave had lost the look of being freshly dug and newer graves now dotted the cemetery, the earth piled high on them, bright and fresh. She had ordered a simple headstone and an iron railing to place around the grave from the undertaker but the headstone would take some weeks to arrive from the monument maker in Sale.

The heavy rains had caused the wooden cross at the head of Will's grave to slip slightly to the right. Weeds had begun to creep through the dirt and stones and the ink bottle that had held Sissy's flowers had been smashed, the pieces glistening brightly in the winter sun.

Eliza straightened the cross and collected the broken pieces of glass. She looked at the shards in her gloved hand and wondered if Sissy had stopped her visits to the grave. Eliza dug a hole with the heel of her boot and buried the fragments. She would have to find a more robust receptacle to replace the bottle.

She looked down at the grave. Knowing her brother, she had no doubt Will had loved Sissy and had, at one point, wanted to marry her. Eliza would have called her 'sister'. Her own feelings about that were mixed. It was one thing for Will to marry 'below his station' but to marry someone who had worked in a brothel? Her parents would turn in their graves. But they were dead and so was Will. Perhaps she owed it to him to find this woman and see what, if anything, she could do to ease her grief. The time had come to pay a visit to the notorious establishment known as Lil's Place.

With a purposeful step she took the path down to the main street, busy with the usual press of people, horses and bullock drays. Despite the lack of a sign, Eliza had guessed some time ago that the well-maintained two-storey building on the Aberfeldy Road, just north of the school, must be Lil's Place.

She stood in the shadows across the road from the hostelry and waited, half hoping she might get a glimpse of the elusive Sissy. A door on the upstairs verandah opened and a red-headed woman stepped out, a thin peignoir her only protection against the cold.

The woman came forward, leaning her forearms on the balcony rail. Her gaze locked on Eliza, drawing her out of concealment.

'What's Will Penrose's sister doing skulking in the shadows?' the woman said. 'What can I do for you, Miss Penrose? Or are you just out surveying the sights of Maiden's Creek?'

Eliza glanced to her right and left. 'I have something to ask, but I don't want to stand here shouting up at you.'

The woman raised an eyebrow. 'Then you better come in, hadn't you?'

The road may have been empty but nevertheless, Eliza felt the eyes of the town on her back as she stepped across the threshold into her first disorderly house.

At first glance, it seemed quite orderly. The floor was clean and swept, tables wiped and stools neatly positioned around them. The redhead leaned against an open doorway, behind which a staircase ran up to the next storey.

'It's all right,' Nell said. 'You're not going to burst into flames or turn into a pillar of salt. We're just ordinary girls, earning an honest living. I'm Nell.'

Eliza collected her wits. 'Please don't mistake me,' she said. 'I'm not like Mrs Russell or the others. My business is with Sissy.'

'Is it, now? And what would that be concerning?'

'I think that is between me and Sissy,' Eliza said.

Nell gave her an appraising glance. 'You're not much like your brother. And one puff of wind'd blow you away.'

Eliza straightened, trying to add the missing inches to her height. 'Can I please speak to Sissy?'

Nell heaved herself away from the door jamb and sauntered across to another door. She threw it open and jerked her head. 'Through here,' she said. 'Don't want you to be seen hanging around the front bar. You'll be givin' us a bad name.'

Eliza bit back the retort that rose to her lips and marched through the doorway. She found herself in a warm, well-lit living area with a fire burning in the grate. Several upholstered chairs decorated with embroidered cushions stood in front of the fire. A clock on the mantelpiece ticked ponderously, the sound loud in the oppressive silence. It could have been her aunt's parlour.

Their entry startled a young woman who had been taking her ease in one of the chairs, her nose in a book borrowed from the Mechanics' Institute Library. She jumped to her feet, pulling a colourful dressing robe around herself.

'Jess, go and find, Lil. Miss Penrose here would like a word.'

Jess, who was probably a lot younger than she looked, cast Eliza a quick, almost frightened, glance as she scampered from the room.

Nell gestured at the round table in the centre of the room. 'Take a seat, Miss Penrose.'

The woman who accompanied Jess on her return took Eliza's breath away. She must have been nearly six feet tall, with a breadth that matched her height, her bulk barely contained by a straining corset that creaked as she moved. She wore her flaming red hair, which probably came from the same bottle as Nell's, piled on top of her head in a bird's nest of a bun.

If this was Lil White, little wonder she kept the most orderly disorderly house in Maiden's Creek.

Lil looked Eliza up and down as if evaluating her for employment. Eliza met the woman's fierce gaze without blinking.

'Not much to you, is there?' Lil concluded, lowering herself into the chair across from Eliza. 'Jess, love, fetch us some tea.' As the girl disappeared into a room beyond the parlour, Lil said, 'What can I do for you, Miss Penrose?'

'I came to speak with Sissy,' Eliza said.

'Did you indeed? Well, you're too late.'

A knot of disappointment gathered in Eliza's stomach. 'What do you mean?'

'She's gone back to Melbourne.'

'But I saw her only a few weeks ago … at the cemetery.'

'She was saying 'er goodbyes.' Lil paused. 'Why are you so keen to speak to 'er?'

Eliza scanned the hard faces of the women. 'I believe she and my brother had some sort of understanding?'

Jess returned carrying a tray with a teapot and four cups and saucers. Eliza had to bite back her impatience as Lil poured the tea with what seemed like deliberate slowness. She accepted the cup she was offered and took a sip. The tea smelled of flowers and had a sweet, unidentifiable taste. Conscious that Lil watched her, she set the cup back on the saucer.

'Like it?' Lil enquired. 'It's jasmine tea. I get it from the Chinese gardeners.'

'You haven't answered my question,' Eliza said.

'Oh yes, they had an understanding, although your precious brother probably never intended to make good on his promises. I've met his like before. Kept the poor girl living in hope for nearly two years,' Nell said.

'Everyone tells me that Will broke it off when he took over the management of the Shenandoah.'

Lil laughed, her corset creaking ominously. ''e could no more 'ave broken it off than fly to the moon. It was all a show for the benefit of 'is uncle and the other do-gooders in the town that 'e needed to impress.'

'You mean—'

'I mean, 'e told Sissy that as soon as 'e 'ad made good with the mine, they could forget the old bastard and 'e'd make it right with 'er.'

'She loved him something fierce,' Jess said, pressing her hands together. 'And for all Lil says, he loved her too. They was good with each other.'

Eliza picked up her cup and took another sip of the jasmine tea. Had Will and Sissy truly been star-crossed lovers? Men were not above using gullible women for their own purposes when it suited them. She hated to think ill of her beloved brother but was he so very different?

'I'm sorry,' she said. 'I wish I'd been able to speak to her. Do you know where I can find her in Melbourne?'

'What? So you can go following 'er, bringing up un'appy memories? No, you leave our Sissy be,' Lil said.

Eliza opened her mouth to protest but Lil raised her hand. 'What's past is past. One thing you learn in this profession is never look back. If Sissy 'ad wanted to speak with you she 'ad 'er chance. She's gone now and that's an end to it. Now, these girls 'ave to get back to work ...'

Eliza took the hint and stood up. 'Before I go, can I ask another question?'

Nell leaned back in her chair. 'Another question? I don't know, what do you think, Lil?'

Before Lil could reply, Eliza said, 'Do you remember the night Will died? I read the coroner's report. You said Will had been here.'

The atmosphere in the room shifted. Even the cheerful fire seemed to dim in the grate.

''e was 'ere,' Lil said. 'That's what I told the coroner.'

'But you didn't say what he was doing. Was he drinking?'

'He came to see Sissy,' Nell said, 'but he was in a right state.'

'They argued,' Jess added.

'That's enough.' Lil quelled her girls with a sharp glance. 'Why do you want to know? Penrose visited 'ere often, no reason why that night should 'ave been any different.'

'Except it was the night he died.'

The three women looked at each other.

Lil rose to her feet, towering above Eliza. 'What we tell you goes no further, promise?'

Eliza nodded. 'You have my word. I just want to know why Will died.'

'Will had come in a few weeks before,' Nell began. 'I'd never seen him so excited. He told Sissy that the mine had hit a major seam and was producing four ounces of gold. You don't live on the goldfields and not learn something of the business. We all know that is a better than good yield.'

The other women nodded.

'And?' Eliza prompted.

'Sis was so excited. She thought this was it,' Jess said. 'He told her their fortune was made. To hell with the town and their gossiping tongues. She was going to have a proper house and coach and servants ...' Jess trailed off, unable to hide the yearning in her own face.

Lil leaned forward, her hands clasped in front of her. 'But that last night, it was like 'e was a different man. Even Sis couldn't cheer 'im up. 'e told 'er 'e'd been to see 'is uncle and they'd 'ad a flaming row.' She cast a glance at Jess. 'Like Jess says, they argued. She was all for telling 'im to go to 'ell.'

Eliza's heart skipped a beat. Here was a detail missing from every account she'd heard of Will's last night. 'The coroner's report said nothing about a meeting with our uncle.'

''e's your uncle, you ask 'im why 'e didn't think fit to mention it.'

'Did he tell you what the argument was about?'

'I was behind the bar. I wasn't listening to the conversation.'

Nell cast her employer a contemptuous glance. 'Go on, Lil, we all know you were listening in. What did Penrose tell Sis?'

'Whatever you might think, Nell, I only caught snippets of the conversation. Something about gold being stolen.'

Eliza's pulse quickened. 'You didn't mention any of this at the inquest?'

'I don't 'old with 'elping the law more than I 'ave to, Miss Penrose, and it didn't seem relevant to 'ow he died.'

'But it might be if he went up to the mine to search Cowper's office for the evidence,' Eliza said. 'That would imply that he thought my uncle was involved.'

'May explain why he went to Cowper,' Nell said. 'God knows they hadn't been near each other for months.'

Eliza took a breath. This all tied in with the information Alec McLeod had in his possession, the stealing of gold from the Shenandoah to bolster the Maiden's Creek returns.

'How much did he drink that night?'

'That I can tell you,' Lil said. 'One whisky.'

'Only one? Everyone seems to think he was drunk, which is why he fell.'

'As I said, just one while 'e was 'ere. Can't account for what 'e did after 'e left. 'e 'ad 'is conversation with Sis and the two of 'em disappeared upstairs for a bit. When 'e came down 'e left without a goodbye to any of us.'

'What time did he leave here?'

Jess looked up at the clock on the mantelpiece. 'Just before midnight.'

And half an hour later he was dead. Hardly time to go and get so drunk that the fall could be attributed to alcohol consumption.

'Alone?'

Lil rolled her eyes. 'Yes, alone.'

'He sometimes took a room at the Britannia if it was too late to get back to the Shenandoah,' Jess volunteered.

But not that night. If Will had left Lil's Place just before midnight and died at the time shown on his watch, what had he done in that last half-hour? Had that been when he slipped his plans under Alec's door? And what about the light a witness had seen in Cowper's office? Had Will been looking for evidence of the missing gold?

Eliza forced a smile. 'Thank you. You've all been most helpful.'

Lil laid a hand on her shoulder. 'Your brother is dead, Miss Penrose. 'e was a good man but not without 'is faults. If I was you, I'd leave well alone. There are people in this town with the gleam of gold in their eyes and cold steel in their 'earts. Take my advice and get on with your school teaching and let the dead lie.'

'Thank you for your advice, Mrs White.'

'From what I hear, you're pretty free with advice too,' Nell said. 'I heard you had words with Mad Annie about her daughter.'

Eliza felt the heat rising to her face. 'That's none of your business.'

'She's right, Nell, it's not your business.' Lil leaned toward Eliza. 'But remember this, Miss Penrose, Annie loves that bairn more than life itself and if there's a reason the child looks like she's been dragged through a log, remember who Annie's callers are. There are some that aren't particular and might 'ave a fancy for the young 'uns.'

It took Eliza a moment to comprehend what Lil meant and when she did, she felt a wave of nausea. In her sheltered upbringing it never occurred to her that such things could happen.

'Does Annie … Is she …?'

'Is she one of us?' Nell suggested. 'No, she's not. If she takes a man to bed, it's cos she likes him. She makes her living selling grog and food but not her body.' She glanced at Lil. 'Told Lil to mind her own business, she did.'

'You seem a good woman, Miss Penrose, and I wouldn't want you to think badly of me,' Lil said. 'I offered Annie a place here, working in the kitchen if that suited 'er. At least she would be safe. But she likes 'er independence and wouldn't take no 'elp or advice from me or the girls. She's made 'er choices in life. Pity of it is, the girl 'as to suffer for 'er mother's sake.' She shrugged. 'But it's an 'ard world. For all of that, she's done 'er best by that girl. But don't you forget the child 'as a mother who loves 'er.'

'Thank you for the advice,' Eliza said, chastened. 'I won't forget.'

Lil gave her a curt nod. 'This way, Miss Penrose. I'll see you to the door.'

Eliza left by the back door and as she trudged up the hill to Cowper's house, her footsteps slowed.

Leave well alone, Lil had said. But how could she? Not now she knew the mine was far from being a failure and that Will knew his gold was being stolen. It seemed as good a reason as any for him to die and whichever way she looked at it, her uncle lay at the heart of her brother's troubles.

A shiver ran down her spine as a chill southerly wind blew up the street, winding icy fingers around her ankles.

Sixteen

15 July 1873

Alec had been waiting on an opportunity to confront Tehan about the break-in and his chance came the following Monday. Cowper requested he go out to the Blue Sailor Mine to sort out a problem with the stamper. The mine had been badly damaged during fires the previous year and the water supply that drove the stamper could be erratic.

Alec set off at first light on Sam, Sones's bay gelding. An hour out of Maiden's Creek, he came on Annie O'Reilly's hut. A thin trickle of smoke rose from the chimney and as he came closer, the woman came to the door, no doubt drawn by the dog's furious barking. She leaned against the door jamb, the swell of her pregnant belly visible beneath the grimy apron.

'Lookin' for some breakfast, McLeod?'

His stomach growled. He had stopped here before and her food was good and plentiful.

She came forward and took the reins of the horse. 'I've fresh eggs and bread if that'll do you?

'That sounds grand, Annie.'

She could have once been beautiful or at least passably pretty, but a hard life had etched lines of bitterness around her eyes and mouth and her smile held no warmth. She'd seen enough of the worst of men to hold no illusions about them.

Alec tethered his horse and ducked his head to enter the gloom of Annie's hut. The scent of brewing hops hung in the air. Despite everything the townswomen may say about Annie O'Reilly's slatternly ways, he always found the hard-packed floor swept clean and the surfaces dusted. A square, roughly made table and four stools were set up in the middle of the room and a couple of chairs made by the same hand stood before the fire over which a large cauldron bubbled. The end of a homemade bed, covered in a faded patchwork quilt, could be seen behind a partially drawn curtain at the far end of the room. Despite the poverty, the simple cottage had a homely feel.

Annie gestured at the table and he pulled up a stool as she turned to her cooking, busying herself with eggs and bacon.

'What brings you this way?' she asked.

'Business up at Blue Sailor.'

The shaggy dog had followed him in and laid its head in his lap. He fondled the silky ears. 'Not much of a watch dog.'

'Kick 'im out, McLeod. 'e knows 'e ain't allowed in the 'ouse.'

Alec shooed the reluctant animal out into the cold and resumed his seat.

A child poked her head around the curtain at the far end of the room. She gave him a shy smile.

'Good morning. You must be Charlie,' he said.

The child gave a quick nod of her head.

'This 'ere's McLeod,' Annie said. 'You best get off to school. There's bread on the table.'

Charlie scurried past Alec, grabbing a couple of slices her mother had cut from the loaf.

Annie waved the knife she was using to tend the frying pan at her daughter. 'Mind you stay outta trouble today.'

Charlie grinned and, with a half-wave at Alec, shut the wonky front door behind her. The door did little to keep out the draughts that whistled in through the cracks.

'Miss Penrose tells me that your Charlie's a bright girl,' Alec said.

Annie sniffed. 'Miss Penrose ought to mind 'er own business.'

She slapped a tin plate, well loaded with food, on the table and Alec tucked in with enthusiasm as she pulled up another stool and sat down with a sigh, her hands resting on her pregnant belly.

'You've got learnin', McLeod,' she said. 'If me Charlie is as smart as Miss Penrose says she is, what good can it do 'er?'

Alec set the fork down and considered the woman. 'I was blessed with a schoolteacher like Miss Penrose,' he said. 'My family had no money and I would have ended up down the pit like my father and his father before him, but the schoolmaster encouraged me to sit for a scholarship to a good school. I did well and got another scholarship to study at university.'

'But you're a man,' Annie said with a curl of her lip. 'It's all right for men.'

'If Charlie has the right opportunities there is nothing to say she can't find decent work.'

'But she won't get those opportunities livin' like this.'

'Then make the opportunities, Annie.'

She gave a snort of laughter. 'Easy for you to say. 'ow's the eggs?'

Alec mopped the last of the eggs up with the bread and pushed the plate to one side. 'Best breakfast in town.'

She stood up and picked up his plate as he fumbled for his wallet and pulled out a pound note.

'For breakfast. Keep the rest for the bairn,' he said.

She looked at the paper he held out to her, her eyes wide as she shook her head. 'I couldn't,' she said.

He dropped the paper on the table. 'I mean it, Annie. For the bairn.'

He left her standing with an empty plate in one hand, staring at the note.

As he swung into the saddle again, he glanced up the track toward Pretty Sally, hesitating only momentarily before turning the horse up the narrow, muddy path. Best to see to his business with Tehan before going on to Blue Sailor.

The ragged township of Pretty Sally clung to a ridgeline and consisted of a few bark huts with mildewed canvas roofs, a general store and a grog shop which, even at this early hour, seemed to be trading. No one acknowledged Alec but he was conscious of the hidden eyes watching his progress.

He had only been to the Shenandoah Mine once during Will Penrose's lifetime and remembered it lay in a gully about a mile beyond the settlement. A rough signpost on the track beyond Pretty Sally pointed to SHENANDOAH and he turned the horse's head down the tortuous slope. As he descended, the steep hills closed on him and the gloom seemed to penetrate his very soul. To his surprise, he found further progress barred by a stout pair of gates he did not recall from his previous visit.

The sound of men's voices drifted up the hill beyond the gate, accompanied by the steady rhythm of the three-headed stamper that Penrose had bought from the Maiden's Creek Mine when he had started up here.

Alec dismounted and tied his horse to a tree. It was not hard to scramble up the hill and around the gate. As he slithered down the slope on the other side, he came face to face with a stocky, black-bearded man sitting on a rock at a point where the track turned back on itself. Alec recognised the black-bearded thug who had caused the commotion at the dance. What had Tehan called him ... Johnstone? No, Jennings.

Jennings thrust his still smouldering pipe into a pocket and fumbled for a rifle that had been leaning against the rock. 'You're trespassing,' he said, levelling the weapon at Alec. 'What's your business?'

Alec decided on prudence and raised his hands. 'I'm unarmed. My business is with Jack Tehan.'

The man frowned. 'You're the boss up at Maiden's Creek. Got a message from Cowper?'

'I told you my business is with Tehan, not with you, Jennings.'

The man's eyes narrowed at the use of his name. 'Do I know you?'

'You upset a lady at the dance the other night.'

Jennings's mouth curved into a sneer and he spat on the road. 'No such thing as a lady,' he said and jerked the weapon up, firing into the air.

Three armed men came running up the hill.

'He says he's come to see Black Jack,' Jennings said.

'What's your business with Jack?' one of the other men demanded.

'My business is exactly that, *my* business. Now either take me to him or bring him here.'

'No need. I'm here.' Tehan pushed through his men. 'Get back to work, I'll see to Mr McLeod.'

Muttering, Tehan's men turned away and shuffled down the hill. Jennings returned to his post on the rock and Alec and Tehan moved down the track out of earshot.

'What are you doing here, McLeod?'

Alec swept his hat from his head and squinted up at the trees. 'I want to know why you, or your men, thought it necessary to rampage through my house while my brother and I were at the dance the other week?'

Tehan's eyes widened. 'I've already had that fool Maidment around asking questions and I'll tell you what I told him: I know nothing about it.'

Alec closed the distance between them and curled his fist into Tehan's shirt, almost lifting the slighter man off the ground. 'I don't appreciate my home being violated. I just hope that whatever you and your men thought to find there, you came away empty-handed.'

Tehan pushed Alec's hand away and took a step back, straightening his waistcoat. 'I repeat. It was not me,' he said in a low voice flaming with heat.

'But you know who it was. What are they after, Tehan?'

Tehan swallowed and glanced up at the slope rising above them. In a whisper, he said, 'What if someone else knows, or suspects, that you have Penrose's design for a new boiler?'

'Then someone would be wrong.'

'You are a logical person, McLeod. I know it wasn't here. I turned Penrose's crib inside out after he died.'

'On your behest or Cowper's? Does Cowper know about it?'

The momentary hesitation gave the lie to Tehan's following words. 'I don't know what Cowper knows. I only manage this bloody mine, I'm not his keeper.'

Alec hesitated, almost, but not quite, prepared to believe him. 'Let's be clear, Tehan. That plan, if it exists, is not yours or mine or Cowper's. It is the property of Penrose's sister and if you or any of your thugs come near my home again, there will be hell to pay.'

'Are you threatening me?' Tehan said. 'Get off my property before I fetch the lads back again.'

The unmistakeable click of a rifle behind him caused Alec to straighten. Out of the corner of his eye, he saw Jennings moving around to stand beside Tehan. Discretion being the better part of valour, Alec half raised his hands in a gesture of surrender. 'Stay away from my family and from Miss Penrose.'

A smile curled Black Jack's lips. 'Or what, McLeod?'

Jennings jerked the rifle in the direction of the gate and Alec sauntered toward it, waiting for the man to unlock it. As Alec passed through, Jennings leaned forward and whispered, 'I don't like cats and I don't like people what keep cats.'

Alec turned to face him but the gate slammed shut.

Seventeen

16 July 1873

Two figures sat huddled together on the top step of the school house when Eliza arrived early on Wednesday morning. As the school gate squeaked, the woman rose to her feet. Swaddled in a grey wool shawl, Annie O'Reilly looked small and slight, despite the bulge of her pregnancy.

'Good morning. What can I do for you, Mrs O'Reilly?' Eliza asked.

Annie hauled Charlie up by the arm and pushed her toward Eliza. The child's face was swollen, tear tracks plain on her pale, sulky face.

'You wanted 'er, well 'ere she is. Give 'er the schoolin' you say she needs, cos I don't want 'er moonin' around me any more: "Miss Penrose this, Miss Penrose that". She's yours, Miss Penrose, make of 'er what you will.'

Annie pulled her shawl closer around her swollen body and walked away without a backward glance.

'Ma—' Charlie said, so quietly that Eliza could hardly hear her. As Annie turned on to the road and out of sight, Charlie's head drooped and heavy tears dripped onto her shabby boots.

Eliza laid a hand on Charlie's shoulder. The child shook it off and raised a face contorted with anger.

'Why'd you have to poke your nose into my business, miss? She was just looking for a reason to be rid of me. Now who's going to look after her when the baby comes?'

'Stay here,' Eliza commanded and ran after Annie. 'Mrs O'Reilly, stop,' she said, but Annie kept walking.

Panting, Eliza drew even with her. 'It doesn't have to be like this. Why don't you come into town? There'd be work here for you.'

Annie stopped and looked at her. 'Doin' what? Cleanin' and cookin' for other people? Workin' 'ere?' She pointed at Lil's Place. 'No thank you, Miss Penrose. I like me own place and me independence but it's too far for Charlie and you're the one who told me she needs to get her education. She's your responsibility now.'

With that, Annie strode away. All Eliza could do was watch her go.

She returned to Charlie.

The girl choked back her tears and she took a shuddering breath. 'What's going to happen to me?'

'We'll work something out, Charlie. Now, are those your things?' Eliza pointed at a bundle wrapped in a faded red kerchief. 'Bring them inside and I'll put them safe in the office. You can help me by setting out the slates and perhaps we can persuade Miss Donald to let you help the little ones with their arithmetic.'

Charlie sniffed, wiping her nose on the sleeve of her patched jacket. 'Me?'

Eliza summoned a reassuring smile. 'Yes, you.'

As she lit the fires, she watched Charlie carefully placing the slates on the desks and wondered what on earth she was going to do with her. She could hardly install her at Cowper's house. Perhaps she could speak with Mrs Russell to see if the charity of the

Ladies' Committee extended to abandoned waifs. She suspected it extended only as far as expecting the abandoned waif to act as an unpaid servant.

When Flora Donald arrived, Eliza explained the situation.

'She just abandoned her?' Flora sounded incredulous. 'What are you going to do with her?'

The answer to Charlie's predicament had come to Eliza and she smiled. 'I have an idea but it will have to wait until after school. Do you think she could help you with the little one's arithmetic today?'

Flora's eyes narrowed and her mouth tightened but in the end she agreed. Charlie struggled with her task, however, not because she did not know what she was teaching but because the ingrained distrust of the scruffy child ran right through the school.

At the end of the school day, Charlie helped Eliza to tidy the room. When she was done, she sat on the step of the teacher's platform and waited for Eliza to fetch her bundle from the office.

'Am I going home with you, miss?' Charlie asked as Eliza handed her the bundle.

Home. What a curious concept, Eliza thought. It had been many years since she'd had a home of her own. Her father's disgrace and death had set her adrift and she certainly didn't consider Cowper's house a home.

'We are going to visit a friend,' she said. 'Ready?'

Charlie hefted her possessions and followed Eliza.

They stopped at Netty Burrell's shop and Eliza stood outside the door, gathering her courage. This would be a huge imposition on their budding friendship but she could think of no other immediate solution for Charlie.

Eliza opened the door of the dressmaker's and ushered Charlie in. Netty, busy with a customer, glanced from Eliza to the child and back again.

'I'll be with you in a moment,' she said.

Eliza settled Charlie in front of the cosy fire and they waited for the customer to leave. Netty shut the door after her and turned the sign on her window to CLOSED.

Hands on hips, she addressed the child. 'It's Charlotte O'Reilly, isn't it? To what do I owe the pleasure?'

'May we speak in your kitchen?' Eliza said.

Netty nodded. 'Can you mind the shop for me, Charlotte?'

Charlie nodded and Netty bustled Eliza into the kitchen.

'Now, what's this about?'

'I have the most enormous favour to ask of you,' Eliza began and explained that Annie O'Reilly had abandoned her child on the doorstep of the school that morning. 'I was hoping,' she concluded, 'that you and Bill could take her in … just until we can find something more permanent for her.'

'Take her in? You mean feed and clothe her? Who's going to pay for that? Annie O'Reilly?'

'Netty, you are the most Christian woman in this town. Charlie's not a bad child.'

'Not what I hear. Her mother—'

'Her mother loves her. She loves her so much that she is sacrificing herself for Charlie to get the life she deserves.'

Netty frowned and Eliza sensed her wavering.

'Very well, but only temporarily, mind and,' she added, almost as an afterthought, 'my Amos would need to agree, but he's a softhearted ninny.'

Eliza smiled. 'Thank you, Netty. I will speak with the Board of Advice and see if some sort of scholarship can be found to help with expenses.'

The women returned to the shop. Charlie had her nose against the glass-fronted counter.

'Ma used to do sewing like that,' she said pointing to an embroidered smock, 'back when we lived in Tasmania. She's been making some clothes for the baby out of old shirts. They're pretty. Wish she'd make me somethin' pretty.' Charlie touched her own raggedy jacket with a naked yearning in her eyes.

'Charlie, you're going to stay with Mrs Burrell and her husband for a few days,' Eliza said.

'Here?' Charlie looked around the immaculate shop.

'Yes, here,' Netty said. 'But I've a few rules, Miss O'Reilly. The first is that anyone staying with me has to take regular baths.'

Charlie took a step back. 'Ma says baths are bad for a body,' she said.

'And I say cleanliness is next to Godliness. Come with me.'

Charlie turned tremulous eyes on Eliza. 'Miss Penrose?'

'While you are under Mrs Burrell's roof, you will do as she says,' Eliza said.

'And I'll see if I can find something more suitable for you to wear,' Netty was saying as Eliza closed the door behind her.

17 July 1873

The following morning, an unrecognisable Charlie O'Reilly came to school. She stood in the doorway, a lunch pail held to her like a shield. Every child turned to look at her and even Flora Donald gaped. In a neatly darned blue dress and a spotless pinafore, with polished boots, thick woollen stockings and her hair washed and brushed, Charlie had become Charlotte.

Flora Donald glanced at Eliza and said in a low voice, 'You think you can make a silk purse out of a sow's ear? We'll see.'

When the children were released for their short lunch hour, Flora took the duty in the playground while Eliza ate her lunch in front of the meagre schoolroom fire, one ear on the burble of children's voices.

She stiffened as the sound turned to an indecipherable chant and Flora Donald's shrill cry of 'Stop that!'

Eliza ran out into the playground to find a fight in progress. Such events were not unknown between the boys; rivalries existed between the children of the town mines and those of the satellite settlements and these quite often devolved on the schoolground.

Every child in the school seemed to have gathered at the fence to the ponies' paddock, cheering the miscreants on while Flora Donald wrestled with the ramshackle gate. Eliza hurried across to lend her assistance but Flora had at last reached the adversaries.

Flora bent over, hauling Charlie off a larger girl. Holding Charlie by the ear, she shook her as Martha Mackie scrambled to her feet, red faced and indignant, her dress and pinafore smeared with mud—and worse.

'She attacked me, miss,' Martha screeched, one finger pointing at the struggling Charlie.

'You deal with Miss Mackie,' Flora ordered. 'I'll deal with this baggage.' Still holding Charlie by the ear, Flora marched the protesting child back to the school house.

'What happened?' Eliza asked Martha.

'She attacked me.'

'She wouldn't have attacked you without reason,' Eliza said. 'So I'll ask again, what happened?'

Martha's jaw jutted and her mouth set in a tight line.

Eliza looked around the gaggle of remaining children. Her gaze fell on Joe Trevalyn. Joe couldn't lie to save himself and she could see from his downturned mouth that he had seen what had caused the affray.

'Joe?'

The boy shuffled his feet. 'Martha said some things about her mother,' he said in a quiet voice. Then, surprisingly, he looked up, his eyes flashing from Eliza to Martha. 'If she'd said them about my mother, I'd have thumped her too.'

'What did she say?'

Joe flushed. 'I don't like to say.'

'She said Charlie's mother was a filthy whore who'd open her legs for any man,' Bert Marsh said.

Eliza turned to look at the prissy Miss Mackie. 'Did you say that, Martha?'

Martha's chin lifted defiantly. 'It's true.'

'Do you even know what it means?'

Martha seemed to deflate a little and she shook her head. 'I heard someone telling my ma,' she said.

'It is probably the worst thing one person can say about another,' Eliza said. 'If anyone is owed an apology, it's Charlotte.'

'I'm not apologising to her. She started it and look what she's done.' Martha pointed to some torn broderie anglaise on her pinafore. 'And I'm filthy.'

'Come with me,' Eliza said, 'and you can explain properly to Miss Donald how this happened.'

In the schoolroom, Flora stood the two girls in front of the platform and asked for an explanation.

'She attacked me for no good reason. She's a menace. Everybody says so.' Martha shot Charlie a hateful glance. 'Just wait till my pa hears about this.'

'Martha,' Eliza warned. 'What did you say to Charlotte?'

Martha's defiance had returned. 'I didn't say anything. She just came at me with her fingers like this.' Martha held up her hands like claws.

'We both know that is not the truth,' Eliza said.

'That's enough, Miss Penrose,' Flora Donald said. 'If Miss Mackie says the attack was unprovoked then I believe her. Martha is not a liar. Charlotte, why did you attack Martha?'

Charlie said nothing.

'Charlie tell her,' Eliza urged.

But Charlie remained obstinately silent, staring at a spider web in the rafters above Flora's head.

'Charlotte, you will apologise to Martha,' Flora said.

'Shan't.'

Flora's thin chest rose and fell. 'Very well. Martha, go and clean yourself up. You are excused from school for the rest of the day.'

Martha gave Charlie a look of triumph as she left the room.

'Well?' Flora said. 'What do you have to say for yourself?'

Charlie maintained her silence.

'Very well.' Flora opened the lid of her desk and produced a heavy leather strap, split at one end. While Flora had always been generous in her application of the cane, Eliza had never seen her use what looked to her something akin to a medieval torture device.

'What is that?'

'It's a tawse. Miss O'Reilly knows what it is, don't you?'

Charlie began to whimper. 'Give me the cane, Miss Donald. I'll be good. I'll say I'm sorry.'

'You had your chance. Now hold out your left hand. Support it with your right so it's good and firm.'

Charlie whimpered, hiding her hands behind her back.

Flora Donald grabbed the child's left arm, forcing it palm up. 'Now your right. Hold still. Miss Penrose will you please hold the child's arms steady?'

'I will not,' Eliza said, aghast. 'May I speak with you in private, Miss Donald?'

'There is nothing to discuss. I am quite satisfied that Miss O'Reilly attacked Martha and she is deserving of punishment.'

'Please,' Eliza said, 'this child was taunted beyond endurance. She is not the one who should be punished.'

'That's enough, Miss Penrose. If you're not going to assist then hold your tongue. Your hands, child.'

Charlie's back stiffened and her chin came up. She stuck out both her hands, palms up, her eyes fixed on the spider web as Flora raised the strap.

The terrible thwack echoed around the room. Silence had fallen on the playground. The lower halves of the schoolroom windows were frosted, for which Eliza was grateful, but she had the impression of shadows pressed against the glass, listening.

Charlie gave a sharp hiss of breath as the strap raised again, coming down with a ferocity that shocked Eliza. This time Charlie screamed, tears rolling down her cheek.

'Leopards do not change their spots, Miss Penrose.' A fierce light gleamed in Flora Donald's eyes as she raised the tawse again. 'Spare the rod, spoil the child. You are the daughter of a whore, Charlotte O'Reilly, and putting you in fine clothes will never change that fact.'

Eliza rushed at Flora, grabbing her arm before she could bring the strap down again. 'That's enough, Miss Donald, you've made your point.'

The arm within her grasp could have been made of iron. Flora Donald's face twisted with hatred. 'That child needs to be beaten and beaten well. If she's not got a mother to do it then I must do it for her. She will see the light of the Lord's grace today and be thankful.'

'Get out, Charlie,' Eliza said. When Charlie didn't move, she said with more urgency, 'Go, now!'

Charlie turned and ran, slamming the door behind her.

Eliza wrested the tawse from the other woman and hurled it into the fireplace. 'I will not see children beaten for crimes they did not commit, Miss Donald. Ask Joe Trevalyn or Bert Marsh what was said to her and you'll understand.'

Flora Donald fixed hot, angry eyes on Eliza, a look that would have done Medusa credit. 'Nothing justifies physical violence in the playground. And as for you, how dare you undermine my authority,' she said. 'Get out, Miss Penrose. Get out of my school. I am advising the board that your employment is terminated. If you know what's in your best interests, you will leave Maiden's Creek and never come back.'

Eliza took a deep breath. Further argument seemed pointless. She collected her belongings and, with her head held high, shut the door on the Maiden's Creek school. The crowd of silent children in the school yard parted before her like the Red Sea.

As she crossed the creek, the enormity of what she had done settled on Eliza's shoulders. She had defied Flora Donald's authority and undermined her in the eyes of her students. It was possibly one of the worse things she, as a mere assistant teacher, could have done. Flora had been right to sack her but she had not been right to beat Charlie with such a hideous instrument.

Eliza had seen the light of a zealot in Flora's eyes. If she had not intervened, what would have happened? Flora seemed more than capable of beating the child senseless.

At that thought, Eliza stopped and leaned against a wall to catch her breath. Yes, she had saved Charlie, but at the price of losing her only source of income.

'Eliza? Are you all right?'

She looked up at the one person she really didn't want to see at this moment.

Alec McLeod.

She managed a watery smile and pushed a stray lock of hair behind her ear with a shaking hand. 'Not really,' she admitted and, looking into his concerned brown eyes, she found herself confiding the story in him.

He shook his head and pushed his hat back. 'I had a tawse applied to me once in my schooling.' He flexed the fingers of his left hand. 'I'll not forget it, but first things first. Let's see to Charlie.'

'I've betrayed Charlie,' Eliza said, fighting back tears. 'Annie trusted me and I let her down.'

Together they hurried down to Netty's shop but Charlie had not returned. Eliza told her about the incident at the school and Netty's kindly face crumpled. 'Oh, the poor lass. You should've seen her face when I gave her the dress and boots. You'd think I'd given her the crown jewels,' Netty said. 'And that spiteful little cow Mavis Mackie ...' Netty drew in a sharp, angry breath. 'What's done is done. I'm guessing she'll have gone back to Mad Annie.'

'In that case I must see she got home safely.' Eliza looked up at Alec. 'I hate to ask this, but can you loan me the money to hire a horse?"

'More than that,' he said. 'I'm coming with you.'

They rode in silence, Eliza too sunk in misery to initiate conversation. It had been her encouragement that had prompted Annie to entrust Charlie to her and she had betrayed that trust.

At Annie's hut the dog lay on the verandah, its head on its paws. It looked up at the newcomers but didn't bark. From within the hut came the sound of gulping sobs. Eliza and Alec dismounted and stood together, staring at the front door, listening to the broken child crying her heart out.

Eliza grasped Alec's sleeve. 'This is my fault.'

He shook his head. 'No, I have to share some of the responsibility. Annie asked me for advice and I put the idea in Annie's head that if Charlie could do well at school then there was a future for her.'

'Good intentions are not enough, are they?'

The door to the hut burst open and Annie stormed out, her face suffused with anger. She pointed at Eliza. 'This is your doin', Miss Penrose. Look at what that cow 'as done to me girl.'

She went back into the hut and hauled Charlie out. Charlie turned a mottled, tear-stained face up to her mother.

'It weren't Miss Penrose. I told you, Ma.'

''old out your 'and,' Annie ordered.

Charlie complied and Eliza drew a breath at the sight of the ugly welts already turning to bruises and swelling across the child's palm.

'Can you bend your fingers?'

Charlie shook her head, tears starting afresh.

The red heat of anger rose in Eliza's chest. She knew Flora had exerted force but this was brutal. Alec McLeod shifted and she glanced at him. His eyes blazed with fury.

'Oh, Charlie, I'm so sorry.' She sank down and took the child's hands in her own, running a gentle finger along the welts. 'Annie, do you have some arnica for the bruising?'

Annie placed an arm around her daughter, drawing her against her. Charlie laid her head against her mother, her shoulders shaking.

'What's to be done now?' Annie demanded. 'She ain't goin' back to that bloody school, not while that cow is in charge.'

'I've lost my position, Mrs O'Reilly,' Eliza said. 'Even if she does go back, I can't protect her.'

The anger leached from Annie's face. 'The bitch fired you?'

'She did, but only after I tossed the strap on the fire,' Eliza said, glad that she'd had that satisfaction.

'That doesn't sound fair,' Annie said. 'But that's life isn't it? You can go back to your respectable little town and tell Mrs Burrell I'll return the clothes she gave Charlie.'

Charlie's lip wobbled. 'The pinny got a bit torn but Ma says she can mend it good as new.'

Eliza shook her head. 'No, the clothes are yours to keep, Charlie. I will make this right for you.'

Annie snorted. 'You can sing to the wind if you like, Miss Penrose, but nothin's goin' to make this right. I'm not lettin' me girl anywhere near that school again.' She looked from Eliza to Alec. 'I know you both meant well, but the likes of us, Charlie and me, this is the hand we've been dealt. We make the best of it as we can. Besides, I'm going to need 'er 'elp soon. No, you tell 'em at that school that they can sleep easy in their beds, Charlie O'Reilly won't be comin' back.' She put a hand on Charlie's shoulder. 'Inside, now.'

Charlie obeyed her mother but not before giving Eliza a look of such despair that her heart tore.

As Alec helped Eliza into the saddle, he said, 'And just how do you think you are you going to make this right?'

Eliza shook her head. 'I don't know.' She managed a smile and curled her fingers around his. 'Thank you for being a friend today, Alec. I needed one.'

'We all need friends,' he said and his fingers tightened on hers.

She huffed out a breath. 'I have no employment now so maybe I can have a look at Will's plans?'

Alec nodded. 'Where do you want to meet?'

Eliza thought about that. Somewhere neutral that would not attract too much attention. 'Can we meet at Netty Burrell's tonight at nine?'

Alec nodded and swung himself into the saddle and they rode back to town in silence.

Eighteen

Eliza had read accounts of the witch trials of the seventeenth century—a woman hauled into a room full of men and forced to recite the Lord's Prayer to save herself from hanging. Under such pressure most failed. No one had asked Eliza to recite the Lord's Prayer but the wrath of Maiden's Creek had descended on her.

While Alec returned the horses, she had paid a call on Netty to reassure her that Charlie was with her mother and to see if Netty minded her parlour being used as a rendezvous. As she had expected, Netty seemed delighted to be involved in such a meeting. On her return to her uncle's house, however, Eliza found the entire Board of Advice and Flora Donald assembled in the parlour. She had never felt quite so alone.

Charles Cowper had evidently been summoned and he came to stand by her side. Given everything she had come to know about him, he seemed an odd ally, but she would take whatever support that was offered.

'Well?' Angus Mackie roared at her. 'Your little protégé attacked my daughter and you have the temerity to prevent Miss Donald chastising the child?'

Eliza hadn't been aware of holding her breath and now she let it out in a rush. 'There is chastisement and there is torture, Mr Mackie, and Charlotte O'Reilly did not deserve either.'

Russell raised a hand. 'That's enough, Mackie. Your Mavis is unhurt. Childhood disputes happen. What we cannot condone, Miss Penrose, is your wilful undermining of Miss Donald's position as head teacher.'

'And I do not condone the punishment of a child who has done no wrong,' Eliza said, 'and neither can I tolerate a teacher who beats a child so hard with a leather strap that her hand is so bruised she cannot move her fingers.'

Russell turned to Flora Donald. 'Miss Donald? What strap did you use?'

'I believe the Scots call it a tawse, Mr Russell,' Eliza said.

'I don't recall the board approving use of such a thing, Miss Donald?'

Flora's chin came up. 'I felt the situation demanded stronger chastisement than the cane. The good Lord knows the cane has not mended Miss O'Reilly's wayward behaviour in the past. The tawse is commonly used in schools in Scotland to no ill effect. I gave her only two lashes across the palm of her hand before Miss Penrose saw fit to interfere. They were not hard.'

'Not hard? I wouldn't be surprised if she hasn't sustained permanent damage,' Eliza said.

'Perhaps the doctor should attend the child,' Charles Cowper spoke for the first time, 'and give his opinion on the severity of the punishment?'

Eliza cast her uncle a grateful glance. 'I think that would be an excellent idea.'

'Nonsense,' Flora Donald said. 'The child is a malingerer.'

'And it doesn't change the fact that Charlotte O'Reilly does not belong in the company of decent, God-fearing children,' Angus Mackie said.

'Who see fit to tell her that her mother is a whore?' Eliza said. 'Do you think Charlotte attacked your Mavis unprovoked?'

Mackie blinked behind his glasses. 'Mavis would never repeat such a thing.'

'Children repeat what they hear adults saying,' Eliza said. 'Charlie can no more be held responsible for her mother than any of your own children can for you, Mr Mackie.'

Mackie bristled. 'I would never—'

'Whatever the reason the quarrel occurred,' Russell said, 'I think we are agreed that it is probably in Charlotte's best interest that she be suspended from school for the remainder of this term, and, unfortunately—much as it grieves us, Miss Penrose— we must concur with the recommendation from Miss Donald and terminate your employment.'

Eliza had been expecting this outcome but it still hit her like a physical blow.

Russell glanced at his watch. 'This incident has already taken up too much time. Miss Donald, please return to your duties. We have received several promising applications for the position of head teacher and expect an appointment will be made soon. Gentlemen?'

The Board of Advice, accompanied by Flora Donald, left the room. At the door, Flora turned and looked at Eliza with such triumph that a shiver ran down Eliza's spine.

Alone with her uncle, she sank onto a chair beside the fire, her head in her hands. She heard the clink of glass before his shadow fell across her. She looked up and he handed her a drink.

'Brandy,' he said.

Eliza rarely drank spirits but she took the glass and drained it in one hit. The liquid burned her gullet but it helped to still her anger.

Cowper sat across from her, nursing his glass. 'I don't know what you did to earn such antipathy from Flora Donald,' he said, 'but I suspect she's been looking for an excuse to get rid of you since the day you arrived.'

'She frightened me today, Uncle,' she said. 'The way she hit Charlie. It was like she wanted to kill her.'

Cowper took a sip of his brandy. 'What did Mavis Mackie say to the child?'

Eliza repeated what Bert had told her.

'Good God,' Cowper said. 'Where would she have heard a thing like that? Not at the Mackies' dining room table, I wager.'

'It doesn't matter. What does matter is Charlie is being punished twice. Firstly by a beating she did not deserve and secondly by being denied her right to education.'

'You're an idealist, Eliza,' Cowper said. 'You can't save every underprivileged child in the world.'

'But she has so much potential,' Eliza said.

'I think, my dear, you need to think of yourself.'

Eliza nodded. 'I needed that position.'

'Ah.' Cowper set his glass down, fished in his jacket pocket and pulled out a letter. 'This came this morning. I took the liberty of making enquiries of an acquaintance in Melbourne. His widowed sister has recently established an academy for young ladies and is seeking suitable teaching staff. I was happy to recommend you.'

'You did this without consulting me?'

Cowper shrugged. 'You knew the position at the Maiden's Creek School was temporary and, as you frequently remind me, you wish to make your way in this world as an independent woman.'

Eliza took the envelope, surprised to see it was unopened and addressed to her.

'*My dear Miss Penrose,*' she read.

I have today received a recommendation that has come through my brother, commending your good self to me for a position in my newly established school. I believe you have a particular proficiency in mathematics and I am desperate for an experienced teacher of that subject. The school is situated in a large, pleasant house in East Melbourne and the salary of forty pounds per annum would include board and lodging. I write in the hope that you will come to Melbourne and meet with me, with a view to making an immediate start. Please advise by return of mail.

I wait in expectation of a positive response.

Yours most sincerely,

Edwina Wallace.

Eliza set the letter down and looked at her uncle.

'Well?' he enquired.

'I did not ask for your help,' she began. But even as she said the words, she saw a way to get to Melbourne and make the enquiries with Will's lawyer without attracting any suspicion. She looked at the letter and sighed. 'But I will write to Miss Wallace and arrange a meeting with her.'

Cowper clapped his hands together. 'Excellent. I am most relieved. Now, if you are sensible, you will leave as soon as possible. The roads at this time of year make the journey somewhat hazardous but it hasn't rained for a few days and you should get through to Shady Creek without a problem.'

In her cold bedroom, Eliza unlocked her writing box and looked at the neat bundle of correspondence between herself and her brother. It would be so easy to walk away from Maiden's Creek but she still owed it to Will to resolve the issues of his death and the situation with the Shenandoah Mine. No, she would not abandon her brother, but the excuse of a trip to Melbourne was a godsend.

She heard muffled voices in the hall and the slam of the front door as Cowper returned to the mine. Despite everything she was coming to learn about him, he could still show her kindness, still be an ally when the world raged against her. She closed her eyes, not wanting to even begin thinking the worst of him.

She glanced at her watch. There was still an hour until her rendezvous with Alec McLeod, which she had every intention of keeping. They needed to make a plan.

She drew out a clean sheet of writing paper and began a reply to Mrs Wallace.

Alec glanced up at the mantelpiece and sighed. He missed the familiar clock, which would need the attention of a skilled craftsman to restore and he lacked the funds for such a frivolous expense. He checked his watch instead and, shortly before nine, he went to his bedroom to retrieve the plans.

When he emerged he found Ian standing with his arms crossed in front of the door.

'Where are you going?'

'I am going to show Eliza—Miss Penrose—the plans and the figures for the two mines.'

'I'm coming with you.'

'No. I don't want you involved.'

'I am.'

Alec shrugged. Arguing with Ian was pointless.

A light shone in the residence at the back of the dressmaker's shop and Netty answered the door, admitting the men into the parlour. Eliza rose from her seat beside the fire, her eyes widening at the sight of Ian.

Alec glanced at his brother. 'He insisted. He knows the whole story and can explain the figures better than I.' He looked around the room. 'Is Amos here?'

Netty shook her head. 'No, he's taken the coach down to Shady Creek. First time in a week.'

She checked the door was locked and the curtains pulled tight and busied herself making tea as Alec pulled Will Penrose's plans from his bag. Eliza let out a hiss of breath as she set the plans on the table. She leaned over them, running her finger down the calculations.

'A fatal flaw ...' she whispered to herself.

Alec drank the tea Netty gave him without tasting it, his breath tightly held.

Eliza looked up and shook her head. 'I can't see where the problem lies.'

'I agree. I've been looking at it for weeks,' Alec said.

Eliza sat and ran a hand over her eyes.

'Are you all right?'

She nodded. 'Just tired. I had to face the Spanish Inquisition after I left you. I am well and truly dismissed from my position at the school.'

The injustice of her situation caused anger to bubble up in Alec. 'The business with Charlie?'

'Yes. But I'm not sorry. I would do it again in a heartbeat.'

'What will you do?' Netty asked.

Eliza shook her head. 'My interfering uncle has secured me an interview for a position in Melbourne.'

A wave of disappointment washed over Alec. 'You'll leave Maiden's Creek?'

Their eyes met. 'I have no intention of leaving while the question of my brother's death remains unresolved, but I now have the perfect excuse to take these plans to Melbourne and secure them with Will's lawyer. I also have some questions for him over the will, and it would be good if I could find Sissy.'

'When will you leave?' Alec asked.

'As soon as possible,' she said. 'Today is Thursday. If I could be in Melbourne by Monday ... but Amos won't be taking the coach back across for a few days—'

'I can hire the horses and take you across,' Alec said. 'But it will have to be Saturday.'

'By yourself? It would hardly be proper,' Netty said.

Eliza turned to her. 'What's improper about having an escort take me across the mountains? Besides, I don't really care whether the matrons of Maiden's Creek think it proper or not. My uncle wants me gone from this town so I doubt he will raise an objection.'

Ian nudged his brother. 'Show her the ledger entries.'

'You should probably take these as well.' Alec unfolded the neat pages. 'Every mine has to complete a monthly return to the mine inspector,' he said. 'Quartz crushed, yield of gold per ton ...'

'This supports my uncle's claim that the Shenandoah Mine is failing,' Eliza said, tracing the figures with her finger.

'Yes, but look at Maiden's Creek,' Alec said.

'It's improving markedly.' She looked at Alec. 'You're the mine superintendent. Does this support your understanding about how the mine is doing?'

He shook his head. 'Maiden's Creek is starting to turn a decent yield but nowhere near this successful,' he said. 'It's about the value of the shareholdings. The higher the yield, the greater the value of the shares.'

'And vice versa. So Will's shares that my uncle now owns are losing value by the day.'

'As are Caleb's and Adelaide's,' Netty said. She looked at the table and added in a quiet voice, 'And mine.'

Eliza laid her hand on the other woman's. 'You have shares in the Shenandoah?'

Netty nodded. 'It was a wedding present to Amos and me from Caleb and Adelaide. As I understand it, Caleb has fifty per cent of the shares, Adelaide twenty per cent, Amos and I, five per cent, and Will had the remaining twenty-five per cent. If they're worthless …'

Alec leaned forward. 'If Cowper now owns twenty-five per cent of the mine, another five per cent would give him a substantial holding, second only to Caleb Hunt's. Has anyone approached you about buying them?'

Netty stood up and took down a wooden box from the mantelpiece. She removed an envelope from it, passing the letter to Eliza, who unfolded it, scanned the contents and passed it to Alec. The letterhead proclaimed it came from a firm of solicitors in Melbourne who advised they were acting for an anonymous client who was keen to invest in the Gippsland goldfields and would buy the Burrells' shares in the Shenandoah Mine situated at Pretty Sally for two pounds a share.

'They were worth five pounds when we got married,' Netty said.

Ian took the letter from Alec. 'It's from Cowper's lawyers.'

Eliza shook her head. 'I am still struggling to believe my uncle would be so—so calculating and heartless.'

Netty's mouth tightened. 'One thing I've learned after my years out here is that gold is a fever, just like they say. It can change a man.'

Alec nodded. 'He has a ruthless streak. I've seen it. Put everything together, Eliza, and there is no other conclusion to reach.'

'Then there is Will's death—' Eliza said quietly. 'It all comes back to that.'

'I have never believed Will would leave his shares in the mine to Cowper,' Netty said. 'The two hadn't spoken in months and, whatever they were worth, it was still all he had. He would never have cut you out of his will.'

'Alec?' Ian broke the silence.

Alec looked at his brother and realised they had been speaking too fast for him to follow. He recapped the conversation.

'If the will was forged, it should be easy enough to prove,' Ian said. 'Miss Penrose, I suggest you take some evidence of your brother's handwriting and his signature with you when you visit the lawyer.'

'Good idea,' Alec agreed.

Eliza picked up the solicitor's letter. 'Can I borrow this?'

Netty nodded. 'Of course. I've no intention of replying to it. Amos and I believed in Will and he believed in the Shenandoah.'

Eliza's lips tightened. 'Netty, when are the Hunts expected to return?'

'The last letter I had from Adelaide indicated they would be sailing from San Francisco toward the end of the year.'

Eliza grimaced. 'That gives my uncle plenty of time to run Shenandoah down to nothing.' She slipped the letter back into its envelope. 'He can't have been expecting me to turn up. While I was thousands of miles away he could have carried his plan out with impunity, but now I'm here and he has to look at me every morning over breakfast, asking awkward questions. The quicker I can get to Melbourne, the better.' She rose to her feet. 'It's getting late. Thank you all.'

Alec pushed back his chair. 'I'll walk you back to Cowper's.'

For a moment he thought she would refuse but she gave a curt nod of her head.

After saying goodnight to Netty, Eliza stepped into the raw night air, her mind reeling with the revelations. Alec waited in the shadows, blowing on his hands.

'Ian's gone home.' He hunched his shoulders. 'I reckon it's below freezing tonight.'

He offered his arm and she slid her gloved hand into the crook of his elbow, grateful for his warmth and solidity. She looked at him, etching his profile into her mind. Leaving aside their first encounter, he'd been her quiet ally since she had arrived and now she had dragged a perfectly honest and respectable man into the murky depths of theft and deception. None of which was any concern of his.

'Will you come back?' he said at last.

'I made a promise to Will,' she said. 'Besides I have grown quite attached to the place.'

He nodded. 'Aye, it's like that. For all its dirt and noise, there's a life to the town that draws you in.'

They reached the path that led up to Cowper's house.

Eliza turned to face him. 'Alec, I should thank you.'

'For what? All I have done is make your situation so much worse.'

'No. I can see it all quite clearly now. If I have to fight my uncle for my brother's legacy, then I will.'

He raised his hand and touched her face with a hesitancy that told her if she jerked away, the moment would be lost. She wanted to be touched, she wanted to be kissed by this man. She wanted— no, she longed for him.

She laid her hand over his, leaning against the hard, callused palm, as he ran his thumb along her cheekbone curving the line of her jaw to brush the soft skin of her throat. She caught her breath as he leaned into her and the moment their lips touched, every nerve in her body caught alight. She pressed into him as his hand slid behind her head, holding her tight against him.

They kissed with the hunger of souls too long alone. When they drew apart, breath clouding in the cold air, they leaned forehead to forehead, fingers entwined.

'I've never—' Eliza began but Alec silenced her with the lightest of butterfly kisses.

'Don't talk,' he whispered, his lips drifting to her forehead, her hair, the tip of her nose ... 'Your nose is cold.'

She shook her head, a bubble of delight welling in her chest. 'I don't want this moment to end. I can't remember a time when I have ever felt this completely happy.'

Alec wrapped his arms around her. 'It's been a long, long time for me.'

But Eliza didn't want to think about his dead love. Catriona's ghost may tug at his sleeve but perhaps he could begin to let her go? Could there be a time for them in the future?

'I'm sorry I have to leave,' she said.

His chest rose and fell beneath her cheek. 'Aye, but it must be done. You'll not find peace until you've sorted out the business with your uncle and laid your brother's soul to rest.'

Despite her brave words she had no confidence in her ability to fight Cowper. 'How can I win? I've hardly a shilling to my name while Cowper has possession of the mine and the money to defend any claim I might make against him.'

'Have faith, Eliza,' Alec whispered. 'You have the plans for the boiler.'

'But they're not worth anything until we can resolve the problem with it.'

Someone nearby coughed and Eliza and Alec sprang apart.

'Ain't interrupting anything, am I?' A woman swathed in a heavy shawl stepped out of the shadows. It took Eliza a long moment to recognise Nell.

'I thought I'd missed you,' Nell said. 'I saw you heading out and figured you'd be back soon. It's been bitter cold waiting for you.'

'What on earth are you doing out here?'

She refrained from commenting that the woman should have been at work, but as if she sensed the question, Nell said, 'Not working tonight.'

She plucked at Eliza's sleeve. 'Come around here. I've got something for you.'

When Alec moved too, Nell looked up at him. 'What? Do you think I'm going to beat her to a pulp and rob her of all her worldlies?'

'No, but—'

'It's all right. Pay me no mind. If you're a friend of Miss P's then you can hear what I've got to say.'

They followed Nell into the shadows behind the Britannia Hotel. Alec leaned against the wall, his back to the women, keeping a watch on the street.

'Lil'll kill me if she knows I'm here, but you want to find Sissy and I know where she is.'

Eliza's breath caught in her throat. 'Where?'

'She's with Lil's sister Maggie Scott in Melbourne.' Nell drew a breath in between her teeth. 'If you think Lil's a force to be reckoned with, you've not met her sister, but here's the address. Just don't tell her where you got it.' She grasped Eliza's hand, pressing a crumpled scrap of paper into it. 'Little Lon's no place for a lady, Miss Penrose. Take care when you go there.'

Eliza looked up and smiled. 'Thank you, Nell. I can take care of myself.'

Nell shrugged. 'Don't say I didn't warn you. Now, I better get back before Lil starts asking questions. That Jess can't lie to save her soul.'

She turned to go and paused, looking back at Eliza. 'I heard what you did for Annie O'Reilly's girl.'

'I think I made it worse for her and I lost my job for my interference. I worry about the child and her mother with that baby due any day.'

Nell patted her arm. 'Don't worry too much about Annie. She has someone looking out for her. He'll see her right when the baby comes.'

'He? Who?' Eliza asked more out of curiosity than anything else.

Nell smiled. 'That'd be telling. Goodnight, Miss Penrose, and you, Mr McLeod.' She bumped Alec with her hip as she passed. 'You know you're always welcome.' She glanced back at Eliza. 'Although I reckon she's as good a prospect as any.'

'Nell!' Eliza said, grateful for the dark that hid the flush that rose to her face, but the woman had gone. She folded the piece of paper and slipped it into her pocket. 'What's Little Lon?' she asked Alec.

He gave a snort of laughter. 'Little Lonsdale Street. It has an unfortunate but deserved reputation for illegal goings-on.'

'Brothels?'

'And opium dens and worse.'

'Charming.'

'Nell was right, Little Lon is not a place to be going by yourself.'

'I'll be quite all right. I'll just have to make sure I go in broad daylight,' Eliza said. 'I'll bid you goodnight, Alec. Thank you for your help tonight.'

He nodded. 'Make your arrangements, Eliza. I'll organise the horses and we can meet at first light on Saturday.'

They stood for a long moment, suddenly awkward. Alec bent his head and kissed her gently on the lips. 'Until then.'

Halfway up the path to her uncle's house, Eliza paused and looked back in time to see Alec's unmistakeable but shadowy figure cross the creek and take the narrow path to his own cottage. She inhaled deeply and touched her lips, which still tingled at the memory of their kiss. A warm glow that began at her toes and fingertips wrapped itself around her, stealing into her heart. Perhaps, for the first time in a very long time, she could allow herself to dream.

Nineteen

18 July 1873

Alec had half-expected Eliza to be wearing the sumptuous green riding habit but she had abandoned it for a plain woollen skirt and a man's pea coat. His disappointment did not last as she swept the shapeless felt hat from her head. Her chestnut hair hung in a thick plait down her back and a heavy scarf around her neck framed her oval face to perfection. She set the carpet bag she carried on the ground.

'I took your advice, Alec, and have chosen something more practical. Netty told me that Adelaide Hunt wore trousers when she went out of town but I could not quite bring myself to do that.' She paused and a small smile caught the corners of her mouth. 'I think I have outraged the ladies of Maiden's Creek enough, and my mother would be appalled.'

Alec managed a casual nod that belied the surge of blood that the sight of her had caused. He longed to take her in his arms and kiss her but here, even in the grey light of dawn, there were too many prying eyes and loose tongues. As Eliza herself had said, it didn't serve her well to be the source of any further gossip.

'Do you have the documents? she asked.

He nodded and handed over the envelope. She excused herself and disappeared into the feed store, emerging empty-handed as Sones led out Sam and Nobby. He didn't ask her what she had done with the plans.

'You'll need to walk the horses up Little John's,' he said. 'Between the mud and the frost, they'll have trouble finding a firm footing. McLeod, I have your word you'll bring Nobby back with you tomorrow?'

They led the beasts out into the dawn. Even at this early hour, there were people out and about and the smell of baking bread collected tantalisingly in the wintry air. Unable to resist the tempting smell, Eliza stopped at Draper's Bakery and brought a knob of bread, still hot from the oven.

Sones had not been wrong about Little John's Sleigh Ride. It took them nearly an hour to ascend it, watching every step and guiding the horses around potholes filled with water on which a crust of ice had formed. The mud itself had turned to ice and both Alec and Eliza went down hard on their knees several times.

They paused when they reached the ridge line and rested for a while to eat some of the bread and catch their breath. Maiden's Creek stretched below them, the rough homes of the miners clinging to the valley sides with the tenacity of barnacles, curls of smoke rising from the morning hearths.

The road followed the ridge line before winding down to a creek crossing. In warmer weather the creek was barely a trickle but after the recent rains, it barrelled across the road.

'Trust the horses,' Alec said at last. 'You go first, I'll follow …'

Eliza's horse took the creek with care and made it across without the water reaching much above its hocks. Alec followed without incident and the road rose again, skirting the side of a hill which rose to one side of them, a steep descent falling away to their left.

They came out onto a flatter piece of ground, and Eliza raised a hand, bringing them to a halt. 'Can you hear something?'

Alec strained his ears and above the wind in the trees a cry rose faintly into the cold air: the bushman's 'Cooee'.

The cry came again, from further down the slope. Alec dismounted, handing the reins of his horse to Eliza. 'Wait here.'

He slithered down the slope, pausing a little way from the road. 'Where are you?' he called.

The unhelpful answer came from his right. 'Over here.'

Alec battled his way through wet ferns and slippery humus, until, through a break in the undergrowth, he could make out a figure slumped against a tree: a man with his hat pulled down over his face. It struck Alec as strange that anyone would be on the side of a remote hill in the middle of nowhere, but he hunkered down beside the stranger.

'Are you hurt?'

The man raised his head. The lower part of his face was wrapped in a heavy scarf and he brought his right hand up, cocking the hammer of a revolver as he did so.

Alec stumbled backward as Eliza screamed his name from the road above them.

'On your feet, McLeod,' the man said. 'Let's go and talk to your lady friend.'

The moment Alec had disappeared from view, three burly men with hats pulled down low and scarfs wrapped around their faces emerged from the underbrush on either side of the road. They carried revolvers, hammers pulled back.

The scream froze in Eliza's throat as one of the men grabbed Nobby's reins. The horse set his ears back and fought the unfamiliar grip.

'Off yer horse, lady.'

'Alec!' She scanned the bush, willing him to reappear.

'He ain't coming to help you.'

Even with a scarf wrapped around his face, Eliza had no trouble recognising the short, solid leader of the ruffians as Jennings, the brute who had caused her so much trouble on the night of the dance.

She kicked out at him as he approached but he just laughed and pulled her from the horse. With one arm around her waist, he carried her across to a fallen tree on the far side of the road. She struggled in his grip but to no avail.

'What do you want?' she demanded, wishing her voice hadn't risen several octaves. He pushed her down on the log with an order to sit and keep her mouth shut.

Eliza complied, fighting down a wave of nausea. What had happened to Alec? She didn't like to think about what these three men had in mind for her. She hoped it was just simple robbery but Jennings's presence boded ill.

A crashing in the bushes on the other side of the road alerted the men and to her relief, Alec came stumbling out. A fourth man had a revolver pressed into his back. He gave Alec a shove and Alec tripped and went down on his knees. He recovered his balance and turned on his heel, his fists balling at his sides but his captor pressed the revolver's muzzle into his chest.

'Go and join your lady friend.'

Seeing Eliza, Alec rounded on the ruffians. 'If you've touched her—'

'She's safe enough,' Jennings said, adding with an ominous sideways glance at Eliza, 'For the moment.'

Alec slumped down on the log beside Eliza, the tension radiating off him.

'I don't know why you're bothered with the scarf, Jennings,' he said. 'I'd know you anywhere. Is this Tehan's work or have you and your friends taken up bushranging?'

'Just keep your mouth shut, McLeod, and no one gets hurt.' Jennings's voice was muffled by the scarf.

In the weeks she had been in Maiden's Creek, Eliza had not heard any mention of bushrangers but yet here they were, four of them. She thought of the only item of value she had with her, her father's locket, and prayed they wouldn't find it.

While one man watched them, a rifle at the ready, another one pulled Eliza's carpet bag from Alec's saddle. He wrenched it open and began rummaging through it. Eliza turned her head, her face burning with embarrassment, as he tossed her chemise to one of his comrades who held it against himself and pranced around to the laughter of his companions, before dropping it in the mud.

'Not here, boss.' The man searching her bag held the bag upside down and shook it to prove his point.

Eliza glanced at Alec. Their eyes met in mutual comprehension. These men were looking for something specific and that something could only be Will's plans.

Jennings tucked his revolver into his belt and approached Eliza, rubbing his hands together. He hauled her to her feet. Alec began to rise but the click of the rifle trained on him forced him back.

'Where is it, missy?'

'What are you looking for?' Eliza said.

Jennings's fingers tightened on her arm and she bit back a cry of pain.

'Your brother's plans. He gave 'em to his friend over there and he's given them to you. Now just hand 'em over and we'll be on our way.'

When Eliza hesitated, Jennings jerked his head at his comrade, who moved closer to Alec, resting the barrel of the rifle just above Alec's ear. Alec flinched.

Eliza's breath stopped in her throat. What price was a man's life—a man she had come to care about?

Alec's eyes met hers, calm and apparently unconcerned. He gave a slight shrug and she frowned.

'They're not worth dying for,' Alec said. 'Let them have what they came for.'

She swallowed and turned her back on the men. Her fingers shook as she undid her jacket and the shirt beneath. She pulled the documents out, warm from her body, and handed them to Alec as she restored her clothing.

Jennings laughed and grabbed up the papers. He held them to his face. 'You smell mighty sweet, Miss Penrose.'

Shock and the cold began to take their toll and, despite the heavy jacket, Eliza shivered.

Jennings opened the envelope and peered at the drawings and indecipherable calculation. He snorted and folded the plans, shoving them without care into his own capacious pockets. He looked around the circle of his comrades. 'Might as well see what else you've got. Make it worth our trouble. Both of you stand up and throw your purses and any valuables down.'

Alec held out his hand to Eliza and they stood up. His hand lingered on hers as he gave her fingers a squeeze. Eliza had only her purse with the last of her hard-earned money. She reached into the inside pocket of her jacket and pulled it out, tears starting as she tossed it on the ground in front of the man's boots. Alec threw his wallet down, his mouth twisted in disgust.

Jennings pocketed the purses and scratched his nose. 'I don't think that's all, little lady,' he said and swaggered over to her. He pulled the scarf from around her neck and smiled, a mouth of yellowing, rotten teeth appearing in the thick bush of his beard. She caught his rank breath, remembering the dance and how he had caught her wrist, breathing into her face. 'Ye're dancing with me, little lady.'

Beside her, Alec stiffened. 'Get away from her, you bastard.'

The man ignored him. His eyes glittered as he came so close to Eliza that the stench of unwashed body and stale alcohol filled her nostrils. 'Never knew a lady without something pretty around her neck,' he said.

She yelped as he ripped open the top buttons of her shirt, revealing the little gold locket. His fist closed over it and he gave it a sharp yank. Pain seared her neck as the chain dug into her, burning her skin as it came away.

'This'll fetch me a few shillings,' he said, turning it over in his dirty hands.

Eliza lunged for the locket but he swung it just out of her reach.

'It's all I have left,' she whispered, too stricken to stop the shaming tears that started in her eyes.

'You should've been nicer to me,' Jennings said. He gripped her chin between a grimy thumb and forefinger and tilted her face up, pressing the muzzle of his weapon to her throat. 'We could 'ave some fun with this one. Give me a kiss, and I might give you back your pretty.' He licked his thick lips in anticipation.

Time stood still. Conscious only of the smashing of her heart against her chest and the vile stink of the man, Eliza was momentarily paralysed. Then, as Jennings leaned into her, she brought her knee up swiftly, connecting with his crotch.

Jennings's eyes bulged. 'You little bitch,' he wheezed, releasing his grip on her.

She stumbled back against the log and caught off balance, she fell backward over it. As she lay winded, gasping for breath, she was conscious of the sickening thud of fist on bone. A cry of pain and the crack of a weapon discharging brought the world back into focus.

She pulled herself to her knees and cowered behind the shelter of the log, trying to get her eyes to focus. Alec stood over Jennings, who was on the ground, blood pouring from his nose, his thick black beard shining with it.

'Shoot him! Shoot the bastard,' Jennings wheezed.

The three thugs glanced at each other, the whites of their eyes bright over their scarves.

'Damned if I'm going to be hanged for rape or murder,' one of the men said. 'I'm off.'

Jennings rolled onto his side and pulled himself up. He staggered like a drunken man, but the attention of his comrades had been diverted by the dull thud of hooves coming down the track.

Eliza could feel the vibration beneath her knees as the horse rounded the bend in the road, sweating and lathered.

The rider, his identity also concealed behind a scarf, yelled, 'Someone's coming.'

Jennings lunged at Alec but he stepped back, swinging his fists as two of the others approached him. Eliza cried a warning but too late for him to avoid the third man, who pressed his revolver between Alec's shoulder blades. Alec let his hands drop. The other two pinioned his arms.

Jerking his head at the new arrival, Jennings gave a curt order to fetch the horses before turning his attention back to Alec.

He wiped his nose with his sleeve, then slammed his fist into Alec's stomach. Alec went down on his knees, gasping for breath as Jennings took a revolver from one of his comrades. He checked the chamber before giving a snort of disgust and reversing the weapon, he brought the revolver down just behind Alec's ear with a sickening crack. The men released him and Alec toppled forward onto the damp earth.

Jennings turned to Eliza, who cowered behind the log. He raised a finger. 'Don't think I've forgotten you, pretty lady. Your turn'll come.'

He strode over to Sam and Nobby and untied their reins, giving them each a firm slap on the rump. The horses needed no further encouragement and started at a gallop in the direction of Maiden's Creek and the safety of Sones's stables.

The newcomer had returned leading four horses and the men swung into the saddles, setting out at a gallop back in the direction of Maiden's Creek, leaving the contents of Eliza's bag strewn across the muddy track and Alec lying motionless on the side of the road, bright blood matting his dark hair.

Eliza scrambled over the log and fell to her knees beside the unconscious man, turning him over. Blood streamed across his face to mingle with mud, forming a grotesque mask. She had no experience of wounds and for all she could tell, Alec could be dead. Only the flutter of a pulse under her fingers gave Eliza the hope that he lived.

She knelt beside him feeling utterly helpless. Never having been blessed with a strong stomach, the world wavered and danced but she would be no use to Alec if she fainted. She took a steadying breath and forced her queasy senses into submission and cast around for something to use as a bandage. Grabbing one of her abandoned petticoats, she balled it up, pressed it to the bloody wound on Alec's head.

'Don't die. Please don't die,' she murmured to him. 'Come back to me, Alec. I need you.'

She looked up at the sound of a woman singing and the jingle of a harness. A cart pulled by a single horse came around the bend. The driver, a woman, wore male garb, her hair tied back from her face in a loose knot at the nape of her neck. She stopped the cart and handed the reins to a stocky man sitting beside her before reaching for a rifle and levelling it at Eliza.

Eliza flinched, raising her hands. 'Please, we need your help. My friend is hurt and our horses have been turned away by the men who attacked us. Can you take us back into Maiden's Creek?'

The woman lowered her weapon and glanced at the man beside her who shrugged.

'*Que vous est-il arrivé?*'

A woman holding a rifle and speaking French was almost more than Eliza could deal with. She spoke French fluently but not here, not now.

'We were held up by bushrangers,' she said.

The woman jumped down from the cart and hurried forward. She moved with the litheness of an athlete, her stride long and easy in her corduroy trousers and long boots. She knelt beside Alec and pulled the petticoat away from the wound. With long, strong fingers, she probed around the wound, nodding to herself.

'I don't think his skull is cracked,' she said in accented English. 'But head wounds bleed a lot.' She picked up the petticoat and thrust it at Eliza. 'Make yourself useful and tear it up properly. Henri,' she said to her companion, 'water.'

The man nodded and jumped down from the cart holding a water flask.

'Will he be all right?' Eliza asked as she handed over the torn remnants of her petticoat.

'Who am I to say? He needs a doctor,' came the curt reply. 'Now, wet one of those cloths and let's try and stop the bleeding.' She looked up at Eliza. '*Tiens*, are you going to faint, girl?'

'No,' Eliza said with more confidence than she felt.

The Frenchwoman dabbed at the wound with the cloth and wiped the worst of the blood and mud from Alec's face before padding the wound and binding it with the rough bandage.

She gave a grunt and sat back on her heels. 'I think he'll have an almighty lump and a headache for a day or two.'

Beneath the woman's hands, Alec stirred and groaned and relief rushed through Eliza.

His first words were unintelligible and Eliza took them to be profane. The other woman just laughed.

'You lie still, *cheri*,' she said, pushing him back as he tried to sit up.

Alec grimaced, his fingers exploring the crude bandaging. 'Who the hell are you?'

'I am Marcelline Guichard, and this is my assistant, Henry Cook,' She pronounced his name in the French style as Henri. 'I think it fortunate we happened on you, *n'est ce pas?*'

Eliza nodded. 'You scared the bushrangers away.'

'How many were there?'

'Five,' Eliza said.

The woman's eyes widened. 'Five. *Mon dieu*. I am not sure Henri and I would be much match for five ruffians.' She rose to her feet, wiping her hands on her trousers. 'Now we must get your friend some proper medical attention. How far to Maiden's Creek?'

'We were about two hours out when we were accosted by the gang,' Eliza replied.

'We will put your friend here in the back of the wagon and you may sit with him. Henri, clear some room.'

Henry moved boxes, spades, mattocks and other digging equipment to make enough space to allow Alec to lie down, creating a rough bed of some empty burlap sacks. Between them they managed to get Alec off the ground and into the back of the cart, with his feet hanging over the edge. Eliza gathered up her scattered possessions and stuffed them into her bag. She climbed into the cart and took Alec's head on her lap to minimise the jolting and, with Marcelline Guichard once more on the reins with the silent Henry beside her, they set off.

The Frenchwoman looked over her shoulder. 'You should try and keep him awake,' she said. 'It is not good to let him lapse into *inconscience* again.'

Eliza looked down at Alec's pale and blood-streaked face. His eyes were closed, but the regular rise and fall of his chest indicated he still lived.

'Alec?'

'I can hear you,' he said. 'I'm just resting my eyes.'

Eliza blew out a breath. 'Thank you for your kindness, Madame Guichard. What brings you to Maiden's Creek?'

'I have a contract to construct a water race to the Antioch Mine.'

Eliza twisted to get a better look at the woman. 'I beg your pardon?'

Marcelline Guichard shrugged. 'It is what I do. My husband was an engineer but since he died I have taken on his contracts.'

'Antioch is the new mine north of Blue Sailor,' Alec murmured. 'Good promise. Your reputation precedes you, madame.'

'Favourably, I hope. I am very good at what I do. And what about you, *cherie*?'

'Eliza Penrose,' Eliza said. 'I am—I was a teacher at the school. I am on my way to Melbourne.'

'And your handsome friend?'

'Alec McLeod. He is the mine superintendent at Maiden's Creek Mine. He was escorting me to Shady Creek.'

Marcelline Guichard nodded. 'We were not warned that the Maiden's Creek goldfield could be so dangerous. Seems we must be on our guard, Henri, *non*?'

'I think it is as safe as anywhere. We were just unlucky.'

But Eliza knew that luck had nothing to do with the attack. They had been expected and the 'bushrangers' knew exactly what they were looking for.

'Alec?' She bent over him, her lips brushing his mud-smeared forehead. His eyes fluttered open and he managed a watery smile.

'Thank you,' she said.

'What for?'

She thought about what might have happened if he hadn't intervened, and shivered. What did they call it? A fate worse than death?

'Don't you remember?'

He closed his eyes, grimacing as he gave the slightest of nods. 'Of course I do. I'm a poor escort. We walked into a trap. They wanted the plans and they knew we had them.'

'Tehan?'

Alec looked up at her. 'Jennings is Tehan's man so I think we can assume he is the one behind it.' The cart hit a rock and bounced and he grimaced. 'If I see that black-bearded bastard again …' He huffed a breath and closed his eyes.

Eliza shook his shoulder gently. 'You have to stay awake, Alec.'

'Do I? I just want to sleep.'

She bent over and kissed him again—this time on the mouth.

A smile curved his lips. 'Do that again.'

She obliged. He raised his hand and she took it, twining her fingers with his. 'What are we going to do?' she whispered.

But if he heard her he gave no answer.

Twenty

Sones had raised the alarm when the two horses returned to the livery stables without their riders and Sergeant Maidment and one of his constables met Marcelline Guichard's wagon an hour outside Maiden's Creek. Eliza briefly related the story of the hold-up and identified Jennings as the ringleader. Maidment despatched his constable to search for Jennings and accompanied the cart back into Maiden's Creek, where a crowd of curious onlookers who had heard the story of the two riderless horses turned out to greet them.

A stretcher was produced and Alec was carried, protesting that he could walk, up to his cottage. The Frenchwoman and her companion departed to find rooms at one of the hostelries and Alec was put to bed with his head bound neatly and orders from Dr Sims that he should be watched for nausea, vomiting and disorientation.

As the evening drew in, Ian knelt by the fireplace in Alec's small bedroom, stoking the flames into life. It did little to warm the bedroom and Eliza pulled the blankets higher over Alec. He stirred and muttered but did not wake. She curled into a chair brought from the living room.

221

Charles Cowper came hurrying down from the mine, enquiring after Alec and insisting Eliza return home with him. She had refused, adamant that she remain with Alec until she was certain he was out of danger. She said nothing more to her uncle although she strongly suspected that he had been behind the hold-up. Robbery was one thing but the thought of what might have happened if it hadn't been for Alec's actions and the fortuitous arrival of Marcelline Guichard made her blood run cold.

Eliza sipped the mug of black tea Ian had made and watched the younger man's deft actions. Apart from the occasional mannerism, physically the brothers were not much alike, Ian was fine boned, slight and light haired while Alec was tall, broad shouldered and brown haired.

As if conscious of her scrutiny, Ian turned to her. 'Are you sure you want to stay, Miss Penrose? I'll watch him.'

She glanced at the man in the bed. 'I will stay. You need your rest and I owe him my life.' *And so much more.*

Ian stood and looked down at his brother. 'That's what he does,' he said. 'If he could save the whole world, he would, but this is a hard life and sometimes people die. He could not save Catriona or the bairn and he's never forgiven himself. Has he told you about his wife?'

'He told me she died in childbirth.'

Ian nodded. 'The winter of sixty-nine …' Words seemed to fail him as his face screwed up in anguish. 'Alec was away in Glasgow when Catriona's time came. I sent for the midwife but she couldn't be found. Catriona'd been in labour nearly twenty-four hours by the time he got home and the doctor arrived too late.'

A large ginger cat pushed open the door and sauntered in. It regarded Eliza with unblinking green eyes before jumping onto the end of the bed, where it settled in a neat ball, one eye still fixed on Eliza. She leaned over and scratched it behind the ear in that special place that only people who love cats know. The cat rewarded her with a low purr.

'Who's this?'

'Windlass,' he replied. 'Alec found him not long after we arrived. Some children were tormenting him and he nothing more than a tiny kitten. Alec can't abide cruelty. He's been with us ever since, but he's Alec's cat.' He paused. 'He'd never let me pet him that way.'

Windlass had turned up his chin to be scritched along the jaw, his eyes closed, and his rumbling purr filling the room.

'I'll throw him out,' Ian said.

'No, leave him,' Eliza said. 'I'll be pleased of the company.'

The young man frowned and cleared his throat.

'Are you worried that people will talk if I stay?' Eliza said. 'Well, they can talk all they like. Go to bed, Ian, I'll wake you if I need your help.'

Ian opened his mouth as if to protest and shook his head. 'I'll relieve you in an hour or so. I am grateful you are here, Miss Penrose.'

'Call me Eliza.'

A smile caught at the corners of his mouth. 'Eliza.'

Despite the fire, cold draughts blew through the floorboards and around the doorframe. Ian stoked the fire and set more wood beside it then left the room returning a few minutes later with extra blankets.

He crossed to the door and looked back at her. 'You will wake me?'

'I promise.'

Eliza pulled the blankets around her, grateful for the thoughtful gesture. Despite the hard chair, the strain of the day caught up with her and she dozed, waking to the cold and realising the fire had died down to bare embers. Forcing her stiff limbs to move, she bent over the fireplace to reignite the flames.

'What do you think you're doing?'

She straightened. Alec was sitting, his night shirt sliding off one shoulder and the hair that had escaped the doctor's bandage sticking straight up.

'Fixing the fire,' she said.

'Do you know how much firewood costs?'

A sharp retort stuck on her tongue and she started to laugh.

'What's so funny?'

'You are,' she said. 'You survive an encounter with bushrangers and your only thought is the cost of firewood. How's your head?'

He gingerly felt around the lump beneath the bandaging. 'Sore.'

'The doctor says you could have concussion so if you find yourself feeling tired or slurring your speech—'

'I know what concussion is. Have they caught the bastards yet?'

'Sergeant Maidment and his men are looking for them. He said he'll come in the morning when you are a little recovered.'

She returned to her chair by the bed. Alec moved his legs and Windlass raised his head to issue a chirrup of protest.

'You know you're not allowed on my bed,' Alec murmured, but his hand reached for the cat, stirring his fur with his fingers. Windlass shifted, snuggling closer and allowing Alec to lay a hand on his head.

Eliza poured a glass of water and gave it to Alec.

'Why are you here? Where's Ian?'

'Ian's in bed and someone has to sit with you to make sure you live through the night.'

'That's a bit dramatic.'

She shrugged. 'The doctor says cracks to the skull are not to be treated lightly.'

Alec winced. 'It does hurt something fierce, but you should go home. A single woman spending the night in a house of men is not likely to be viewed well by the town gossips.'

'As I told Ian, I don't give a fig for the town gossips, besides which my uncle's house is not my home,' she said. 'If he set those ruffians on us today then he is no better than them. A home is somewhere safe, somewhere you are loved.'

Alec's eyes, dark pools in the light of the single candle, were fixed on her. 'Aye,' he said, 'when you lose that, there is nothing.'

The pain and yearning on his face told his story. His gaze flicked to his desk and Eliza picked up the leather-bound travelling photograph frame.

'May I?'

He shrugged and she held the image to the light. Through the cracked glass she could see that Catriona McLeod had probably never been a beauty but even in the cold formality of the photographer's studio, a sense of fun and life radiated from her. Behind her, a younger Alec—clean shaven, his hair neatly combed— stood, one hand on her shoulder, exuding pride.

'You would have liked her,' Alec said. 'Everyone who met her loved her.' Eliza passed him the frame and he touched the ghostly image of his dead wife with his forefinger. 'We talked of leaving Wishaw for Australia so often but I was reluctant to leave a good job for uncertainty. If only ...'

Eliza reached for his hand, squeezing his fingers in her own. 'No. Don't ever talk like that, Alec. We none of us know our fates or the consequences of our actions.'

He turned away from her. 'I—I miss her. Every day that passes, it's as if she died yesterday.'

Eliza knew those were words that he would never have spoken in daylight, nor if he'd been hale and hearty. She searched for the right response to convey that she understood loneliness, but she had never known the close companionship of a partner, had never been in love …

In the short time she had known Alec McLeod, she had come to see him as more than just her confidante in the puzzle of her brother's death—she had come to rely on his quiet solidity and his strength. More than that. Her heart and her breathing quickened at the sight of him, and when away from him, she yearned to be in his company. Was it possible that she was falling in love?

That thought frightened her. Everyone she had ever loved had abandoned her. What if Alec were to do the same? What if he did not return her feelings? How could she ever hope to replace the memory of Catriona?

She looked down at her hand, her fingers twined in his. His eyes had closed and his breathing slowed. She tucked his hand under the blanket and, with only the dozing cat for company, sat in the chill dark, her feet tucked under her and a blanket wrapped around her shoulders, watching as he slept.

Twenty-One

20 July 1873

The grey early morning light had begun to creep over the hills as Eliza, leaving Alec in his brother's care, picked her way along the treacherous path to her uncle's house on the hill. It would have looked strange if she had taken lodgings at one of the hotels, and she needed a bed and time to gather her thoughts before she tried once more to get to Melbourne.

She climbed the steep path, went around to the back and knocked on the kitchen door. Not hearing any movement inside, she knocked again. Mrs Harris answered the door, dressed only in her nightgown with a shawl clutched over her shoulders. The woman's eyes widened and she glanced at the door to her bedroom. Eliza glimpsed the neatly made bed while the door to her uncle's bedroom stood ajar, and she understood. Eliza wondered why she hadn't noticed the arrangement before. Perhaps this was another reason her uncle had been so anxious for her to leave.

Not that it mattered. She had no interest in his domestic arrangements.

'Forgive the hour,' she said. 'I've been sitting with Mr McLeod and I'm very tired.'

Mrs Harris nodded. 'Your room is made up. After your uncle told me what you had been through, I expected you home. Just let me heat the coals for a warming pan and I'll fix you something to eat.'

'Don't trouble yourself, Mrs Harris. I just want to sleep.'

Her uncle came out of his bedroom, tying his dressing gown. 'I thought I heard voices. Eliza, my dear, how is McLeod?'

'He'll be fine, Uncle.'

'And you?'

He laid a hand on her shoulder, his eyes earnestly searching her face. Her flesh shrank from his touch but she forced herself not to flinch. The hypocrisy of his concern sparked the flame of anger and she had to fight the urge to rail at him for what he had done. Now was not the time to bring the accusations that were mounting against him.

'Just very tired. Excuse me.'

She pushed past him and retreated to her room, shutting the door behind her. She threw her carpet bag into a corner, pulled off her boots and outer garments and fell onto the bed, curling into a ball as the tears of exhaustion and betrayal trickled unchecked from her eyes.

She woke to full daylight. Someone had pulled a quilt over her. Mrs Harris, she supposed. She threw the quilt to one side, conscious of her stiff, aching muscles. The drama of the hold-up and a night spent in an uncomfortable chair at Alec McLeod's bedside had taken their toll.

A jug of clean but cold water stood on the washstand along with a towel. She looked at her filthy bag and her flesh crawled at the thought of those vile men touching her intimate garments and worse, parading around with them. Her ruined clothes could go on the fire at the first opportunity. Fortunately Eliza had left sufficient clean clothes in her travelling box and she selected a dark green gown.

Washed and dressed, Eliza stepped out to face the world.

She found Mrs Harris in the kitchen, humming to herself as she peeled potatoes. Tom sat in his favourite place by the stove, absorbed in the task of scraping carrots. He looked up and smiled at Eliza.

The housekeeper brushed her hands on her apron and set the kettle on the stove.

'You look quite washed out,' she said. 'A good cup of tea will see you right, and I've a pie in the oven that'll be ready shortly. Your uncle has been detained at the church.'

Eliza sniffed the air, the delectable scent of pastry reminding her she hadn't eaten in twenty-four hours. She picked up a wizened apple from the fruit bowl and bit into it. The floury texture would normally have repelled her but it filled the gap until the pie would be done.

A loud rapping on the front door caused both women to start. Smoothing down her apron, Mrs Harris left the room, returning with Sergeant Maidment.

'Good morning, Miss Penrose. I trust you are recovered from your ordeal of yesterday?' the policeman asked.

She nodded. 'A little sleep works wonders.'

'I have some questions for you. Is there somewhere we can talk?'

Eliza took him through to the parlour and they sat at the small table. At the policeman's prompting she recounted everything she could recall of the previous day's events. She glossed over the unpleasant advance Jennings made on her but when Maidment asked how Alec had sustained his injury she admitted that one of the men had threatened her.

Maidment shook his head. 'You were fortunate the Guichard woman came along.'

'Have you found Jennings?'

'Constable Prewitt went up to the Shenandoah at first light, but no one claims to have seen him and if Jennings knows you recognised him, he'll be halfway to Melbourne by now, if he's any sense.' Maidment scowled. 'That one's been trouble since he arrived. Nothing that can be proved, mind. Now, apart from Jennings, did you recognise any of the others?'

She shook her head.

'What did the rogues take?'

Eliza's hand went to the place where her locket had hung. 'My gold locket and our money.'

Maidment's mouth tightened and he nodded his understanding. 'Nothing else?'

As Eliza hesitated, they were interrupted by the arrival of Charles Cowper.

'Eliza, good to see you up and around.' He turned to the policeman. 'Maidment, why are you bothering my poor niece? Shouldn't you be out trying to find these ruffians?'

Eliza couldn't help but stare at the effrontery of the man. In all probability he had been the one to set the rogues on them.

'I assure you, Mr Cowper,' Maidment said, 'I have men out there now but it helps to get a better description of who we are looking for. Miss Penrose is of the opinion that at least one may have come from the Shenandoah Mine. That's your mine these days, isn't it?'

Cowper sighed. 'Which of the fellows are you looking for?'

'Jennings.'

Cowper shook his head. 'I told Tehan that one would be trouble, but as you and I both know, we can't always pick and choose our men the way we would wish. Good miners are worth their price and if one or two of them have turned to the bad to supplement their income, that is hardly the fault of their employer. Do you want me to speak to Tehan?'

Maidment stood. 'No need, I've got men out there. Now if you'll excuse me ...'

Eliza pushed her chair back and stood up. 'I will see you to the door, Sergeant,' she said. 'I haven't given you a full description of my stolen locket.'

She walked with him until they were out of earshot of the house.

'Is there something else bothering you, Miss Penrose?' Maidment enquired after she had supplied the missing description.

'Sergeant, this is nothing to do with the robbery but is it possible my brother did not die by accident?'

Maidment frowned. 'What do you mean?'

'Just a feeling, but there are aspects of his death that simply don't make sense to me.'

Maidment gave her a sympathetic look. 'We all look for reasons for such tragic events, but your brother had no enemies, Miss Penrose. There's no reason that I could discover why anyone would want to take his life. Do you have proof to support any conclusion other than that reached by the coroner?'

What could she say? She had no concrete evidence that Will's death itself had been brought about by a third person, despite the plots against him. Eliza could go through the growing list of inconsistencies: the falling out with her uncle; the gold being channelled from the Shenandoah to the Maiden's Creek Mine; the theft of the valuable plans. There were elements that pointed to foul play but nothing concrete, nothing that would convict anyone.

'If I could produce some evidence, would you reopen the case?'

'Of course, but Miss Penrose—'

She held up a hand. 'I know. You think I am being a foolish woman grieving her brother's death, Sergeant. Forget I spoke.'

His shrewd eyes studied her face. 'I don't think you're foolish, Miss Penrose, and between us, there were certain matters that concerned me. No one was able to furnish a reason as to why your brother was up at the mine at that hour of the night, for example. You be sure to tell me if you find something, won't you. In the meantime, I will speak with McLeod.' He raised fingers to the peak of his hat and nodded to her. 'Good day, Miss Penrose.'

Eliza returned to the house, where her uncle waited in the parlour. He greeted her with a frown.

'What other matters did you have to discuss with Maidment?'

'You interrupted us before I had given him a description of my locket.' She poured them tea from the teapot on the table and sat down beside the fire. 'I mourn the locket. It was a piece my father gave me and it contained the only images I have of Mama and Will.'

'I'm sorry, my dear, but if a stolen locket is the worst of the events of yesterday ... I was foolish agreeing to let you go to Melbourne without the coach and I am angry with McLeod for not taking better care of you.'

She stared at him. 'There were five of them, Uncle. Five. I assure you, Mr McLeod was injured in the very act of taking care of me. If anything, he deserves commendation rather than condemnation.'

'What do you mean?'

'The robbery was not the worst of the whole business. I believe that Jennings had the intention of ... of—if it hadn't been for McLeod's intervention, I shudder to think what would have happened.'

Cowper's eyes widened as comprehension dawned. 'Oh, my poor girl.' He shook his head. 'That is unthinkable. Not here. I hope they catch the scoundrel.'

'As the sergeant says, he will be long gone and I must still get to Melbourne. If it is agreeable with you, I will be on the Shady Creek coach tomorrow morning.'

Cowper took a sip of his tea. 'Yes, of course. As long as it doesn't rain, Burrell is a sturdy fellow and I very much doubt there will be a reoccurrence of such an unnerving incident.'

Eliza studied her uncle over the rim of her cup.

No, because you now have the plans.

Alec woke with a splitting headache and a mouth that felt like sandpaper. Windlass had managed to manoeuvre himself so he took up most of the bed, leaving Alec with what felt like a few inches. He pulled himself up, shifting the unprotesting cat, and squinted at the window. It had to be late morning or early afternoon.

He swung his feet out of bed, shivering as they touched the cold floor. He stood up with care but even so the world lurched and tilted and he had to grab the bed to steady himself.

'What are you doing?' Ian leaned against the door jamb, arms crossed.

Alec glared at his brother. 'By my reckoning I've spent long enough in bed and nature calls.'

Ian left him to it, returning with a jug of warm water for the wash basin. Alec unwound the bandage and inspected the damage in his mirror. Blood had matted his hair and he gently washed out as much as he dared, wincing as he worked.

His brother helped him dress and Alec sank gratefully into a chair by the fire in the main room where he was immediately joined by Windlass, who seemed determined not to miss a single moment of attention. Alec leaned his head against the back of the chair and stared into the fire. The headache had subsided to a manageable throbbing and he didn't feel nauseous, all of which he took to be good signs. He did, however, have the strength of a kitten and a nagging suspicion that he may have said things to Eliza in the dark of the night that he now could not take back.

Ian lifted the lid on a pot on the stove and stirred the contents. 'Bridget O'Grady came around first thing this morning. She'd heard about what happened and she's left some broth.'

While Alec had not felt nauseous before, the aroma drifting from the pot turned his stomach. 'What sort of broth?'

Ian pulled a face. 'I have no idea. Want some?'

'No, thank you.'

'I'll try and find something more appetising to eat.'

As Ian organised bread and cheese Alec closed his eyes, trying to recall the events of the previous day, but he saw only the fear in Eliza's eyes and Jennings's lascivious leer. If they hadn't been interrupted by the arrival of the peculiar Frenchwoman, what would have happened?

The gentle crackle of the flames and the warmth worked into his bones and he drifted off to sleep. A knock on the door woke him from his doze.

Ian went to answer it.

'I heard what happened and I've brought some barley broth, fresh baked bread and oatmeal biscuits. Nothing like food from the old country to strengthen a body,' Flora Donald said from the doorstep.

'My brother is not up to visitors,' Ian insisted. Flora pushed past Ian—evidently she did not consider herself part of that category—set her basket on the table and turned to Alec.

'Oh, you poor man.' Flora's hands flew to her breast at the sight of him. 'You're as white as a sheet. I heard at church what had happened and when Ian did not turn up for the service, I feared the worst. You just sit there and I'll warm the broth for you.'

Ian shot his brother an apologetic glance. Alec glared back.

'That's very kind of you, Miss Donald, but really I'm fine. And Bridget O'Grady has left us some broth,' Alec said, but Flora had already lifted the lid on the pan supplied by the brothers' housekeeper and recoiled.

She thrust the pan at Ian. 'Throw that out,' she ordered and to Alec's horror, she divested herself of her outer garments and tied a pristine white apron over her dress.

Alec endured Flora's fussing for the next hour. She put pillows at his back, tucked blankets around his legs and fed him barley broth and oatcakes. He had to admit he was hungry and the soup and the oatcakes, lathered with fresh butter, were a huge improvement on anything Bridget had provided. But there was a price to pay and Flora had just settled into Ian's chair with the bible open on her knee when a knock on the door saved him from a reading from the good book, no doubt followed by a suitable homily.

Sergeant Maidment ducked his head under the lintel as he entered. The house had been built for miners and Alec had learned by hard experience that anyone over six feet had to duck to enter.

'Ah, Mr McLeod, it's good to see you up and around.'

Maidment cast a glance at Flora, who showed no sign of moving. 'Miss Donald, I must speak with Mr McLeod in private,' he said.

'Oh,' Flora said. 'I'm sure there's nothing he can't say in my presence.'

'Please, Miss Donald,' Alec said. 'Thank you for your kind attentions but I assure I shall be quite all right.'

Flora closed the bible with a thump and stood up, setting the book and her apron back in the basket. 'I shall call again tomorrow,' she promised.

'There really is no need ...' Alec began, but she had gone, closing the door behind her with a bang that rattled the windows.

'Thank you, Sergeant,' Alec said, throwing off the rug and removing the pillows from his chair.

'She's a good-hearted woman,' Maidment said, taking the seat Flora had vacated.

'You are being ironic, I trust, Sergeant,' Alec said.

Maidment shrugged. 'Maybe I should say, a good Christian woman.' He cleared his throat. 'I've just come from speaking with Miss Penrose. She believes the ringleader was one of the men from the Shenandoah: Jennings.'

Alec nodded. A mistake. He winced and touched the lump on his head. 'He shouldn't be too hard to find. He has a broken nose.'

'That's the problem with these remote mines,' Maidment said. 'Got to take workers where they can get them.'

Alec hesitated. 'I have no proof, but I believe Jack Tehan may have been behind the robbery.'

'Why do you say that?'

'The bushrangers took something from Miss Penrose. Something very specific.'

Maidment cocked his head to one side. 'Her locket?'

'They also took a set of designs done by Miss Penrose's brother.'

Maidment raised an eyebrow. 'She didn't mention those. What are the designs for?'

Alec silently cursed himself but he'd committed now. 'An industrial design. She was taking it to Melbourne.' He paused. 'Penrose left them with me before he died and I suspect that the men who ransacked my home were possibly the same as those who held us up yesterday.'

'And why do you think Tehan is behind it?' Maidment asked.

Alec hesitated. 'He is the only person I know who knew, or at least guessed, I had them.'

Maidment huffed out a breath and pushed his hat back to scratch his head. 'Black Jack Tehan may have come with a reputation but he's done nothing I am aware of to put him on the wrong side of the law. Still, if you're sure at least one of his men is involved then that gives me the excuse to speak to him and maybe do a more thorough search of their camp, but I don't think he'll fall at my feet, confessing all.'

Alec tapped his fingers on the arm of the chair. 'This is confidential, Maidment, but would you consider it a possibility that a thing of value like that may lead someone to take another's life?'

'Are you saying Penrose may have been murdered for the plans?'

Alec shrugged. 'I don't know. It just seems a great many coincidences are all pointing to one conclusion.'

And the greatest coincidence of all was the possible involvement of Charles Cowper, but now was not the time to start throwing accusations at one of the town's most prominent citizens. The way to Cowper was through Tehan.

Maidment stared into a corner of the room for a long, long moment. 'Strange you should say that. I've just had a similar conversation with Miss Penrose. As I told her, the coroner didn't find Penrose's death suspicious and in the absence of new evidence of foul play, there's nothing I can do.' He straightened. 'I suggest both you and Miss Penrose get on with your own business and leave me to mine. Good day to you, Mr McLeod.'

After the policeman left, Alec closed his eyes, allowing himself to drowse in front of the fire as the winter evening drew in.

Another knock on the door jerked him awake again.

'If that's Flora, tell her to go away,' he said to Ian, making sure his brother understood every word.

Ian smiled. 'You don't fancy the tender ministrations of Miss Donald?'

'No.'

Ian answered the door and he heard a woman's voice at the door. He shivered as the cold air crept in dissipating the warmth.

'Shut the bloody door,' Alec said.

'My, my, Mr McLeod, you do sound out of sorts.'

Alec's heart lifted at the sound of Eliza Penrose's voice. He waved a hand at the other chair. 'Come and sit down, Eliza. Ian, can you offer Miss Penrose tea?'

Ian shot his brother an amused glance. 'The amount of tea I'm making today, I think I'll seek employment in a tea room.'

Eliza smiled as she shut the door behind her and came to stand beside the fire, rubbing her hands together. 'It is perishing out there.' She gave him a quick smile. 'It's a relief to see you up.'

Alec touched the lump on his head. 'A bit sore and sorry, but better for seeing you—' He broke off, the heat rushing to his face as the trite words fell into the space between them.

Eliza reached for his hand. 'And I'm better for seeing you.'

She curled her fingers in his, soft and slender and very, very cold. He covered her hand with both of his, trying to instil some warmth back into her.

'I can't stay.' She pulled her hand from his grip. 'I came to say I am leaving on the coach tomorrow.'

A hollow feeling formed in the pit of Alec's stomach but apart from the theft of the plans, nothing had changed. She had to make this trip to Melbourne.

Eliza glanced out the window at the lowering sky, the gloom of a winter's evening already spreading across the valley. 'I don't want to leave, but …'

'You've only been here a short time, Eliza, and you'll be safer in Melbourne. I think you should stay there.'

'But time is immaterial. I—I feel I belong here. Will brought me to Maiden's Creek for a reason.'

Her grey eyes filled with tears and he realised that the brave face she put on for the world was not matched by the grief and loneliness of a life without her brother.

He kissed her fingers, wishing he could take her in his arms. 'It need not be forever. Put some distance between you and Cowper. He may yet make a mistake. Ian and I will watch out for your interests and if you are worried for me, don't be. Cowper needs me.'

She smiled. 'You're very sure of yourself.'

'I'm very good at what I do.'

'And modest too.'

They sat in silence for a long moment, watching the crackling of the logs.

'I'm sorry I lost the plans,' she said at last.

Alec looked up at her and smiled. 'You haven't.'

'What do you mean?'

'I made a copy.'

She stared at him.

'Hidden in my bedroom. There's a floorboard under the bed. You'll find the plans and the ledger entries there.'

She stood up, thumping him lightly on the arm. 'Why didn't you say?'

'I felt it would have been irresponsible to send the only copy out of my custody without some insurance.'

She and Ian went to Alec's room and returned with the copy of the plans. She spread the pages out on the table, running her finger over the design and the calculations. She straightened and stood for a long time, chewing her bottom lip. When she looked up at him he saw an unfamiliar gleam in her eye.

'Do you have something stronger than tea?' she asked.

'Yes. In that cupboard. Pour me one too,' Alec replied.

Eliza pulled out the whisky bottle, found two glasses and poured them both a couple of fingers.

'Not with a head wound,' Ian protested but Alec held up his hand.

'I take full responsibility for my own negligence.'

Eliza paced the floor several times, taking sips of the whisky before she stopped in front of him, a small, defiant figure in a dark green gown. 'I think I know where the error lies,' she said. 'The design is predicated on cast iron. Cast iron won't take the pressure of the extra heat and energy in the firebox. It will cause a catastrophic explosion.'

Heedless of his sore head, Alec rose and joined her at the table. He reached for pencil and paper and together they redid the calculations for the Carnot cycle.

'You are wasted teaching children,' Alec said. 'Why did you see that and neither Penrose nor I did?'

'Because you were too close to it. With the right material like a wrought iron—'

'Or a steel alloy.'

She looked at him with shining eyes. 'I will redo the calculations and instruct the lawyer to lodge it with the Patents Office. Perhaps Ian can leave it with Amos Burrell for safekeeping tonight? I dare not take it away with me, although ...' A smile lifted the corners of her mouth. 'If my uncle did go to the trouble of arranging the theft of the original, then all he has is a worthless piece of paper.' She threw her arms around him. 'Alec, if we can build a prototype we'll make a fortune.'

For a fleeting moment he stiffened but her excitement was contagious and he wrapped his arms around her, drawing her into him.

'You,' he whispered into her hair, 'you will make a fortune. It's your design, not mine.'

'No. It has to be both of us. Partners.'

Distantly Alec heard the click of the back door as Ian made a tactful exit. Eliza fitted in his embrace as if she had always belonged there and her shining eyes and parted lips drew him like a magnet. He kissed her and found her lips soft and sweet and yielding. The world beyond the two of them vanished. He closed his eyes and she gave a soft sigh, returning his kiss with a passion of her own. It had been so long, so very long. She wasn't Catriona and he didn't want her to be Catriona. She was Eliza ... his Eliza.

They drew apart and she cupped his face in her hands, looking at him with wonder. 'No one has ever kissed me like you do.'

He meshed his fingers in her hair, marvelling at the silkiness of it. 'So much to teach you then.'

He tightened his arms, never wanting to let her go. She looked at him and he saw tears in her eyes. Appalled at the thought he could be the cause of distress, he released her. A tear sparkled on her lower lash and, in the light from the fire, blazed a golden trail down her cheek. He wiped it away with his thumb.

'Eliza, I'm so sorry. It's been a long time and I'm a clumsy fool.'

She laughed and caught his hand. 'You darling man, if there are tears, they are tears of happiness. I don't know what it is to love or be loved, but if this is what it feels like, I don't ever want to leave you.' She paused and the smile slipped. 'But I must go to Melbourne.'

The thought of parting from her tore at his heart. How could he protect her when she was a hundred miles away?

She smiled and touched his face, sending sparks of fire through his body. 'From the moment you knocked me into the mud, I thought you were different. Can we—dare we—'

He caught her hand, closing his eyes as he brought the palm to his lips. A hundred inadequate words jostled in his head but when it came to speaking, all he could manage was an inarticulate grunt.

She pulled her hand away. 'I have to go, Alec. Poor Ian is probably freezing outside.'

'Eliza, I ...'

She looked at him expectantly. He wondered if he could say the words he'd said to only one other person in his life.

'I ... will be waiting for you.'

She nodded. 'I will be back, Alec.'

By the time he had summoned a coherent sentence, she had gone.

I love you ...

Twenty-Two

23 July 1873
Melbourne, Victoria

It had only been a matter of weeks since Eliza had left Melbourne with hope in her heart, bound for Maiden's Creek and reunion with her brother. Now she had returned, her journey uneventful but tiring. She had no compunction in accepting her uncle's offer of accommodation at the Menzies Hotel in Bourke Street, a magnificent modern hotel and reputedly the best in Melbourne.

Installed in relative luxury with fresh linen sheets, a thick rug on the floor and a fire burning in the hearth, she should have been content, but her mind kept returning to Maiden's Creek and the people she had left behind. People she had grown fond of. People she might have even grown to love.

The bleak weather and the cold wind blowing down Collins Street reflected her mood. The shops with their bright merchandise held no interest as she trudged the crowded footpath, the paper on which she had written the address of Will's solicitor clutched tightly in her gloved hand.

Will Penrose's lawyers were to be found up a flight of stairs in a solid, respectable red brick building at the top end of Collins Street. Eliza, used to the steep paths of Maiden's Creek, took the stairs without pausing for breath and pushed open the solid cedar door to step into the plush offices of Messrs Kennedy, Bolton and Briscoe.

'Miss Penrose.' Mr Kennedy himself came out to greet her, a man in late middle age with sparse grey hair and a pallid complexion. He took her gloved hands in a firm grip and with a suitably sorrowful expression, said, 'Please accept my condolences on the death of your brother.'

'Thank you.'

'It was my great pleasure to conduct the legal work for your brother and of course his partners in the Shenandoah Mine. Have you had the pleasure of meeting Mr and Mrs Hunt?'

'No, they are still abroad.'

Kennedy ushered her into the office, pausing only to order 'tea for our guest'.

As the clerk set down the tray and poured, Kennedy said, 'Now, what can I do for you?'

Eliza laid the envelope with the copy of Will's plans on the desk. 'My brother drew up these plans for a new design of an industrial boiler,' she said. 'I would like you to lodge it with the Patents Office as soon as possible.'

Kennedy drew out the plans, frowning as he studied the calculations. 'There is a great deal of crossing out. I'm not sure the Patents Office will accept it in this form.'

'The important thing is to lodge it,' Eliza said. 'It's a copy of the original design which was recently stolen and I do not wish the stolen copy to be lodged before this one.' She paused. 'Apart from anything else, the calculations on the original are wrong. Those are the amendments you can see.'

'What does it do?' Kennedy asked.

'The improved firebox will ensure better combustion which in turn will produce hotter steam. It will be a boiler so much more efficient that it will reduce the size needed, use less fuel and have a higher energy output.'

Kennedy stared at her. 'You sound like you understand these plans. Hardly a matter for a lady such as yourself. Your brother's work, I presume?'

Eliza bit back the sharp retort. 'I do understand these matters and a friend and I have reworked the calculations to ensure the correct Carnot cycle.'

Kennedy shook his head and laughed. 'I have no idea what you are talking about, Miss Penrose, but I see the urgency and will ensure this is properly lodged this afternoon.'

Relief flooded Eliza and she thanked the lawyer.

'Is there anything else I can assist you with?' He looked at her expectantly.

'Yes, I have a concern about my brother's will. Did you handle the probate?'

'No, alas. Your uncle saw fit to use his own firm of lawyers, Prendergast and Pratt, for that.'

'But you drew up the will for him?'

'I did draw up a will for Mr Penrose at the time he entered into the business arrangements for the Shenandoah Mine.' Kennedy gave the impression he was choosing his words carefully.

Eliza took a steadying sip of the tea. 'And what were the terms of that will?'

'He left a bequest to a friend and everything else to you, his sister. It could not have been clearer.'

The cup rattled in its saucer as she set it back down on the table. 'Everything?'

'That's correct. In fact, I recall him saying quite clearly that he was pleased to be in a position to see you established for life should anything happen to him.' Kennedy shook his head. 'Sadly prophetic in the circumstances. Which is why it surprised me to hear of a second will.'

She picked up the hesitancy in the lawyer's manner and asked, 'Do you have a concern about the second will?'

'It's not uncommon for people to change their wills and he was at liberty to make another with, say, Prendergast and Pratt, or simply draw it up himself. Although that often leads to difficulties with the legality of such a document. The stories I could tell you—'

Eliza leaned forward. 'I have been told that under the terms of his last will, the one I presume was approved in court, his interest in the Shenandoah Mine passed to my uncle. All William left me was cash in hand and his personal possessions, and there was little of either.'

The man's eyebrows lifted. 'That is certainly not the document I settled with him.'

'I don't wish to sound ungrateful, Mr Kennedy. My uncle tells me that the mine has not lived up to its early promise and is worthless, that my brother did not wish to saddle me with the possible debts its failure would entail.'

Kennedy sat back in his chair, steepling his fingers. 'Really? That does surprise me. I helped your brother and Mr Hunt draw up the prospectus and there was nothing to indicate that the early promise would not be realised.'

'That is what I suspected. It seems I need your help if I am to dispute the will, Mr Kennedy.' She swallowed. 'But you should know that in my present circumstances I do not have the money to pay you immediately.'

He spread his hands. 'We are at your service, Miss Penrose. I liked your brother and if there is something I can do to alleviate your situation, then I hope I can be of help.'

'I suspect that my brother's second will may be a forgery. Is it possible to see the will that was presented for probate?'

Kennedy nodded. 'It is a matter of public record at the Supreme Court.' He studied her. 'Is there something else troubling you?"

She nodded. 'It is related to the issue with the will. I believe gold from Shenandoah is being used to bolster the returns of the Maiden's Creek Mine. I have seen the ledgers for both mines and there is a definite lift in the returns from Maiden's Creek at the same time Shenandoah is diminishing.'

She took out the papers Ian had copied and walked the lawyer through them.

He nodded. 'It certainly looks like you may be right. Are you suggesting your uncle may be stealing the gold?'

Eliza took a breath. 'Yes, and I suspect him of forging my brother's will. Thanks to the terms of my brother's second will, my uncle now has unfettered access to the mine and the gold.'

Kennedy tutted. 'Dear oh dear. This is unfortunate.' He pulled a magnificent gold watch from his waistcoat. 'I have an hour to spare. If you don't mind a short walk, we can pay a visit to the court and inspect this will. You may be able to tell me if your suspicion is correct.'

The man seemed to take an age fiddling with his coat and hat and a silver-topped ebony walking stick before he was ready to go. They traversed several blocks from Kennedy's office to the Supreme Court building on the corner of Russell and Latrobe Streets. To Eliza's irritation, Kennedy took his time, pointing out the sights of Melbourne as he went, as if they were on a guided tour not an urgent mission.

'We are getting a grand new court,' he said, gesturing with his stick down Lonsdale Street where the skeleton of an enormous building could be seen rising on a hill. 'Until then, our judiciary are somewhat pressed for accommodation. Ah, here we are.'

The present court buildings looked like they had been cobbled together with bits added when extra space was required.

The interior was a rabbit warren of corridors and doors but her guide knew the building well and the staff in the registrar's office greeted him by name. Kennedy requested to see the recent probate of one William Josiah Penrose and a folder was handed to him with strict orders about not removing documents. Kennedy waved the concerns away and led Eliza to a tall bench where he opened the file and began turning over the heavy court papers with a frustrating slowness.

'Here we are,' he said. 'Your brother's will.'

Eliza took the document from him. The body of it had been written in a clerical hand and it confirmed everything Cowper had told her. All interest in the Shenandoah Mine passed to Charles William Cowper. The rest and residue of Will's estate to his sister, Eliza Jane Penrose. No mention of the boiler plans but Cowper hadn't known about those until recently. Kennedy confirmed that the plans fell under the 'rest and residue'.

And there at the end of the document, Will's signature and the two witnesses. She drew a sharp breath: Jack Tehan and Mary Harris. She set the document down on the desk with shaking hands and stepped away.

'That's not his signature,' she said.

'What do you mean?'

She pointed at the twisting characters of the signature. 'It's close, but it's not Will's writing.' She opened her handbag, her fingers closing on the much folded and read paper she carried. 'Here … this is the last letter he wrote me. He always signed himself WJ Penrose in his letters to me. It was a joke between us.'

Kennedy unfolded the letter and set it against the signature at the bottom of the will.

'See, the W is wrong and he always looped the J,' Eliza pointed out.

Kennedy nodded. 'This is very interesting and even to my untutored eye would seem conclusive.' He refolded the letter. 'What do you want to do?'

'I want what is mine, what Will intended me to have,' Eliza said. 'Mr Kennedy, what do you need to challenge this will?'

Kennedy tapped the letter. 'I have some examples of his handwriting from correspondence I've had with him but if I could keep this for a little time, I shall find a graphologist to study this document.' He hesitated. 'It is one thing to know the document is a forgery but proving it will be a costly business.'

A heavy stone sank to the pit of Eliza's stomach. 'I understand.'

The money would have to be obtained from somewhere and she had no security for any loans.

The lawyer gathered the legal documents together and gave them back to the clerk.

On their return, Kennedy gestured for her to enter his office and shut the door.

'Do you know what may have become of the original will? Of course I advised your brother to leave it with me for safekeeping, but he insisted on taking it with him.'

Eliza shook her head. 'I can only assume that whoever forged the second will destroyed the first.'

The lawyer sat behind his desk and steepled his fingers. 'I fear you may be correct. The question is, who perpetrated such a fraud?'

Eliza stared at him. Surely it was obvious. 'Why, my uncle,' she said. 'Who else benefits the way he has done?'

'And do you believe your uncle may be responsible for the theft of the boiler plans?'

She nodded.

'Dear, dear. I have not met Mr Cowper, but this tale of duplicity concerns me, and I hate to say this of my fellows in the law, but Prendergast has some explaining to do.' The lawyer shook his head. 'Do you think your uncle will try to lodge these plans?'

'I would imagine so, no doubt using his lawyers. That's why my copy must be lodged today.'

Kennedy leaned forward. 'I am becoming extremely concerned for your safety, young lady.'

'Thank you for your concern but while my uncle believes he has the plans and the mine, I am no threat to him.'

'But if he suspects that you have uncovered his deception? I've seen gold lust before, Miss Penrose, and blood kin or not, if Charles Cowper has his eye on the gold then God help anyone who stands in his way.'

A shiver ran down Eliza's spine. 'I hope you are wrong, sir,' she said. 'But I have friends.' She glanced at the clock on the mantelpiece. There were still a couple of hours until her meeting with Mrs Wallace. 'If you will excuse me, I have an interview for a post at a school here in Melbourne this afternoon.'

They shook hands at the door and Kennedy laid his hand over hers. 'Please do not hesitate to call on my help, my dear. As I said, I liked your brother and if your suspicions are correct, it may well be his death was not accidental. You must take care.'

As she descended the stairs, Eliza allowed herself to smile. The thoroughly respectable Mr Kennedy would have been appalled and not a little concerned that after that interview she would be visiting the notorious Little Lonsdale Street.

Clutching the piece of paper bearing the scrawled address that Nell had given her, Eliza walked the few blocks from the opulence of Collins Street to Little Lon, the street of brothels, opium dens and criminals. Eliza had seen poverty in the industrial cities in England but the grim lanes and dark passages of Little Lon, even in the middle of the day, filled her with trepidation.

Nothing from the outside of the single-storey red brick cottage, one of a row of six in Casselden Place, proclaimed its purpose and she presumed that to be a promising sign that Lil's sister could be choosy about her clientele. Eliza had no doubt that the proximity to the legislative chambers of the colony attracted the prosperous and the powerful to Maggie Scott's door.

A girl hung out of the doorway of an adjoining cottage. She looked barely old enough to be out of pinafores, her skinny frame visible beneath a soiled chemise and a much-mended scarlet petticoat. Seeing Eliza glance her way, she thrust out her hip, pouted her lips and curled a lock of lank brown hair provocatively around her finger, her dead eyes willing Eliza's disapproval.

A wave of nausea washed over Eliza. She wanted to take the child home and ensure she had a bath and a decent meal. She'd read the accounts of Josephine Butler, the social reformer who campaigned for the rights of women such as this. These girls had no future, pregnant by fifteen, infected with syphilis or similar by twenty and dead before thirty.

She steeled herself and turned back to the door of Maggie Scott's house of ill repute, lifted the well-polished brass knocker and let it fall.

A maid in a conservative black dress and frilled white apron and hat answered her knock. The girl's face had been disfigured by a burn that had melted the left side like wax and Eliza had to school herself not to react. The maid bobbed a curtsey before enquiring Eliza's business. On being told she wished to speak with Mrs Scott, the maid showed Eliza into the front room. It could have been the parlour of her mother's house, filled with heavy furniture, overstuffed chairs, dead animals in glass display cabinets and copies of famous paintings.

'Who can I say is calling?' the girl asked.

Eliza gave her name. She declined the offer of the overstuffed red velvet day bed and settled into a comfortable chair beside the fire.

She did not have to wait long, and stood up as a tall woman entered the room. Maggie Scott could have passed unnoticed in the most respectable salons. As tall as her sister but slender, she wore a gown of dark blue figured satin in the latest cut, with a sizeable bustle behind and good quality lace at her wrists and neck.

Eliza held out her hand. 'Mrs Scott?'

The woman smiled and after a small hesitation, lightly touched Eliza's fingers. 'I apologise for keeping you waiting. Can I offer you some refreshment?'

Eliza declined.

Maggie Scott tilted her head to one side and considered her visitor. 'What brings you to my door? I have no need of—'

The heat rose to Eliza's cheeks as she realised she may have given the impression she had come seeking employment. 'Oh no. You mistake me. I have come to speak with one of your girls—Sissy.'

'Have you indeed. Did Lil send you?'

Eliza shook her head. 'No. My business with Sissy is personal.'

'Sissy's time is money,' Maggie Scott said.

Eliza looked around the parlour. 'It is somewhat early in the day for business, Mrs Scott. I promise you I will not be long. Sissy was acquainted with my brother and I just have some questions to ask her about Will's last days.'

'Did you say your name is Penrose? Ah yes, the man Sissy believed was going to marry her.' Maggie Scott threw back her head and laughed.

'I'm not sure what you find so amusing?'

'Because Sissy's not the first whore to be taken in by the sweet talk of a man. He would never have married her.'

'I don't know what William's intentions were and, as he is dead, I can hardly ask him, but I have every reason to believe his feelings toward Sissy were genuine,' Eliza said. 'Sissy was one of the last people to see him alive and I have a few questions for her, that's all.'

Maggie Scott put her hands on her hips and studied her for a long moment. 'Aye, well, as you say, he's dead, so what's done is done. You can see Sissy if she wishes to see you. Wait here.'

The woman swept from the room and the minutes ticked by before the maid appeared at the door.

'This way, miss,' she said.

The maid led her down a narrow corridor. Eliza counted four closed doors. The maid stopped at the last door and knocked, opening the door before whoever was inside the room responded. She stood aside for Eliza to enter.

Despite it being midday, the only light came from a narrow window, thinly disguised by a lace curtain. The window offered an unedifying view of the narrow yard of the house, flanked by brick walls that cast the room into gloom. A white iron bedstead covered in a scarlet silk bedcovering took up most of the room.

Sissy sat before a mirror at a dressing table, brushing hair an unflattering shade of blonde and clearly from a bottle. Eliza struggled to recall the girl's hair colour on their first and only meeting but would have sworn it was darker. She wore a silk peignoir over corset and petticoats in an artful arrangement, designed no doubt to charm the gentleman visitors, but seeing Eliza in the mirror, she set the brush down and rose to her feet, swinging around in a cloud of silk and lace to face her, pulling the robe closed in a fetching display of modesty.

'What are you doing here, Miss Penrose?'

Eliza held up a hand. 'You left Maiden's Creek before we had a chance to talk. I have so much to ask you.'

Sissy resumed her stool, crossed her legs and laid her hands in her lap. She waved at the bed. 'Take a seat, Miss Penrose. What do you want to ask me?'

Eliza perched on the edge of the bed. 'Can we start with why you have left Maiden's Creek?'

Sissy shrugged. 'Nothing to keep me there. And maybe I didn't want to have to put up with you asking me questions.'

'I knew nothing about you,' Eliza said. 'Will never mentioned you.'

Sissy gave a humourless laugh. 'He wouldn't have done, would he? He ran into enough trouble with that uncle of his—of yours. What he and I had was special but he had his reasons for keeping it quiet.'

Hardly quiet when the whole of Maiden's Creek knew about the affair.

Eliza leaned forward. 'Sissy, you can trust me. There are things I have discovered about my uncle. Things he has done.'

Sissy looked up. 'He hasn't hurt you, has he?'

It took Eliza a moment to get her meaning. 'No, nothing like that, but I have very good reasons not to trust him.'

'Yes, well, he stole Will's mine,' Sissy said with such certainty, Eliza caught her breath.

'Why do you say that?'

'Will told me that you were to get everything if he died. Unless we were married, but he said he would leave me some shares in the mine, even if we weren't married. After he died, I went to see old man Cowper and asked him when I could expect my shares. He laughed and said that Will had been leading me on. There weren't no shares for me or you. He had 'em all. I knew that wasn't right. But who'd take any notice of me?' Sissy curled a lock of hair around her finger. 'It was only a matter of time before …

before he worked out that the split between Will and me was a sham and I knew more than was good for me.'

'Did my uncle threaten you?'

'That one wouldn't dirty his own hands when he has a dog to do his biting for him.'

'Tehan?'

Sissy looked genuinely startled at the mention of that name. 'No, not him. That goddamned Jennings. Ugly sod with a black beard.'

Eliza's face must have revealed her revulsion because Sissy laughed.

'Met him, have you?'

'Yes.' Eliza shuddered at the memory of his filthy hands on her body. 'How did he threaten you?'

'He said what happened to Will could happen to me if I didn't leave Maiden's Creek.'

Eliza's breath caught. 'He implied Will had been murdered?'

Sissy nodded. 'Jennings caught me in the cemetery. I'd been visiting Will most days and he must have been following me. No one to hear … no one to see.' Her eyes filled with tears.

'Did he hurt you?'

She shook her head. 'He called me a dirty lying whore and said if I didn't keep my mouth shut, I would end up in the cemetery like Will.'

'So he didn't exactly say Will had been killed?'

'No, but he scared me, Miss Penrose. I didn't care about the shares. Cowper was welcome to them. I told Lil I wanted to go back to Melbourne.' She fixed Eliza with an unblinking stare. 'Did I do wrong?'

'No. You did what you had to do.'

Tears stained Sissy's cheeks and the kohl she had drawn around her eyes was beginning to smudge. 'Nothing'll bring Will back.' She swept a hand around the room. 'This is it for me. The doctor says I have consumption. I'll not make old bones. Will was well shot of me.'

In the dismal light from the window, Sissy's artfully painted face looked like that of a doll, but Eliza could see now that the fetching colour in her cheeks came from a pot, not from nature, and her eyes were strangely large and bright. If she had consumption there was little that could be done for her, except make her last days comfortable. Her heart broke for this girl who never had a chance, and her brother, who had loved her.

'I'm sorry, Sissy.' The words seemed inadequate.

'Don't be. Maggie's good to work for. Like Lil, she looks after her girls. Makes sure I see a doctor regular.'

'She knows you're sick?'

Sissy nodded. 'She's promised to send me to a place in the country when I can't work no more. I've said I want to be buried with Will, but I guess that won't be possible. Doesn't matter— we'll be together.' She cast her eyes at the ceiling and forced a smile. 'Don't look at me like that, Miss Penrose. You should know that's how it is for us working girls.'

She picked up a handkerchief from the dressing table and wiped her eyes, smudging the paint further. She coughed, pressing the handkerchief to her mouth. Eliza crouched in front of her, waiting until the coughing had finished.

Sissy twisted the square of linen stained with the tell-tale spots of blood.

'What can I do, Sissy?'

Sissy shrugged. 'Spare me your pity, Miss Penrose.'

'I think, for all his faults, my brother truly loved you,' Eliza said.

'I'd like to think that too, Miss Penrose. God knows, I loved him.'

Eliza stood up. 'Just one last thing to ask you, Sissy. Did you see Will on the night he died?'

Sissy nodded. 'He came to Lil's Place in a right state. He was ranting about Cowper and Tehan. Said there was no one in the world he could trust. Said that someone was stealing the gold from the mine and he would prove it.'

'He didn't say who?'

Sissy shook her head. 'He wouldn't even have a drink with me. Went storming out and I never saw him again.'

Eliza blinked. 'He didn't have a drink?'

'No. He may have downed one whisky, but when he walked out the door, he was sober as you and me.'

Sissy's recollection confirmed what Lil had told her: Will had not been drunk when he went up to the Maiden's Creek Mine.

Eliza took Sissy's hand. 'Thank you, Sissy.' She smiled. 'Is that really your name?'

The young woman smiled. 'I was christened Cecily Brown,' she said, 'but I've been Sissy since I was fourteen years old. I don't remember Cecily any more.' Her fingers tightened on Eliza's. 'It's been nice to talk to you. I can see Will in you. Do you miss him?'

Unbidden tears sprang to Eliza's eyes. 'Like a wound in my chest that refuses to heal.'

'I'm not so good at my words, Miss Penrose, but is there anything I can do to help you with that bastard Cowper?'

'Would you be prepared to come with me to my lawyer and sign a statement of what you just told me?'

Sissy seemed to consider this proposition for a long moment. 'I've nothing left to lose,' she said. 'I'll do that for you and for Will, but it'll have to be tomorrow. Got to get Mrs Scott to agree to give me the time off.'

'I'm staying at the Menzies,' Eliza said.

'Ooh, lah-de-dah,' Sissy said with a smile. 'Give me the address for your lawyer and I'll meet you there at ten tomorrow morning. I'd like to see old man Cowper brought down. My sister's husband was working in his mine up in Bendigo. When he broke his leg, Cowper turned him out without a penny in compensation.'

'I'm sorry. What did he do?'

Sissy laughed. 'Mrs Scott employs him to ensure a gentleman does not outstay his welcome and my sister works for a seamstress in Flinders Lane. Between them they manage.' She turned back to her mirror, squinting at the damage caused by her tears. 'Now, if you'll excuse me, I got to get ready for my callers. I'll see you tomorrow, Miss Penrose.'

Maggie Scott waited in the parlour, working on a piece of embroidery. She looked up as Eliza entered the room, setting her needlework in her lap. 'Did you get what you came for?'

'I did, and I'd be grateful if you could give her some time off tomorrow.'

'What for?'

'I've asked her to come with me to my lawyer and make a statement.'

Maggie Scott considered her for a long moment. 'Very well. Was there something else, Miss Penrose?'

'Yes, she told me she is ill. She has friends in Maiden's Creek who would help with her care when the time comes. Be sure to let us know.'

Maggie nodded. 'My sister knows Sissy's not long for the world. I write to Lil every week and report on her health.'

Feeling lighter than she had for a long time, Eliza stepped back into the foetid lane. The girl still stood in the doorway of the neighbouring house, her thin arms blue with cold. Eliza had deliberately not brought much money with her on this excursion to Little Lon, but what she did have she gave to the waif with orders to hide it from her employer and buy herself a decent feed.

Eliza's appointment with Mrs Wallace had been set for four o'clock, which gave Eliza time to return to the hotel to wash and change. Her visit to Little Lon had left her feeling soiled and depressed. She had no doubt the fancy politicians from Spring Street and the businessmen from Collins Street used and abused the powerless women and girls of the brothels and the streets and left them to die too young.

Sissy had probably been more fortunate than most—she had employment in a good establishment with a madam who looked after her girls—but it remained a degrading and dehumanising occupation.

Eliza eked out her shillings for a cab ride to the address in East Melbourne, which proved to be an elegant villa of recent build. She was admitted to a spacious front room by a neatly dressed maid. A tall, slender woman in her early forties stood to greet her with outstretched hand.

'Edwina Wallace,' she said. 'Welcome to Ormiston House, or as I should now more properly call it, East Melbourne Academy.'

'It's a lovely house,' Eliza said, looking up at the gilded archi-traves and heavy velvet drapes.

'Built by my husband. Sadly, he only lived long enough to enjoy it for a couple of years.' Edwina Wallace sighed. 'And bills still have to be paid so I decided to pursue the opportunity for the advancement of education for young women. One day, Miss Penrose, women will be admitted to study medicine or law and the walls of the august University of Melbourne will shudder with horror.'

Eliza smiled. 'I once told my father that I wished I could be an engineer like my brother. I thought the poor man would have an apoplexy. He said he should never have allowed me to share my brother's lessons, it gave me ideas.'

'Ideas, Miss Penrose. We should all have ideas! Now, do take a seat and I shall send for tea.'

The interview with Mrs Wallace went well. Eliza found the lady to be intelligent and passionate in her pursuit of education for women. The school had just twenty pupils and only one other teacher apart from the principal.

Mrs Wallace perused Eliza's credentials, lingering on the glowing reference from the ladies' academy in Devon. 'This all looks perfectly satisfactory,' she said, passing the letter back to Eliza. 'I would like to offer you a position, but I sense a restlessness in you, my dear.'

Surprised by the insight of the woman, Eliza said, 'I have unfinished business in Maiden's Creek, Mrs Wallace.'

'Then you must see to that business, Miss Penrose. If the position remains unfilled when it has reached a satisfactory conclusion, then it is yours.'

Eliza rose to her feet and held out her hand. 'Thank you, Mrs Wallace. I will let you know.'

Despite her exhaustion, Eliza lay awake long into the night, listening to the sounds of the city around her, so different from the steady beat of the Maiden's Creek stampers. She had wanted desperately to believe some good of her uncle but the evidence of her eyes, the forged signature on the will, told their own story.

She rolled onto her side and drew her knees up to her chest. The betrayal of Will and herself was so raw she wanted to rush back to Maiden's Creek and confront Cowper about his perfidy, but Mr Kennedy had been right: she had to build the evidence for her case first.

Forgery. She turned the word over in her mind. Where had she heard the word 'forger' in her time at Maiden's Creek?

She was just beginning to doze when it came to her.

Tom Harris had said, 'I hear things. No one pays me much mind so I hears what they say and I heard Mr Tehan telling the master his da were a forger.'

Tehan's father had been a forger. Had he taught his son some of the tricks of the trade?

As if the forged will were not enough, there were the stolen plans and, most devastating, the increasingly suspicious circumstances of her brother's death.

Tehan and Cowper … Whichever way she looked at it, the two names seemed to go together. She had no choice—she had to return to Maiden's Creek.

Twenty-Three

31 July 1873

Alec McLeod did not make a good patient. Unfortunately, it took a few days for the dizziness to subside and Alec found he could not stand upright for more than a few minutes without the world coming up to meet him. The doctor seemed unconcerned and told him it would pass, it just needed time and rest.

In the meanwhile, the number of explosions coming from the mine during the week concerned him. The practice had always been to spend the week preparing the face of the mine wall and laying the explosives to go off on Saturday. That gave Sunday for the dust to settle ready for extraction and clearance to start on Monday. It was a well-tried and relatively safe routine.

Ian reported that Cowper was in a foul mood and anyone with any sense avoided him. He had Trevalyn in his office on several occasions but Ian had not been able to make out what was said and, as Cowper appeared to be going out of his way to find fault with Ian's work, he judged it prudent to keep his head down. Like Alec, he had noticed the explosions but when he asked the miners they just shook their heads.

Despite Dr Sims's strongly voiced protests, on the Thursday after the hold-up, Alec donned his heavy coat and boots and stomped through the rain up the hill to the mine. A quick inspection confirmed his growing concern. Stooped over in a tunnel that did not have the height to accommodate him, Alec made quick notes. In his short absence the work on the deep lead had progressed faster than he would have considered prudent, the mine workings hastily shored up with the sugar gum props, and the explosives team were already preparing holes in the wall that were too shallow to be truly effective. Even more worrying was the water ingress. They were at creek level and the continual rain meant the groundwater was rising. It pooled at his feet, several inches deep.

'This is wrong, Trevalyn.'

'Cowper's orders,' Trevalyn said. 'He wants at least two breakthroughs a week. You're the one who has to have it out with him. He won't listen to me. I just have to do the best I can.'

Alec stormed into Cowper's office without waiting to be invited. He found the mine manager in earnest conversation with Jack Tehan. Both men looked up, startled, as the door banged open.

'Tehan!' The lump on the side of his head throbbed, reminding him who he suspected of being responsible for the hold-up. 'Just the man I want to talk to.'

The Tasmanian rose to his feet. 'I heard about the incident on the road, McLeod. How's the head?'

Alec touched the still tender but healing wound above his right ear. 'Fine,' Alec snapped. 'No thanks to you.'

'Me? I had nothing to do with it.'

'No? It was your men, wasn't it? I recognised that thug with the black beard.'

'So Maidment said, but Jennings is long gone. If he's chosen to take to the road, it's nothing to do with me.'

'It's everything to do with you, Tehan. Where are Will Penrose's plans?'

'What are you implying, McLeod?'

'I'm saying that you staged the hold-up to get Will Penrose's plans for a new boiler.'

'Mind what you're saying, McLeod,' Cowper said. 'You can't go making allegations like that.' He jerked his head at the door. 'Leave us, Tehan. We'll talk later.'

Tehan had to pass Alec to reach the door and as he did so, Alec grabbed his sleeve. 'Do you know what Jennings could have done to Eliza?'

Tehan looked at him with what seemed to be genuine bemusement. 'I told you, I had nothing to do with it, McLeod. Now unhand me.'

Alec released his grip and watched as Tehan left the building, slamming the door behind him.

Ian looked up from his ledger and his hand moved in the sign they had developed between them for *What's happening?*

Alec shook his head as Cowper closed the door.

'You know, I thought it might be to my advantage to have a company clerk who is deaf, but it seems I underestimated your brother.'

'Everyone underestimates him,' Alec said.

'And you, McLeod.' Cowper moved behind his desk. 'My niece has, as you know, returned to Melbourne, and I hope that will be the end of her meddling and poking her nose into matters which are none of her business. Grief clouds a person's judgement. I would not like to see you and Ian make the mistake of seeing shadows and conspiracies where there are none.'

Alec controlled his anger with difficulty. 'If there is no gold at Shenandoah, then why are you still wasting your efforts up there?'

'As I have repeatedly told Eliza, I feel I am honour-bound to do so until the Hunts are in a position to make a decision on the future of the mine,' Cowper said. 'Penrose knew the mine would just be an anvil on his sister's back so he left his interest to me. Plain and simple. The will is quite legal and duly proved. Do we understand each other, McLeod?'

Alec bit back the retort that rose to his lips and changed the subject. 'I have a more immediate concern, Cowper. The deep lead ... we're progressing too fast and we've a problem with water ingress.'

'Just get some more pumps down there,' Cowper said. 'The shareholders are getting anxious. They are beginning to see some return on their investment, and are keen for more. I've assured them there is good gold-bearing quartz in the deep lead and I want it out as soon as possible. You are moving too slowly.'

'I will not risk the safety of the miners.'

'McLeod!' Cowper stood nearly a head shorter than Alec but he seemed to inflate with anger. 'You forget yourself. I have over-looked your unfortunate liaison with my niece and I will excuse your impertinence today on account of your recent injury, but don't ever presume to come in here and tell me my business again, or you—and your brother—can find yourself other employment. Without references.'

'My brother is as fine a bookkeeper as you will find anywhere, Cowper.'

'Then he should learn to keep his mouth shut.'

As if conscious he was being talked about, Ian, in the outer office, raised his head, his brow furrowed as he cast his brother another questioning glance.

'You can threaten me all you like,' Alec said, 'but not my brother.'

'Get back to work. I want my orders carried out, or …'

'Or?'

'I will be looking for a new mine superintendent.'

Alec gave a hollow laugh. 'Good luck with your search, Cowper. There aren't that many of us. Unless you are thinking of Tehan?'

'Get out.'

Alec slammed out of the office, causing the glass panes to rattle.

Ian slipped off his stool and caught him by the arm. 'What was that about?'

'Nothing. Professional disagreement. Get back to work, Ian. Don't give the man the satisfaction of finding an excuse to fire you.'

'Fire me? Why?'

'We'll talk tonight.'

'Where are you going?'

'Down the mine. I have to see what can be done to ensure the men's safety and get the water out of the workings.'

Alec spent a frustrating day trying to rectify Cowper's meddling. In addition to substituting the reliable Huon pine for the brittle sugar gum, Cowper had increased the spacing between the supports. Alec got home late, covered in mud, exhausted from the effort of trying to bring some sense to Cowper's orders.

'I think Cowper knows,' he told Ian as he choked down dinner.

'About what?'

'That we suspect him of stealing the gold from the Shenandoah.'

Ian paled. 'What's he going to do?'

'He's warned me off. Behave or we both lose our jobs.' He rubbed his hand over his eyes. His head throbbed. 'I'm sorry, Ian. I should never have involved you.'

'I involved myself,' Ian said. 'But Eliza has gone and we have to survive in this town. It's nothing to do with us. Perhaps Cowper is right, we should just—'

'Just forget what we know? Forget that the man is no better than a thief? Forget that he is quite possibly a murderer?'

Ian looked at the floor.

Alec pushed back from the table and circled it, laying a hand on his brother's shoulder. 'Sorry, Ian,' he murmured, knowing Ian would sense rather than hear the words. He squatted beside the younger man, forcing him to look at him. 'You're right, it's nothing to do with us.'

'But we just wanted to help Eliza,' Ian said.

'And we've done all we can. I have enough problems at the mine without worrying about things I have no control over.'

Ian studied his brother's face for a long moment. 'Do you love her?'

Alec tried to laugh but there was no humour in his heart, just an aching loneliness. He shrugged and straightened, going in search of the whisky bottle.

Ian pushed his chair back and caught the bottle as Alec lifted it from the cupboard. 'This is not the answer to your problems, Alec.'

'Aye, but it numbs the pain.' He wrestled the bottle from his brother's grip and set it down on the table. Placing both hands on the table top, he looked up at his brother. 'You asked if I love her and the answer is I don't know.'

Ian touched his arm. 'Yes, you do.'

'For all the good it'll do me. She's in Melbourne and I'm here. No, best I forget her.' He picked up the bottle. 'And this helps.'

Ian shook his head. 'Don't give up, Alec.'

'Aye, well, you'd know all about love. How are things with Miss Susan Mackie?"

Ian blushed and Alec clapped him on the shoulder. 'Don't presume to lecture me on love, little brother.'

Long after the light beneath Ian's door had been extinguished, Alec remained by the dying embers of the fire, Windlass on his knee and the bottle of whisky beside him. Ian had seen what he had been denying to himself. There was so much he wanted to say to Eliza: how much he missed her; how he wanted to hold her again; to feel her heart beating against his; and above all, the ache of his own loneliness.

Twenty-Four

Over the next three days, the rain continued and Maiden's Creek rose, overflowing its banks and sloshing over the ramshackle bridges. Down in the mine, the pumps were working at their maximum to keep the water level manageable but it left the men working in ankle-deep mud and slush in the deep lead.

Alec had ordered extra shoring for the new area but he had to make do with the brittle sugar gum, not the sturdy Huon or even the mountain ash he needed so badly. To compensate, he placed the posts closer together, prompting an angry tirade from Cowper about the cost of the timber and a forceful directive to space the props further apart, which he ignored.

On the positive side, the quartz seam they were following had begun to show some genuine promise, with the glint of gold visible in the light of the lantern Trevalyn held up to inspect the exposed rock face. He ran his hand along the tell-tale line of yellow, glinting in the light. 'That'll please Cowper.'

'Aye, but we'll leave it till morning before we tell him. I want to be sure this part of the lead is secure before we go blowing any more of it.'

Trevalyn nodded and the two men parted.

Dark clouds hung over the town, obscuring the tops of the hills around them as Alec walked up the hill to the mine the next morning. He found Trevalyn deep in conversation with Cowper at the entrance to the mine adit.

'Ah, McLeod.' The mine manager had a glint in his eye that Alec did not like. 'I've just been down to the workings. Trevalyn has shown me the gold in the seam we are following. Good solid gold. I want it out.'

Alec cast his foreman a sharp glance. 'We need to move carefully. The rock in that area is unstable.'

'Nonsense. That face is to be blown today.'

Alec bridled. 'It's not ready to be blown. We need another day at least.'

'Today, McLeod.'

Alec turned to Trevalyn. 'Back me up, Trevalyn.'

'Whatever the boss wants,' the foreman mumbled.

Finding no support, Alec turned back to Cowper. 'The holes aren't deep enough to set the explosives yet.'

'Then make them deep enough,' Cowper said and stalked off, avoiding the puddles that had formed in the courtyard.

Alec glanced at the mine manager's office, anger and frustration rising in his chest. 'You'd think he didn't care about the safety of the mine. And you—you know what he's asking is dangerous.'

Trevalyn licked his lips and his eyes slid sideways. 'I've a wife and three children, McLeod. I need this job.'

'So I'm on my own,' Alec said, fixing his gaze on the administration building.

'What are you going to do?'

'Try to reason with him.'

Trevalyn placed a warning hand on his sleeve. 'If you see him now, you'll say something you'll regret.'

'My father died in a mine, Trevalyn. I won't have the mine's safety compromised for one man's greed.' He shook off the warning hand and stormed into Cowper's office, slamming the door behind him.

Cowper rose from the desk, his face flushed. 'I've told you before. You are not to enter my office without knocking,' he roared.

Alec leaned his hands on the desk and faced the manager across the expanse of cedar. 'And you're interfering in matters that you are not qualified to make decisions on.'

'I've had years of working in mines, McLeod.'

'Then you should know that the spacing of the timber supports, the quality of the wood you have chosen and this mad decision to blow the face prematurely is reckless, if not negligent.'

'Enough.' The tone of Cowper's voice had dropped to glacial. 'I will not be spoken to in this manner. As far as I am concerned, McLeod, this insubordination is the final straw. You are fired.'

Alec straightened, his anger a roaring inferno. 'I resign,' he said. 'I will not have the safety of this mine compromised by your penny-pinching greed.'

Cowper shot a glance at the outer office where Ian's high desk was unattended. 'You and your brother. Don't think I don't know the stories you are spreading. Slanderous lies.'

His words doused Alec's anger like cold water. 'What do you mean?'

'Some ridiculous tale about how I am using gold from Shenandoah to falsely inflate the returns from Maiden's Creek.'

'They're not lies and you know it,' Alec said. 'You've been stealing the gold from Shenandoah for months. Anyone who knows what they're looking at can see the correlation. The mine inspector—'

Cowper laughed. 'Only sees what I pay him to see.'

Alec's blood ran cold. The mine inspector was in Cowper's pocket? That would explain why the theft seemed so blatant: the only person who would notice was paid to turn a blind eye.

Before he could think of an adequate response, an explosion shook the building.

Alec glared at Cowper. 'Too soon,' he said. 'You're an idiot.'

'Get out, McLeod, and don't think for a minute you get a reference from me.'

Alec's lip curled. 'I don't need your reference. Ian and I will do just fine. Tell me where he is and we'll collect our things and be gone.'

'I sent him down to do an inventory of the fuses.'

'You sent Ian down the mine?'

'Yes. He regularly takes inventories for me.'

'Knowing you were about to blow it?'

Cowper's gaze shifted to Ian's empty desk and his moustache twitched. 'He's safe enough.'

Alec ran across the courtyard and down the long tunnel to the main cavern. A haze of dust hung in the air above the mine shaft, a testament to the recent explosion. He went straight to the storeroom but it was locked and empty. He asked the men working in the cavern if they had seen his brother.

'Aye, he asked to see the new workings so Trevalyn took him down,' one of the men said.

Alec flung himself onto the ladder, half-sliding to the level of the deep lead. His nostrils filled with cloying dust and the smell of cordite. The powder monkeys were tucked into the cubby, their faces covered with cloths.

'Where's Ian?' Alec yelled.

'What did you say?'

'My brother.'

'I think they've gone forward to check on the fall,' the man replied.

Alec glanced down the tunnel. It turned a corner to follow the seam, which minimised the impact of the blast, but the air was still thick with dust. He let out a breath, seeing the muffled light that indicated the path of the miners, the faint glow disappearing as they rounded the corner.

Curiosity. It had got Ian into trouble before, just as it had led him to re-examine the figures for the two mines that had unmasked the theft of the gold from the Shenandoah.

Holding a dampened kerchief to his nose and mouth and with head bowed to avoid the beams, Alec started down the corridor after his brother, following the sound of muffled voices ahead of him and ... something else. He paused, every nerve in his body tingling with a miner's instinct. He laid his hand against the wall and his blood ran cold. The vibration in his fingertips grew and there it was again—a faint knocking sound, like the tap-tap of a small hammer.

He straightened, his ears straining in the dark as the knocking became louder. A definite rapping as if the hammers of the Knockers were beating out a warning.

'Get out!' Alec yelled.

A cry came from the end of the tunnel as the miners, sensitive to the nuances of the mine, also picked up the sound.

The timbers set in the mine for the purpose of warning the miners of a shift in the earth let out a warning growl that was followed by the roar and crash of tumbling rocks. Alec turned as the ceiling came down just feet from where he had been standing. The impact knocked him flat and he lay in the dark, choking on the dust and debris falling around him.

Coughing, he got to his knees as men ran forward with lanterns. Strong hands helped him to his feet and he hunched over, hands on his knees, gasping for breath as the light illuminated a miner's worst fear: the tunnel ahead was now completely blocked with dirt and rocks.

'Which team is working down there?'

'Morgan's team,' a man said.

Alec closed his eyes. David Morgan had four children. George Tregloan, who had stepped in to help Eliza on the night of the dance, was newly married. And then there was Marsh, the dour Yorkshireman with his brood of youngsters. And Trevalyn ... and Ian.

Alec thought for a moment he would be sick. Five men trapped by the fall of rubble. At best the fall only took up the tunnel to the dog leg, leaving the site where the men were working clear, but with no air and rising water ... The last part of the tunnel may have been shored up with sugar gum but the supports were closer together, the ceiling bracing tighter. That thought gave him hope that the men at the far end of the tunnel had survived.

Conscious of shouts from above, he looked around at the circle of filthy faces.

'What do we do, boss?' one of the men asked.

'We start clearing the rubble,' Alec said. 'We'll need every able-bodied man and boy.'

'McLeod!'

He closed his eyes at the sound of Cowper's voice coming from above him. The mine manager had to be faced.

Cowper waited at the head of the shaft, where rescue teams were moving into action. 'How bad is it?'

Alec gave a succinct report on the collapse and the five trapped men.

'Are they alive?'

'We have no way of knowing,' he said. 'If they are, the best we can do is clear a way to them as fast as we can, before they run out of oxygen.'

'Do whatever is needed,' Cowper said and walked away.

Alec rallied the rescue team and the operation began. At least they now had the new boiler and engine available to lower buckets down the shaft and operate water pumps. That would help, but it was still hot, muddy, manual labour. He lent his own strength to the effort, his hands bleeding from pulling the jagged rocks away. It was only when someone tapped him on the shoulder that he stopped.

'Cowper wants you in his office,' the young lad behind him said.

Alec wiped his hands on his trousers and nodded, suddenly conscious of his own exhaustion. It took a supreme effort to climb the ladders out of the shaft and he was surprised to emerge into darkness. The yard bustled with activity. A crowd had gathered at the gate to the mine and lights blazed from the crib room, where it looked like the women had set up a kitchen. The scent of fresh bread and soup drifted from that direction, reminding Alec he hadn't eaten since breakfast.

In the manager's office, Cowper was not alone. Osborne Russell and Sergeant Maidment were at the table, poring over plans of the mine. Angus Mackie sat at the desk going through a pile of papers.

'You sent for me, Cowper.' Alec was in no mood for niceties.

Cowper looked up and his eyes gleamed with a cold hatred that chilled Alec to the bone.

Mackie rose to his feet. 'Mr McLeod,' he began in the voice of one about to deliver a lecture. 'I am shocked—shocked. Such a callous disregard for the safety of a mine. I should order Sergeant Maidment to arrest you here and now.'

Alec ran a hand over his eyes, not certain he had heard the man correctly. 'What do you mean, callous disregard? Everything I have done is for the safety of the mine.'

Mackie held up a stack of papers. 'These are purchase orders for the timber used in the shoring of the mine. Sugar gum! You have used sugar gum. Even I know that is a wood unsuitable for mine supports.'

Alec straightened. 'I never ordered sugar gum. My orders were always for Huon pine. The order for sugar gum came from another source.' He glanced at Cowper but the man's face revealed nothing.

Mackie stabbed a finger at the topmost paper. 'Is that your signature?'

Alec crossed to the desk and picked up the paper. It was indeed a purchase order for sugar gum for use in shoring the mine and the signature at the bottom of the paper appeared to be A McLeod, but Alec had never seen this paper before. The signature may have been a passable replica of his but he had never signed it. Ian could have told them it was not genuine but Ian was not here.

'And then there is the matter of the spacing of the shoring,' Mackie said, taking the forged order back from him.

'Those were Cowper's orders, not mine,' Alec protested, the red mist of rage starting to film his eyes. 'Trevalyn can confirm—'

But Trevalyn was not here either.

'And the ordering of the explosion that caused the collapse?' Russell spoke for the first time.

'That was Cowper,' Alec said.

Everyone turned to look at him. Cowper assumed an expression of affronted shock. 'I deny I gave such an order.'

'Can anyone corroborate your story?' Russell asked.

'Trevalyn,' Alec said, uselessly. He scanned the grave faces of his interlocutors and saw no softening. Only Maidment's eyes, watchful and assessing, offered him any sympathy.

His gaze came to rest, unblinking, on Cowper. He had called the man ruthless and now he knew just how ruthless. With the only witness to Cowper's orders among the trapped men, the mine manager would make sure the blame for the entire collapse would rest on Alec's shoulders.

Osborne Russell regarded Alec over the top of his glasses. Alec had always found Russell a reasonable and thoughtful man to deal with but the banker shook his head. 'These are serious allegations, McLeod. I don't know what to think.'

'Just leave me to do my job and get the men out, then I will more than answer them to your satisfaction,' Alec said.

Russell glanced at Cowper and shook his head. 'I think in the circumstances, Mr Cowper has every right to relieve you of that responsibility, McLeod. He informs us that he terminated your position this morning.'

Cowper straightened. 'McLeod had no business being in the mine.'

'I went to fetch my brother. *He* had no business being down there and now he is trapped, possibly dead. Do you expect me to just leave him? No … I am not leaving.'

'You are not required. Trevalyn's offsider, Williams, is quite capable of seeing to the rescue effort.'

'At least let me help with the digging.'

Cowper glared at him. 'I don't want you anywhere near the mine. Is that understood, McLeod? Get off my property now or I will request Maidment and his men remove you bodily. Maybe a night or two in the gaol cells will make you reconsider your negligent conduct.'

Maidment stepped forward and laid a hand on Alec's sleeve. 'Go home and get some rest, McLeod, you look dead on your feet.'

The floodgates of anger burst and Alec swept the contents of Cowper's desk to the floor. 'You bastard. Maidment, ask this charlatan about the Shenandoah Mine, ask him about the stolen gold.' He paused, his chest heaving. 'Ask him who killed William Penrose.'

'Enough!' Russell roared. 'There is a time and place for the airing of grievances and this is not it. The priority is getting those men out alive.'

'One of those men is my brother!'

'Get out, McLeod. Go and get some rest and we'll discuss matters when those men are back with us—alive or dead. I'm sorry Ian is trapped, but there's nothing more you can do here,' Russell said.

Cowper turned to the policeman. 'Maidment, remove this man. He is trespassing.'

'This is your doing, Cowper,' Alec cried. 'Yours! I warned you time and time again that you were compromising the safety of the mine. If my brother dies, I will hold you responsible and I will see you pay.'

Cowper's stony countenance did not twitch. 'You gentlemen are all witnesses to the fact this man has threatened me.'

Alec took a step toward the mine manager and swung at him with a fist honed on the rough streets of Wishaw. Cowper managed to avoid the worst of the impact but Alec connected with his nose and he staggered back with a howl of pain, blood pouring from between his fingers.

At the sight of the blood, Alec's fury subsided. The impact had jarred his hand and he shook it, mortified that he had lost control of himself.

'Get him out,' Cowper yelled. 'I want him in a cell, Maidment. A cell!'

Maidment stepped forward, holding up his hands. 'Enough. This isn't helping. Come with me, McLeod. Let these men get on with the job at hand.'

Outside, the cold air hit Alec like a dousing of water. He collapsed against the wall of the building, his head in his hands.

Maidment touched his arm. 'I'm not throwing you in the cells, McLeod, but I want you to go home and stay there. I heard what was said. I know you and I know Cowper. The truth will come out, but for now, you need to stay out of Cowper's way and out of trouble, understood?'

Alec nodded, suddenly too weary to even think straight.

He headed for the gate. Among the crowd he recognised Morgan and Tregloan's wives. Mrs Morgan held a fretful baby on her hip while a small child clutched at her skirts.

She stepped in front of him, her hands on her hips, her eyes anxious. 'What's happening, Mr McLeod?'

How could he answer? 'Everything that can be done is being done,' he said.

'Are they alive?' Mrs Tregloan asked, hope bright in her eyes.

'I hope so. The chances are good but we won't know until we've shifted more of the rubble.'

'Why aren't you down there?' A man's voice, angry and frustrated.

'Is it true you've been sacked?'

Alec turned to confront John Butcher, the owner of the *Maiden's Creek Chronicle*, who had notebook and pencil in hand.

A murmur went around the crowd.

'The priority is getting our loved ones out of there, my own brother among them,' Alec said. 'Now excuse me, I must get some rest.'

He dragged his weary feet down the path to his cottage and unlocked the door, slamming it behind him. He found the whisky bottle where he had last concealed it. Ian would not approve.

Ian injured, afraid and in the dark.

Ian ... dead.

Windlass butted his head against Alec's shaking hand and he picked the cat up. 'Not dead,' he said. 'I don't—I won't believe he's dead.'

Windlass wriggled free and Alec poured a glass of the whisky, downing it in one draught. The liquor burned his throat and he felt the fire course through his veins.

He looked at the hand that held the glass: black with dirt, the fingernails torn and ragged, blood welling from cuts he hadn't even noticed. He poured water into the wash basin in his bedroom and tried his best to remove the dirt from his face and hands, but he just seemed to turn the water to mud and drive the dirt deeper into the pores of his skin.

He stripped off his filthy clothes and had another go at washing before slumping into the chair beside the unlit fire with the whisky bottle, too tired to do anything except brood on the injustice of his situation and how he would answer the charges that would be brought against him.

If Ian were here, he would have some wise counsel, some sharp words that would bring sense to Alec's world.

Alec had lost everyone else he cared about—his parents, his wife, his child. He couldn't lose Ian. That would be unthinkable.

He poured another glass. And another.

Twenty-Five

30 July 1873

Eliza leaned her head against the woodwork of the swaying coach and closed her eyes. Her fellow passengers, all as tired and put out as she, also drowsed in the dark. It had taken thirty-six hours for the coach to make the eighteen-hour journey. The heavy winter rains had turned the road into a quagmire and the boggy ground into a waterway. The poor horses had to be changed several times and that had slowed the coach even further.

They rattled to a halt. Eliza peered around the leather shutter, her heart leaping at the light burning on the verandah of the Shady Creek Hotel. Warm food, warm water and a warm bed beckoned.

The coachman threw open the door and lowered the steps, helping the stiff and weary passengers into the chill night air. Eliza placed her hands in the small of her back and stretched. Tomorrow she would be back in Maiden's Creek with all the information she had discovered. She could hardly wait to share it with Alec.

As she stepped into the parlour where Mrs Gulliver was setting out bowls of hot soup and fresh bread, a burly red-headed man rose from one of the benches.

'Miss Penrose.'

Eliza smiled at the sight of the coachman's familiar face. 'Amos. How good to see you.'

Something was amiss. Amos Burrell shifted his weight and scratched his stubbled chin. 'You won't have heard,' he said.

'Heard what?'

'There's been an accident at the mine.'

'When?'

'Tuesday morning.'

'Alec?' The name came out in a hoarse whisper.

Amos Burrell shook his head. 'No, but his brother and four others are trapped below. There was a collapse …'

Eliza subsided onto one of the benches, too tired to comprehend what the man had just told her. 'The trapped men … are they alive or dead?' she said between stiff lips.

'No one knows.'

'Alec must be desperate—' Seeing Amos's frown, a cold fear clutched her heart. 'What else has happened?'

'Cowper fired McLeod, just before the collapse. He's holed up in his cottage. No one's seen him since Tuesday night and the whole town is blaming him for the collapse.'

She stared at Burrell. 'No—Alec couldn't … he wouldn't.'

'You and I know that, Miss Penrose, but there's a lot of angry folk in town who want to see the blame placed somewhere and McLeod's been nicely set up to take it.'

'My uncle,' Eliza said with bitterness.

Amos nodded. 'They say McLeod had been ordering in shoddy wood for the supports and pushing through with the blasting when it wasn't safe.'

Eliza buried her head in her hands. All her excitement at the prospect of returning to Maiden's Creek evaporated. She was returning to a disaster of monumental proportions.

1 August 1873

The remaining miles to Maiden's Creek took all the following day and it had gone dark by the time the coach drew to a halt outside the Empress Hotel.

'What'll you do?' Burrell asked Eliza as he handed down her bag.

'I don't know.' In truth, she didn't feel able to return to her uncle's, not knowing what she had discovered in Melbourne.

'There's a bed at our place,' Burrell said, 'and Netty'll be pleased to see you.'

Eliza nodded, grateful in the knowledge she still had friends in the town. Netty's welcome was everything she needed, a warm hug, hot tea and a bowl of fragrant stew from the huge pot bubbling on the stove.

Netty poured her own cup of tea and sat down at the table. 'You heard about the accident? I suppose Amos told you?'

Eliza nodded. 'Is there any more news?'

'No. They've been down there for near on three days.' She paused. 'People are saying ... well, they're saying that they don't expect they'll be found alive.'

Eliza ran a hand across her eyes. 'And Alec?'

'No one's seen him since your uncle threw him out. Everyone's saying he's responsible and Cowper sacked him for his incompetence.' Her face crumpled. 'Alec, of all people! It's lies, of course.'

Eliza's blood ran cold. Ian possibly dead, Alec disgraced and herself conveniently banished to Melbourne. While certainly not everything could be blamed on Cowper, she felt that he must have guessed that she was getting uncomfortably close to the truth of his duplicity and she couldn't have done it without help. Alec was being punished for helping her.

Netty hauled the pot off the stove and placed it in a basket on the table. 'I was just going to take this up to the mine,' she said. 'They've men from the whole district working around the clock.'

'I'll come with you,' Eliza said. She gestured at her travelling bag, 'Can I beg a bed off you, Netty?'

'Of course, but don't you wish to return to your uncle?'

'I never want to set foot in his house again.' Eliza gave her friend a quick summary of her discovery regarding the will.

Netty shook her head. 'I always felt there was something not right about that. But that's for tomorrow. Can you help me here?' She lifted the basket with the pot of stew as Eliza wrapped one of Netty's shawls over her head and shoulders. In the dark, she wouldn't be recognised.

An ominous silence hung over the town. Every stamper battery in the valley had been shut down as a mark of respect. Lights blazed from the Maiden's Creek Mine, flickering as figures passed in front of them. At the gate, a small crowd waited, huddled around a makeshift brazier with tin mugs of tea in their hands.

'Any news?' Netty asked.

One of the men shook his head. 'Nah. Word is McLeod was taking shortcuts with the mine props. He'd better keep his head down. If those men are dead, he'll be too.'

Eliza's stomach lurched. 'Where is he?'

'Hiding in his cottage,' the man replied. 'No one's seen him since Cowper threw him out.'

'And him with his brother one of 'em that's trapped,' one of the women said. She peered at Eliza. 'Here, ain't you Eliza Penrose?'

The crowd moved, cutting her away from Netty's side. They circled her and a man grabbed her arm.

'This is your doing,' he said. 'I saw you the day you came poking your nose around the mine.' He looked around the crowd. 'You know what they say, never let a red-headed woman near a mine or disaster will befall.'

Eliza shook off the hand. 'Don't be ridiculous.'

'You and McLeod. You've both doomed this mine,' another woman screamed.

Eliza scanned the dirty, strained faces, looking for sympathy, finding none.

'That's enough! Let Miss Penrose pass.'

The crowd fell silent and moved away from Eliza as Jack Tehan swung off his horse. Leading the horse with one hand, he tucked the other under Eliza's elbow and propelled her through the gates.

'I thought you'd left Maiden's Creek,' he said.

'That would have pleased you,' Eliza said, pulling her arm from his guiding hand.

'Me? Nothing to do with me.' He glanced at the administration building. 'Does your uncle know you're here?'

'Not yet. He has enough to concern him. I've just arrived in town. What are you doing here?'

Tehan shrugged. 'See what help I can be.'

Netty had pushed her way through the crowd, huffing under the weight of the heavy basket. She thrust it at Tehan. 'If you want to help. You can carry that to the crib hut.'

Tehan hefted the basket and, still leading his horse, crossed the courtyard. A light glowed from the mine's adit and the sound of men's voices and the rumble of carts bringing the detritus out echoed dully around the space.

Eliza glanced at the mine manager's office. Through the lighted window she could see Charles Cowper in earnest conversation with another man.

'Who's that?' she asked Tehan.

Tehan's steps faltered and he swore. 'It's the bloody mine inspector.'

'He doesn't look happy.'

'He's never happy and if I've any sense, I'll keep my head down until he's gone. If you see your uncle, tell him I've gone back to Shenandoah.'

He handed the basket to Netty and led his horse down the dark gap between two buildings where the trolleys ran to the batteries.

The crib room seemed to have been taken over by the Ladies' Committee, with Mrs Russell and Mrs Jervis in command. Flora Donald stood at the door, handing out bowls of soup and bread.

'Brought you a mutton stew,' Netty said.

Flora stood aside. 'Come in and set it on the table.'

Eliza pulled the shawl closer around her head as they stepped into the light.

Netty asked for news again.

'They say it could be weeks before the rescue party gets through to them. If they're still alive, they won't last until Sunday,' Mrs Jervis said.

One of the women bent over a pot on the fire straightened, wiping her hands on her apron. Eliza realised it was Mrs Harris.

Their gaze met. 'Miss Penrose. You're back,' Mrs Harris said with little warmth.

Flora swung around, her brow furrowing. 'What are you doing here?'

Eliza did not feel she needed to explain her return to either woman. 'I am here to see if I can be of any help.'

'Best help you could have offered was to stay in Melbourne.' Flora set her empty tray down on the table with a thump.

'At least Cowper's not left his office. He's no coward. Not like McLeod. The collapse is his doing and if he shows his face, he'll be torn apart,' Mrs Harris said.

'What do you mean it is his doing?' Eliza said.

'Mr Cowper says he's been taking shortcuts with materials and pushing through the tunnel faster than he should have done.'

'But that wasn't his doing—' Eliza began but Mrs Harris fixed her with sharp, angry eyes and she knew argument would get her nowhere. The woman's loyalty lay with Cowper.

She glanced at Flora, expecting the same righteous anger as Cowper's housekeeper, but Flora just shook her head and turned to her work.

'There's nothing for you to do here,' Mrs Harris said in a softer tone of voice. 'If it's a bed you're wanting, the back door's unlocked. No one's home. Even Tom's helping with the mine.'

'Miss Penrose?'

Jenny Tregloan sat with two other women, older but just as haggard. She crossed to them, crouching in front of Jenny and taking her icy hand in her own. 'Mrs Tregloan, what can I say?'

Tears welled in Jenny's eyes. 'If I lose him ...'

'It's our husbands down there,' one of the older women said. 'I'm Ada Morgan and this here's Janet Marsh.'

Ada Morgan put an arm around the younger woman's shoulders. 'She's with child, Miss Penrose.'

Eliza looked at the other two women, seeing the faces of the Morgan and Marsh children in the school room.

Janet Marsh, the oldest of the three women, lifted her chin. 'I have faith in the Lord, Miss Penrose. I don't believe for a minute they're dead.'

But Eliza knew mines. She knew that even if they had, by some miracle, survived the fall of rock, air would be running out. If they weren't reached soon, it would be too late.

She had no words of assurance nor of comfort. 'All we can do is pray,' she said and rose to her feet.

With a quick, knowing glance at Netty, Eliza left the crib room. She didn't have much time. A mad plan had come to her as soon as Mrs Harris had said the house was unlocked but empty. This could be her one opportunity to search for her brother's missing will and the plans—if her uncle had them.

But first there was the matter of Alec McLeod.

The crowd at the gate had dissipated as the night deepened so there was no one to pay her any heed. She took the narrow path to the McLeods' cottage. No light burned in the living room and the house was in silence. Her concern increased and she slowed her step as she approached the front door. Even in the dark she could make out the word 'Murderer' daubed across it. She stared at the ugly word for a long moment before knocking.

Getting no response, she went to the back door and found it unlocked. She pushed it open. The room was in darkness and no fire burned in the hearth. The icy air was heavy with a miasma of whisky and unwashed male. She groped on the dresser for a candle and match box.

'Who's that?' a muffled voice came out of the dark.

'Eliza.'

'Go away.'

She found the candle and its thin light illuminated the room. Alec sat slumped over the table. She set the candle down on the mantelpiece and crossed to him.

His head was buried in his arms and an empty bottle lay at his side. His fingers, curled around another half-full bottle, told their own story. He had been subsisting on nothing more than whisky and self-pity for the last few days.

'Alec ...' She touched his arm and he jerked upright. The bottle he'd been holding slewed its contents across the table.

'Whatcha doin' here?'

Eliza righted the bottle. 'What's happened since I've been away?'

'Ian's trapped in the mine ... he could be dead.'

Eliza moved to the fireplace and found the embers were completely cold. 'And drinking yourself into oblivion and dying of cold is going to help him?'

'Seemed like a good idea.' His fingers found the bottle again. 'Ian ... Is there any news?'

She squatted beside him and laid her hand over his. 'None. I've just come from the mine. Everyone is blaming you. What happened?'

'Cowper ordered the last explosion that brought the mine down.' He took a shuddering breath. 'And now Ian is down there. He shouldn't even have been there ...

She tightened her grip on his hand. 'Why did Cowper take that risk?' she asked.

'Greed.' He blinked and she thought she detected the glint of tears in his eyes. 'My signature is on the purchase orders but I never signed them. You have to believe me, 'liza.'

'He's a forger, Alec ... or he knows a forger. The will, my brother's will, that is forged too. I've seen it.'

Alec frowned, clearly too befuddled by the whisky to comprehend what she was saying.

'When I stood up to him, he fired me ... me and Ian.' His head collapsed on his arms and his shoulders shook.

Eliza picked up the whisky bottle. 'And did you think you'd find the answer in a bottle?' she said, setting it on the dresser out of his reach.

The candlelight flashed in his eyes as he raised his head and rose unsteadily to his feet. 'Don't lecture me, Miss Penrose. It's your fault—'

'Yes,' she said, her gaze holding his. 'Yes, it is all my fault. I should never have involved you or your brother. I'll make it right, Alec. I promise.'

'How?'

'I don't know.'

She touched his face, her fingers rasping on his unshaven chin. She half-expected him to pull away but he put his arms around her. She longed to provide some comfort, tell him everything would be fine, but there were no words to ease his pain. They held each other in silence, the anguish leaching from him. His brother missing, possibly dead, his reputation destroyed ... Small wonder he had taken to the bottle.

She laid her hands on his chest and pushed him away. 'Alec, you need to sober up. You're no good to anyone—least of all Ian—like this.'

He shook his head and ran a hand over his eyes. 'I'm no good to anyone. Couldn't save Catriona or the bairn and now Ian—'

She grabbed his arms and shook him. 'Stop it! Feeling sorry for yourself is not the answer. You are good at what you do and what we need now is someone to tell us how to get those men out. Drinking yourself into oblivion is not helping anyone.'

'But they don't want me. You saw my door.'

'They need you. You'll see, Alec, they'll come looking for you. You're not a coward and you've lost two days wallowing in self-pity. Get some sleep, tidy yourself up and face the naysayers.'

He reached out and touched her hair, curling a lock around his finger. 'You're a stronger man than I am, Eliza Penrose.'

She smiled and rose on her tiptoes to kiss him on the cheek, his bristles rough beneath her lips. 'I can't stay,' she said. 'There is something I have to do while I have the chance.'

'What?'

'I am going to find the evidence that my uncle is a liar and a thief.'

As she turned away, he caught her arm. 'Not now. He's cornered and dangerous.'

She snorted. 'Now is exactly the time,' she said. 'I don't believe he knows I'm back and there's no one at the house.'

'Don't do anything rash.'

'I'll be careful.' She gave him a gentle shove. 'Go to bed, Alec. Sleep off the whisky. Tomorrow is a new day.'

Eliza skirted the shadows, crossing the valley to Cowper's house on the hill. No lights shone from the windows and she slipped around to the rear of the house. An emergency candle and tinder box stood on a shelf inside the back door but before she lit the candle, Eliza took the precaution of ensuring every curtain on every window was tightly drawn. The last thing she needed was for someone to report a light in the house.

Only when she was completely satisfied the house was in darkness did she light the candle and try her uncle's bedroom door. Her heart leaped when she found it unlocked. He must have been so distracted by events at the mine that he had neglected to secure it. She smiled. More fool him.

The furnishings were plain and good quality: a large bed, washstand, chest of drawers, desk and nightstand, with a rag rug on the floor to add colour and warmth. She began by systematically searching drawers and cupboards. She discovered nothing of any interest, except her uncle's predilection for silk handkerchiefs. That left his desk, a massive roll-top in the corner. She searched the drawers and found a small strong box but both the box and the shutter itself was locked. She searched the room again, this time looking for concealed keys, but found nothing. She could only assume that her uncle had the keys to both.

She replaced the box and leaned against the bedstead to look around the room. It reflected her uncle's fastidious nature. Only one picture adorned the walls, an amateur watercolour of a Georgian country house, the crumbling facade of elegant columns immediately recognisable as Cowper's childhood home in Devon. Her mother's family had, like her own, fallen on hard times and the house had been sold some twenty years ago but she remembered visiting it as a small child. The sole resident had been her grandmother, a crusty old dame who was quick with the cane if she caught Eliza slouching.

She walked over to the painting for a closer look, her heart giving a jolt as she recognised her mother's initials in the corner. Up close, the painting stood oddly proud of the wall and, with shaking hands, she took it off its nail and laid it on the bed. Hardly daring to breathe, she turned it over and could have given a whoop of joy: the paper lining had been slit down one side. Gently she pried the slit open and her excitement increased as she withdrew a heavy envelope. She unwound the string fastening the envelope and pulled out the contents, giving a gasp of pleasure at the sight of Will's plans, the set that had been taken from her by the bushrangers, identifiable by her brother's signature and Alec McLeod's scribblings. With it was another document, heavy legal paper with the words LAST WILL AND TESTAMENT OF WILLIAM JOSIAH PENROSE inscribed in an elegant hand on the outside, along with the name of the law firm that had drawn it up: Messrs. Kennedy, Bolton and Briscoe.

Tears welled in Eliza's eyes and she sank to her knees beside the bed, holding her brother's original will. This would go a long way to proving the other a forgery.

The sound of men's voices coming up the path to the front door made her shoot to her feet, her heart hammering. She hurriedly replaced the documents in the envelope, rehung the painting, extinguished the candle and headed for the kitchen as a key turned in the front door. In her haste her hip caught the kitchen table and a cup and saucer crashed to the floor.

She froze.

'Who's there?' Her uncle's voice.

No time to hide and nowhere to conceal the documents on her person. As a light flared in the hallway, she tripped over Tom's boot box and, lacking any other ideas, thrust the documents as far down into the depths of it as she could.

She had time to regain her feet and take several steps away from the box before her uncle burst through the kitchen door, a small pistol in his hand. Eliza's gaze went from the pistol he held to his face. His nose was swollen and reddened and his eye blackened.

Seeing her, he took a step back, lowering his weapon.

'Eliza, what the hell are you doing here? I thought you were in Melbourne. I could have shot you.'

'I secured that teaching position and I was on my way back to Maiden's Creek to fetch my belongings when I heard of the mine collapse. I only got in this evening and went straight up to the mine to see if there was anything I could do to help but the ladies didn't need an extra hand and I'm exhausted from the journey. Mrs Harris told me the back door was unlocked and I was looking for a light.'

Cowper frowned as he pocketed his pistol. 'Were you indeed?' His gaze fell on the broken cup and saucer.

Eliza edged toward the back door. 'If it's not convenient, I will go and stay with Mrs Burrell.'

As she reached for the door handle, the back door swung open. She stumbled backward as the black-bearded Jennings stepped into the kitchen. He closed the door behind him, leaning on it as he leered at her.

'Good evening, my pretty.'

'Jennings!' Her uncle's voice held command and warning. He took a step toward Eliza, a humourless smile curving his lips. 'I am glad to see you, my dear. I had a letter from my lawyers warning me that you were poking your nose in where it is none of your business. Asking questions. Why couldn't you just be content with a comfortable post at the school I organised for you?'

'I told Mrs Wallace I had unfinished business here,' Eliza began but the weeks of mounting anger and disillusionment rose in her chest. 'And, yes, I have been asking questions and finding the answers. I know you for what you are: a liar and a thief. You forged my brother's will and stole my inheritance just as you have been stealing the gold from Shenandoah to bolster the profits of Maiden's Creek.'

Cowper rolled his eyes, his hand slipping back into the pocket that held the pistol. 'This is not the time, Eliza. I warned you when you first came that you shouldn't stay, but no, you had to involve the McLeods in your fancies and now look what has happened.'

'You're punishing them because of me?'

Cowper let out a snort of humourless laughter. 'Trust me, I didn't plan a mine collapse. The last thing I need are government officials coming here and asking questions. Fortunately, I have a useful scapegoat. As far as the world is concerned, this is Alec McLeod's doing. It's not going to be hard to prove that he took shortcuts and foolish risks.'

Eliza stared at her uncle. 'If there were shortcuts and foolish risks they were your doing, not his.'

'It's his signature on the documents.'

'Forged, like my brother's will. And they were your orders to push the blasting through.' She raised her chin and drew herself up to her full height. 'If you'll excuse me, Uncle, I am weary from the journey. I will leave you and return to Netty Burrell's and we will continue this discussion when the men are free from the mine.'

'Leave? I don't think so, Eliza. I have enough trouble without you spreading these foul rumours and innuendos.'

A flicker of fear rose in her stomach. 'What do you mean? Are you threatening me?'

'I rather think I am. Such a shame because I am really rather fond of you, as I was of William. But he started to ask questions too.'

Her breath caught. 'Did you—did you kill him to keep him quiet?' The words came out as a hoarse whisper.

Cowper didn't reply for a long moment. 'He saved me the trouble.'

Eliza's blood turned to ice. What did he mean? That he'd intended to kill Will but something or someone else had intervened?

'We are your flesh and blood,' she said. 'Your only family.'

Cowper sighed. 'I know, but I don't need family. You and your brother were just a burden to be borne.' He straightened his shoulders and ran a hand across his eyes. 'Like you, I'm tired and I need to rest.' He turned to Jennings. 'Let's deal with her now, Jennings.'

Jennings took a few steps toward Eliza, leaving the back door exposed.

Eliza made a dash for the door, wrenching uselessly at the handle.

Jennings held up the key. 'You're not going anywhere,' he said.

'Let me out!' She turned to face Cowper. 'Uncle!'

Cowper ran a hand through his thinning hair. 'I'm sorry, Eliza,' he said. 'I have enough to worry about without you shouting your fanciful little tales to the world. I am sure when the trouble at the mine is settled we will be able to come to some arrangement, but until then, I am going to put you somewhere out of the way. Jennings, my niece has often expressed a desire to visit Shenandoah. Why don't you take her and show her the delights of her brother's mine while I decide what to do with her?'

Jennings grinned and grasped Eliza by the forearms and she opened her mouth to scream but he whirled her around, one brawny arm pinioning her arms to her side while the other hand clapped across her mouth.

Cowper frowned and glanced at his bedroom door. Eliza saw now it had failed to click shut and stood ajar. 'Hold her, Jennings. I am just going to check on something.'

He left the kitchen carrying the lantern. A stream of invective came from his bedroom and he returned to the kitchen eyes blazing and his colour high.

'Where is it?'

Jennings dropped his hand from Eliza's mouth but maintained his hold on her even as she tried to wriggle free.

'Well? Answer me, damn you!'

'What are you talking about?'

'You know damn well.' He took a step toward her and struck her across the face.

She slumped back against Jennings, her ears ringing and a blinding pain in her head as her uncle's face came close, snarling and unrecognisable.

'You're nothing better than a sneak thief. I should just put a bullet in you now and get it over with. You know damn well what I'm talking about—the documents you took from behind the painting.'

'What documents? I don't have anything belonging to you. Look at me, where would I conceal it? You came home before I had a chance to even look.'

Cowper's chest rose and fell as he struggled to get his anger back under control. 'You should have stayed in England, my girl, and when I am done with you, you will wish you had. Get her out of here, Jennings.'

'What do I tell Tehan?' Jennings said.

'Tell Tehan I want her held until I've made a decision about what to do with her. And if he decides to be difficult, remind him of our arrangement.' He raised a finger. 'And Jennings ... she is not to be touched. Do you understand me?'

The black-bearded man grunted and Cowper tossed him the pistol.

'Good. I'm going to bed.' And with that he turned on his heel, slamming his bedroom door behind him.

Jennings changed his grip on Eliza, holding her by one arm as he traced the line of her throat down to the buttons of her jacket with the muzzle of the weapon.

'So, pretty lady, it's you and me. No Scottish hero to save you now.'

The bile rose in Eliza's throat but she met his gaze, determined not to show fear. 'You heard my uncle.'

Jennings glanced at the door and shrugged. 'Don't think for a minute anyone who cares about you will see you again. You're dead, my girl. One way or another. May as well have some fun.' He tugged her arm, thrusting her toward the door. 'And just in case you are thinking of screaming—' He pulled off the sweaty rag he wore around his neck. 'Open your mouth.'

The cold metal of the pistol's barrel on the tender skin beneath her jaw convinced Eliza that she should cooperate. She retched as he gagged her with the ghastly fabric before pushing her into the night.

A horse snuffled in the dark and Jennings shoved her toward it. As he untied the animal, she covertly pulled her handkerchief from her sleeve and let it fall, grinding it into the mud with her heel. Jennings hoisted her into the saddle, swinging up behind her and pulling the reins around her. As he did so, his hand cupped her breast and he laughed.

'I thought you'd be a good handful,' he said.

Eliza held back a moan of fear. She would hate for him to think it was one of desire. The stench of the man sickened her, and bile rose again behind the loathsome cloth wedged in her aching jaw.

Her last hope of being seen as they left the town evaporated as he turned the horse up the hill, following a path she had never noticed before, which took them up to the ridgeline and north, beyond the town boundaries. When they descended to the Aberfeldy Road they were well away from Maiden's Creek.

The cold cut through her clothing and she shivered, fighting back the tears generated by the real fear that, as far as Charles Cowper was concerned, she was better off dead. Just like Will.

They approached Annie's hut but no light nor sound came from the shabby building. Even the dog was silent. On such a cold night it was probably inside.

They turned on to the Pretty Sally Track, which rose steadily, winding through dark gullies until they reached a small settlement perched high on a mountainside. Eliza stiffened, casting her eyes to right and left, looking for a light, for someone to help, but they rode unchallenged through the dark, silent settlement before turning onto a steep track that wound down from the ridge to a gully from which the familiar *ka thump*, *ka thump* of a battery stamper echoed around the hills. As they rounded a bend in the track she could finally see lights. Her heart quickened its beat. This had to be the Shenandoah Mine.

They entered through a pair of solid wooden gates and the track flattened out as it passed through a cluster of rough sheds that made up the mining settlement. From a tall, corrugated-iron building the steady cadence of the stamper reverberated. For a mine not producing any gold, it had the air of an enterprise in full operation.

'Tehan!' Jennings shouted.

Jack Tehan came out of a small hut, pulling on his jacket. 'Jennings! What the hell are you doing here? I thought you were long gone.'

'Boss has sent you a package. You can have her.'

As Jennings shoved Eliza sideways, she gave a muffled cry. Tehan moved fast and caught her as she tumbled from the horse, setting her on her feet. He pulled the noisome gag from her mouth, keeping a grip on her arm.

Relieved of the cloth, Eliza leaned over, retching.

'What the hell's going on, Jennings?' Tehan said.

'Cowper wants her kept somewhere out of the way until the business at the Maiden's Creek Mine is done.'

'Water, please,' Eliza croaked.

Tehan appeared not to hear her. 'Why?'

'This little lady has been asking questions. She knows about the gold.'

Tehan's grip tightened on Eliza's arm and he swore under his breath.

Jennings had dismounted and stood with his horse's reins looped over his arm. 'I think we both know what Cowper will want done with her,' he said and handed Tehan Cowper's pistol.

'Get me the lantern from my hut.'

When the man entered the small hut, Tehan leaned forward. 'What did you think you were doing, Miss Penrose?' he said in a low voice. 'And what am I going to do with you?'

Jennings re-emerged carrying a lantern and handed it to Tehan.

Tehan took Eliza by the arm and led her away from the main camp. When Jennings followed, he turned. 'Go and find a crib, Jennings. I can manage Miss Penrose.'

'Want her to yourself?'

'Get out of my sight.'

He waited until Jennings turned and made his way back into the main encampment.

'Did he touch you?' Tehan asked.

Eliza didn't answer and Tehan grunted, taking her silence as an affirmative. 'I'm sorry,' he said. 'I'll make sure he can't get to you.'

Eliza stumbled along an uneven path, coming to a halt before an unused mine adit, little more than a hole in the cliff face.

'You'll be safe enough in here,' he said.

He led her into the tunnel, which went into the hillside for about twenty-five yards. The end had been secured with a metal grille, and Tehan pulled out a set of keys, fumbling for the right one. He unlocked the heavy padlock and thrust her into the dark interior.

The light of the lantern illuminated a rugged cave filled with wooden boxes and piles of sacking. She sank to the floor and covered her face with her hands, willing herself not to cry.

Tehan hunkered down in front of her and took her hands, pulling them away from her face. 'I'm sorry, Miss Penrose. This is all I could think of. It's the most secure place on the site.'

'What do you mean by that?'

He shook his head and ran a hand over his eyes. 'It's more for your own protection. I know Jennings, and you need a stout lock between him and you. You must be tired, so I suggest you try and get some rest. I'll fetch you some things to make your stay more comfortable. It's going to get perishing cold before daylight. Fortunately, you're far enough into the hill that it stays quite warm.'

'What is this place?'

'It's the original adit,' Tehan said. 'Your brother moved the mine workings up the hill and made this the storeroom. It's dry and secure and I'm the only one with the key, so Jennings and his crew won't get to you.'

He stood up and suddenly she didn't want him to go, didn't want to be left alone in this place.

'Are you going to leave me here?'

He gestured at the lantern. 'I'm just going to fetch a few things to make you more comfortable. I'll leave you the lantern.'

After he left her, she sat with her back to a stacked pile of timber supports, breathing in the unusual sweet scent of the cut wood. She recognised it from her visit to Maiden's Creek Mine. What had Alec called it? Huon pine, an expensive but strong wood they had been bringing in from Tasmania. Had this shipment of wood been intended for Maiden's Creek? If so, the theft of the wood could be added to her uncle's crimes.

She inspected the boxes but failed to find anything of any use. Even if she knew how to pick the substantial lock that secured the door, she had no idea how to get herself to safety or indeed, who she could trust. It said much about her predicament when the only person she had any confidence in was Black Jack Tehan.

It seemed an age until he returned with blankets and other objects, which he deposited on the floor, and squatted down across from her.

'There's spring water in this flask and a bucket for your convenience,' he said. He handed her a flask and she drank deeply, grateful to rid herself of the taste of Jennings's neck cloth. Restored, she put the flask down and Tehan handed her a package wrapped in brown paper.

'Bread and cheese,' he said. 'I thought you might be hungry.'

At the mention of food, her stomach growled and she pulled the paper apart in her haste. The bread was stale and the cheese hard but she ate both with gratitude.

Tehan leaned against a wall, watching her as she ate. 'So you know what Cowper's been up to. I'd say you've as good as ruined his plans and he's not a man who takes well to being thwarted. If he wants you dead ...'

Eliza looked at Tehan, his face no more than a pale oval in the gloom. 'Are you going to kill me?'

'Me? I'm many things, Miss Penrose, but I ain't a killer.'

'But Jennings is.'

Tehan straightened. 'There's a stack of sacking in the corner—I suggest you get some sleep.' He jerked his head in the direction of the mouth of the adit. 'I'll be right there. You'll be quite safe.'

'You're not going to leave me?'

He shook his head and smiled. 'Let's see what the day brings.'

He secured the lock and settled down in the mouth of the adit, wrapped in a blanket, his rifle across his knees. For the first time in hours, Eliza relaxed; although quite why she would find Black Jack Tehan's presence reassuring, she could not have said.

Sitting around in the cold and the dark feeling miserable would gain her nothing so she made a bed from the sacks and wrapped herself in the blankets. She extinguished the lantern and lay down. She needed to rest and gather her strength to see what the daylight brought.

Twenty-Six

1 August 1873

In the dark hours before dawn, Alec stood in the shadows watching the comings and goings at the mine. His pounding head reminded him that a copious amount of alcohol on top of a still healing head wound may have been a mistake. It had taken a small, chestnut-haired firebrand to bring him to his senses.

Feeling sorry for yourself is not the answer. You are good at what you do and what we need now is someone to tell us how to get those men out. Drinking yourself into oblivion is not helping anyone.

He'd taken her advice, drunk several cups of tea and fallen onto his bed but the alcohol-fuelled sleep had not been restful. Images of the men trapped in the pitiless dark screamed at him until they had driven him from his bed. He could no longer stand by and do nothing.

'Can't sleep, Mr McLeod?'

He started, turning sharply at the woman's voice, recognising Eva Trevalyn.

'Mrs Trevalyn. I—'

'You don't have to defend yourself to me, McLeod. I know the truth. I know what Cowper's been up to. I've got it all written down.'

'I don't understand.'

'Cowper was undermining your orders, substituting substandard wood for the Huon and driving the blasting forward. My husband couldn't say anything for fear of losing his job, but he told me. He wrote it down and signed it. Gave it to me for safekeeping. He had a feeling the Knockers would come. They don't take kindly to such bad practices.'

Alec let out a breath that clouded in the cold air. 'Thank you, Mrs Trevalyn. Thank you for believing me.'

She laid a hand on his sleeve. 'They've been down there too long, haven't they, McLeod?'

'I won't lie to you, Mrs Trevalyn.'

'You're needed. Have you the courage to face them?'

'My brother is down there,' he said. 'I would face the devil himself to save him.'

Her fingers tightened on his arm. 'Then come with me.'

Alec thrust his hands deep into his pockets and hunched into his jacket, prepared for the reception he would receive at the mine. Seeing him coming up the hill, the men gathered in the courtyard turned and arranged themselves in a line barring his way, arms crossed and belligerent expressions on their faces.

'What are you doing up here, McLeod?' one demanded. 'We've been told you're banned from this mine.'

'My brother is trapped down that mine, I have every right to be here.'

'Word is you're not fit to set foot on the mine workings,' a second man said.

'I have worked with you day and night for the last twelve months, John Brierley. Have I ever given you cause to doubt my competence?'

Brierley's expression folded. 'No, but—'

'When this is over, when the whole story is known, *then* you can pass judgement on me, but not before … not now. Let me through.'

Muttering, the men parted and Alec entered the Maiden's Creek Mine.

Flora McDonald stood at the door to the crib hut, a mug of tea in her hand. Even in the poor light he could see the lines of exhaustion on her face. All her fight and fire seemed to have died and she just looked at him.

'What news is there, Miss Donald?'

'None. They've been working day and night and they've cleared some of the rubble. Someone reported hearing a tapping yesterday but there's been nothing more.'

'Tapping?'

'Yes, like a pick on rock, apparently.'

Alec thought of the Knockers and their warnings about mine collapses. 'Human?' he said.

'That's what they said.'

He turned to Brierley and the others. 'Is this true?'

Brierley nodded. 'Aye, but we've heard nothing since.'

A wave of relief swept over Alec. So, there was hope that some or all of the trapped miners had survived, but they'd been down the mine for three days and air would be thin.

'There's a lot of people very angry with you, Mr McLeod,' Flora said. 'They're saying the collapse was your fault. Was it?'

Alec sighed. 'It's easy to pass blame, Miss Donald. I would hope that you might find it in your heart not to believe the stories you're hearing.'

'I'm not a miner, but I believe you're a good man, and your brother likewise. I am praying for you both.'

He touched his fingers to his hat. 'Thank you. We need your prayers.'

'What are you going to do?'

'I'm going to see if I can be of any help. Even if it's just the digging. I can't sit by and do nothing,'

'Do you want something to eat before you go down?'

Alec accepted the mug of tea she held out to him and drank it without taking breath, his hangover forgotten. No one stopped him as he strode across to the mine. The adit yawned before him, dark and uninviting, as if the very mine he had carved from the earth had turned against him. He took a lantern from the entrance and made his way down the long, familiar tunnel, his boots sloshing in the mud and water.

The cavern glowed with light and seemed to be filled with men clustered around the shaft, hauling out buckets of waste and debris. The silence in which they worked gave the scene an otherworldly feel. No one noticed him until he stepped into the light, then, one after another, the men turned to look at him.

'What are you doing here, McLeod?' Williams, the assistant foreman stepped forward.

'I'm here to help,' Alec said.

The men looked at each other and someone handed him a shovel.

'You can help with loading the trolleys,' Williams said.

Alec worked without a break, grateful both for the physicality and the mindless repetition. It gave him time to think, to work through the problems of the mine rescue. Even if all he could do for the moment was manual labour, at least that was useful.

He was so lost in his work that it took a moment or two to realise that one of the boys who pushed the trolleys was tugging at his sleeve.

'Mr McLeod, there's a woman here to see you. Says it's urgent.'

Alec laid down his shovel and brushed his filthy, bleeding hands against his trousers. *Eliza?*

Outside, he blinked in the daylight, even though the morning was grey and dank with a tedious drizzle, slicking the muddy cobblestones. He turned his face up to the sky, allowing the cold darts of rain to wash away the dirt, but the fresh air and rain left a residue of helplessness that would not be assuaged until the men were free of the mine.

'Alec!'

He brought his attention to the sturdy figure standing in the doorway of the crib hut. Netty Burrell stood aside to let him enter. He looked around, relieved to see they were alone. Realising he hadn't eaten for a long time, he picked up a hunk of bread, some cheese and a piece of cold meat.

She faced up to him, her hands on her hips. 'Where is she?'

'Who?' he said, taking a bite of the rough meal.

'Eliza.'

He frowned. 'I don't know. I haven't seen her since last night.' He ran a hand through his hair, trying to force his clouded brain back into working order. 'Why do you ask?'

'Because she left her travelling bag with me yesterday evening and I was expecting her to return to spend the night, but she hasn't come back. I've been up to Cowper's house and the Harris woman says she hasn't seen her since yesterday evening when she came here. I thought maybe she was with you?'

Alec caught his breath. Had Netty really thought to find Eliza warming his bed? That would have been very pleasant and a twinge of regret passed through his mind. He had been in no state to woo a woman last night.

'No. She came, gave me a lecture and said she was going to speak with her uncle. That's the last I saw of her.'

Netty sat on one of the benches. 'I have a bad feeling, Alec,' she said. 'We need to look for her.'

Alec worked through the possible scenarios. All of them left him with a sense of dread.

He had a choice: continue in a menial role at the mine or go and look for Eliza. There were plenty of willing hands at the mine but Eliza was on her own.

'They can manage without me here, so I'll go and look for her.'

'I don't know if he's got anything to do with it, but Jack Tehan was here last night. When he saw the mine inspector was here, he took off. Said he was going back to Shenandoah.'

Before Alec could respond, the door opened, admitting a damp Flora Donald.

'Miss Donald, have you seen Eliza Penrose?' Alec asked.

Flora's lips tightened. 'Aye, she was here yesterday evening with Mrs Burrell. Asking about you. She headed to the gate, so I assume she went in search of you. Gone missing, has she? Well, I've enough to do without fretting about the likes of Eliza Penrose,' she said with a sniff. 'Mrs Burrell, that soup is burning.'

Netty jumped up and hurried to the pot that bubbled over the fire, uttering an unladylike curse as she did so.

Alec slipped out the door, hunching against the rain as he crossed the courtyard. The small crowd at the gate lacked the energy to throw anything more than hostile glances at him as he passed. He stopped at his house to wash and change before crossing the valley to Cowper's. As he neared the house he could see the silhouette of the mine manager through the windows of the front room. He was seated at the table, no doubt enjoying his breakfast. Alec had nothing to lose so he firmed his stride, letting the brass knocker on the door fall with a firm rap.

Mrs Harris answered. Like everyone else, the woman looked like she hadn't slept in days, her face drawn and her eyes sunk in dark circles.

'I want to speak with Cowper.'

A well-trained servant, she met his gaze without blinking. 'He's not here,' she said.

'I beg to differ. My apologies, Mrs Harris.'

Alec pushed past her and she hurried after him, her hands fluttering in distress as he threw open the door to the parlour.

'Mr Cowper, he—'

Cowper stood as Alec entered the room, dabbing at his moustache with his pristine serviette.

'How dare you—'

The sight of the man's swollen nose and black eye gave Alec a perverse sense of satisfaction. He leaned both hands on the table. 'Where is she, Cowper?"

'Who?'

'Your niece, Eliza Penrose. Where is she?'

Cowper shrugged. 'She's not here. I don't know why you would think—'

'Because when I saw her last night, she was coming here and now she has disappeared.'

Cowper glanced at the woman hovering behind Alec. 'Disappeared? Have you seen her, Mrs Harris?'

'No, sir. The Burrell woman was also here this morning looking for her. You were still abed and I didn't want to disturb you.'

Cowper frowned. 'If Eliza has, indeed, gone missing, then this is a matter of concern, but as you well know, McLeod, Maiden's Creek is a dangerous place to go wandering at night.' He tossed the serviette down. 'To be frank, I cannot worry about a foolish woman at the moment. Now get out of my house before I summon the police. And this time I'll ensure Maidment locks you up.'

Alec cast the man a withering glance and straightened. 'Is that your answer for everything, Cowper? Get other people to do your bullying for you?' He paused, scanning the man's bruised face for some sign of compassion. 'Do you really not care that your niece is missing?'

Cowper glared at him. 'Of course I care, but she is a grown woman and not my responsibility, as she is wont to tell me.' He pointed at the door. 'Get out, now.'

The front door slammed behind Alec. He paused for a long moment, looking up and down the valley, seething with anger.

How could Eliza just vanish?

He had no wish to walk through town again so he took the side path that led to the road just north of the town's boundaries. The mud beneath a small stand of trees had been churned and sodden droppings indicated a horse had been present in recent days. In any other circumstances he would have thought nothing of it, but a flutter of dirty white pressed into the mud caught his eye. He stooped to pick up the slip of cambric with a fine lace edging, and rinsed it in a puddle. His breath caught as he traced the embroidered initials in the corner: *EP*.

He sat on a fallen log and turned the handkerchief over in his hand. Had Eliza dropped her handkerchief deliberately? Whose horse had waited for her in this lonely place? The sense of dread returned and he turned his face to the rain.

Where is she, God?

Twenty-Seven

1 August 1873

Eliza woke and lay quite still. Despite being wrapped tightly in the blankets, she had never felt so cold. She stared at the small patch of daylight beyond the iron gate and caught her breath as a shadow, too broad to be Tehan, blocked it.

The lock on the door rattled. Whoever it was gave a grunt of exasperation. He grasped the bars and shook the gate. Eliza scrabbled back against the cave wall, her stomach roiling as she recognised Jennings.

'Just bidin' my time, pretty lady,' he said. 'Had to wait for Black Jack to leave his post.'

'Go away,' she said, ashamed at how high and tight her voice sounded.

Jennings laughed, a chilling sound. She cringed as he gave a commentary on what he intended to do with her when he had his chance.

'Get out of here, Jennings.'

At the sound of Tehan's voice, she let out her breath.

'Think you're going to have her all to yourself, do you?' Jennings retorted, but to Eliza's relief he backed out of the cavern and stumped away.

Tehan unlocked the door and set down a plate with more bread and cheese and a pannikin of hot, black tea. He looked as rough as she felt, his eyes bleary and lost in dark shadows. She wondered if he had slept at all as he watched over her.

'Sorry about Jennings,' Tehan said. 'I just went to fetch some victuals.'

'Sorry is not really good enough,' Eliza said, conscious that she shook from head to foot. 'You didn't hear what he was saying.'

'I did.'

'I presume you know he was one of the thugs you sent that waylaid us,' Eliza said.

'I've told you, I had nothing to do with that.' Tehan sounded indignant. 'That was Cowper's work. Contrary to what you might think, Jennings is in his pay, not mine.' He waved at the food. 'I thought you might be hungry.'

Her rebellious side told Eliza to knock the plate from his hand, but the sensible side prevailed. She took the plate, sitting down on a sturdy wooden box.

After a couple of mouthfuls, she looked up at him. 'What do you mean Jennings is not in your pay?'

Tehan took a long moment to answer. 'Jennings has been Cowper's man since the Bendigo days. Whenever he wanted someone ... persuaded to his way of thinking, he would send Jennings.'

'But Cowper brought you here. You're as much his man as Jennings.'

Tehan drew in a harsh breath. 'It suited me to come to Maiden's Creek and I'll be honest with you, Miss Penrose, I'm not going to deny that I haven't been complicit in some of your uncle's dealings, but I don't do the dirty work and I most certainly had nothing to do with Jennings and his crew holding you up on the Shady Creek Road, or the business up at McLeod's place.'

She studied him, not sure whether to believe him or not. 'So how do you keep him in line?'

'I'm not sure I do. Maybe it just suits him for the moment.'

'That's not very reassuring.'

'I know. That's why I kept watch last night.' Tehan pointed to the rifle propped against the wall just inside the cavern.

Eliza swallowed. 'He's that dangerous?'

'I didn't want to take any risks.' He stood up and walked to the iron grille and stood looking out at the mine workings beyond the adit.

He turned back to her and reached into his pocket, pulling out a small object which he held up by its chain. It glinted in the early morning light and her heart gave a leap. 'Yours, I believe.' He tossed the locket to her and she caught it, pressing it to her heart.

'Thank you, but why are you returning it?'

'Call it a gesture of good faith,' he said. 'Took a little persuading for Jennings to hand it over.'

She wanted to dislike Tehan but he made it very difficult.

'McLeod said you knew about Will's plans. Did you tell my uncle about them?'

Tehan shook his head. 'Cowper already knew about them. Your brother must have discussed it with him in better times. But you know they'd fallen out? It didn't take much to work out who Penrose had left them with and your uncle sent Jennings and his crew to search McLeod's house. When they didn't find them, Cowper guessed McLeod had passed them on to you and you would have them with you when you left for Melbourne.'

'So what does Cowper hold over you?'

Tehan gave a snort of laughter. 'He did me a turn on the Bendigo goldfields but as you and your brother both know, he expects repayment for his favours, and at the end of the day, I need the employment.'

'So when my brother employed you, you were already working for my uncle?'

Tehan cleared his throat. 'Cowper wanted to know what was happening up here so, yes, he suggested it might be in my interests to get on the right side of your brother. He was paying me and your brother was paying me, so life was pretty sweet.' He shook his head. 'But Cowper wanted more—wanted me to start stealing the gold for the Maiden's Creek Mine. Just small amounts at first. Not so your brother would get alarmed, but he'd begun to suspect. Asked if one of the men may have been salting it away.' He paused. 'He started asking too many questions.'

'Did you kill him?'

Tehan's eyes flashed. 'No. I told you—I haven't killed anyone.'

'But my uncle has?'

Tehan shrugged. 'Not one to get his own hands dirty. As far as I know, your brother's death was an accident.'

Eliza let that pass. 'But you forged my brother's will?'

Tehan pushed himself off the wall. 'Why would you say that?'

'You signed as a witness … you and Mary Harris, and I know for certain that my brother's signature was a forgery.'

'And I am the son of a convicted forger?' His tone was bitter but he didn't deny his involvement.

Eliza took a sip of the lukewarm tea. 'You're in deep trouble, Tehan,' she said. 'Forgery, theft and now kidnap. I could help you. I could put a case forward—'

He gave a snort of laughter. 'And what case would that be? I come from bad stock, Miss Penrose. My father was a convict. I am stained with his crime. That's why I left Tasmania. There's no court in this land would look favourably on me.'

'But if, as you say, you haven't killed anyone, they won't hang you.' She paused before voicing the thoughts that had churned through her mind all night. 'But I know what my uncle intends for me. What will it be ... lost in the bush or a trip down an abandoned mine, or maybe a snake or spider bite?'

For the first time, the bravado seemed to leach from the man. He swallowed, his eyes darting to the open door. 'I'm not a killer of men or women. For what it's worth, you have my word that you're safe enough with me. I won't let either your uncle or his men harm you.' He paused and glanced outside. 'But I'm only one man and even I don't know who here is loyal to me.' He straightened and held out his hand. 'Finished?'

She handed him the empty plate and mug.

'Uncle Jack, Uncle Jack ...'

The familiar voice brought Eliza to her feet. 'Charlie!' She made for the door but Tehan caught her around the waist as Charlie came racing into the adit.

'Wait outside for me, Charlie.' Tehan thrust Eliza back into the cave and slammed the door. She rushed at the door but he snapped the padlock shut.

Too late. Charlie had seen her.

'Miss Penrose?' Charlie stood in the old adit's entrance looking from the man to the woman. 'What's Miss Penrose doing here, Uncle Jack? Why've you locked her up?'

'None of your business,' Tehan snapped. He put a hand on the child's shoulder. 'Outside, now.'

'Uncle Jack?' Eliza said.

He looked down at the child. 'Charlie's me brother's girl,' he said.

What had the girls at Lil's said? Annie had someone looking out for her? Could it be Jack Tehan?

Charlie pulled at her uncle's sleeve. 'It's Ma,' she said. 'The baby's coming and she needs help.'

Tehan swore and hit the rock wall of the adit with his fist. 'Jesus, Mary and Joseph, I don't need this now.'

'Tehan, you need to fetch the midwife,' Eliza shouted after him as he left, pushing Charlie in front of him. 'Tehan!'

But he had gone, leaving her in the gloom, both physical and metaphysical. She pressed against the gate and strained to make out Charlie's breathless, panicked voice and Tehan's attempts to calm her over the day-to-day noise of a working mine.

After an interminable time, Tehan reappeared at the entrance and stood looking at her. 'Do you think you can bring yourself to trust me, Eliza?'

Eliza ignored the use of her given name. 'Do I have a choice?'

'Something you said just now,' Tehan said. 'I don't want to hang for a man like Cowper, so I'm going to try and make this mess right. In the meantime I need your help.'

'How?'

'Annie sounds to be in a bad way so I'm going down to Maiden's Creek to find the midwife. I can't leave her alone with only the child.' He paused. 'For her sake, not mine, do you think you could stay with her?'

'I don't know anything about childbirth.'

'You're a woman.'

'I am completely useless in these matters. I've never even—' She bit her lip. It was hardly the time or place to admit to her lack of experience of any kind, beyond a few chaste kisses from suitors … back in the days she had suitors.

'Please.' Tehan sounded desperate.

'And your relationship with Annie?' Eliza asked, curiosity getting the better of her.

'I told you, she was my brother's … wife, I suppose you'd call it, not that they ever formalised matters in a church. After he died she got in with a brute of a man. He'd hit her around so I rescued her and the child and brought them over from Tasmania.'

'And you let her open a grog shop and … and …' Eliza struggled for words.

'I did what I could but Annie's got her own mind and she made her choices,' Tehan said. 'She made that clear to me. I kept an eye on her, made sure Charlie was all right.'

'Well, you didn't do a very good job.'

Colour flooded his handsome face. 'This is not the time to be arguing my suitability as Annie's guardian. Whatever she is—or might have been—she's in trouble and she's scared and she needs someone who isn't a ten-year-old child to be with her. Can you help?'

Chastened, Eliza nodded.

'Good, we don't have time to waste. Come with me now.'

Eliza left the Shenandoah Mine riding a skewbald pony of uncertain temperament, Charlie perched on the saddle in front of her uncle on his tall bay. Eliza looked neither right nor left but her skin prickled as if something evil was watching her. Something by the name of Jennings.

No smoke came from the chimney of Annie's hut and an ominous silence hung over the building. Even the birds had fallen quiet. The only life came from the dog, which jumped to his feet, his joyful bark breaking the silence of the bush. Tehan let Charlie down and the child made a dash for the cottage.

'I'll just see to your horse and then I'll head into town and fetch Ellen Bushby,' Jack said as he helped Eliza to dismount. 'Look after her, till I'm back.'

While Jack led the skewbald into the yard behind the hut, Eliza pushed open the door to the cottage, afraid of what she might find. The curtain separating the living area from the bed had been drawn back and Annie knelt beside the bed, her head on her arms, dark hair, sodden with sweat, spread out across a faded patchwork quilt. Charlie stood beside her, one small hand on her mother's shoulder.

Annie looked around as Eliza entered. Even in the poor light of the cottage she was unnaturally pale, her eyes huge and bright.

'It's all right, Ma. Uncle Jack's brought Miss Penrose to help,' Charlie said.

'She'll be as much use as tits on a bull,' Annie managed as another contraction contorted her face.

Eliza swallowed. Annie couldn't have been more correct. When it came to childbirth, she knew nothing beyond what she had witnessed in the barnyard or the stables, and animals seemed much better at dealing with birth than people.

'Charlie, light that fire and boil the kettle. We all need tea. And bring me a basin with water and a cloth,' she said with more authority than she felt.

She crossed to Annie and knelt beside her, smoothing the strands of hair from her forehead. Annie's lower lip was swollen from where she had bitten it and blood stained her chin and her neck.

'How long have you been in labour, Annie?'

Annie shook her head. 'Dunno. Since yesterday mornin', I think. I—' Her face contorted and she doubled in pain.

Yesterday morning? Eliza's blood ran cold. 'But I came past last night and your cottage was in darkness.'

Annie shot her a sharp glance. 'The dog 'eard an 'orse. I told Charlie to douse the light. I didn't want no unwelcome visitors. Where's Jack? I need Jack.'

'Gone for the midwife.'

Tehan's absence tore a hole in the insubstantial fabric binding the two women and the child together and Annie began to weep.

Charlie looked up at Eliza, her eyes filled with unshed tears. 'What are you going to do?' she asked in a small voice.

While Eliza knew nothing about the intricacies of childbirth, she had her own basic instincts and common sense. 'Let's start by making your mother comfortable. Help is coming,' she said with more confidence than she felt.

They stripped Annie of her soiled clothes and dressed her in a clean, surprisingly respectable, nightdress. As another contraction came, Eliza held her, encouraging her to breathe.

'Scream, Annie,' she said. 'There's no one to hear you.'

And Annie did, an ear-piercing scream of despair that echoed around the cottage.

They settled Annie on the bed and she fell back on the rough bolster, her breath coming in short gasps, her eyes wild as she gripped Eliza's hand so tightly the bones crunched.

'It's not comin', Miss Penrose. Somethin's wrong. I know it.'

Eliza wiped the woman's face. 'Hush,' she said. 'The midwife will be here soon. It'll be fine. Try and rest between the contractions.'

Annie's eyes closed. 'So tired. So tired ...'

'She'll be all right, won't she?' Charlie sounded impossibly young and very frightened.

Eliza held out her hand to Charlie. 'Do you know how to pray, Charlie?'

Charlie shrugged. 'Ma taught me the Lord's Prayer,' she said.

'That'll do. Let's say it together, it'll help your mother.'

The inadequate gesture seemed to calm Annie and she pointed to Charlie. 'Fetch me box, Charlie.'

Charlie pulled a stone from the fireplace and brought out a small tin box, the sort that would have once held chocolates.

'Pass me rosary.'

Charlie rummaged in the tin and brought out an old rosary, the beads worn smooth from handling.

'It was me grandma's,' Annie said, twining the beads in her fingers. 'She'd say the rosary every mornin' and night. Do you know the rosary, Miss Penrose?'

'I'm Church of England, Annie.'

The woman closed her eyes. 'Of course you are. Say the Lord's Prayer again.'

Eliza glanced at Charlie and the two recited the prayer again. When they finished, Annie said a round of Hail Marys.

'ail Mary, full of grace,
the Lord is with thee.
Blessed art thou amongst women,
and blessed is the fruit of thy womb, Jesus.
'oly Mary, Mother of God,
pray for us sinners,
now and at the 'our of our death. Amen.

The world shrank down to the pattern of Annie's distress. Minutes, even hours could have passed, but Annie's laboured breathing and contractions became the focus of Eliza's world.

In a lull between the contractions, Annie managed a watery smile. 'You ever 'ad a man?'

'No,' Eliza said. The situation demanded an honesty she would never have considered at any other time.

Annie shook her head. 'A bloody virgin. I might've known. Well, you mark me, Miss 'igh and Mighty Penrose, men will do you no good in this life.' She glanced at Charlie, who sat tending the fire, and her face softened. 'I loved Matt Tehan though, and 'e gave me Charlie and then the bastard up and died. What was I supposed to do?'

Eliza didn't have an answer and the conversation was curtailed by another massive contraction. She wiped Annie's sweating face and the tears that fell from her eyes.

'I chose a wrong 'un and if it weren't for Jack, Charlie and me would be dead now.' Her hand tightened on Eliza's. 'Jack's done wrong in 'is life but 'e ain't bad at 'eart.'

Eliza had reached that conclusion herself.

Annie shifted her weight slightly. ''e asked me to marry 'im.'

'Why did you refuse him?'

'I was done with men,' Annie said. 'Thought I could make a go of it by meself.' She opened her eyes and looked up at Eliza. 'If anythin' 'appens, you'll look after Charlie for me? Jack's a good man but 'e's not—' her face contorted, '—reliable.' Annie ran a hand over the swell of her stomach. 'This one's been trouble from the moment—'

'Who's the father of the child, Annie?' Eliza ventured.

Annie's face closed over. 'Dunno. Could be the bastard who thought I gave favours out for free.'

Eliza mulled this statement over. A nasty, ugly word came to mind.

'Rape?' She whispered the word.

Annie opened one eye and looked up at her. 'There's some as might call it that, but it ain't the baby's fault. 'e didn't ask to be born.'

'I'm sorry, Annie,' Eliza said.

Outside the dog began to bark, wild, angry yaps that ended in a squeal and a whimper and then silence.

Charlie jumped to her feet and started for the door as it burst open. She froze for a moment before scuttling across the room to the bed. Eliza stood to confront the man framed by the doorway, a rifle carried loosely in the crook of his arm, finger resting on the trigger, and a bloodied knife in the other hand. Behind the man, the dog lay still, its brindled coat wet with more than rain.

'I hate animals,' Jennings said, stowing the knife in his belt. 'McLeod has a cat. What sort of man keeps a cat? Bloody beast scratched me when I tried to catch it.'

Charlie whimpered and cowered behind Eliza.

'Get out of here,' Eliza said. 'This is no place for you.'

'Oh, but it is,' he said and jerked the rifle up, moving it from Eliza to Annie, who stared up at him with wide, too-bright eyes. 'That's my spawn the whore is carrying. I've every right to be here.' Something that most normal people would call a smile lifted the ugly beard away from his yellowing teeth. 'And you and I have a score to settle, Miss Penrose.'

Annie screamed as another contraction took her.

'Shut the bitch up!' Jennings demanded.

Eliza responded by pulling the curtain across the bed. Jennings had no interest in Annie or the baby. If he wanted to hurt anyone it was her, but at least he had given her a reprieve. 'Sit down and shut up yourself,' she said. 'If it's your child, it sure as hell doesn't want to meet its father and I'm not going anywhere until this is done.'

Jennings's finger tightened on the trigger and Eliza closed her eyes, her breath held tightly. She heard the rasp of a stool being pulled back.

Eliza opened her eyes to see he had sat down at the table, his boots up on the scrubbed surface. He crooked his finger at Charlie. 'Fetch me a beer.'

Charlie looked at Eliza.

'Do as he says,' she said and watched as Charlie pulled the man a tankard from the cask in the corner. She set it down on the far side of the table out of arm's reach. He laughed and pulled it toward him.

'I prefer me women a bit older,' he said, but he caught Charlie's arm as she tried to scuttle past him. 'No, you don't. You can stay with me and behave yourself or I'll give you another slap.' He thrust the child behind him and Eliza knew who was responsible for Charlie's blackened eye.

Charlie cast a frightened glance at Eliza.

'Go and sit by the fire, Charlie,' she said. 'Keep it going for us.'

Jennings grunted. He set the rifle on the table and picked up the tankard. 'Get on with it,' he said.

Eliza forced herself to move, returning to Annie's side. The woman was shaking, whether from the prolonged labour or fear of Jennings, it was impossible to tell.

Annie grabbed her arm, tears in her eyes. 'Don't let him hurt us,' she whispered.

'You just concentrate on getting this baby out,' Eliza said, 'and let me worry about Jennings.'

'Under me bed,' Annie whispered.

Eliza covertly bent over and her heart jumped at the sight of Annie's double-barrelled shotgun.

'It's not loaded but it might scare 'im.'

Eliza nodded. The way things stood there seemed no point in playing this card: they only needed time, time enough for Jack Tehan to return with the midwife.

Twenty-Eight

Alec glanced across the valley to the Maiden's Creek Mine, torn between his anxiety about Ian and the promise he'd made to Netty to find Eliza. Enough people were working on finding the miners but no one seemed to care about Eliza except Netty and himself. Her mysterious vanishing had to be his priority and he would start with Tehan. He had been seen in Maiden's Creek yesterday evening. Alec had no proof that the man was in any way connected with Eliza's disappearance, except for his own deep-seated dislike and distrust of the Tasmanian. Tehan made as good a starting point as any.

He hired a horse from Sones and set out for the Shenandoah Mine at a hard canter, scattering pedestrians in his haste. When he reached the haunted smallpox house on the far side of the Chinese gardens, he slowed. No point in driving the animal into the ground and he needed time to cool his own head before he confronted Black Jack Tehan.

The Aberfeldy Road climbed and as Alec rounded a corner, he saw a horse coming down the hill toward him, ridden hard. He recognised both horse and rider and swung his own animal across the road, forcing Jack Tehan to a stop. Tehan's horse went down on its haunches, its eyes rolling as its rider hauled on the reins.

'What the hell are you doing, McLeod? Stand aside and let me through!'

'You're going nowhere until you tell me what you've done with Eliza Penrose.'

Tehan pushed his hat back. 'I don't have time for this.' Seeing Alec showed no sign of moving, he tossed his head. 'She's fine. She's with Annie O'Reilly.' All trace of Tehan's usual bravado leached from his face and for the first time, Alec saw the man behind the sardonic smile. 'Annie's in trouble. The baby's coming and she needs a doctor or a midwife or both.'

Alec narrowed his eyes. 'Eliza is safe?'

'I told you—she's with Annie. I didn't take her, McLeod, if that's what you think. Cowper ordered Jennings to bring her to Shenandoah. I've kept her as safe as I can. Now let me through. If you don't believe me, go on to the hut. She'll be glad of you.'

Alec glanced at Tehan's horse. He'd ridden it hard and it was blowing. He nodded. 'Your horse is spent. Take this one and I'll go on to Annie's hut.'

Tehan flashed a brief smile. 'Thank you. I appreciate that.'

They swapped horses. Alec dared not ride Tehan's animal while it was in such distress, so he set out on foot leading the exhausted beast. They moved in relative silence, the horse's slow step muffled by the damp earth. The hut had just come into sight as a woman's scream pierced the bush. The horse started, nearly dragging the reins from Alec's hand. He calmed it and his own breathing, realising that the scream had probably been Annie in the throes of labour.

A horse, tethered to one of the posts holding up the lean-to verandah, turned its head and nickered. An ugly skewbald horse grazed in the yard behind the hut. Alec's nerves stretched. Two horses. Allowing for Eliza to be responsible for one animal, that was one horse too many. Someone else was at the hut, someone who had no business there.

He tethered Tehan's horse to the side of the track and crept forward, watching every footfall, although with a screaming woman inside the hut, the chance of being heard seemed minimal. The dog did not greet him as he had on his last visit and as he came closer, he saw the brindled body lying on the ground. The dog raised his head and whimpered faintly, the stringy tail beating the dirt.

Alec knelt beside the animal and stroked his head. It had blood on his coat and death in its eyes. Even as he stroked the poor beast's head, the animal gave a small shudder and lay still. Alec's stomach lurched. He loved all animals and he shuddered to think how close Windlass had come to the same fate. He now knew the identity of the unwelcome intruder.

Another scream seemed to shake the leaves on the trees, sending parrots flying up in squawks of indignation. Alec took advantage of the distraction to get closer to the hut. The shutters on the mean little window had been closed but they had enough gaps to allow him to look inside.

He could make out a pair of men's boots resting on the table and, alarmingly, a rifle beside the boots. He changed position and saw the curtain across the bed space. The women, he hoped, were behind the curtain. Where was Charlie?

He sought another gap in the shutters and squinted. Now he could see Jennings watching the curtain, his big hand wrapped around a tankard, and behind him the child hunched beside the fire.

Alec crouched and considered his options. He had to draw Jennings out of the house, or he risked the man using the women and the child as hostages but he had no weapon. One unarmed man against an experienced criminal with a rifle. The odds were not good.

He returned to Tehan's horse to see if the man carried anything useful. He found a length of rope and a small axe. Neither of these objects surprised him; trees blew down across the tracks on a regular basis and they would be useful in clearing the track. He cast around in the bush and found a solid branch. Neither an axe nor a branch was much use against a rifle but Alec had the element of surprise and he intended to use it.

He tucked the axe into his belt, walked down to the creek and collected a handful of pebbles. With his heart in his mouth, he came within a couple of yards of the hut and threw the pebbles at the door before making a bolt for the side of the house.

He heard Jennings bellow and the front door crashed open. Alec strained his ears, waiting to see which way the man would go and thanked the gods that his first instinct was to turn right, in Alec's direction. As Jennings rounded the corner, Alec brought the heavy branch crashing down. He aimed for the man's head but at the last second, Jennings twisted away and the branch caught his shoulder. It was enough force for the rifle to drop to the ground and Alec kicked it away as Jennings roared, coming for him with all the fury of a man who would stab a dog to death.

Alec had the advantage of height but Jennings had brute strength. The force of the onslaught sent Alec crashing back against the house and onto the ground. The man's fingers locked on his throat, his face a snarling, rabid mask. Alec pushed back, keeping the man at arm's length while trying to break the grip on his throat.

The world began to blur and he felt himself losing strength. Shadows danced into his peripheral vision.

'You bastard!' a woman screamed and something large and heavy swung down on the back of Jennings's head.

The bearded man went limp, collapsing on to Alec in a sweating, stinking heap.

Alec caught his breath and looked up to see Eliza standing over the miner, a shotgun in her hand and her eyes blazing. *Hell hath no fury ...*

Eliza waited, letting Alec McLeod extract himself from beneath the unconscious man. He rested on his hands and knees, catching his breath, but Eliza's eyes were only for Jennings. The man was down and as far as she cared, he could stay down forever. He had raped Annie, he had threatened to rape her—he had probably killed Will.

She raised the shotgun, pointing the barrel at Jennings. If it had been loaded, she would have fired, but Alec found his feet and caught her arm.

He shook his head. 'Enough, Eliza.'

She let him take the shotgun from her. Alec had a rope and, putting one knee on Jennings's back, he bound the man's hands tightly and dragged him over to the nearest tree where he wound the last of the rope around Jennings's chest. Eliza watched him, her hands balling at her sides as she tried to still the red beast that still roared inside her.

Her fear and hatred of the bearded man had awakened something that frightened her. She had wanted to kill Jennings, wanted to beat him until he was a pulp, fire both barrels of the shotgun.

Alec returned and picked up Jennings's rifle, cracking it open. Satisfied that it contained a charge he closed it again and cocked it, taking aim at the burly miner who groaned and looked up at Alec with unfocussed eyes.

'Does your head hurt?' Alec asked.

For an answer Jennings spat in his direction.

'Give me one reason why I shouldn't kill you here and now,' Alec said, bringing the rifle up to his shoulder.

'Because you ain't the sort,' Jennings said. 'Bloody man of honour, you.'

Alec took a deep breath and lowered the weapon. He looked up at the sky. 'I think it's going to rain,' he said. 'Let that cool your temper, Jennings.'

A cry of distress from Charlie made Eliza turn. The child knelt by the body of her beloved dog, cradling its head in her lap.

'I wish you'd killed him,' the child sobbed.

Eliza laid a hand on Charlie's shoulder. 'That would be wrong,' she said. 'What was his name?'

'Bernie.'

Alec squatted beside the child and stroked the dog's head. 'We'll give Bernie a proper funeral,' he said. 'He died trying to protect you and your mother and we owe him that.'

Gulping back sobs, Charlie allowed Eliza to raise her to her feet and lead her back into the hut.

Annie propped herself up on her elbows, her fevered gaze going from Eliza to Charlie. 'What happened? Did I hear McLeod?'

'It's all right, Annie, Alec McLeod managed to overcome Jennings,' Eliza said.

'Did he kill the bastard?"

'No, but he's not going anywhere. You're safe, Annie.'

Annie let her head fall back on the pillow, tears streaming from her eyes. 'I can pick 'em, Miss Penrose. I can really pick 'em.

Thought Jennings was properly sweet on me, until he ...' Her words were lost in another contraction.

'Charlie, stay with your mother. I'm going to talk to McLeod,' Eliza said.

She found Alec leaning against a post in the shelter of the verandah, the rifle crooked in his arm and his gaze firmly on Jennings.

'How's Annie?'

Eliza shook her head. 'It's not going well. She's losing strength.'

Alec propped the rifle against the post and came to her, wrapping his arms around her. She curled into him with a sigh.

'I wanted to kill him,' she said and, her voice muffled by his coat, she told him how Jennings had raped Annie. 'And you know that given the chance he would have done the same to me.'

Alec said nothing but held her closer, kissing her hair. Beneath his shirt, the muscles in his shoulder tightened and his breathing quickened.

He pulled away from her and, holding her at arm's length, he said, 'As soon as Tehan gets here I'll go for Maidment. I'll see Jennings hang for what he's done.'

She let out a long breath and nodded.

Inside the hut, Annie screamed.

Charlie came running out. She tugged at Eliza's sleeve. 'Ma needs you.'

Alec released her. 'I'll be here,' he said, taking a seat on one of the benches outside the door, Jennings's rifle across his lap.

The afternoon wore on and despite Eliza's chivvying, Annie hardly had the strength left to ride the contractions. The dark closed in and Eliza set Charlie to light the lanterns and stoke the fire. None of them had eaten all day and Eliza left the bed and stood looking at the contents of Annie's food safe, easing the cramp in her back. Some dry bread and salted meat seemed to be the only edible items.

Alec opened the door. 'Tehan's back and he's got the midwife with him.'

Relief flooded Eliza and she leaned on the table, conscious of her own hunger and exhaustion as Ellen Bushby entered, shaking off a bedraggled cloak. Tehan followed her, taking the cloak and hanging it from a peg by the door where it dripped water onto the earthen floor. The town's midwife wasted no time in niceties. Her eyes were only for Annie and she went straight to the patient, pulling the curtain behind her.

Tehan jerked his head at the door. 'What have you done to Jennings?'

Alec gave him a brief account and Tehan ran a hand over his eyes.

'I knew I should have damn well locked him up before I left the mine, but I couldn't find him. What are we going to do with him?'

Alec glanced at the curtain. 'Now you're here, I'll take Jennings in to the police.'

Ellen Bushby came out from behind the curtain, her brow furrowed. 'The baby's breech. We need the doctor and we need him soon.'

Tehan frowned. 'What does that mean?'

'Baby's in the wrong position—feet first. He's well and truly stuck.' She paused. 'I'll do what I can but she needs a doctor, and even then ...'

Alec sucked in his breath, his hand going to the table as if he needed to steady himself. Eliza looked into his pale, drawn face and remembered his wife and child had died in similar circumstances. It must all be coming back. She took his hand.

'If you're going back to town, go for the doctor.'

'The doctor, yes ...' He nodded. 'Give me a hand with Jennings, Tehan.'

Ellen turned to Eliza. 'Make yourself useful, Miss Penrose. Tea, please.'

Eliza set the kettle to boil and watched from the shelter of the verandah as a sodden Jennings was thrown onto the saddle of his horse. The man seemed surprisingly cooperative but he had spent several hours exposed to the elements and the thought of a nice warm gaol cell must have seemed a good alternative.

With Jennings secured by his hands and feet, Alec turned to Eliza. She raised her hand but he left Tehan holding the horses and ran to her, folding her in his arms. He kissed her gently before reluctantly releasing her and swinging himself into the saddle of the freshest horse. He laid the rifle across the bow of the saddle and Tehan handed him the reins of the horse carrying Jennings. Alec jerked the reins and both horses moved forward. As he rode away, he twisted in the saddle and raised his hand. Eliza's heart jolted. Whatever the next days held, she and Alec would face them together and to hell with what the town thought.

Twenty-Nine

Alec made good time into town and found Constable Prewitt behind the desk at the police station. He saw Jennings incarcerated in irons in one of the cells and went in search of Dr Sims.

Mustering every shred of courage, Alec turned the horse up the track to the mine where the doctor's housekeeper advised he would be found. An ominous silence hung over the mine site and the crowd at the gate parted to let him through without a word. In the yard, filthy, exhausted miners gathered in silent knots, watching Alec's progress. He found the absolute silence worse than the earlier abuse and his instincts prickled. Something had changed in the hours he had been away.

Osborne Russell appeared at the door to the administration building. 'We've been looking for you,' he said.

'I'm only here to fetch the doctor. Annie O'Reilly's in trouble and he's needed.'

Russell held up a hand. 'Step inside for a moment.'

'I don't have a moment and there is nothing I have to say to Cowper that won't wait.'

'Please.'

A man came forward to hold Alec's horse and Russell ordered the nearest boy to find the doctor.

A hundred questions boiled over in Alec's chest as Russell stood aside to admit Alec to the manager's office. 'What's happened? Have they found—are they ...?'

Angus Mackie sat at the table and beside him was Edward Gutteridge, the mine inspector for the Maiden's Creek goldfields. Sergeant Maidment stood beside the fireplace, poking the fire in the grate with the toe of his boot. Cowper was conspicuous in his absence.

'Where's Cowper?' Alec shook his head. 'A woman is dying, I don't have time—'

Russell cleared his throat and said, with a sweeping glance that took in everyone in the room, 'You are owed an apology, McLeod.'

'Cowper's gone,' Mackie said. 'And certain knowledge has been brought to us that clears your name.'

Maidment turned around. 'Eva Trevalyn came to me this morning with notes she had been keeping of conversations with her husband. They corroborated your story. I went up to the house to confront Cowper but I found he had packed his bag and told his housekeeper he was headed for an urgent meeting in Melbourne. He took off on one of Sones's horses. We've alerted the police posts at Buneep, Port Albert and Sale, but no one's seen him since this morning.'

Russell straightened. 'Interestingly Mary Harris had her own story to tell. It would appear she had certain expectations of her relationship with Cowper that have not been realised so she was happy to tell us everything she knew about the theft of the gold from the Shenandoah Mine. Gutteridge here has confirmed the figures for the two mines and it would seem you were right, there has been a systematic theft of gold from Shenandoah.'

Maidment left his rearrangement of the fire and stepped forward. 'We are now most concerned with the disappearance of Miss Penrose,' Maidment said. 'Mary Harris had no information beyond the suspicion that some sort of struggle took place in her kitchen last night. She found broken crockery.'

So Mary Harris had been lying.

'Miss Penrose is safe. She was abducted on Cowper's orders by his man Jennings, who is now, I am relieved to say, in the custody of your constable. She was—' he couldn't believe he was saying this, '—rescued by Jack Tehan and she's with Annie O'Reilly. While I would like to talk more, I must get the doctor to Annie.'

Dr Sims appeared at the door. 'What's this about Annie O'Reilly?'

'Ellen Bushby's with her. She's been in labour for nearly thirty-six hours and Mrs Bushby tells me the baby is breech. Doctor—'

Sims nodded. 'My horse is outside. I'll go now.'

Alec moved toward the door, but Russell laid a hand on his sleeve. 'We need you here, McLeod. There's been another fall. All the rescuers managed to get out of the way, but the water level is rising and we're running out of time.'

Alec ran his hand through his hair as his mind surged with the possibilities. Rising water, lack of oxygen, further falls. Even if Ian and the others had survived the first fall, they may already be too late. Without another word, he turned and ran from the building.

As he passed the crib room, a woman in the doorway shouted, 'Get them out, McLeod. You're their last chance.'

He turned to acknowledge Eva Trevalyn. She had been joined by three other wives: Ada Morgan, Jenny Tregloan and Janet Marsh. They stood by the door, their arms around each other, and an unfamiliar prickling started in the back of his throat.

Everything Eva Trevalyn had done for him would be worth nothing if he could not get to the trapped men. These women would lose their husbands and their children, their fathers. He couldn't fail them.

Ducking his head, he entered the main tunnel of the mine. In the brightly lit cavern, groups of rescuers worked in silence.

At the head of the shaft, the assistant foreman, Williams, confirmed the second collapse and the threat of rising water.

Alec glanced at the two boilers in the cavern. 'Stoke up the new boiler,' he ordered, 'and open up the steam valves on the engine all the way. We have to get the pumps to maximum.' He straightened, narrowly avoiding hitting his head. 'I want as much shoring brought in from wherever you can get it. I'm going below.'

Below ground the situation was as bad as he had feared: the men were sloshing around in calf-deep water and the second fall of rock had undone whatever they had managed to achieve. The men had been trapped for four days; if they were still alive it would be a miracle.

'We need to keep moving the material from the top part of the fall,' Alec said to Williams. 'God willing, there is enough of a void left by the fall to allow someone to get through to the other side.'

Williams nodded. 'We were doing well until the second fall.' He paused, his eyes weary in the mask of dust and dirt. 'Glad to have you back, Mr McLeod.'

Ellen Bushby stood and sighed. Her eyes caught Eliza's and she gave a slight shake of her head. 'She's not much strength left,' she whispered. 'We can't wait for the doctor. This baby's got to come out or they'll both—'

She didn't say the word but it hung between them. Eliza had lost a childhood friend to childbirth, and she had been in the hands of the best doctor and midwife her husband's money could buy. All Annie had was a midwife, a useless woman and a child.

Ellen turned back to Annie. 'Next contraction and I want you to really push,' she said. 'Can you do that for me?'

Annie nodded and moaned as the contraction came. Later, Eliza had trouble recalling the exact sequence of events that followed. Annie's screams and Ellen's shouted orders became a blur. First the legs, then the body and finally with a twist and a final push, a baby ... a baby that hung limp and blue in Ellen's arms.

Annie struggled to prop herself up on her elbows. 'Let me see,' she begged.

'It's a girl, Annie,' Ellen said, 'but she's not breathing.'

Annie gave a ragged cry and fell back on the bed. From the other side of the curtain, Charlie began to sob.

Ellen cut the cord, wrapped the child in a cloth and handed the limp bundle to Eliza. 'See if you can get some life into the child while I see to Annie.'

Eliza looked down at the perfect little face of the child who might never be and thought about a wax doll she had owned as a child. 'What do I do?'

'Try rubbing her,' Ellen said.

Eliza laid the baby on the end of the bed and, using the cloth, chafed the tiny body, willing life to return. But the child remained unresponsive.

'Let me.' Charlie pushed in front of her. She picked the baby up and held her close to her own little body, crooning to her and rocking her.

'Charlie ...' Eliza said, holding out her arms.

'She's not dead,' Charlie replied, holding on fiercely. 'She's not dead.' She bent her head to kiss the fragile little face. There was a moment of absolute silence, then came a small sneeze followed by a cough and a high, indignant, fretful wail.

'I told you she wasn't dead,' Charlie said.

Ellen took the baby from the child and unwrapped her, checking fingers and toes while the new baby mewled her protests.

She laid the child in Annie's arms. Tears rolled silently down the woman's cheeks and Eliza marvelled that a woman who had just endured the most horrific labour could look so content, so happy.

'Is Jack 'ere?' Annie whispered.

'He is,' Eliza said, adding, 'keeping out of the way.'

A smile curved Annie's generous mouth. 'Look at 'er, Miss Penrose. She ain't Jennings's. She looks just like Charlie.'

It took a moment for Eliza to get her meaning. Charlie was Tehan's niece, Tehan's blood. 'You mean she's Jack Tehan's child?'

'Only one of two men could be 'er da and if it ain't Jennings ...'

Eliza found Tehan out in the stable, grooming his horse.

'I couldn't take her screaming,' he said, without looking around. 'Never felt so bloody useless in me life. Is it over? Is she ...?'

'She's fine and so is the baby. She wants to see you.' To her shame, Eliza began to tremble uncontrollably, tears pouring down her face. 'I thought we were going to lose her.'

'We breed them tough in Tasmania,' Tehan said. He clapped a hand on her shoulder and squeezed as he passed her. 'You did grand, Miss Penrose. Thank you.'

Eliza followed Tehan into the hut, watching from the doorway as the man bent and accepted the child from Annie.

'You 'ave a daughter, Jack Tehan,' Annie said.

'Does she have a name?' Ellen Bushby asked.

'Sarah, after me ma,' Annie answered.

'Sarah it is,' Tehan said.

He had eyes for no one else in the room, just the little bundle in his arms. Eliza had never seen a man so captivated. Maybe one day it might be Alec and the child in his arms would be theirs.

She turned away from the tableau at the bedside and stood fighting back the exhaustion, arms wrapped around herself. The man, the woman and the two children were as far removed from a perfect family as they could be and yet they looked as if they belonged together.

She wiped the shaming tears from her eyes as a horse came cantering up the road and Dr Sims halted in front of the hut. She went forward and took the reins as he threw himself off the horse, reaching for the bag strapped to the back of his saddle.

He looked at her face and shook his head. 'Too late?'

She nodded and his shoulders slumped.

'No … I meant Annie and her baby are still with us,' Eliza said.

Sims huffed out a breath. 'Doesn't mean they're out of danger,' he said. 'Take me to them.'

Charlie lay curled up on the bed next to her mother. Jack sat beside her, the baby in his arms. He looked up at the doctor. 'Ain't life grand?' he said to no one in particular.

'That's as may be, but the doctor needs to see to Mrs O'Reilly. Everyone out,' Ellen Bushby ordered. 'Miss Penrose, could you make some more tea?'

As Eliza set the kettle to boil once more, Jack subsided into a chair and lifted Charlie on to his lap. The child's eyelids fluttered and in a minute she was asleep.

'What now, Jack?' Eliza asked.

He glanced at the curtain, behind which Dr Sims and Ellen Bushby were speaking in low voices. 'I thought when I brought her over from Tasmania I could make things better for her, but I failed.'

'Is that why you involved yourself in my uncle's schemes?'

He nodded. 'I was saving the money to buy us a farm, but I guess I need to find another job now.'

'Leave Maiden's Creek? Leave Annie and the girls?'

'You think I should marry her?' Jack said. 'Well, it ain't for want of asking. She won't have me. Besides I think I need to make meself scarce. Last thing they need is me banged up in gaol. I could do with something a bit stronger than tea. Annie's got a whiskey bottle in that cupboard. Let's wet the baby's head.'

The doctor and midwife came out from behind the curtain. They glanced at each other.

'Mr Tehan, I gather you are Mrs O'Reilly's next of kin?' Sims said.

Tehan transferred Charlie to Eliza's care and rose to his feet, thrusting his hands into his pockets.

'She's not out of danger,' Sims said. 'She needs proper care and rest and she's not going to get it here. Is there somewhere in town she can lodge?'

Jack looked at Eliza, his face blank.

'Maybe we could ask Mrs Burrell. She's taken Charlie in before now and she has as kind a heart as anyone,' Eliza said.

Sims collected his hat from where he'd thrown it on to the table. 'I must get back to Maiden's Creek, so I will speak to Mrs Burrell. In the meantime, can I ask you to remain here and keep her as comfortable as possible? Mrs Bushby will stay too. Let's get them both through the night.'

'What's the news from the mine?' Eliza asked.

Sims frowned. 'I suppose you haven't heard. Your uncle has absconded. Packed his bag and went at first light today. From what I heard, he has been up to his elbows in dirty dealings and it had gone past the point where he could cover it up any longer.

McLeod's owed an apology by the town. When I left they'd put him back in charge at the mine.'

'Have they got the men out yet?'

Sims shook his head. 'There's been another collapse and hope is fading.'

Thirty

2 August 1873

Netty and Amos Burrell came to the hut in the early hours of the morning, in a wagon drawn by one of the coach horses. Annie had no strength to do more than protest feebly as Tehan carried her out to the cart, where a mattress had been laid. They wrapped the woman and the baby in blankets and Charlie snuggled in beside them. Eliza covered them all with the patchwork quilt.

Tehan collected and saddled the horses and, as Ellen fussed over her patient, Tehan helped Eliza mount her horse.

'Are you coming?' she asked.

He shook his head. 'Time to go, before Maidment comes looking for me. Just got to pack me bags.'

'What about Annie and the children?'

He scratched his beard and shrugged. 'I'll send money when I can.'

'Jack …' Eliza began, but he had already mounted and turned his horse on to the track to Pretty Sally. She wondered if she or Annie or Charlie would ever see him again.

They reached Maiden's Creek in the dead hours before dawn. Burrell carried Annie into the house and settled her and the baby in their spare bed. Netty made up a little trundle bed for Charlie and Eliza fell asleep on the day bed in the parlour, too tired to even take off her boots.

She woke to the smell of eggs and bacon cooking. Netty handed her her travelling bag and after a wash and a change of clothing, Eliza felt more human. As Netty served up breakfast she looked in on Annie, surprised to find the woman propped up in bed with the contented baby happily nursing. Charlie sat cross-legged on the end of the bed, reading a book. She looked up and, seeing Eliza, flew at her, wrapping her scrawny arms around her.

'And good morning to you too,' Eliza said, disengaging the child. 'Annie?'

Annie managed a wan smile. 'I've been better, Miss Penrose, but I don't want to be imposing on Mrs Burrell—'

'Nonsense,' Netty said, bustling in with a tray. 'Now, I want to see all of that eaten up. Yours is on the table, Eliza.'

'Is there any news from the mine?' Eliza asked as she sat down to a plate heaped with eggs, bacon and fresh, crusty bread.

'No. Amos has gone up there this morning to see if he can be of any help, but the word around town is there's not much chance of finding 'em alive now.'

Eliza set her fork down, thinking of the Morgan children and Bert Marsh and Joe Trevalyn, who could now be without fathers, and pretty Jenny Tregloan, whose child would never know a father ... and Ian, who should never have been in the mine. Ian with his wisdom beyond his years and his love for Susan Mackie.

She stood. 'I'm going up to the mine.'

Netty didn't attempt to stop her and Eliza set off with a purpose-ful stride, conscious that she was Charles Cowper's niece and his disgrace was now reflected on her. But the watchers at the gate, huddled beneath makeshift shelters, only lifted weary eyes to her. After nearly five days, they were probably as exhausted as the rescuers.

The door to the manager's office stood open and she stepped inside.

Alec was at the table studying what seemed to be a plan of the mine. He looked up and the exhaustion lifted from the lines in his face.

'Eliza!'

She stumbled toward him and he took her in his arms. She closed her eyes as she leaned against him, breathing in the scent of damp earth and sweat. At that moment, she did not wish to be anywhere else.

'Amos Burrell told me that Annie and the child are safe,' Alec said.

'Yes, the whole family is with Netty now.'

'Best place for them. Tehan?'

'He's gone. I don't know where.'

Alec nodded and let out a breath. 'When I saw how bad Annie was, I feared the worst. It all came back to me.'

'Catriona?'

'I would have given the blood from my veins to save her.' He pushed away from Eliza, sinking onto a chair, his face buried in his hands. 'I swore on her grave that I'd not ... I'd not risk my heart again.'

The breath left Eliza's body as certainly as if he'd punched her in the stomach. What did he mean?

He looked up at her. 'And then you stood in my path, Eliza Penrose.'

She crouched in front of him, taking his hands in hers. 'No one is meant to be alone, Alec, and sometimes we just have to take a risk.'

'Would you be willing to take a risk on me, Eliza? I've not much to offer except my heart.'

She smiled and laid her hand on his chest, her fingers firm over the steady beat. 'And it is a good heart, Alec McLeod. Yes, yes, I would be prepared to take such a risk.'

He cupped her chin in his hand and drew her face toward his. Her lips brushed his in a question that he answered by pulling her to her feet. Time and space seemed to merge into the soft winter light, leaving just the two of them.

The clanging of the mine bell and a clamour of voices forced them apart. Alec threw open the outer door as Williams and half-a-dozen men came running across the yard.

'They're alive,' Williams said. 'We heard 'em calling out. They're alive, McLeod.'

It seemed to Eliza that every man, woman and child in Maiden's Creek were converging on the mine from all directions. The exhausted rescue crew emerged from whatever corner they had found to rest and the courtyard filled with people eager for news.

Eliza pushed through the crowd to reach the crib room where the women waited with the exhausted wives. Unfortunately the first person she encountered was Flora Donald.

'Miss Penrose, I heard you were safe,' she said. 'You want to make sure you're not dragged into your uncle's disgrace.'

'What do you mean?'

'I don't mean anything,' Flora said. 'But you and your brother before you … It might be said you knew what he was up to.'

Eliza said nothing. She wasn't going to lie for Charles Cowper but neither did she need to share the whole sordid story with Flora Donald.

A commotion went up and standing on her tiptoes, she could just make out Alec standing at the entrance to the mine but whatever he had been trying to say was drowned out by the noise. He held up a hand and the crowd went silent.

'We've cleared enough of the rubble to get within striking distance of where the men are trapped. We don't know anything about their condition and we won't until we can get through and for that we need a volunteer, someone small enough to crawl through the space we've cleared—' His voice rasped with the dust and exhaustion.

'Me, sir!'

Eliza recognised Bert Marsh pushing his way to the front of the crowd.

'Not you, lad.'

'Please, sir, it's me dad in there. Me name's Bert Marsh,' the boy said.

'No—'

'I have to do it for Da.'

Eliza pushed her way to the front of the men. 'I'm small and I know mines as well as any man here. Let me go.'

Alec stared at her. 'Eliza, no!'

'Not a woman,' one of the miners said.

Eliza rounded on the crowd. 'This boy has his whole future in front of him. I have no one. Let me go.' Her gaze held Alec's, silently pleading with him to understand that what she had just said was not true. She had this man, this extraordinary man.

Willliams shook his head. 'Miss Penrose, it is too dangerous.'

'But you would let a boy go? I know mines. I've lived around them all my life.'

Alec stared at her, his face unreadable. 'Eliza, Williams is right. It's too dangerous.'

She held his gaze. 'I have to do this, Alec. It's one thing I can do.'

'Find her some clothes,' Alec said, and turned back into the mine.

Ten minutes later, dressed in rough trousers, stout boots and a heavy woollen shirt that was far too large, Eliza presented herself at the head of the mine shaft. She had tied her hair in a tight bun and jammed a workman's cap on her head. Williams handed her a pair of thick leather gloves that swamped her hands.

Alec drew her to one side. 'Eliza, please don't do this. I can't risk ... I don't want to lose you too.'

She laid a hand on his arm. 'I have to do it, Alec. Don't you see? I have to make it right with this community.'

'You are not responsible for your uncle's actions.'

'But I am tainted by them.'

He studied her face for a long moment before giving a brisk nod of his head. 'Follow me.'

She descended into the dark shaft, her heart hammering. A circle of filthy, exhausted men gathered at the foot of the ladder. They stared at her but none of them made any comment. She could see the damage extending down the tunnel to her right, a heap of broken rock and spoil.

'We've cleared a way across the void,' Alec said. 'What we need you to do is find a way through the last few feet.'

She nodded, too nervous to trust herself to speak.

Alec tied a rope around her waist and handed her a pick, a miner's lantern and a flask of water. 'We'll be at the end of the rope,' he said. 'Give three tugs if you need help—'

'Four if you get through,' another man said.

Alec drew her into his arms. 'Not too late to change your mind,' he said.

'I haven't,' she replied.

'Eliza ... come back to me,' he whispered in her ear and released her.

She scrambled up the fallen spoil heap, picking her way on hands and knees through the gap that had been made. The light from the working face of the collapse disappeared as she moved cautiously forward. She reached a wall of rock and dirt; now the only connection she had with the men behind her was the rope around her waist. She took the pick and knocked. Holding her breath, she waited, letting out a gasp as she heard an answering knock. It sounded close.

She surveyed the rubble in front of her and carefully began to chip away at the softer earth closest to where the collapse had occurred. It was hot, dusty work and she took a small swig of the water, conscious that the precious liquid should be saved for the men, who had a greater need of it than her.

A scrabbling noise on the far side of the spoil caused her to halt and she heard a voice, the lilt of a Cornish accent. Trevalyn?

'You're nearly through. Keep digging, lad.'

Hope lent her strength and she hacked at the hole she was making, expanding it, listening to the sound of someone else digging from the other side. She broke through with a triumphant cry. Heard an answering cry.

She held up the lantern, illuminating a man's face, almost unrecognisable beneath the grime.

'Put that down,' Trevalyn said. 'We've had no light and it'll blind us. Who's that?'

'Eliza Penrose.'

The man gasped.

'Bloody pleased to see you, Miss Penrose. Pardon the language.' Trevalyn paused. 'We're all here, but young McLeod and Tregloan are both in a bad way. The air's not good and we're in water up to our knees. To be honest, I don't think we could have lasted much longer.'

Eliza remembered the instructions and gave the rope four sharp jerks. Distantly she heard a cheer.

'Now, lass,' Trevalyn said. 'You go back to McLeod and tell him to go careful. We'll get the youngsters out first. They need the doc.'

Eliza passed him the water flask and the pick. 'I need the lantern,' she said. 'But I'll come back with light and food.'

Trevalyn chuckled. 'A little while longer in the dark won't hurt us.'

The crawl back the way she had come did not seem to take as long and as she emerged at the end of the shaft, she was greeted by another cheer. Alec caught her as she slithered down the last few feet.

'Well?'

'Ian's alive,' she said, 'but not in a good way. We need to get him and Tregloan out first.'

'*We* don't need to do anything,' Alec said as relief flooded his face. 'You've done more than enough. Go back up, Eliza, and tell everyone out there what you've told me and then have a rest. You've earned it.'

She would have protested but he had already turned away, ordering the men to continue the clearance.

Eliza climbed the ladder and walked to the end of the long tunnel, where the crowd waited for her news.

Over the next few hours, the men worked with a feverish energy, clearing a pathway wide enough to allow air to the trapped men. Food, water and lanterns were passed through, but it would still be some time before the rescuers had secured a safe space to allow the men to come out.

Chafing with impatience, Alec could stand by no longer and took his turn at the excavation. A man came behind him with timbers for shoring and props. They worked in silence except for the grunts of their effort and moved with agonising slowness. Sweat poured from Alec, his skin caked with dirt that turned to mud. He had dust in his eyes, his mouth and his ears. And despite the gloves he wore, his fingers bled. None of it mattered. He worked like a man possessed with one end in mind: getting Ian out of this hellhole.

Others offered to take his place but he ground on, determined to see it through. He only paused when he heard voices and the faint light from the lantern that had been passed through to the miners. Laying his head on his arms, he took a deep breath.

'Ian McLeod, are you there?' he called, realising his foolishness as soon as he spoke. Ian couldn't hear him.

'He's here, McLeod,' Trevalyn replied.

Relief and hope drew Alec on and he worked feverishly, clearing his way through to the trapped men. He crawled on torn and bleeding elbows through the space, tumbling out with a splash into the foetid, water-filled cavern that had saved the four miners and his brother.

'Took your time, McLeod,' Trevalyn remarked as Alec stood.

Trevalyn had been correct. The water had reached the men's knees but they had used some of the spoil to create a platform on which the two injured men lay.

Alec knelt in the water beside his brother. In the light of the lantern, Ian could have been dead. He lay quite still, his face ashen and his eyes lost in dark hollows. He brushed the mud from his brother's face.

'Ian, I'm here. Where are you hurt?'

Ian licked his dried and cracked lips but said nothing.

'His arm,' Trevalyn replied. 'Might be other injuries, but we've tidied the arm up as best we can.'

Alec drew his brother to him as though he were a small child. 'Ian, how can you forgive me?' he whispered into his brother's filthy, matted hair, knowing the younger man couldn't hear him.

'I always knew you would come,' Ian said.

Thirty-One

Eliza spent the rest of the day working in the crib room, providing meals and endless cups of tea for the men working below. Finding the men alive was one thing, getting them out, quite another.

Long after it had gone dark, she retired to her uncle's office to rest. She lit the fire and sank into a chair at the table where she laid her head on her arms, too tired to make her way back into town. Even though she craved a bed, she didn't want to leave Alec. He would need her as much as she needed him.

She must have slept, because she woke with a start as the office door slammed. She looked up, brushing hair from her eyes. The fire had burned low and the candle on the desk was nearly a stub and for a moment she thought she was seeing a ghost. The hope that it would be Alec with news slipped away and she stiffened, every nerve taut. She had never seen the resemblance between her uncle and her brother but the dishevelled figure standing in the doorway staring at her looked younger than his years, and for a moment the likeness took her by surprise.

She pushed back the chair and rose. 'They said you'd left.'

Cowper gave a bitter laugh. 'You know the ways in and out of this town, Eliza. Leaving is not that easy.' He jerked his head at the safe. 'I left something important in there.'

'Take it and go.'

He pulled a small pistol, similar to the one he had handed to Jennings the night before, from his pocket and levelled it at her. 'Just be a good girl and sit there and be quiet.'

She complied, poised for flight if the opportunity arose, but Cowper's nerves were strung tight and if she so much as shifted her weight in the chair, he'd swing the pistol in her direction.

The safe stood in the corner beside the fireplace, a sturdy model opened with a key, which he selected from the ring he carried. He flung the door open, stuffing bank notes and documents into a canvas bag. When he was done, he sat back on his heels and surveyed the empty safe.

'You know this is all your fault,' he said. 'If you had left town when I advised—'

'I would never have discovered the extent of your perfidy? How long do you think it would have been before the discrepancy in the mine returns would have been noticed? As for forging my brother's will, that is unforgiveable. You're a thief—worse than a thief. You stole from William and I, the two people in the world who most trusted you.'

Cowper screwed up his face, running his hand through his hair. 'Eliza, I'm sorry—sorry for everything. I cared deeply for Will … and for you. I didn't mean to hurt either of you, but the opportunity was there and I took it.'

'Did you kill my brother?'

His eyes widened. 'No. As God is my witness, I would never have hurt him.'

'But you thought nothing of allowing that brute Jennings to carry me off. Do you know what he threatened to do to me?'

'You were safe enough.'

'If it hadn't been for Jack Tehan, I would not be here now.'

'Tehan?' Cowper gave a short, derisive laugh. 'Tehan trims his sails to the wind. I suppose you think him pure as snow now?'

'No. I know he forged the will and was complicit in the theft of the gold, but he has something you lack—integrity. What do you intend to do now?'

Cowper lifted the bag and looked at it as if seeing it for the first time. 'You've left me no option, have you? I have to go. I've got enough set aside to establish myself in another forgotten corner of the empire.'

'But first you have to get out of Maiden's Creek.'

He glanced at the door. 'You might just have to help me.'

Eliza's breath caught, understanding his intention. 'Just go,' she said. 'I'll say nothing.'

But her uncle had a wildness in his eyes she'd never seen before. He shouldered his bag and grabbed her arm, jerking her out of the chair and pushing her toward the door.

'Come with me.'

She pulled back. 'No. You're in enough trouble already, Uncle.'

He shrugged. 'I am beyond caring. Now, just keep your mouth shut.' He twisted her arm behind her back and pushed her ahead of him.

Outside, she cast wildly around, looking for help. The crowd had long since dispersed and the courtyard was deserted except for a few men at the mouth of the adit. She willed them to turn but they were engrossed in a conversation. A light burned in the crib hut and she could make out figures moving within but in the shadows nobody would notice the two figures, even if they did happen to glance in their direction.

Cowper pushed Eliza down the dark lane between the workshop and the administration building, following the tram lines toward the battery and the tailings.

'What's going on?'

Cowper swung around at the sound of Flora Donald's voice, drawing Eliza to him, the pistol pressed against her ribcage.

'He has a weapon, Miss Donald,' Eliza said. 'Just turn away.'

The Scotswoman emerged from the shadows between the buildings and put her hands on her hips. 'Is that so?' she said. 'And are you really going to kill her, Mr Cowper?'

'I will,' Cowper said. His voice had risen and Eliza could smell the fear oozing from him.

'Well, I don't think I can permit that.'

From behind Flora Donald came the sound of upraised voices and the thunder of feet and the men who had been standing at the entrance to the mine pulled up at the sight of the two figures standing at the head of the tailings. Eliza's breath hitched at the sight of Alec.

Alec took a step in front of Flora. 'Let her go, Cowper.'

Cowper shook his head. 'This is your fault, McLeod, as much as hers. Why did you have to start asking questions?'

'Let Eliza go and we can talk about what's been done to this mine and to your niece.'

Cowper's fingers tightened on her arm and Eliza was reminded that trapped rats will fight for their survival. He took another step back, his foot slipping on the loose rock. He regained his balance and glanced behind him.

From the corner of her eye, Eliza could see that they were now poised precariously, the sheer drop down the tailings only inches behind them.

Alec took another step forward. Cowper shifted but did not move. Time seemed to slow and the men who stood with Flora Donald faded into the background as the world contracted to just Eliza, her uncle and the man approaching them.

Alec stretched out his hand. 'Let her go, Cowper. You don't want to die like Will.'

Cowper whimpered as the rocks skidded beneath him, one large rock dislodging and falling with a dull thud.

'Please, Uncle,' Eliza whispered.

With a sharp, anguished cry of disgust mingled with fear, Cowper flung her away from him. Alec caught her as she stumbled, holding her, his arm almost pressing the breath from her.

Cowper raised his face to the sky and stretched out his arms. The pistol fell from his hand and for a heartbeat, Eliza thought he would throw himself from the tailings heap. But the fight went from him and he fell to his knees, burying his head in his hands.

Two burly miners pushed past Alec and Eliza and grabbed Cowper by the arms.

'Take him to the office and watch him,' Alec said. 'Someone fetch Maidment.'

The arm around her relaxed and Alec drew her into a gentle embrace, his head resting on hers. 'I thought,' he murmured. 'I thought he would take you with him.'

'I think that makes the third time you have saved my life, Alec McLeod.'

'I just have to keep a better eye on you, Miss Penrose. I think you and I need to talk about that—when this is over.'

She nodded, suddenly too tired to speak.

He pushed her away from him. 'You're exhausted, Eliza. Go back to Netty's and get some sleep. It'll be morning before we get the first man out.' He turned to Flora Donald. 'Can you see to her, Miss Donald? I've got to get back.'

Eliza raised her head to look at the unsmiling Scotswoman. 'Thank you, Miss Donald.'

'You've nothing to thank me for. I didn't do it for you. I happened to see you pass the hut and thought something was not right. Now, you need to get to a bed. I know Mrs Burrell has been waiting for you. I'll see you down there.'

Thirty-Two

3 August 1873

'Eliza! Eliza!'

Woken from a deep, dreamless sleep by Netty shaking her, Eliza rolled over and looked up. It took a moment for the blur of her friend's face to come into focus.

'What is it?'

'They've got the first man out!'

Eliza sat bolt upright on the daybed and ran a hand through her hair. From beyond the cottage came the din of bells, as if every church in Maiden's Creek had extra reason to ring as loudly and as joyfully as it could this particular Sunday morning.

'I have to get up there.'

Netty put her hands on her hips. 'You're not going anywhere until you've had a good wash and some food. I thought you were halfway dead when Flora Donald brought you in last night.'

'What time is it?'

'Ten in the morning. You've had a good eight hours' sleep.'

'Where's my uncle?'

'Locked up with that dreadful man Jennings. Amos says Maidment plans to take 'em both down to Melbourne on Monday.'

Eliza stared at Netty as the memory of the previous night came back. 'I really believe he would have killed me.'

Netty gasped. 'Did he admit to killing your brother?'

'No.'

The outside door opened and Charlie walked in carrying something pressed to her chest. Something small and furry that mewed and wriggled in her grasp.

'Joe Trevalyn gave me this to me,' she said and held up a small ginger kitten. 'Said he heard about me dog. Isn't he lovely?'

Netty opened her mouth to speak but closed it again.

Eliza smiled. 'He's lovely, Charlie. He looks a bit like Windlass.'

'Windlass?'

'Mr McLeod's cat.'

'Can I keep him?' Charlie looked from one woman to the other.

Netty shrugged. 'I think that's up to your mother.'

'How is Annie?' Eliza asked.

'She's grand and so's the baby,' Charlie answered.

Netty picked up a tiny baby's smock from a pile she had been folding. 'Amos went up to the hut this morning and packed a box. I thought I'd just give everything a wash.'

The little garment was made from what could have once been a linen sheet, but it had been beautifully smocked and decorated with embroidered roses.

'Who made this?' Netty asked Charlie.

'Ma. She made it when I was born. She's good with a needle. She's tried teaching me, but I'll never be as good as she is.'

Netty folded the little smock and restored it to the others in the pile and handed the clothes to Charlie. 'Take these into your mother and tell her I'll bring her a cup of tea shortly.'

As the door closed behind Charlie, Netty lowered her voice. 'I've a foolish notion of offering Annie employment. You know I've more work than one person can manage.'

Eliza laid her hand over her friend's. 'I think that is an excellent notion, but you need to tread carefully with her, she's fiercely independent.'

'Aye, but I think some of the fight's gone out of her. The baby gave her a bad scare and she's not out of the woods yet. Now, you wash and change. I've some pie for you.'

Netty set the kettle to boil and as Eliza sat at the table, enjoying Netty's excellent pie, there was a soft rapping at the door. Netty opened it to Nell and Jess, neatly dressed in Sunday best, as if they were on their way to church. The two women stood on the doorstep as if reluctant to enter, despite Netty's invitation.

'We heard about Mad—about Annie,' Nell said, 'and we've brought something for the bairn.' She handed over a leather pouch.

Netty opened it and looked inside. 'That's kind of you,' she said. 'Every bit will help.'

'It's not much but we know what was done to Annie and—' Nell glanced at Jess, '—I hope that bastard Jennings hangs.'

Eliza rose to her feet. 'If you knew, why did no one tell the police?'

Nell stared at her. 'The police? Think they'd care? Jennings tried it on our Sissy, but Lil took to him with the shotgun and he never came back. Reckon that's when he—' She shrugged. 'Never mind.'

'I saw Sissy in Melbourne,' Eliza said. 'Did you know she was dying?'

Netty shot her sharp glance. 'Dying?'

There had been no chance to tell Netty about her meeting with Sissy.

'Consumption,' she said.

Nell nodded. 'When Penrose died, she gave up. She just let the consumption take her.'

Jess tugged her friend's sleeve. 'Gotta go, Nell.'

Netty stood at the door, watching the two women slip away. She turned to Eliza. 'What you said about Sissy ... That grieves me,' she said. 'I was that fond of her and Miss Adelaide will be sorry to hear it too.' She picked up the pouch of coins and opened the door to Annie's room.

Eliza was relieved to see Annie had some colour in her cheeks and the baby asleep contentedly in a wooden cradle beside the bed.

Netty patted the cradle. 'Amos made this for me when I thought we might ...' Her mouth tightened. 'But it wasn't to be. Dr Sims says I'm too old.' She handed Annie the purse. 'Lil's girls sent that for you.'

Annie took the purse. 'For me?'

'For the bairn.'

Annie nodded and took Charlie's hand. 'First I've got to get you some decent clothes and things you'll need for school.'

Charlie's face fell. 'But I'm not allowed to go to school.'

'I think you'll find the situation is a little different now,' Netty said. 'Annie,' she continued, 'I have a proposition for you.' She put her offer to Annie.

The woman stared at her. 'Me? Work here?'

'Your needlework is exquisite,' Netty said. 'Truth is I need a good needlewoman like you, Annie. And I know a small cottage you and Charlie can rent.'

Charlie let out a squeal. 'Please say yes, Ma. We can live in a proper house and I can go to school and Sarah can go to school and—' The child's desperation for normality radiated from her, and Annie nodded.

'I'd like that,' she said. She looked at Eliza. 'Jack's not coming back, is he?'

'I don't know. He said he'd send money.'

Annie looked at the sleeping baby. 'I've no wish to go back to the way things were without Jack to keep an eye on us.'

'You never have to go back,' Eliza said. She saw the hope in Charlie's eyes and thought of Mrs Wallace and her wonderful school. If Charlie could get a scholarship, perhaps ... One thing at a time.

Netty beamed. 'That's settled then. Now I'd like to go up to the mine and see how things are. Eliza?'

'Can I come too?' Charlie asked.

'We'll all go,' Netty said.

It seemed like the entire town had gathered at the gates of the mine, stretching down the approach road to the bridge over the swollen creek. The throng parted to allow the two women and the child to reach the two police constables at the mine's gate.

'What's the news?' Netty asked the larger of the two, Prewitt.

'They've got Tregloan out,' he said.

'Please let us pass, Prewitt,' Eliza said.

The constable nodded and lifted the latch on the gate.

'Miss Penrose!' Susan Mackie pushed her way through the crowd. The girl looked as if she'd had no sleep since the initial collapse, her eyes red with exhaustion. 'I've been desperate. They won't let me in, but I have to see Ian ...' Her face crumpled.

Eliza put her arm around the girl. 'Come with me. Let her through, constable.'

The women crossed the courtyard to the crib room, where the men were resting after their rescue. Jenny Tregloan knelt beside her husband, holding his hand and talking to him. If the young man heard her, he gave no sign, but the rise and fall of the blanket indicated he still breathed.

Dr Sims came forward and steered Netty and Eliza away from the others.

'I haven't had a chance to look in on Mrs O'Reilly. Is she faring well?'

'Ellen Bushby has called a couple of times,' Netty said.

'No sign of fever?'

'No.' Eliza glanced at the young man on the stretcher. 'How's Tregloan?'

'A bit early to tell. Looks like he had a blow to the head and he's badly dehydrated, but he's young and fit. He should be fine.'

'What about the others?'

'We'll have to see.' A ragged cheer went up from outside. 'Ah, here comes another one. Should be young McLeod.'

Susan Mackie gave a sharp cry and ran to the stretcher, her fingers closing on Ian's good hand as they carried him in.

As they set the stretcher down, Ian's eyes fluttered open and he gave the girl a lopsided grin. 'Miss Mackie, what a pleasure to see you.'

'And you, Mr McLeod,' she replied and burst into tears.

Eventually, David Morgan and John Marsh were carried out, to be greeted by their relieved wives and children.

It was dark before the last man came out on his own two feet. Enoch Trevalyn waved to the cheering crowd but once inside the crib room, he collapsed into his wife's arms.

The Maiden's Creek Mine drama had concluded with all five men alive and well. Down at the gate, the reverend gentlemen of the town led the townspeople in hymns and fervent prayers of gratitude for their safe delivery.

Eliza watched from the door of the crib room as the weary rescuers began to filter out of the mine, their feet dragging. The last man to leave was the tall, broad-shouldered Scot. He stopped when he saw her and smiled. They stood looking at each other, overwhelmed with feelings that ran too deep for expression.

'You're filthy,' she said at last.

'I can wait,' he said. 'I've come to check on the lads.'

Seated by the fire, a blanket around his shoulders, Trevalyn pushed aside the spoon his wife was offering him. 'I take back what I said about it being bad luck to have a red-headed woman in the mine, McLeod. She saved our lives,' he said without rancour.

Alec gave a low chuckle and put his arm around Eliza's shoulder. 'Get used to it, Trevalyn,' he said. 'I think we'll be seeing more of this particular red-headed woman.'

Thirty-Three

4 August 1873

On Monday morning, Eliza packed her bag and left Netty's comfortable but crowded cottage to return to her uncle's house on the hill. She had no particular right to stay there, but at the very least she needed to collect the last of her belongings and retrieve the papers she had hidden in Tom's boot box.

As she passed the police station, her steps slowed. A heavy wagon waited in front of it and Constable Prewitt was leading Charles Cowper out. Manacled, unshaven and filthy, her uncle bore no resemblance to the dapper mine manager he had been.

He glanced in her direction and a smile lifted his haggard features.

'Can I have a word with my niece, Constable?'

She hesitated. 'I have nothing to say to you, Uncle.'

He nodded. 'I don't blame you, Eliza. I just want you to know that I'll make it right.'

She gave him a scathing look. 'And just how do you propose to do that?'

'I intend to admit everything,' he said. 'The forgeries, the will, the theft of the gold, everything.'

'That is the least you can do.' She raised her chin and looked him in the eye. 'What about Will's death?'

'I did not kill your brother and I won't admit to something I didn't do. You have my word that you won't see or hear from me again. I am truly sorry, Eliza.'

'I would like to believe you, but I'm not ready to forgive you.'

Cowper nodded and turned to Prewitt. 'I'm ready, Constable.'

She stood, unable to move, as Prewitt shoved Cowper into the back of the wagon, then slammed and locked the door.

As she turned away, she heard him call her name. She turned back. He clutched at the bars on the door of the wagon.

'Eliza, I ask only one thing of you. Look after Mary Harris and the boy for me. She's a good woman and she deserved better.'

Eliza nodded. 'That is one thing I can do.'

'Thank you.'

She did not linger to watch the wagon drive away. She climbed the hill to the mine manager's house, but no one answered her knock at the back door and when she turned the handle, she found it unlocked. It came as no surprise to find Mrs Harris sitting at the kitchen table staring at an undrunk cup of tea. No fire burned in the hearth and only the faintest heat came from the oven.

'Come to gloat, have you?' Mrs Harris asked.

'No,' Eliza said. 'I've come to claim what is mine.' She crouched beside the boot box and lifted the lid, relieved to find the envelope, now stained and crumpled, where she had left it.

'I did love him, you know.'

Eliza sat back on her heels. 'Then I'm sorry for you,' she said. 'I did too, but he betrayed us both.' She paused. 'Tell me, was he Tom's father?'

Mrs Harris shook her head. 'No. My husband deserted me when Tom was born. Said he would have naught to do with an idiot child.' Her face twisted in pain. 'I made do but it were hard, until Charles found me. He did have a kind heart, Miss Penrose. Back then …'

Eliza held back the observation that it probably suited her uncle very well to have a bed mate who happened to be a good cook and was happy to be his housekeeper.

Mrs Harris pushed a key across the table. 'That's the key to his desk,' she said. 'He kept records of everything.'

'You knew what he was doing?'

'Some of it. But he was doing it for us … for Tom and me. Tom'll never find his own way in the world.' She paused. 'And I think in his own way he loved us. And you and William.'

'But he loved gold more.' Eliza picked up the key, weighing it in her hand.

'What will become of us now?' Mrs Harris looked up at her. 'I can't hold my head up in the town again.'

Eliza looked around the kitchen. 'A new manager will have to be appointed, Mrs Harris, and no doubt he will need a house-keeper. You've done nothing wrong and I don't see why you and Tom should be punished for my uncle's misdeeds.'

The woman nodded, the light of hope sparking in her weary face. 'It would be proper for you to stay up here until—or at least for a little while, Miss Penrose. That would help make it right for Tom and I.'

Eliza nodded. 'I'll stay.'

Mrs Harris stood and smoothed her skirts. 'Then I'd best be making up your bed and getting the fires lit, and you'll be wanting a cup of tea.'

Eliza let the woman bustle around her, glad that she could help. Why was it always the women who suffered? The Mary Harrises and Annie O'Reillys never asked for the life that had been thrust on them.

The evening was gathering in as Eliza sat at the table in the parlour, her uncle's papers spread out around her, the true extent of his crimes now clear. She hoped he would keep his promise and plead guilty to what would be a multitude of charges, but Maidment would still need the evidence to present to the court.

She was so engrossed in her work that the click of the door opening startled her. She looked up, expecting Mrs Harris with yet another pot of tea, but Alec McLeod stood in the doorway, washed and shaved, his hair still clinging damply around his face in curls. An uncertain smile caught the corners of his mouth, but his eyes were bright as he surveyed the table.

'Quite the businesswoman, Miss Penrose,' he said.

'The extent of my uncle's dealings surprises and saddens me.' She swept a hand across the ledgers and papers. 'You said he was ruthless and I have it all here. As soon as any mine showed signs of struggling he closed in. I can't even begin to believe the dreams he destroyed, the men he put out of work ... but until the business with Will, it was always legal. What made William and I different?'

Alec picked up a sheaf of papers, leafing through them. 'You both trusted him.' He set the papers down. 'Have you seen him?'

'This morning, before Maidment took him down to Melbourne. He says he'll plead guilty to the charges brought against him. He'll go to prison but he won't hang. He has spared me a trial and for that I should be grateful, but I never wish to see him again.' She held up a legal document. 'I have my brother's genuine will and once that is dealt with, I suppose that really does make me a part owner of the Shenandoah Mine.' She ran a hand over her face. 'How's Ian?'

'Susan Mackie and her mother appear to have him well in hand. I left them ladling more good Scotch broth into him. Susan seems to fancy herself as Miss Nightingale, fluffing pillows and wiping brows.' He rolled his eyes. 'Even my cat seems to have succumbed. I left him by the fire, curled up in Miss Mackie's lap.' Alec's face softened, sinking into lines that told of his exhaustion. 'To answer your question, Ian is weak and his arm's badly broken but the doctor doesn't seem to think that there will be a fever and his arm should mend.'

Eliza pushed her chair back and took her hands in his. She turned them over, noting the cuts, the torn fingernails and the ingrained dirt that would take many washes to loosen. She kissed each palm in turn, before looking up into his face. 'And you, Alec? You've been to hell and back in the last few days.'

His fingers tightened on hers and he raised her hand to his lips and kissed it. 'And so have you, lass. Do you have time? Perhaps we can talk—'

Eliza laughed. 'Talk? Alec, we have all the time in the world to talk.' She wanted to say. *Forget talking, just kiss me …*

A brisk knock at the door caused them to jump apart. Mrs Harris entered setting down a tray bearing a bottle of wine, glasses and cold pie. She cast Eliza a prim look as she said, 'I must apologise, Miss Penrose. Thomas and I have been called away this evening. We will not be back until late.'

Eliza bit her lip to hold back the grin. 'Thank you, Mrs Harris. I am sure we will manage.'

The door shut behind the housekeeper and Alec frowned. 'What's so amusing?'

'She is leaving us alone and unchaperoned, Mr McLeod.'

'Oh, well, in that case what is a gentleman to do but to leave you in peace.' He turned to go and she lunged at his arm, pulling him back into the room.

'Please do not leave me alone and unprotected. You never know what trouble I might find myself in.'

He entered into the spirit of the moment, advancing on her. 'Hmm … what sort of trouble would that be?' He took her hand and kissed each finger. 'This sort of trouble?' His lips moved to the inside of her wrist. 'Or this?'

She cupped his face in her hands. Care and responsibility had etched lines there that belied his age but his brown eyes were soft and it seemed that she saw her face reflected in their depths, as if they had always belonged together.

His fingers meshed in her hair, dragging it out of its neat coil.

'I'm the son of a miner,' he said. 'I don't know any poetry or grand ways to woo you. I only know about mines and rocks. You deserve better than me …'

'And I'm a goldminer's sister and the daughter of a miner. Don't be such a fool, Alec McLeod. Mines and rocks are in my blood and I love you exactly because you are who you are. I don't want grand romantic gestures. I want a man who will come home to me, a man with whom I can talk about leads and seams and boilers. A man I can share a life with, not be a pretty ornament in his front parlour.'

'You mean what you just said?'

'All of it.'

'That you love me?'

She made a fist and hit his chest. 'Yes, of course I love you!'

She willed him to say the words she longed to hear, but once again Catriona's ghost caught at her sleeve. He had loved another before her. Maybe he could never love again? Never mind, she would take whatever he could offer.

Seemingly oblivious to her sobering mood, Alec gathered Eliza into his arms, lifting her from her feet and spinning her around until they both collapsed, giddy and laughing, onto the rug in front of the fire. He stretched out, pulling her on top of him. Her hair had come loose and now tumbled down, brushing his face.

'Lass, I love you with every part of my being.' He curled a lock of hair around his fingers. 'But your hair's getting in my eyes.'

Her heart gave a leap of pure joy. He had said those three precious words.

He caught her hand, threading her fingers through his. The humour had gone from his eyes and he seemed to be studying her with a curious intensity.

'Alec?'

'Eliza, I couldn't bear to lose you. Catriona—'

She laid her head in the hollow of his shoulder, holding him tight. 'You've lost one love, Alec, and Catriona will always hold a part of your heart. I understand that. I just hope there is room for another.'

He pulled her close, burying his face in the fall of her rich, chestnut hair. 'My heart's been empty for a long while now and there is room enough for you. Will you marry me?'

Tears pricked her eyes. She had existed in a world devoid of happiness for so long that she wanted this moment to last forever. Nobody knew what the future held so she couldn't think about the what ifs. She had been blessed to find love and she would cherish every second, every minute, every hour, every day they shared.

'I'll marry you, Alec McLeod, as soon as it can be arranged.' She took a deep breath, her heart hammering as she said, 'Stay with me tonight, Alec. I don't want to be alone any more. Not tonight or ever again.'

He locked his fingers behind her neck, drawing her to him.

Eliza lay awake in the grey light that heralded dawn, curled against the man beside her. His arm encircled her, holding her as close as two people could get. Beyond the window, the township would be waking, the shifts at the mines changing. Except at Maiden's Creek Mine, which remained closed.

She turned in Alec's arms and he stirred. A smile curved his lips and she ran a hand along his unshaven jaw. Her body still tingled from his touch and the narrow bed could have been floating ten feet above the floor.

'It's getting light,' she said. 'You should leave.'

'I don't care,' he said.

'But I do. It would be good to keep the shreds of my reputation intact for a little while longer.'

He screwed up his nose and sighed. 'Aye, you're right.'

Neither of them moved and his hand slid down, curving her breast, his fingers causing her mind to cloud with desire.

'No,' she said firmly, removing the questing hand. 'You have to go.'

He sat up, cold air invading their cosy nest, and pushed the hair back from his eyes. 'Will you be married in the Presbyterian or the Church of England?'

'I don't care.' She paused. 'Yes, I do. The church is important to Ian and Ian is important to you. Reverend Donald can do the honours.'

'I'll speak to him today,' Alec said. He squinted at the lightening sky. 'You're right. I must get going, much as it grieves me to leave you.'

He bent and kissed her. She stretched her arms above her head, as contented as a cat, as his lips slid down her throat, brushing against the soft skin. She closed her eyes, giving in to the delicious sensations he aroused, but somewhere in the house a clock struck seven.

He gave a strangled grunt and slid his feet to the floor, his shoulders hunching against the cold. She ran a hand across the muscles of his back and the breath stopped in her throat. She had never understood what desire meant but now just the sight of this beautiful man banished all sense except the wish to never leave this bed.

Alec collected his clothes from where they had been abandoned on the floor in their haste and dressed slowly, almost provocatively, as she leaned on one elbow watching every movement, every twist of a button.

He caught her watching him and smiled. 'There's no modesty in you, is there, lass?'

She shook her head. 'I never thought a man could be described as beautiful, Alec.'

Half-dressed, he bent over her and kissed her softly. 'I've got to go. Shall I call on you tonight?'

She smiled. 'And tomorrow night, and the night after that.'

'I'm not one to deny a lady.'

'And I don't think you can describe such wanton desires as I am experiencing as those of a lady. Go, before I turn the key in that lock and keep you here for the rest of the day.'

His face sobered and he took her hands in his. 'Have I told you that I love you, Eliza Penrose?'

'You may have mentioned it,' she said.

He bent to kiss her, a long, slow, lingering kiss that she wished would never end, but the clock struck the half-hour and he straightened.

'I really must go,' he said and, pulling on his jacket, slipped out of the house to make his way home before too many curious eyes saw him.

Eliza curled up and went back to sleep, soothed by the lingering scent of man and desire.

Thirty-Four

5 August 1873

Eliza woke late to the sound of Mrs Harris singing as she swept the hallway outside the door. She'd never heard the dour house-keeper sing before and she had quite a sweet voice. Could it be that Cowper's disgrace had released her from an obligation that dragged down her soul?

Eliza left her bed, hurriedly pulling on her nightdress, and threw open the bedroom door.

'Good morning, Mrs Harris.'

The woman leaned on her broom. 'And a fine one it is, Miss Penrose.'

'I'm to be married.'

The girlish dreams of being a bride in the ancient parish church where her parents, her grandparents and great-grandparents had been married had long ago vanished and, confined to the stric-tures of being a teacher in a ladies' academy, the opportunity to even meet a man had seemed an impossible dream. Now she had a wedding to organise and the realisation that she had nothing to wear dawned on her. A professional visit to Netty Burrell was definitely called for.

She ate, dressed and, with a lightness in her step, all but skipped down the street to Netty's shop.

Netty did everything expected of a good friend. She squealed with excitement and dragged Eliza inside, combing her stock for something suitable that could be adapted to a wedding dress. They settled on a soft grey-green silk and Netty assured her that with some help from one of the other women in the town, she would have it done within days.

Charlie watched the activity, her hands clasped together, hanging on every word, and when Eliza asked if the child would care to be part of the wedding party, Charlie burst into tears.

'I've never been to a wedding,' she said between gulps. 'I don't have nothing to wear.'

'Anything to wear,' Eliza corrected and folded Charlie in her arms. 'You shall have a new dress, the prettiest Mrs Burrell can make for you.'

Netty's eyes widened but she bit back whatever retort she was going to make when Eliza added hurriedly, 'At my cost. After all, when the legalities are sorted, thanks to my brother, I am now a shareholder in one of the richest mines on this goldfield.'

She left the shop, mind racing with arrangements that had to be made, but first someone important had to be told.

She climbed the hill to the cemetery and stood looking down at Will's grave. The monumental mason had yet to deliver the headstone but the local blacksmith had erected a neat wrought iron fence.

'I hope you approve, Will' she said. 'I know he was your friend ...' *And you should be here to stand beside him*, she thought, tears catching at the back of her throat.

'Seems we always have to meet over Will's grave.'

Eliza looked up. A woman in a dark cloak clutching a bunch of golden wattle stood on the far side of the grave.

'Sissy!' Eliza scrambled to her feet. 'I didn't expect to see you back here.'

'After you visited, I knew I had to come and say goodbye.'

Eliza moved aside and let the woman lay the wattle at the base the wooden cross. Eliza found the other woman's hand and they stood with fingers entwined in silence for a long few moments before Sissy eased back the hood of her cloak. Without the paint and the trappings of her trade, her deterioration was apparent, her face grey and gaunt and her eyes sunken.

'I've come back to die,' Sissy said, nodding as if in agreement with something Eliza had said. 'It's right.'

'Where are you staying?'

'Lil found a little cottage for me, out of the way so I won't be a bother to the town. The girls will see to everything but I want to be buried here, beside him.' She started to cough, pressing a handkerchief, already bright with blood, to her lips. Eliza slid an arm around her shoulders and eased her onto the slab of a nearby grave and the two women sat side by side.

'You need to be somewhere warm, not out here in the cold.'

Sissy shook her head 'It won't make any difference to me now, but there's one last thing I must do. I have to make my peace with you, Miss Penrose.'

'Me?'

Sissy nodded. 'It's the other reason I've come back. I thought long and hard about what you said when you came to see me and I haven't told you the whole truth about what happened that night.' She held up a hand before Eliza could respond. 'Let me say my bit and then you can speak.' The breath rattled in her chest and she swallowed. 'Will was in a right state ... said Cowper was stealing the gold from Shenandoah and he had to find proof.' She coughed again. 'I know how to open locks so I went with him to the mine office. We got into the office but I couldn't open the safe. He was cross. I called him a few names and we argued. I—I was that vexed with him that I ran out into the night but he followed me … He tripped and lost his footing just by the head of the tailings. He didn't even have a chance to cry out as the rocks gave way. He couldn't hold on and he fell. I swear it was an accident, Miss Penrose.' Tears shone in her eyes. 'I loved him. I'd never have hurt him. Can you ever forgive me?' Sissy reached for Eliza's hand, her fingers tightening on hers.

Eliza stared at her brother's grave, not knowing how she should feel. Relieved that it really had been an accident? Anger that this woman had caused her brother to fall and not come forward?

After all the weeks of wondering, grieving, seething, she felt nothing, just a deep emptiness. It no longer mattered how Will had died—nothing could touch him now—but this dying woman needed her forgiveness.

'There is nothing to forgive,' Eliza said. 'It was an accident. Will should have known better than to go so close to the tailings.' She paused. 'I think he loved you very much.'

'I like to think he did. I loved him and that was enough,' Sissy whispered. 'I'm going to see him soon, I know he'll be waiting for me.'

Eliza swallowed her own tears. 'Tell him—tell him I came. Tell him I miss him … Tell him I am to marry Alec McLeod and that I am happy.'

Thirty-Five

14 December 1873
Melbourne, Victoria

The large crowd filling the auditorium of the Melbourne Athenaeum fanned themselves as the heat in the space rose with the noise. In the wings of the theatre, Alec had gone ashen, his face sheened with sweat.

'I can't do this,' he said.

Eliza straightened his cravat. 'You can. You know everything there is to know about the boiler.'

'Aye, but I'm not a salesman.'

'And that's why you'll do well.' Eliza turned to Ian. 'Am I not right?'

Ian nodded.

A man's voice tinged with an American accent reached them from backstage. 'We are friends. Let us through, my good man.'

Alec and Eliza exchanged a puzzled look as a fashionably dressed couple picked their way over the stage ropes toward them. He wore a bright gold and green brocade waistcoat, and the elegant gown of the tall woman beside him betrayed the roundness of a woman carrying an advanced pregnancy. A lad of about twelve, as fair as both his parents were dark, trailed behind them.

The gentleman shifted the brass-handled cane he carried to his left hand and held out his right to Eliza. 'Miss Penrose?'

Eliza glanced at Alec as she took the man's hand. 'Eliza McLeod,' she said. 'William Penrose was my brother.'

'Please accept our deepest condolences,' the woman said. 'He was a good friend to my husband and me. We didn't get Netty's letter until we reached San Francisco, so it came late. Ill news to receive when we were so far away.'

Eliza looked from one to the other, realisation dawning on her. 'You are the Hunts,' she said, resisting an urge to throw her arms around them.

The man smiled. 'Caleb Hunt. My wife, Adelaide, and our son Daniel.'

'You're here! You're home.' Eliza took a breath. 'Excuse me, it is just so wonderful to finally meet you. Are you back to stay?'

'We are,' Caleb Hunt replied. 'We've been travelling a long time. Pretty much seen the world but—' he glanced at his wife, '—Australia is home and we wanted our child born here. We've purchased a property up near Mansfield and young Danny is going to start school at Melbourne Grammar after Christmas. But we will have plenty of time to discuss our plans. You will dine with us tonight at the Menzies.?' Caleb Hunt turned to Alec. 'You must be McLeod.'

Alec shook the man's hand and ran a finger around his high, tight collar. 'You'll have to forgive me, Hunt, but you have caught us at a bad time.'

'Ah yes, that is why we have come,' Adelaide Hunt said. 'We only docked yesterday and I read it in the paper this morning. Caleb and I could not believe we had the opportunity to meet you today. We are, of course, coming to visit everyone at Maiden's

Creek and I believe you are now the manager of Maiden's Creek Mine, Mr McLeod.'

Alec glanced at Eliza. 'And I have been managing the Shenandoah until such time as you arrived and a decision made about its future.'

Caleb Hunt glanced at his wife. 'Of course, but all of that can wait. We want to know all about Will's wonderful invention.'

He nodded toward the stage. 'I think you'd better get going. The crowd is becoming restless. Who'd have thought a boiler would excite such interest?'

'Not just any boiler,' Eliza said. 'This one will revolutionise all industry, not just mining.'

'Really? Do you think we should invest in it, Adelaide?' Caleb Hunt turned to his wife.

'Let's hear what Mr McLeod has to say first,' Adelaide replied.

Eliza looked up at her husband. 'Ready?'

Alec nodded and took her hand. He squeezed it tightly as he managed a smile. 'Ready.'

Side by side, they walked onto the stage in front of the drawn curtain. The restless crowd grew silent as Alec cleared his throat.

'Ladies and gentlemen, thank you for your attendance today. My wife and I are delighted to see such an interest in the Penrose boiler.'

On cue, the curtain was raised to reveal the neat prototype of the boiler that they had fought so hard to make real. With the confidence of someone who truly knew his subject, Alec spoke of the boiler's virtues, demonstrating its capabilities as Eliza stood to the side.

Her brother had written to her: *I feel confident in saying we can make a good life for ourselves here …*

'Thank you, Will,' she whispered. 'Thank you for bringing us together and for making this happen. We will make a good life here.'

Author's Note

Thank you for reading *The Goldminer's Sister*, which, like *The Postmistress*, is set in the fictional town of Maiden's Creek.

Maiden's Creek is based on the town of Walhalla in Gippsland, Victoria, which in its heyday was one of the most successful gold mines in Australia. The Maiden's Creek Mine is loosely based on the Long Tunnel Mine, which tourists can still visit today. The goldfield spread well out from Walhalla and there were many satellite settlements like the fictional Pretty Sally, now lost to the bush. If you are feeling intrepid you can still find a water wheel in a deep gully that once belonged to the Morning Star Mine. But the countryside is a warren of abandoned gold mines and snakes, so watch your step.

I took the inspiration for the mine collapse from the terrible Creswick Mine Disaster, one of Australia's worst mining tragedies. In December 1882, a mine shaft at the Australasian No. 2 Mine flooded. It took over three days to break through to the trapped miners. They were too late. Twenty-two miners died.

One minor character worthy of her own story is the woman I named Marcelline Guichard. She is based on Pauline Bonfond, who died in Blackwood in 1867. Pauline is described in a contemporary newspaper report:

> *Madame Pauline Bonfond, a French woman, made an excellent living contracting to cut races for the diggers. She built the water races for sluicing gold around the hills on the opposite side of the gully from Golden Point, Blackwood. The story states that many a thievish miner carried the marks of her shovel to their grave, when they thought they could get the better of her.*

Many Cornish tin and copper miners came to Australia in the nineteenth century, my husband's ancestors among them. We have visited the mine at Geevor on the rugged north coast of Cornwall where they worked in appalling, cramped conditions. They really were a tough breed.

The danger of research is it becomes a rabbit warren down which the unsuspecting author can spend many interesting hours in researching matters that are just touched on in the text:

- The term 'Mongolian Idiocy' or Mongoloid, is, thankfully, the now obsolete term coined by Dr John Down in the early 1860s to describe what we now call Down syndrome. The descriptions persisted well into the 1960s but are thankfully long gone now!
- I mention briefly the work of Josephine Butler (1828–1906) one of the great social reformers and campaigners for the rights of women (particularly underage prostitutes) of the nineteenth century and commend anyone with an interest in this area to explore her achievements further.
- And the work of Frederick Rose, the founder of the Victorian College for the Deaf (the Victorian Deaf and Dumb Institution) as early as 1860 and the origin of Auslan

(the Australian version of sign language). Rose was a well-educated deaf man who saw a desperate need to assist those people, described in the language of the day as 'deaf mutes'. If you are interested in what happens to characters after you close the book ... Ian goes to work for Mr Rose as a teacher (and marries Susan Mackie)!

- *The Education Act 1872.* In 1872 a new, government funded, secular, compulsory education system was introduced in Victoria under the control of the first Education Department. From the legislation itself, I gleaned the structure, pay and curriculum that the Maiden's Creek School would have been forced to adopt under the guidance of its Board of Advice.

And finally an embarrassing disclaimer. I failed maths in Form 3 and I cannot, for the life of me, explain why Eliza informed me she was a mathematical whizz kid, but characters tend to take on a life of their own and if there are any glaring errors or inconsistencies in Eliza (or Alec's) mathematical forays, the errors are mine, not theirs.

It was great fun writing *The Goldminer's Sister.* I hope you enjoy reading it as much as I enjoyed reimagining our mining past!

Alison Stuart

Acknowledgements

I dedicated this book to my hero and husband of many, many years, David. As a mechanical engineer himself, he asked me to write a story with an engineer for a hero. I have to admit Alec provided me with some interesting challenges, but I hope I have succeeded in bringing him to life and making him a worthy match for my heroine, Eliza. David is my technical consultant, beta reader and sounding board, sharer of the highs and lows—I couldn't imagine writing a book without him. Best of all we share a love of the Australian bush and the area around Walhalla, which we first visited as a newly engaged couple.

I would also like to acknowledge the wonderful guides at Sovereign Hill in Ballarat who, finding a willing subject, were delighted to spend time explaining the process of hard rock gold mining to me. It makes a difference to see the machinery in action from the boilers to the battery stampers. I also enjoyed visiting the goldfields schools and seeing the teachers in action. Living history is worth a thousand words!

Another essential element in my support crew is my wonderful writing group, the Saturday Ladies Bridge Club, who are always there to cheer, commiserate, make endless cups of tea (or ply me with alcohol), brainstorm and just be the best friends ever.

And finally, of course, I am enormously grateful to my team at Harlequin Mira (HarperCollins Australia): Jo Mackay, Nicola Robinson, Chrysoula and Kylie, Sarana and all the back room staff. Thank you for your faith in me!